NEED YOU NOW

Also by James Grippando

Afraid of the Dark*+

Money to Burn+

Intent to Kill

Born to Run*+

Last Call*+

Lying with Strangers

When Darkness Falls*+

Got the Look*+

Hear No Evil*

Last to Die*

Beyond Suspicion*

A King's Ransom

Under Cover of Darkness+

Found Money

The Abduction

The Informant

The Pardon*

And for young adults
Leapholes

* A Jack Swyteck Novel
+ Also featuring FBI agent Andie Henning

NEED YOU NOW

James Grippando

A Novel

HARPER

An Imprint of HarperCollinsPublishers
www.harpercollins.com

HarperCollins books may be purchased for educational, business, or sales promotional use. For information, please write: Special Markets Department, HarperCollins Publishers, 10 East 53rd Street, New York, NY 10022.

FIRST EDITION

Library of Congress Cataloging-in-Publication Data
  Grippando, James.
    Need you now : a novel / James Grippando.—1st ed.
      p. cm.
    ISBN 978-0-06-184030-2
    1. Investment advisors—Fiction. 2. Wall Street (New York, N.Y.)—
Fiction. 3. Fraud—Fiction. I. Title.
    PS3557.R534N44 2012
    813'.54—dc22   2011014345

12 13 14 15 16 OV/RRD 10 9 8 7 6 5 4 3 2 1

In memory of Maria Hellendoorn.

God needed you more.

DECEMBER 2008

Miami

1

GERRY COLLINS KNEW THAT IT WOULD END. AND END BADLY. The entire operation was a fraud. His fraud, as much as anyone's. Still, the breaking news on the Financial News Network left him numb.

"Abe Cushman, a former chairman of the NASDAQ Stock Market and a force on Wall Street trading for nearly fifty years, has reportedly taken his own life this morning."

Collins stared at the plasma screen on the wall. The Harvard-educated anchorwoman with the beauty-queen hair was almost giddy with excitement, as if the real-time development of a story like this during her midmorning time slot were the journalistic equivalent of winning the Super Bowl.

He did it, thought Collins. *Abe really did it.*

"Cushman's apparent suicide has sent shock waves through the financial community," the anchorwoman said, "as it comes just hours before he was to surrender to federal authorities in Manhattan on charges of massive securities fraud."

The telephone rang. It had been ringing off the hook all morning. Collins ignored it. He went to the window and soaked in one last view of sparkling Biscayne Bay, the port of Miami, and sun-drenched South Beach beyond.

The south Florida office of GC Investments was a lavishly appointed penthouse in Miami's Financial District. Not bad for a kid from Jersey who had started out selling pre-owned cars. A keen eye for big spenders ready to part with their money was his gift. A little car knowledge and a lot of smooth talking had paid his way through business school, where he'd graduated in the bottom 10 percent, good enough to launch a ten-year string of completely unspectacular career moves. Then his father—buddies with Abe Cushman since grammar school—landed him a dream gig. GC Investments became an approved "feeder fund," one of a select few investment firms that could funnel cash to Abe Cushman. His bonus the first year had been a million dollars. By age thirty-five he was earning twice that much—*per month*.

And now this. Collins was glad his father wasn't alive to see it.

Again, the desk phone rang. Collins crossed the room and yanked the cord from the wall jack. There was no one to answer telephones anymore. No financial advisers, no assistants, no receptionist. The office had closed its doors for good at five P.M. the day before. Collins was alone.

"We go now to FNN reporter Charlie Hughes," said the anchorwoman, "who is at the Midtown headquarters of Cushman Investment, where frantic investors are gathering to demand answers about the money they entrusted to Mr. Cushman."

Collins turned his attention back to the TV screen.

"Shock and anger," the reporter on the scene said. "Those are the prevailing sentiments right now, as clients of Cushman Investment receive the startling news that the trusted name partner—who may well go down as the worst financial demon in the history of Wall Street—will never answer for his crimes."

Collins stepped across the silk rug, closer to the television. The FNN reporter was standing in the chrome, glass, and granite lobby of the Cushman office tower on Third Avenue.

Behind him, a distraught elderly woman was shouting at a security guard, as if some poor guy with a clipboard and the building's sign-in register were hiding the keys to the vault where Cushman kept all the stolen money.

"As those of us on Wall Street know," the reporter continued, "Abe Cushman distinguished himself as one of the most successful and sought-after investment advisors in the business, earning an annual return of ten to twelve percent even in down markets. In the recent financial crisis, however, clients like the ones now standing behind me requested a reported $7 billion dollars in redemptions. This marked the end for Cushman, who apparently never bought or sold anything. Sources have told FNN that Cushman met with his family and lawyer last night and admitted that the business was all a lie, a giant Ponzi scheme in which investors were paid not with earnings from investments but with money collected from other clients. His sons were reportedly prepared to turn him over to the authorities this morning."

Collins switched off the television and returned to the floor-to-ceiling window of his corner office. He leaned forward, pressed his forehead to the glass, and cast his gaze downward— forty-one stories. The skyscraper's facade was as flat as a mirror, and he could see all the way to the pavement. Traffic below was a stream of toy cars. The hurricane-proof windows were sealed shut, and there was no way to open them, but for a split second he could almost feel the wind on his face, hear the sounds of the city, and sense the rush of adrenaline that Abe Cushman must have felt. He wondered what had gone through the old man's head in those final moments of his seventy-one years, as he stood on the balcony outside his bedroom, climbed over the railing, and jumped from the fifty-fifth floor.

Collins closed his eyes tightly, then opened them. It was hard to get his mind around this, but he had to focus. Since his father's death, he'd heard Cushman say over and again that he was "like a son" to him. The real Cushman sons oversaw the firm's proprietary trading and market-making operations—the legitimate front. Cushman ran a separate investment-advisory business that managed money for investors. He shied away from individuals, no matter how rich; they asked too many questions. Cushman's bread and butter were his approved "feeder funds" that only pretended to perform the due diligence a reasonable investor would perform. Gerry Collins at GC Investments was one of Cushman's gatekeepers—spigots of private wealth who questioned nothing and profited handsomely from Cushman's fraud. Collins' big hits were the famous winter playgrounds for billionaires—Ocean Reef Yacht Club in Key Largo, Fisher Island on Miami Beach, the Palm Beach Country Club, and the like. Collins was the master of the Cushman pitch, the golden boy who made investors feel privileged to hand over their life savings or mega inheritance to Cushman. It was like the old days of selling cars, except that "Lemme go back and talk to the manager" was "Lemme talk to Abe, see what I can do for you, my friend." Same bullshit, bigger numbers. Much bigger.

His BlackBerry vibrated in his pocket. It was nonstop—clients in a panic, demanding to know where their money was. Collins was in no position to talk.

He went to the wall safe behind his desk. It wasn't nearly big enough to hold the billions that had vanished in the Ponzi scheme, but it was adequate to safeguard his emergency provisions. Stacks of hunded-dollar bills. An equal number of euros and sterling notes. A Glock 9-millimeter pistol. An extra ammunition clip. British and U.S. passports under an assumed name. He stuffed everything into a leather travel bag and hurried out of the office, no time to turn out the lights or even lock the doors. He stopped himself, however, just before pressing the call button for the elevator. The image from FNN flashed in his mind: swarms of irate clients gathering in the ground-floor lobby of Cushman Investment in New York. On second thought, he headed for the stairwell.

He tried to control the pace of his descent, to be careful not to trip and tumble down the stairs, but he gained momentum with each passing floor. Thirty-nine. Thirty-eight. Thirty-seven. Soon his feet were moving like Gregory Hines on too much caffeine. His pulse pounded, and he could hear his own breathing, but he'd found his rhythm and was flying down the stairwell. He was taking two steps at a time as he rounded the landing on the tenth floor. Thirty seconds later he reached the parking entrance on level four. He pushed through the metal door to the garage and stopped to catch his breath. His BlackBerry vibrated yet again, which he ignored, but the call triggered a thought. There was one item of unfinished business. He dialed as he walked quickly down the ramp to his car, but the call went straight to voice mail. No surprise there. It was the middle of the night in Singapore. He left a quick message for his banker.

"It's blown up," he said into the phone. "I'll call you when I can. Talk to no one until I reach you."

He tucked the phone into his pocket and climbed into his Bentley. It felt good to slide into the driver's seat and get the weight of the travel bag off his shoulder. He pulled the door shut and buckled his seat belt, but as he reached for the ignition, his head snapped back against the seat—pulled by a wire around his neck.

"*What?*" he started to say, but he had no voice. His legs churned with kicks and stomps to the floorboard. His spine arched. His whole body twisted in desperation as he tugged at the wire around his neck, unable to pry away the death grip. It only drew tighter against his throat—so tight that he could feel the heat of his own blood on his skin. The noose around his neck wasn't smooth like piano wire. This thing had the teeth of a piranha.

Stop!

He banged on the horn, but he heard nothing. His head pounded with congestion, like the worst sinus headache imaginable. His temples throbbed. His vision blurred, and in the struggle, his eyes allowed barely a glimpse of his attacker in the rearview mirror.

I'll tell you anything! Anything!

The silent reply came quickly: a quick jerk from left to right, and the wire slid against his throat, those tiny teeth ripping into his skin like a cable saw.

Did they not believe him? He really would tell all, give them whatever they wanted—if only they would let him. A final jerk of the wire sliced even deeper, cutting through his vocal cords and into the carotid artery. The trickle of blood down his neck was suddenly a fountain that sprayed across the dash, soaked his shirt, and stained the saddle-leather seats with pools of crimson.

In his mind's eye Collins could see himself falling like Abe Cushman, the streets of New York racing up to meet him. Collins screamed, but the sound was only in his head. No one could hear him.

No one was even listening.

THREE YEARS LATER

New York

2

IT WAS TOO GOOD TO BE TRUE: A WALL STREET WHIZ WHOSE performance was the statistical equivalent of a baseball player with a career batting average of .962. For years, critics had voiced their skepticism. Whistle-blowers had laid out dozens of red flags for the Securities and Exchange Commission. Yet no one would listen. The entire law enforcement arm of the U.S. government—tireless teams of federal agents and prosecutors who had dedicated their careers to fighting sophisticated financial crimes—was just a bunch of incompetent, bumbling fools who couldn't spot a massive Ponzi scheme that had unfolded right under their regulatory nose for more than a decade. It was the Wall Street version of the Keystone Kops.

Or so the world was led to believe.

I sure bought into it, hook, line, and sinker. Perhaps a financial advisor—even a relative newbie in his twenties—should have been more skeptical.

I worked in private wealth management at the Midtown Manhattan office of the International Bank of Switzerland—that's "BOS," mind you, as the German-speaking founders of this century-old juggernaut were quick to appreciate the unfortunate English-language connation of bankers with business cards that read "IBS." Over the decades, bright minds and bank secrecy had swelled the bank's total invested assets to $2 trillion. I was the junior member on a team of high-net-worth specialists who managed a nice piece of that pie. Clients counted on us to know fraud from legit. I never steered a dime of their money toward Cushman, but it wasn't because I *knew* anything. My reaction to Cushman's scheme was like everyone else's. I was stunned as the estimated losses climbed ever higher—$30 billion, $40 billion, $60 billion. I felt sorry for the innocent victims. I wondered if I knew any of them. I wondered who else was a crook. I joined in speculation around the watercooler as to where in the world all that money had gone. And then I went home at night, switched on cable news, and nodded off as politicians debated whether Wall Street needed tighter regulation. I was convinced that nothing would really change—until somebody did something from the inside. So I did something. Something a little crazy. I'm still not sure I learned the truth. But I did learn something *about* the truth, especially where unimaginable sums of money were involved. The truth can get you killed. Or worse.

The epiphany came right after my return from Singapore.

I'd been away from New York longer than planned—months longer. Asia was a BOS stronghold, even stronger than Europe. Our weakness was in the United States, where the bank was generally regarded as a mere shadow of itself. "Uncertainty" had been the market watchword before my gig in Singapore. A new management team was about to change all that, if the BOS press releases were to be believed. Wall Street wasn't exactly whistling with optimism on the day of my return, but the fact that the bank's managing director wanted to meet with me—a junior financial advisor—put a spring in my step. I rode the elevator to the executive suite, breezed into a lobby that showcased museum-quality art—*Is that a van Gogh?*—and announced my arrival to the receptionist.

"I'm here for a meeting with Ms. Decker," I said.

The young woman at the desk smiled pleasantly. "And you are?"

"Patrick Lloyd. I'm an FA here in New York."

"Oh, my. You're in the wrong place. The meeting for financial advisors is in the Paradeplatz Conference Room."

Paradeplatz was one of Switzerland's famous squares, near the end of the Bahnhofstrasse and Lake Zurich, home to BOS headquarters. BOS/America was filled with such reminders of whom we answered to.

"But the message said to meet Ms. Decker in her—"

"You need to hurry," she said. "You don't want to be late."

Apparently, my one-on-one meeting with the managing director was a group session. The message from Decker's assistant had made it sound more personal, and I had spent half the night pondering what it could be about. A promotion? The recognition of "rising stars" in the new world of BOS/America wealth management? It had been silly to let my imagination run wild. I picked my ego up off the carpet and rode the elevator down to the seventeenth floor.

It was straight up on ten o'clock, and the last of the latecomers were filing into the Paradeplatz Conference Room at the end of the hall. I caught up as the carved mahogany doors were closing. It was packed inside. The room could comfortably seat about fifty, but the head count was easily double that number. The meeting was about to begin, and all chatter had ceased—which meant that the door closed with an intrusive thud behind me. Like a reflex, heads turned toward me, the only guy still looking for a seat.

A distinct uneasiness gripped me as my gaze swept the room. It was my first time in the Paradeplatz, and under different circumstances I might have been taken with the rich maroon carpeting and burnished walnut paneling. Adorning the longest mahogany table I'd ever seen was the emblazoned gold insignia of BOS: three golden cherubs that symbolized the bank's core principles of discretion, security, and confidentiality. What I noticed most, however, was all the gray hair around that table. A second row of chairs lined the walls, like the back benches of Parliament—less gray hair, but plenty of salt and pepper. The financial advisors in this room were not like me. These were senior advisors, some from New York, and others I recognized only from press coverage of their accomplishments.

"Patrick?"

The voice was little more than a whisper, but I recognized the gravel in my team leader's delivery. Jay Sussman was one of the salt-and-pepper advisors in the second row. I skulked my way over, like a theatergoer arriving halfway through the first act, and took the empty chair beside him.

"What are you doing here?" he asked under his breath.

A door opened on the opposite side of the conference room. In walked the managing director of BOS/America, Angela Decker, with whom I had been scheduled to meet. Or so I'd thought. With her—and my quick double take confirmed it—was the chief executive of the International Bank of Switzerland, Gerhardt Klaus.

"Is this the meeting for FAs?" I asked through my teeth.

"Yeah, the *top one-hundred-producing* FAs."

BOS had more than eight thousand financial advisors in the United States. My invitation from Decker's office had obviously come by mistake. "Should I leave?"

"Stay," he said, smiling with his eyes. "Watching you squirm will keep me awake."

The chief executive walked to the head of the table and remained standing as the managing director took a seat at his side. I'd never met Klaus, of course, but it was well known that he never allowed anyone to introduce him at internal bank gatherings. A vice president had sucked up so badly in Zurich last year that Klaus had forever banned all *Willkommen* speeches.

"Guten Morgen," he said. "And thank you for coming, especially those of you who are visiting from out of town."

Klaus had a booming voice that required no microphone. Disciplined living and cross-country skiing kept him fit and looking younger than his years. He'd been born into a family of Zurich bankers at the height of World War II, at a time when his country couldn't decide which side it was on. It has been said that certain Swiss banks had suffered no such indecision.

"Each of you was invited to this meeting because we wanted you to be the first to hear a major announcement, one that is vital to the future of the worldwide operations of BOS. Without further ado, I'm pleased to tell you that a final settlement agreement has been reached between the International Bank of Switzerland and the U.S. Department of Justice."

A chorus of murmurs coursed through the room like a breeze through a wheat field, followed by sparse and nervous applause. Then silence.

"As you all know," Klaus continued, "both the Swiss government and BOS officials have been engaged in discussions for several months with U.S. authorities. These discussions . . ."

Discussions. Talk about a fudge word. Justice had BOS by the short hairs. The same excesses and mismanagement that had rocked the largest Wall Street investment banks had forced BOS to write down $50 billion in subprime losses in the fall of 2008. The market was in free fall, the world economy was in shambles, and investors from New York to Hong Kong were in a state of panic. The oldest and largest Swiss bank had been on the verge of collapse when the government had come to the rescue with a bailout. At that precise moment, the Justice Department swooped in. With the treasury secretary and the New York Fed warning that the collapse of institutions "too big to fail" could unleash another Great Depression, someone at Justice had the presence of mind—nay, the stroke of genius—to realize that the time was ripe to make Swiss cheese of the secret Swiss banks. The DOJ officially demanded the names of "serious tax evaders." When BOS balked, they arrested a top financial advisor who was silly enough to state publicly that he'd smuggled a diamond in a tube of toothpaste for a client. When BOS stalled again, they indicted the bank's head of private wealth management. They threatened to indict the chairman himself. They demanded a "collateral consequences" report from BOS lawyers, which is typically the final step before the indictment of an entire company. Finally, BOS—still in a weakened state, despite the multibillion-dollar bailout—blinked. It turned over the names of 280 of the most serious tax avoiders. *Poof.* A century of Swiss bank secrecy went up in smoke, just like that. Justice had been hammering away for more names ever since.

Apparently not everyone who worked for the U.S. government was a dumbass. Yet Abe Cushman had gone unnoticed by law enforcement. Those Ponzi schemes sure are hard to sniff out, especially the ones that last for only two decades and involve a measly $60 billion.

Hmmm.

"As part of this settlement," the chief executive continued, "we have agreed to release the names of four thousand additional clients over the coming year."

"Four thousand?" my team leader whispered. "This is *good* news?"

I leaned closer. "Actually, the good news is that the bank is offering a free box of *Depend* to each of our clients."

My boss snorted with laughter, a reflex. The chief executive stopped, clearly annoyed. His steely-blue-eyed glare silenced the room—and it nearly sent me running for my own box of adult diapers.

Klaus leaned forward, his palms resting on the polished wood tabletop as he spoke. "I want to underscore that the only names on this list are clients of our cross-border business. This settlement agreement respects the fact that the cross-border business of BOS consists only of wealth management services offered to American residents outside the United States, that it operates entirely out of Switzerland, and that it is completely separate from the BOS/America wealth management business. In other words, this settlement affects less than one percent of the bank's total invested assets. To put an even finer point on it, the settlement does not affect our U.S.-based private wealth management clients."

Yet, I wanted to say.

"Which brings me to even more important news," said Klaus, "and to the real purpose of this meeting. With the DOJ settlement behind us, it's time to look forward. Ladies and gentlemen, I am pleased to introduce the new head of private wealth management for BOS/America, a man who truly needs no introduction, Joe Barber."

My supervisor and I exchanged glances. His expression matched my unspoken sentiment: *Joe Barber? You must be joking.*

Advisors and their clients had been walking away from BOS since the fifty-billion-dollar write-down of subprime losses. The recent threat of a criminal indictment over bank secrecy had pushed the total loss of assets for the year to over 200 billion Swiss francs. BOS was on the fast track to number two—not in the world, but in *Switzerland.* The much-anticipated announcement of a new head of private wealth for the United States was supposed to restore faith and calm everyone's concerns. The chosen one, however, had earned his stripes at Saxton Silvers.

Barber entered the room, the picture of Wall Street confidence as a photographer captured him and the chief executive smiling and shaking hands.

It was Bear Stearns, Lehman Brothers, and Saxton Silvers—in that order—on the list of Wall Street investment banks that had gone the way of *T. rex* and the dodo bird, swept away by the financial tsunami of subprime lending and mortgage-backed

securities. Barber had sown the seeds of disaster at Saxton
Silvers before accepting a presidential appointment as deputy
secretary of the Treasury, the department's number two post.
Government service required him to liquidate his holdings,
which meant that he had cashed out at the height of the market. He took $28 million out of Wall Street, and a year later
he orchestrated a government bailout that pumped billions of
taxpayer dollars back into the disaster that he and others like
him had created. It still wasn't clear what indictments might
come out of the Saxton Silvers collapse. But there he stood,
handpicked by the top executive in the world of bank secrecy:
Joe Barber, our new leader, the power-drunk pilot who had
put Wall Street on autopilot, headed straight for the side of a
mountain, only to watch the crash from Treasury's ivory tower.

"Gee, I feel better already," my boss muttered.

"Me, too," I said, joining in the lukewarm applause.

I left the conference room quickly, as soon as the meeting broke,
before anyone could ask what the heck I was doing there.

My palms were sweating as I hurried down the hall to the
elevator, but I tried to keep things in perspective. I wasn't the
first junior advisor in BOS history to end up in the wrong place
at the wrong time. Any number of my predecessors had surely
crashed a meeting of top producers. In the hallowed Paradeplatz
Conference Room. With the chief executive from Zurich, the
managing director of U.S. operations, and the new head of private wealth management in attendance.

Good God, what was I thinking?

The chrome elevator doors parted, and a man wearing a
black suit was already inside. I entered and pressed a button, but
the man froze the control panel with a turn of his passkey.

"Patrick Lloyd?" he asked.

"Yes."

He looked like a Secret Service agent, and my impression wasn't far from the mark. "BOS Corporate Security," he said as he punched the button for the executive suite. "I need you to come with me."

My jaw dropped. I expected some good-natured ribbing from colleagues about the mix-up, perhaps even a brief reprimand from a divisional manager. But calling in security was over the top.

"It was a mistake," I started to say, but he wasn't interested. We rode up to the executive suite, and he escorted me into the lobby. I was hoping the receptionist would recount our earlier conversation and clear things up, but she was away from her desk. My escort from Corporate Security directed me to a leather couch by the window, and he sat in the armchair facing me, as if keeping guard. The expression on his face was deadpan, even by Swiss banking standards. Had I still been in Singapore, I would have thought I was in line for a public caning.

I surveyed the lobby. A Jasper Johns original oil painting hung on the wall opposite the van Gogh. Fresh-cut flowers were placed tastefully around the room in crystal vases. A table by the window displayed a small vase so priceless that there was actually a plaque to identify it as being from the Ming dynasty. A row of Swiss clocks on the wall caught my attention, each set to the time zone of a different trading market. New York. London. Frankfurt. Tokyo. Hong Kong. Singapore.

Singapore. I thought of Lilly. She worked with BOS/Asia. Our relationship had been purely business at first, but we ended up dating for six months. Arguably the best six months of my life.

I looked away, then checked the clock again, and a song popped into my head. In Singapore, it was a quarter after one, and I had a sudden vision of Lilly, all alone, and listening to that megahit by Lady Antebellum that seemed to be playing nonstop on the radio since our breakup. *Need you now.*

Yeah, right.

It was four weeks, exactly, since Lilly and I had gone for our last swim at Changi Beach. Anyone who worked at a place like BOS understood that "lose" was a four-letter word, but Lilly and I tried not to let that competitive spirit spill over to our personal relationship. I was better about it than she was; or it could be said that Lilly was better about it than I was. It depended on whom you asked—not that we were competitive about not being competitive. Swimming, however, was where the gloves came off. We did a mile every Saturday morning. This time, as we headed down to the ocean's edge, Lilly broke custom. She didn't snatch my goggles from my hand, pitch them deep into the seaweed, and shout her usual "Loser buys breakfast" as she hit the water with a good three-minute head start. Rather, she led me over to a large piece of driftwood, sat me down, and delivered the solemn words that no man in the history of the world has ever seen coming: "We need to talk." The way she looked on that day would never leave my memory—the sad smile, her honey-blond hair blowing in the gentle breeze, those big eyes that sparkled even in the most dismal of circumstances. She didn't exactly say, *"It's not you, it's me,"* but she might as well have. I couldn't find words, just like the first time I'd laid eyes upon her, only this time there were no violins playing. I was about to speak, and then it had started to rain. At least I'd thought it was raining. I felt a drop on my head, and Lilly promptly lost it right before my eyes. She was embarrassed to be laughing—not at me but at the absurdity of the situation. It was then that I heard the shrill screech in the sky, saw the winged culprit swooping down from above the coconut palms to mock me. A seagull had shit squarely on my head.

Some signs should not be ignored. I transferred back to New York, and Lilly and I said good-bye for life.

An executive assistant entered the waiting area. "Ms. Decker will see you now."

Great. More shit to fall from the sky.

I still couldn't believe the big deal this had become. The assistant showed me into the office, and it wasn't just the managing director inside. Joe Barber, who'd been head of private wealth management for all of one hour, was with her. So was the general counsel. Executives at this level traveled like international diplomats, and it was rare indeed for three of them to actually be in New York at the same time. For the holy trinity of BOS/America to be in a meeting with a junior FA was preposterous.

"There is a perfectly benign explanation for what happened," I said.

"Sit down, Mr. Lloyd," said Decker.

The managing director returned to the leather armchair between Barber and the general counsel, neither of whom rose to greet me. This had the feel of an inquisition, not a meeting. I took the hot seat opposite them.

"This has nothing to do with this morning's meeting in the Paradeplatz," said Decker. "I told my assistant that I wanted to see you this morning, and she put you on the list of FA's for the ten o'clock meeting. An honest mistake on her part."

I breathed a sigh of relief, but it didn't last. The purpose of *this* meeting clearly wasn't to show me the BOS secret handshake.

"Is there some kind of trouble?" I asked.

The general counsel spoke. "As I'm sure you're aware, Lilly Scanlon's employment at BOS/Singapore has been terminated."

I caught my breath. "No, I was not aware of that. When did that happen?"

"Ten days ago."

"I haven't spoken to Lilly in . . . I don't know, exactly. Longer than ten days. Can you tell me what happened?"

"To the extent that it pertains to you, yes. Broadly speaking, it has to do with the Abe Cushman Ponzi scheme."

"Cushman?" I said. "I can't believe Lilly would have anything to do with that. I can assure you that I didn't."

Barber took over. "Mr. Lloyd, why did you go to Singapore?"

His body language made the question anything but innocuous. I tried not to become defensive.

"It seemed like a good career move," I said. "I saw the writing on the wall for Swiss banks. It's no secret that the BOS strategy is to shift to super-high net worth and Asia."

"Why not Hong Kong or Tokyo?" asked Barber.

I could have recounted my decision-making process; instead, I took the offensive. "Is that what this is about? You think my transfer to BOS/Singapore has something to do with Cushman?"

Barber ignored my question. "How well did you know Lilly Scanlon?"

"I didn't know her at all before leaving New York. We met in the Singapore office. She was an FA, just like me."

"This is my first official day," said Barber, "but I've been fully briefed. Don't waste our time trying to pretend that your relationship was purely professional."

Obviously, they already knew the answers to most of the questions on their list. This was a test of my truthfulness, not a search for information—so far, at least.

"We dated," I said. "It ended before I left. I've had zero contact since."

"Tell us about her," said Barber.

I didn't know how to respond. "What do you want to know?"

"We're asking the questions here," said the general counsel.

"I'm just trying to get some color."

"Color" was synonymous with "background" in the BOS lexicon—*"Call Goldman for color on the Tesla Motors IPO"*—but from the look on Barber's face, the operative color here was red. His temper was legendary.

"Listen to me, asshole," Barber said.

"Joe, please," said the general counsel.

"I'm sorry, but this needs to be said. I spent the last twenty-six years of my career in one of two places—in Washington in public service or on Wall Street with Saxton Silvers. It pained me to watch that firm go down. I've seen the kind of arrogance that can breed disaster for a bank, and it starts in puppies like you. I'm not going to put up with it. Are we clear on that?"

"Crystal."

"I could have gone anywhere when I decided to leave Treasury. I chose BOS/America. And the first thing on my plate is an internal investigation into a junior FA's possible involvement—*criminal* involvement—with Abe Cushman. If you haven't figured it out yet, let me spell it out for you: I intend to put out this fire immediately. I will not allow it to heat up and sidetrack my plans to make BOS number one in private wealth management. Again, are we clear?"

"All I can say is that I had absolutely nothing to do with Cushman."

"Did you and Ms. Scanlon ever talk about Gerry Collins?" Barber asked.

Of course I knew the name, especially in the context of Abe Cushman. Collins' gruesome murder had been front-page news everywhere from the *Wall Street Journal* to *People*.

"Talk about him in what way?" I asked.

"Don't be cute," said Barber.

"I'm trying to understand your question. Are you asking me if we talked about him as a person in the news?"

"No, I'm speaking of Gerry Collins in a very different capacity: as one of Ms. Scanlon's most important sources of business."

It was the bomb, and all three executives measured my reaction when it dropped. I tried not to squirm, but my voice tightened. "Lilly never told me about that."

"You worked in the same office and slept in the same bed, but she never mentioned Gerry Collins?"

Asking how he knew I'd occasionally spent the night at Lilly's wasn't going to get me anywhere. "If you're telling me that Lilly had a business relationship with one of Cushman's front men, that never came up. Never."

Barber glanced toward the general counsel. Then his gaze returned to me. "I'd like to believe you, Mr. Lloyd."

"Did you ask Lilly? I'm sure she would tell you the same thing."

"Ms. Scanlon was fired after she was caught red-handed trying to access confidential information about BOS numbered accounts. She refused to discuss it. I suggest you start talking, unless you'd like to join her in the ranks of the unemployed."

I couldn't believe what I was hearing about Lilly, but if it was true, she was in serious trouble. "I have nothing to hide."

"Good," he said. "Tell us about Ms. Scanlon."

Again, I wasn't sure how to respond. "What do you want to know?"

"Everything," said Barber, his tone deadly serious. "Absolutely everything there is to know about that woman."

3

I TOOK MY LUNCH BREAK ALONE BUT DIDN'T EAT. COULDN'T EAT.

At least you still have a job.

For some reason they hadn't fired me. I wasn't even on probation. That was the silver lining I clung to as I walked down Seventh Avenue, destination unknown, trying to get my head around the worst day of my life since . . . I wasn't sure when. An hour earlier, I would have said it was Lilly's it's-not-you, it's-me speech on the beach, but if she was connected to Cushman, our split had actually been a blessing.

Worst day . . .

Probably October 2004, when the Yankees made postseason history by blowing a 3–0 advantage in a seven-game series, which allowed that team from Boston to advance to the World Series and break the eighty-six-year curse of the Bambino. On a bet, I had to wear a Red Sox cap for a month. Very hazardous attire on a New York subway, but who was I kidding? I was twenty-nine years old, I was a lifelong Mets fan, and the two worst things in my life that I was willing to recount were getting dumped and losing a bet on two teams I didn't even care about. It wasn't that I was actually that shallow.

I was in denial—and had been, for years.

A sudden scream jarred me from my thoughts. I'd walked

all the way to the TKTS kiosk at Forty-seventh Street, where two college-aged women had just scored half-price tickets to a Broadway show. They jumped, hugged, and generally made a spectacle of themselves. After my grilling from BOS senior management over a $60 billion Ponzi scheme, it made me nostalgic for the days when saving fifty bucks felt like winning the Lotto.

"Mazel tov," I said, and kept walking.

Times Square, in its Vegas-like splendor, stretched before me. Flashing JumboTrons and spectaculars brought life to an otherwise gray winter afternoon. Building owners in the square were required by law to display illuminated signs, which had to be the only zoning ordinance in New York that garnered 100 percent compliance. It was hard to ignore the five-story-tall Victoria's Secret model, but my gaze drifted to the famous high-tech display that wrapped around the cylindrical NASDAQ building. The financial news of the hour was the Justice Department's settlement with BOS over bank secrecy, and the gist of it scrolled across the marquee over Broadway.

"Justice Department cracks secret Swiss vaults of alleged tax evaders."

The story was getting none of the perky positive spin that our Swiss CEO had attached to it.

A strange ping emerged from my iPhone. A wide range of bells and whistles came with two smartphones—I carried an iPhone in addition to the bank-issued BlackBerry—but this one was unlike any chirp or ringtone I'd heard before. A quick check revealed no new call or message. Nor was my battery running low. A suspicious thought came to mind.

Are they tracking me?

Remote GPS tracking or an eavesdropping device in my iPhone wasn't out of the question. The Corporate Security gurus for the largest Swiss bank had plenty of gadgets. Barber had laid down the law at the conclusion of our meeting: "Do not speak to Lilly Scanlon about this." I promised not to, but perhaps they were making sure of it.

I checked my phone again. Lilly and I truly hadn't spoken since that day on the beach in Singapore, but for whatever reason, I had yet to delete her from the number one slot on my speed-dial list. One touch of the screen and we'd be connected, but just the thought of calling her to find out what she'd done with $60 billion had that Lady Antebellum song playing in my head again, albeit my own version of it:

And she'll wonder if I've lost my freakin' mi . . . ind.

I put the phone away before I could do something stupid. Barber and his fellow BOS executives had been careful to reveal very little about the internal investigation, but Lilly clearly had some serious explaining to do. I was dying to hear her take on Gerry Collins and the pipeline of cash to Cushman Investment by way of BOS/Singapore.

A dark SUV screeched to a sudden stop in front of me at the curb. Had I taken one more step, my toes would have been ground beef.

"Watch it!" I shouted, slapping the fender.

The rear door on the passenger side flew open. Before I could react, someone on the crowded sidewalk pushed me from behind, and I fell inside as the door slammed shut. The vehicle sped away, my head snapped back against the headrest, and the muzzle of a pistol was at the base of my skull.

"Don't move," a man said.

It was a big American SUV, the kind with a third row of seating in the back, and the man was directly behind me. "What—" I started to say, but he jammed the muzzle forward, silencing me.

"Don't say a word."

His voice was like a snake hissing in my ear. My eyes darted toward the driver. I noted the heavy black beard and white turban, but he could have been a Westerner in disguise. Dark-tinted windows dashed any hope that someone on the sidewalk would notice my plight and call the cops. The traffic light changed, the SUV continued through the busy square, and straight ahead I spotted an enormous billboard that said WICKED.

No shit.

"Eyes forward," he said, and I took the warning to heart. The ride was surreal, the glow of a billion colorful lights ahead and the cold sensation of gun metal at the back of my head. The north face of One Times Square was approaching, the building famous for the dropping of the New Year's Eve ball, and I could see both the FOX News Astrovision Screen and the even larger ABC SuperSign at Forty-fourth Street. It made me wonder if I was going to be on the evening news—and if I'd be alive to see it.

"This message is for your girlfriend," the man said. "Our patience is at an end. It's time to see the money. Cough it up, or you will both end up like Gerry Collins. Do you understand?"

This was the second time the name Collins had come up in the span of an hour. There was no mistaking what money this thug was talking about, but I had a burning need for more information, even at the risk of playing dumb.

"What money?"

In the blur of an instant the muzzle slid across the back of my head, and with a muffled pop a silenced projectile whizzed below my ear. Gunpowder and the hot gases of a muzzle blast stung my neck as the bullet buried itself in the back of the passenger seat in front of me. Before I could react the gun was back in place, pressed against my head.

"The next one will be much more than a flesh wound," he said. "Do you understand?"

I wasn't nearly stupid enough to think it would matter that Lilly was no longer my girlfriend.

My right ear was ringing, and it was even worse when I swallowed the lump in my throat. "Yes," I said. "I understand."

The SUV stopped. We were in the Fashion District, just beyond Mustang Sally's Saloon, a place I'd visited one night after seeing the Knicks get thumped at the Garden. The SUV was at the corner, perpendicular to the yawning entrance to the Twenty-eighth Street subway station. I felt the man's breath on the back of my neck as he delivered his final warning.

"Don't even think about calling the cops," he said in a chilling whisper, "or the next bullet is in your brain. You got that?"

"Yes."

"Now get out and walk straight into the subway. Don't stop and don't look back, or I'll put a bullet in you."

I heard the mechanical release of the child lock, and the gun slid away from my head. I pushed open the door and stepped onto the sidewalk. The SUV pulled away so quickly that the door closed itself. I was tempted to glance over my shoulder and get a tag number, but the convincing threat of a bullet with my name on it kept me in check. The subway entrance was directly down the side street, less than thirty yards away from the curb at Seventh Avenue. I started walking and was thinking of Lilly, my hand shaking as I checked the welt on my neck. I wondered what secrets Lilly was hiding, and it occurred to me that there was definitely one thing more dangerous than knowing where the Cushman money was:

Not knowing—and having a trained killer think that I did.

Don't even think about calling the cops.

That warning echoed in my mind with each step down the stairwell, louder and louder as the sound of Midtown traffic yielded to the rumble of an approaching train.

4

——

I EMERGED FROM THE SUBWAY IN TRIBECA, A FEW BLOCKS FROM MY apartment. The northbound train would have taken me to the Midtown office, but word was probably out that I was officially the first FA to get slapped down by Joe Barber, and the last thing I needed was to return to work with the burn marks of muzzle blast on my neck, as if I'd spent the lunch hour trying to shoot myself—and missed. Talk about unbearable.

"Hey, it's Patrick Paradeplatz, Super FA."

"Really, dude, suicide hasn't been the Wall Street way since 1929. Now we resign in disgrace and go buy a vineyard."

I was making light of it, but I was pretty shaken. I stopped on the sidewalk to examine my neck and lower jaw in a plate glass window. Nothing serious, but it was plenty ugly—a red, black, and purple combination of a bruise, a burn, and a scrape. Somewhere in my closet was one of those black mock turtlenecks that Steve Jobs had made acceptable, if not exactly fashionable. That was just what the doctor ordered, at least until I decided what to do. It would have been easy to lose all perspective, and I reminded myself that people got assaulted at gunpoint every day in New York. Some of those victims were close friends of mine. It wasn't fun, but it was important to keep your wits about you. The most troubling part was that I'd been warned not to contact the police, and this had the feel of something that was bound to get bigger. The trick was to figure out who was in the best position to help me.

It was chilly in the shadows of Tribeca's iron-facade architecture of another century, and after a brush with death and a ride on the subway, the fresh air felt good on my face. The Irish immigrants who built the Romanesque Revival–style gem near the Franklin Street subway station could hardly have imagined that, someday, a four-bedroom apartment there would go for 12 million bucks—no extra charge for the quaint cobblestone street. Hell, it had even given my boss sticker shock. My much smaller condo was down the street. I passed a flower shop and a Jewish bakery on the way. Across the street was a coffeehouse with free Wifi for people who didn't mind sharing personal information with every two-bit hacker in Manhattan. The familiar haunts of my old neighborhood were comforting. Singapore had never felt anything like home, and if my assault had happened there, I might have been too shaken to think straight.

"You probably should see a doctor."

I said it aloud to see if the flesh wound on my neck made it painful to talk. Not bad. I'd felt much worse pain after flag football games in Central Park.

My iPhone rang. I let it go to voice mail, but the intrusion had me thinking about that funny noise again—the ping I'd heard moments before landing in the back of an SUV with a gun to my head. I stopped at the corner and tried to duplicate it. I couldn't. My guess was spyware. Before the attack, it would have been paranoia to think so. But now the only question was *who* was tracking me. BOS Corporate Security? The gentle folks who had hired a professional hit man to come within a half inch of blowing my brains out?

Footsteps sounded behind me. As I looked up I caught a glimpse of a woman fast approaching.

"Stay cool," she said.

On some level I recognized the voice, but before it could fully register, her arm locked with mine and she was pulling me along. It took only a step or two to feel the familiarity of her body against mine.

"Yes, it's me," she said, still moving. "Don't react."

I felt her hand slip into my pocket, and she removed my phone.

"It's bugged," she whispered, and she dropped it into a trash can on the sidewalk. "It picks up conversations even when you're not on the phone."

Lilly's grip tightened around my forearm as she led me into the bar at the corner.

We found the darkest booth available, and I stared at her from across the table, trying to absorb both the surprise of her return and the change in her appearance. She'd cut her hair to a stylish length that barely covered her ears, and it was dyed much darker, more of a chestnut color. It suited her, but what a different look it was.

"What the hell is going on, Lilly?"

"Do you mean what am I doing here?"

"That's only the beginning. Do you have any idea what just happened to me?"

"Yes, I do." She turned her head slowly, offering her profile. In the dim glow of a neon beer sign on the wall, I noticed the swelling on her neck, just below the jawbone. Her makeup was hiding the remnants of a flesh wound just like mine. It was an upsetting sight, and given our personal status, I probably cared too much and in ways that I had no business caring.

"Are you okay?" I asked.

She drew a breath, and on the exhale offered a weak response. "For a while, I suppose. Until they figure out that I decided not to hang around for the mock execution to turn into a real one. I cut my hair and got on a plane out of Singapore so fast that I barely had time to pack a bag."

"Who are *they*?"

"Are you sure you want to know?"

"Well, so far today I've learned that you may have hidden God only knows how many billions in Cushman's Ponzi scheme, that the bank fired you for trying to access information about numbered accounts, and that a professional hit man has promised to send both of us the way of Gerry Collins if you don't tell him where the Cushman money is. How much worse can it get?"

She looked away, presumably in shame, but my sympathy had its limits. "That thug who threatened me said not to call the police," I said, "but I'm in serious need of some answers, Lilly."

Her eyes welled, and she was suddenly on the verge of tears.

"I'm sorry," I said, not sure why I was apologizing. I didn't deal well with tears in general, and the fact was that, until our breakup, my previous record for staying mad at Lilly had been about eight seconds.

"I don't blame you if you can't stand the sight of me," she said.

"It's not that."

"I wanted to call or text you, but there's no such thing as a secure electronic communication. I was even going to send a handwritten letter by old-fashioned snail mail, figuring that was the only way to make sure they wouldn't intercept it. But I was afraid you wouldn't open it."

My head was starting to spin. "Every time the conversation starts to sound slightly normal, you throw in another layer that sounds completely crazy. Why would anyone intercept your calls and texts to me?"

"Bad stuff is going on. Has been going on since . . . we talked on the beach."

"Must be why that bird shit on my head."

My sarcasm made her smile a little, and I almost regretted the fact that I'd elicited a glimpse of the old Lilly. Almost. *Love that smile.*

"No," she said, turning serious again. "This is bad, Patrick. It started when we were together, and I knew it might come to the point where it would hurt you. I tried to tell you more on the beach, but . . . I couldn't. I chickened out, I guess. I opted for the clean break."

"So, you dumped me . . . to protect me?"

"I could lie to you and say that I'm the best person on earth and was just trying to insulate you from all this. But my thought process wasn't that clear. I needed out. With everything that was going on, you were . . . it was too much to handle."

"Okay," I said, trying not to seem too deflated. "Honesty is good. Not good for the ego, but overall—in a cosmic, utopian, Judeo-Christian, don't-get-your-hopes-up kind of way—good."

"Stop," she said. "All I'm saying is that it was not black and white. Of *course* I was afraid something might happen to you. That's why it almost killed me when I found out they had you."

"But how did you find that out?"

"They called me and said, 'We have your boyfriend.' Then they tapped me into some kind of eavesdropping device they'd planted on your iPhone."

That explained the strange ping I'd heard. "If you knew I was in danger, how about calling the cops?"

"Then they really would have killed you."

Again I recalled the thug's warning to me: *Don't even think about calling the cops.* "How did you know they weren't going to kill me anyway?"

"They told me."

"They *told* you?"

"If I'm going to find the money, they know I need a helper

inside the bank, now that I got fired. I'm sure you heard about that."

"Yes, I just heard. But hold on a second. Is that why you're here—to ask me to help you find the money?"

"No. I'm here because I'm sorry you had to become a part of this. But you need to understand the message they are sending me. What happened to you today . . . they want me to know that they can—and will—hurt people I care about if I don't meet their demand."

Part of me wanted to follow up on "people I care about," but I stayed on task. "By 'demand,' do you mean handing over the money you put in Cushman's hands?"

She nodded.

"How much are we talking about?"

"Two billion."

"Whoa. I didn't know it was *that much*."

She leaned across the table, held my hand, and looked me in the eye. "Patrick, I had no idea Abe Cushman was running a Ponzi scheme. I wish I knew what happened to all that money, but anyone who thinks I do is flat wrong."

Her hand felt nice in mine, but old feelings weren't the way to the truth. I withdrew and said the same thing Joe Barber had said to me. "I'd like to believe you."

"You have to believe me."

"You're going to have to explain an awful lot."

"All right. Where do you want me to start?"

She was touching my hand again, and despite my effort not to get caught up in old memories, my mind pulled up a funny one. Lilly and I shared a passion for old movies, and we'd rented *The Sound of Music* after working late one night at our Swiss bank, only to laugh our way into bed upon realizing that the DVD was entirely in Chinese and that the original story was set in Austria, not Switzerland anyway. It was one of my favorite nights with Lilly—sort of the standard by which our future lovemaking would be measured.

"We could make like von Trapps and start at beginning," I said in a lame Chinese accent.

The *Do-Re-Mi* allusion seemed to trigger the same pleasant memory for her, even if she did screw up her line:

"Not a bad place to start."

5

"I MET GERRY COLLINS ABOUT FOUR YEARS AGO," SAID LILLY.
"At a conference in Maui."

I was massaging behind my ear as she spoke. The ringing
had stopped, but even with a suppressor, a gunshot at such close
range was enough to cause serious discomfort.

"It was more than business," she said.

That was enough detail for me. "How long did it last?"

"I was working in New York then, and he came to the city
on business pretty regularly. We probably saw each other eight
or ten times over the next few months."

"Then what?"

"Then it just sort of fizzled out. No big dramatic breakup,
no speeches."

"No seagulls."

She gave me a weak smile. *Enough with the jokes about the
breakup.*

"We completely lost touch until I was in Singapore. He
called me. This time, it was purely business."

"What kind of business?"

A waitress came by, but there was no pressure to order.
Puffy's Tavern is one of the few remaining places on lower
Hudson Street where you can sit as long as you like and not

feel obligated to buy a fifteen-dollar bottle of sparkling water to justify your stay. Amid a spate of trendy restaurants and pricy bars, Puffy's is a blue-collar throwback to old Tribeca, a shot-and-a-beer haven for artists and truck drivers alike, still with its original tile floor and an old-fashioned bar that dates back to Prohibition. Lilly ordered a diet soda. I could have used a couple of aspirin, but I went for a shot of tequila. To each his own, I say, when it comes to pain management.

Lilly continued when the waitress stepped away.

"Gerry had a client roster that read like a social register of south Florida—professional athletes, Grammy-winning singers, all high-net-worth individuals. You have to remember that Cushman was very clever. One reason his operation didn't look like a Ponzi scheme was that he didn't accept every client who threw money at him. Gerry was able to draw in heavy hitters with guaranteed access to the Cushman fund, but not all of them wanted to be a hundred percent in Cushman. Gerry was too busy networking to manage the non-Cushman part of the investment portfolios, so he needed someone else to do it. I was someone he trusted not to steal his clients away. The fact that I was on the other side of the world and would never meet his clients was actually a plus. I handled the non-Cushman part of the portfolios from BOS in Singapore."

"So Collins matched you up with clients you never met?"

"There was always an introductory conference call."

Like most banks, BOS abided by the KYC rule: "know your client." But in this business, KYC didn't require anything nearly so onerous as actually *knowing* your client. Perfunctory conference-call introductions—"intro-functories," we called them—made Lilly no different from any of the other private wealth managers in the Singapore branch.

"But if you were helping these clients invest outside Cushman, how does that connect you to the Ponzi scheme?"

"That came later. Gerry had other clients. Super-high net

worth. Some with numbered accounts in Zurich, some with funds in other systems. I don't know all the details, but over time, the relationship with Gerry was working very well for me and BOS. That was when he asked me to arrange for one of his super clients to meet with the head of our numbered account services in Singapore."

"Surprise, surprise. The link to Cushman is bank secrecy."

"The flag wasn't nearly so red at the time."

A burst of cold air brushed my face, and I looked past Lilly to see who had entered the tavern. Puffy's wasn't exactly a Wall Street hangout, but you could never be too careful when discussing bank secrecy. The guy making a beeline to the bar seemed harmless enough. He actually looked ridiculous, a little fortysomething white man wearing one of those flat-billed rapper caps.

"Who was the client Gerry wanted you to assist?" I asked.

She shrugged. "I arranged for the meeting, but the identity of the account holder was known only to Gerry and the manager of numbered accounts."

"You had no other involvement?"

"I didn't say that."

Our drinks arrived, and the waitress left us alone. Lilly sipped her soda. I belted back my tequila, but I should have known better than to order without specifying a brand. The man at the bar pretended not to notice, but he was clearly amused by my reaction to Puffy's firewater. Lilly waited for my face to unwind, then continued.

"After the account was created, Gerry wanted me involved. We had to jump through some administrative hoops in the bank, but we finally got it approved so that I could deal directly with his client."

"A client with no name."

"Or face," she said. "Only the top brass knew who he was. To me, he was just a voice on the phone with a personal identification code. I was getting a glimpse into the private banking business that had put BOS on the financial map. I was excited, actually, but after a while it was fairly routine. Gerry's client would call me, identify himself through the proper codes, and tell me what to do with the money."

"So you moved funds from a numbered account at BOS/ Singapore to Cushman Investment."

"I didn't physically push the buttons to make it happen, no. I filled out the transfer-of-funds paperwork and personally walked it over to one of the guys in Payments Traffic. They did the actual wire transfers."

"But the wiring instructions had your name on them?"

"Yes."

"And the transfer slips showed that the money was routed to Cushman Investment?"

"Usually to offshore accounts, and then it went to Cushman."

"How do you know it actually went from the offshore accounts to Cushman?"

"The transfers were done in a very compressed time frame, usually the same business day. I spoke to Gerry every day to make sure there was no glitch in the pipeline. He gave me verbal confirmation when the money hit Cushman Investment."

"How big were the transfers?"

"On average, about ten million dollars. A day."

"For how long?"

"Like I said: It came out to just over two billion. You do the math."

Math was something I was good at. Two hundred days. "And that's the same two billion that my Times Square tour guide wants back."

"That would be correct."

"So the two-billion-dollar question is . . ."

"Who was Gerry's client," she said, finishing for me. "The bank, of course, won't divulge that information. The secrecy laws in Singapore are just as tight as Switzerland's. Unless there's evidence that the client used a secret account to assist in the commission of a crime, the bank itself violates the law by revealing any information about the account. Bankers in Singapore actually face more jail time than bankers in Switzerland for violations of bank secrecy. As far as BOS is concerned, their client isn't a criminal. He's a victim of Cushman's fraud."

"I'm guessing that's how you got yourself fired—trying to attach a name to the numbered account?"

"I was desperate. With the threats I was getting, I wanted to know who I was up against."

I looked down into my empty shot glass, thinking. "What if we went up to the BOS executive suite right now and told the general counsel that we've both been threatened?"

"First of all, we can't prove that it's a BOS client who is threatening us."

"Who else would it be? It's either him or someone working for him."

"It's him," she said. "I heard his voice every day on the phone. There's no doubt in my mind that I heard the same voice when he had the gun to my head, and when he called to tell me you were in the back of that SUV."

"Then we have to go to the bank," I said.

"Forget it. I've already taken it all the way to the Zurich headquarters. I flew six thousand miles from Singapore to meet with two stuffed shirts in Finanz Kundenbetreuung Abteilung," she said, mangling her pronunciation of the German equivalent of Financial Client Management. "It was like talking to the wall. Trust me, Patrick: the bank is never going to help on this."

"Maybe you just didn't find the right set of ears."

"Listen to what I'm saying. Eight figures a day moved into that secret account in Singapore. It was my job to execute the transfer orders going out, but I never knew who put the money there in the first place, or where it came from. It's clear to me that if we go through the proper institutional channels," she said, using her fingers to put *proper* in quotation marks, "the bank will do everything in its power to make sure that no one ever finds out."

I rested on my elbows, running my fingers through my hair. "How did you allow yourself to be put in this position?"

"What was I supposed to do—forget where I worked and become one of those people who automatically assumes that anyone who's rich and has a Swiss bank account is a criminal? I respected the lines of authority at the bank. You would have done the same thing, and you know it."

She was right. I would have—with the exception of sleeping with Gerry Collins, of course. "Have you . . ."

I stopped without even realizing I was in midsentence. That guy at the bar was pretending not to notice me again, but this time I hadn't choked on my tequila or done anything else to draw his attention. *What's so damn interesting over here, buddy?*

"Have I what?" asked Lilly.

I regained my train of thought. "Have you tried going to the authorities? The FBI, Interpol, whoever?"

"Patrick, has one shot of tequila gone straight to your head?" she said as she took my empty shot glass away from me and put it aside. "The message to me was crystal clear: call the cops, die an instant and unpleasant death."

Like a reflex, I rubbed my neck. "Ditto. But let's not rule it out."

"It's not an option. Law enforcement won't help."

"How can you say that?"

"This arrangement with Collins has put me dead center in the hunt for the Cushman money. Treasury thinks I'm hiding the money, the same way these thugs think I'm hiding the money."

"You can't assume that."

"I'm not just assuming. I've seen it with my own eyes."

"Seen what?"

She paused, and her voice lowered a notch, as if we were moving into an area of heightened sensitivity. "I've seen an internal memo written by someone high up at Treasury."

"How'd you get that?"

"I don't actually have it. I said I'd seen it. The guy who attacked me in Singapore showed it to me."

"How did he get it?"

"I don't know."

"Why did he let you see it?"

"After about the tenth time I told him I knew nothing about the Cushman money, he got fed up, said he knew I was lying. He stuck the memo right under my nose. It says it in black and white: Treasury's most promising lead as to concealment of proceeds from the Cushman fraud remains Gerry Collins' banking activities at BOS/Singapore. And the memo identifies me *by name* as the point person for those activities."

"But you were feeding money into the Cushman Fund, not taking it out."

"To them, it must be like the law of gravity: what goes up, must come down; what goes in, must come out. My point is that if I go to law enforcement, you can bet they'll be happy to protect me, but only if I give them information I don't have: what happened to the money I funneled to Cushman."

She was definitely in a box, but my focus had drifted again to the guy at the bar. Even though he was on his cell phone, I was still feeling watched.

"Lilly, don't be obvious about it, but when you get a chance, glance toward the bar and tell me if that guy looks familiar to you."

"What?"

"Just take a look," I said as I brushed her napkin off the table. She took my cue, picked up the napkin, and stole a glance in the process.

"Not anyone I know," she said. "I think I'm making you paranoid."

I wasn't so sure.

"Stay with me on this," said Lilly.

"Sorry. You were saying?"

"I was going to say that calling the FBI or whatever agency is not only dangerous, but pointless. Even if they wanted to help, the simple fact is that the bank isn't willing to give up any information about the account holder. They fired *me* for trying to get it. How quickly do you think government lawyers can get into court and force the Singapore arm of the biggest bank in Switzerland to give up the name on a numbered account? These thugs gave me two weeks to come up with the money. *Two weeks.*"

"That's a short fuse."

"And it's even shorter now."

"Why?"

"Because . . ."

"Because *why*, Lilly?"

"I didn't want to say this before. I'm not the kind of person who gets people in trouble and then looks for a pat on the back for getting them out of it. But that's the deal I struck when I was freaking out on the phone, listening to what they were doing to you in the back of the SUV in Times Square. I promised to deliver their money in one week, instead of two, if they didn't hurt you."

"You shouldn't have done that."

"It's done. So if the bank won't help us, we have to find someone inside the bank who will. Someone who can work around the regular institutional channels and tell us what we need to know about numbered account 507.625 RR."

"Why would anyone stick his neck out like that?"

"Because not everyone who works for BOS is interested in protecting organized crime. You just have to find him."

"*Me?*"

"I don't work for BOS anymore, remember?"

I could have used another shot of tequila; any brand would do. "Do you have any proof that the money flowing to Cushman was from organized crime?"

"I've done some digging. Do you remember the name of the man who murdered Gerry Collins?"

I felt another puff of cold air. That guy at the bar was heading out the door, leaving a full beer untouched.

"I'm sure I heard it in the news," I said, "but the name escapes me."

"A semiretired guy in his late fifties who lost his entire life savings in Cushman's Ponzi scheme. Never stood trial. He entered a guilty plea in order to get a life sentence instead of the death penalty. His name was Tony Martin."

"Singapore Mall," I said.

"What?"

"That's where I've seen that guy before. It was one of our first dates. I was taking your picture in front of the fountain at Singapore Mall, and he's the guy who came up and offered to snap one of the two of us."

"Patrick, that was months ago and on the other side of the world."

I jumped from the table, ran out the door, and stopped cold on the sidewalk. I looked left, then right. Parked cars lined the street, a delivery truck passed, and an old woman was scooping her poodle's droppings into a plastic bag. I had no idea which way to go. I stood frozen, not sure what to do. There was no sign of the man in the bar, and as the moments passed, I became less and less sure that I'd actually seen him before in Singapore or anywhere else.

You're getting a little crazy.

I went inside and returned to my seat at the table.

"What the hell was that about?" asked Lilly.

"Sorry, I—I just had this strange feeling that we were being watched."

She looked at me with concern. "Welcome to my world. The paranoia will take over if you let it. You need to get a grip. This is important. Please listen to what I'm telling you."

"I'm sorry, but I actually have been listening. You said the guy who killed Gerry Collins was Tony Martin."

"That's my point. His name is not Tony Martin. It turns out his *real* name is Tony Mandretti."

"Who is Tony Mandretti?"

The waitress returned. Either she'd read my mind, or Lilly had ordered a shot of tequila for each of us while I was chasing after nothing.

But why would he order a beer and not drink it?

"Now there's a really good question," said Lilly. "Who *is* Tony Mandretti?"

She leaned over her brimming shot glass, and I saw a distinct sparkle of excitement in her eye. "This is where things really get interesting."

6

—

NIGHT FELL AS WE LEFT PUFFY'S TAVERN.

Our bar talk had drifted well away from Ponzi schemes and bank secrecy, and I lost count of the empty shot glasses. Tequila had been known to loosen my tongue, and regrettably I found myself confessing that thoughts of Lilly had crossed my mind whenever I heard Lady Antebellum singing "Need You Now." This she found even more hilarious than bird shit on my head. There's a line in the song about being a little drunk, and we definitely were, so we sang our own rendition on the way back to my place, adjusting for the fact that we didn't really care what time it was:

. . . *a quarter after something / I'm out of milk / and I need your cow.*

Okay, so we were more than a little drunk.

My apartment was on the third floor. After several stabs at the keyhole, I managed to unlock the door and get us inside. It occurred to me that the first woman to visit my New York apartment was the same woman who had dumped me in Singapore, but there was no time to appreciate the irony. It took longer to find the light switch than to end up in the loft, though the decision wasn't completely without discussion.

"Should we do this?"

"Yes."

"You make a very persuasive argument."

Knew I shouldn't call / but I've lost all my clothes / and I need your towel.

The rest was a blur, which was a shame. I'd experienced "make-up sex," before, but this was better than make-up sex, since I wasn't just mad at Lilly; I had actually lost her. That put us in the realm of *reunion* sex, a rare combination of the excitement of a first-time lover with the joy being with someone who knows exactly what you like. This was one of life's greatest pleasures—and I was bumbling my way through it on too much tequila. Suffice it to say that it wasn't our best performance—far short of our Chinese *Sound of Music* watershed—but Lilly fell asleep in my arms, and all was well.

For an hour or so, anyway.

The pain in my neck—literally—woke me. I sat up in bed and gave the burning sensation a minute to subside. Lilly was sleeping soundly, and it was nice to see the curve of her body beneath the bedsheet beside me. Morning couldn't possibly have come so soon, and a check of the clock confirmed that the night was still young: 8:38 P.M. I quietly rolled out of bed, took a quick shower, and went to the dresser. We'd left a lamp burning downstairs, and it provided just enough of a glow for me to move around the loft without stubbing a toe. My overnight suitcase was packed when Lilly finally stirred.

"Wow," she said as she rose up on her elbow. "I've heard of guys dashing off after sex, but I must be the first girl in New York to send a man running from his own apartment."

I went to her side of the bed and sat on the edge of the mattress. "I was supposed to be on a seven o'clock flight out of LaGuardia. If I hurry I can catch a later one."

"Do you really have to go?"

I nodded. "It's just for a day. I'll be back tomorrow night."

"How will I reach you? Your phone's in the garbage."

"I still have my BlackBerry," I said. Everyone on my team had both an iPhone and a BlackBerry, as the head of BOS security had laid down the law that a bank-issued BlackBerry was the only way to access the bank's e-mail system.

"I guess I'll be okay," she said.

Even in the dim light, I could see the concern on her face. She'd spent the previous three nights in a hotel on Eighth Avenue, and I sensed that she didn't want to go back. "You can stay here, if you want."

"Are you sure?"

"Yeah, this is a very secure building. You'll feel safer."

"Safe is good. Apart from that . . . are you sure?"

She was giving me an out, but after what had happened to me that afternoon, it would have taken a total jerk to say, *On second thought, go sleep in your hotel room and see if anyone comes knocking in the middle of the night.*

"Yes, I'm sure."

She kissed me and smiled. "I'll go over to the hotel in the morning and check out. I only have one suitcase, so don't worry about me taking over your closet."

My mouth opened, but no words came. "Uhhhh," was all I could say. My invitation had been for tonight only. Although I wasn't dead set against her staying longer, there was still too much left unsaid between us to know where we were headed.

"Are you okay?" she asked.

"I'm fine," I said. "I think my head is starting to throb from all that tequila."

"I hope it doesn't explode on the airplane."

"What airplane?"

"The one you're trying to catch."

"Right. That one. I'd better get going."

She pulled me toward her, looking me in the eye. "It's true what I told you at Puffy's," she said. "When I found out I was under investigation for helping Cushman hide his money, my biggest fear was that they'd lock me up in a third-world jail and throw away the key before I was even charged with a crime. I had to get out of Singapore."

"I understand."

"What I'm trying to say is that I couldn't stay in Singapore. But I didn't have to come to New York." She blinked twice, as if to underscore, in a tender way, what she was telling me. "Now I'm glad I did."

I was tempted to climb right back into bed with her. "Me, too," I said.

We kissed good-bye, and I slipped away. I grabbed my overnight bag, gave Lilly one last look, and went downstairs. My coat was on a hook in the foyer, along with an extra key to the apartment.

"Lilly," I said in a voice loud enough to carry upstairs, "there's an extra key right by the—"

"I saw it," she called out.

You did?

"Hurry back," she said.

I made sure the door was locked when I left. My thoughts and emotions swirled as I headed down the hall to the elevator. I was glad to have Lilly back, and it was good that she'd filled in some of the biggest blanks for me at Puffy's. At that particular moment, however, I was mostly relieved that Lilly hadn't asked too many questions about my trip.

That 7:00 P.M. business flight had been a complete fabrication, and I wasn't on my way to LaGuardia. I hated lying to Lilly, and if she'd pressed for details, I would have been forced to come up with an even bigger one.

No way could I have told her that I was going to see Tony Mandretti.

7

JOE BARBER WATCHED THE ELEVEN O'CLOCK FINANCIAL REPORT from bed. Even with the volume blasting, he could barely hear the television over the noise of his wife pounding the treadmill.

She'd been fitness crazed since her fortieth birthday, but the late-night routine hadn't begun until after her husband's first infidelity. It was the same drill every day: start drinking at noon, go to bed at ten, lie awake calculating the staggering number of calories in a bottle of Chardonnay, freak out, jump on the treadmill, and punish her body until midnight. Of course their seven-bedroom estate in Greenwich had an exercise room, but after three years in Washington, Vanessa was still getting reacquainted with her old house. Their first night back, Vanessa had been so drunk that she'd fallen down the stairs. It was a miracle that she hadn't broken her neck. Moving the treadmill into the master suite was easier than caring for a quadriplegic wife, even if he did have to stomach the nauseating smell of alcohol exuding from her pores every night.

"Joe, that's your new bank they're talking about!"

Barber raised the volume. A further expected drop in the price of BOS stock in tomorrow's markets was the lead story on Financial News Network. "Investors are clearly wary," the FNN reporter stated, "seemingly unconvinced that the bank's settlement with the Department of Justice marks the end of the assault on bank secrecy."

"Oh, my God," Vanessa said as she stepped off the treadmill. "I told you not to take that job."

Barber shushed her, and the report continued: "This is just more bad news for Switzerland's largest bank, which last quarter reported a fifty-three percent drop in earnings, due to a slowdown in its trading and investment banking businesses."

"Damn it, Joe. You could have written your own ticket. Goldman, JPMorgan. They all wanted you. What the hell were you thinking?"

"Will you please just listen," he said.

The telephone rang. The "news" had digressed into pointless speculation and rumor, the raison d'être of real-time financial reporting. Barber lowered the volume with the remote control and took the call. It was the general counsel of BOS/America.

"Yes, I'm watching FNN," said Barber.

"That's not what I'm calling about. I have an update on Patrick Lloyd."

"Anything of interest?"

"Yeah. Patrick Lloyd is not his real name."

Barber's wife had reverted to treadmill mania, and the noisy machine forced him out of bed and into the bathroom, behind a closed door, where he could hear.

"What are you talking about?" he said into the phone.

"The bank's normal prehire background check goes back to college. Everything on Patrick Lloyd checked out that far. But when I asked Corporate Security to take it back earlier, there's nothing on this guy."

"There's nothing," said Barber, "or they just couldn't find it?"

"Swiss banks are nothing if not secure. Trust me: if it existed, our security department would have found it. The Patrick Lloyd who went to work on Wall Street simply didn't exist before he enrolled as an undergraduate at Syracuse University."

"Then who the hell is he?"

"We don't know. Security has just scratched the surface."

Barber fell silent, thinking. His general counsel asked, "Do you want me to prepare the paperwork to support his termination?"

"No," said Barber. "We stick to the plan."

"I still don't agree. You know my view from this morning's meeting: we should have fired him on the spot. Keeping him around now is playing with fire."

"He's a snot-nosed junior FA. Not for one minute do I believe that he and his girlfriend cooked up this kind of trouble alone. They're working for someone. Lilly Scanlon is gone, but Patrick Lloyd—or whatever his name is—is still under my thumb. Let him run, and see who he leads us to."

"The lack of clarity as to his true identity makes me very uncomfortable."

"Then we'll get some clarity."

"I'll instruct Corporate Security to continue looking into it."

"Things can get really dirty when you dig deep, and I don't want BOS fingerprints on the shovel. Let in-house security try its usual contacts, but if nothing pans out, outside security is the way to go here."

"Do you have someone specific in mind?"

"I do."

"Who?"

Barber returned to the bedroom. His exhausted wife had collapsed on the bed, and the treadmill was silent. The FNN assault on BOS continued, working in file footage on the "billions in bailout money" that the troubled Bank of Switzerland had received just two years earlier "in order to avert financial disaster."

"Someone who will give the boy just enough rope to hang himself," Barber said into the phone.

8

THE HOLLAND TUNNEL WAS LESS THAN TWO MILES FROM MY
apartment, and luckily for me there was a flight out of Newark,
just on the other side of the river. I was in Raleigh/Durham in
time to catch the late news coverage of the "continuing plummet
of BOS stock."

My visit to Tony Martin was all the more timely, but a
decent night's sleep had been impossible. I couldn't stop wondering what those stock analysts would have said if they had
heard rumors that BOS/Singapore was directly connected to
the disappearance of billions of dollars tainted by the Cushman
scheme. If they had known about my ride through Times
Square with a gun to my head. If they had known what I was
doing in North Carolina.

"Turn here," I told the taxi driver.

"That's the road to the prison."

"That's where I'm headed," I said. "Central Prison Hospital."

Tony Martin was one of the lucky ones. His plea of guilty
to the charge of murder in the first degree had landed him in
the custody of the Florida Department of Corrections, where he
would have been treated just like any of the other 800,000 inmates nationwide who suffered from chronic illness that required
regular medical attention. Two years into his sentence, when the

disease progressed, strings were pulled for transfer to a facility that could better treat his cancer. Central Prison in North Carolina had a 230-bed hospital and an even bigger one under construction, and it was just minutes away from the Duke University Medical Center in Durham for more specialized treatment. It was about as good as it got for inmates who required maximum-security confinement. It was the best deal around for a seriously ill mobster who was without health insurance and had lost his entire life savings to Abe Cushman's Ponzi scheme.

The taxi stopped at the entrance gate to the prison grounds. Directly ahead was a sprawling redbrick building that looked like a multilevel office complex, but for the guard towers, sharpshooters, and double perimeter of chain-link fence topped with razor ribbon. The corrections officer at the checkpoint was telling the cabdriver how to get to the hospital on the other side of the parking lot when my BlackBerry rang. It was Lilly.

"Where are you?" she asked.

"Atlanta." I lied. It was getting to be a habit, and I didn't like it. But the truth was not an option.

"You need to come back to New York."

"I'll be back tonight," I said.

"Come as soon as you can. Everything's changed."

The guard at the gatehouse allowed my taxi to pass. I wasn't entirely comfortable talking in a cab, but the driver was having a heated cell phone discussion about his fantasy football "mock draft"—whatever that was—and seemed sufficiently distracted. I spoke as softly as I could.

"What do you mean everything's changed?"

"I was so sure I was right." She was talking fast, which was what Lilly did when she got nervous. "Tony Martin was Tony Mandretti, Mandretti worked for the mob, the mob killed Collins for losing their money with Cushman, and now the mob is after me to get its money back. Now that's all out the window, and I don't have a clue who is trying to get back the two billion dollars that Gerry Collins funneled through me."

The cab stopped, and my heart thumped. It was freaky the way Lilly had mentioned Mandretti's name the moment I had arrived at Central Prison.

"Slow down, Lilly. Why is that out the window?"

"I was lying in bed, going over in my mind everything the guy in Times Square said to you. His exact words. He said: 'It's time to see the money. Cough it up, or you will both end up like Gerry Collins.'"

"Right, I remember."

"Don't you get it?"

I didn't see her point at all, but even with the cabdriver trying to work out a fantasy trade for Peyton Manning, I wasn't in a position to talk about it. Lilly was talking too fast for me to jump in anyway.

"He threatened to do the same thing to you and me that he did to Gerry Collins. *He* killed Gerry!"

"I'm not sure you can make that leap of logic," I said.

"Yes. That's clearly what he was saying. You have to take into account the way he said it, not just what he said."

"I agree, but still . . . I'm not sure."

"This is so obvious to me. If the guy who killed Gerry Collins is still out there—threatening you, threatening me—then Tony Mandretti is sitting in jail for something he didn't do."

"Lilly—"

"I know, I know. The man entered a guilty plea, and I understand he lost all his money to Cushman thanks to Gerry Collins. But I don't care. Something's not right."

The cabdriver was off the phone. He called my attention to the meter, which was still running. "Sir, if you're gonna sit here and talk, I gotta charge you."

"Lilly, I need to go. I'll be back in New York early this evening."

"I'm scared. Maybe it's time to go to the police."

"You're ignoring your own instincts," I said, lowering my voice, my hand over my mouth to prevent the cabdriver from overhearing. "You said it yourself before: he threatened to kill us if we call the cops. It's too soon to say he's the same guy who killed Collins."

"I'm going to call the police."

"Lilly, don't!" My tone was harsher than I'd intended—harsh enough for the driver to throw me a look in the rearview mirror.

"What's wrong with you?" she asked.

"I'm sorry. I have a lot on my plate today. Please, don't do anything while I'm away. Don't worry about going over to the hotel to check out. Just stay in the apartment until I get back."

She didn't answer right away. When she finally did, it was in a weak voice. "If you really think that's the right thing."

"I do. It's okay. We're going to be just fine."

"I want us to be more than just fine."

It was a nice sentiment, just enough to ease some of the tension. "Me, too," I said. "I'll call you this afternoon from the airport."

We said good-bye, and the driver turned off the meter.

"That'll be fifty-two fifty."

I paid and asked him to come back in an hour for my trip to the airport. I grabbed my bag and started up the sidewalk to the visitation center, where visits to both the penitentiary and prison hospital were coordinated. The corrections officer seated on the other side of the Plexiglas divider looked up and asked, "Can I help you?"

I had to catch myself and make sure I asked to see Tony Martin, not Mandretti. The officer inspected my bag, checked my identification, and gave me a printed form to complete. My name wasn't on the list of preapproved visitors, so there was even more paperwork. He made a phone call while I was filling it out, and he seemed a bit flummoxed after hanging up.

"Is there something wrong?" I asked.

"Have a seat, please. Someone will be out to see you in a minute."

I went with the flow and found a chair by the vending machines. I checked my watch. Lilly had sounded completely freaked on the telephone, and I wondered how long it would take her to call again to see when I was coming back to New York. I felt guilty again for having lied to her, pretending that I didn't know that Tony Martin was Tony Mandretti. She was so sure of her detective work on the mob connection to the Cushman money, but she was still poking at the tip of the iceberg.

I knew all about Tony Mandretti, the former New York mobster who had become Tony Martin upon entering the witness protection program. More than a decade had passed since Mandretti's testimony against the Santucci family. It had been front-page news, though many in law enforcement had been opposed to a deal that, in their view, didn't give Tony enough jail time. I had no firsthand knowledge, but those same critics must have seen it as poetic justice when, years later, they'd nailed him as Tony Martin for the murder of Gerry Collins. Assuming, of course, that they knew he was really Tony Mandretti. Very few in law enforcement had that information.

Outside of law enforcement, even fewer had it.

A buzzer sounded, and a man dressed in a polyester business suit entered through a secure metal door. He conveyed all the warmth of an IRS auditor. "Mr. Lloyd?"

"Yes," I said, rising.

He introduced himself as the warden, which told me right away that something was up.

"I've been advised that you're here to see inmate Tony Martin."

"That's right," I said. "It was my understanding that he is hospitalized."

The warden drew a breath. "He was."

"Was? Is he back in his cell?"

"No. I'm sorry to have to tell you that Mr. Martin passed away last night."

If the warden was expecting the news to upset or move me in some way, I completely let him down. Not because I was cold and indifferent to the death of a confessed killer. Not because I couldn't believe, or wouldn't believe, that he was dead. My reaction—or lack of it—was for a reason he couldn't have begun to fathom.

I positively *knew* it was a lie. A complete, bald-faced lie.

I thanked the warden for his condolences, grabbed my bag, and headed for the parking lot—before he could ask how I had known Tony Martin, or why I had come to see him.

9

———

TWO MINUTES AFTER MY RETURN FLIGHT FROM RALEIGH TO Newark hit the runway, I powered on my BlackBerry. The usual flood of messages crammed my in-box. One was not so usual. Opening it required the use of a decryption algorithm to unravel the cipher. Even then, the message would have meant nothing to anyone but me: "They know. Meet me at Position Three. 4:30."

Sunset was near as I crossed Fifth Avenue at Seventy-second Street and entered Central Park, and less than a half hour of daylight remained by the time I followed the long concrete crescent of sidewalk around the west side of the Conservatory Water and up to "Position Three."

The Alice in Wonderland sculpture is one of the park's most popular destinations. True to an original John Tenniel illustration from the first edition of Lewis Carroll's classic, the work depicts Alice perched on a giant mushroom reaching toward a pocket watch held by the March Hare. Peering over her shoulder is the Cheshire Cat, surrounded by the Dormouse and the Mad Hatter, and finally the White Rabbit. It is an unusual bronze, not just because of the magical subject matter, but also because the artist intended for children to play on it. Thousands have answered the call, their busy hands and feet polishing parts of the statue's patina surface smooth. This was a place I had visited as a child, in one of the handful of trips my family made into Manhattan from Queens. Burned into my memory was the look on my father's face as he approached the granite circle surrounding the sculpture and read the engraved line from "The Jabberwocky," a poem by Lewis Carroll: " 'Twas brillig, and the slithy toves did gyre and gimble in the wabe." Then he put his hands on his hips, faced my mother, and said exactly what you'd expect a native New Yawker to say: "What the fuck language is that supposed to be in?" It had sent a team of nannies from the Upper East Side hightailing it over to the carousel.

Years later, when I was asked to create a list of public sites in Manhattan to serve as potential emergency meeting places— "Position One" through "Position Five"—Alice made the cut.

The list was for FBI agent Andie Henning.

"I got your message," I said, my breath steaming in the chilly air.

Henning turned at the sound of my voice. She was seated on the same bench that, years earlier, my mother had nearly fallen from in embarrassment. I sat at the opposite end. She was looking out toward the sculpture, her hands buried in her pockets, her leather jacket too short and stylish to be of much good in the long, cold shadows of a late afternoon in January. It was hard to tell in the twilight, but I would have bet that her lips were turning purple.

"Next time we meet at the zoo," she said, fighting off shivers, "in the nice, balmy rain forest. Let's make this quick."

"Fine by me. Which *they* were you talking about in your message? And what exactly do 'they know'?"

"BOS Corporate Security. They know you haven't always been Patrick Lloyd."

I froze. That was my biggest fear since I'd agreed to this assignment.

It wasn't a job I had gone looking for. Eight months earlier, Henning had contacted me on the premise that an inside view of BOS/Singapore could uncover millions—perhaps billions—for the victims of Cushman's Ponzi scheme. That was a serious upside. The downside was obvious. Get fired. Get blacklisted in the industry. But there were even bigger risks.

"How do you know they're onto me?"

"The assistant director of BOS security called one of our field agents in New York. They have some kind of relationship that goes back a few years. Our agent didn't give up anything, but he was able to string out the conversation long enough to figure out that BOS is determined to find out who Patrick Lloyd really is."

My head rolled back, and the winter sky suddenly seemed even darker. "Shit," was all I could say. "What am I supposed to do now?"

"Stick to our agreement."

"Meaning what?"

"So long as BOS hasn't fired you, I want you to stay put."

"What happens when I'm called up to the executive suite to answer questions like 'Who is Patrick Lloyd'?"

"You can't tell them about me; you can't tell them why you went to Singapore; you can't tell them anything about our agreement."

"So that's your position—I'm on my own?"

"We have too many positives working for us to bail out now. We know that Lilly is in New York. She followed you from Singapore, just as I predicted she would. It shows that she's desperate, and that she trusts you. Expect her to make contact with you anytime now."

"She already has."

"Good. How did that go?"

I hesitated a little too long.

Andie groaned. "Don't tell me . . ."

"She spent the night."

"Men are so weak."

"Yes, but I'm all you've got. And even though we don't see eye to eye on Lilly, I do have something useful to pass along to you."

"Talk to me."

I tugged at the collar of my sweater to reveal the powder burn on my neck.

"What is that?" she asked.

I wasn't convinced of her ignorance, but I indulged her for a moment, telling her about the SUV in Times Square and the threats that had come with powder burns.

"You should have told me about this immediately."

"I got a little distracted. That's right when Lilly showed up."

"That's no excuse. Forensics could have gathered gunpowder, other trace evidence. You've washed it all away."

"Yes, I'm doing fine, thank you. Very kind of you to ask."

"Sorry. What happened to you was unnerving, I'm sure."

"Lilly got the same threats in Singapore. And more."

" 'More' in what way?"

I essentially parroted Lilly's description of the Treasury Department memo that the same thug had shoved in front of her face to refute her professed ignorance about Cushman. "Apparently someone inside Treasury has determined that the most promising lead on the location of the proceeds from the Cushman fraud is Lilly's connection to Gerry Collins."

"Who in Treasury?"

"I don't have a name. Surely the memo isn't news to you."

"This is the first I've heard of it."

I had expected the leak to surprise her; I had not expected any show of surprise as to the memo's existence. "I find that hard to believe," I said.

"Why would I lie?"

It was a question with many answers, but this wasn't the first time I'd heard her complain about the lack of interagency cooperation. Still, I wasn't sure I believed her.

"Let's talk logistics for a minute," I said. "Lilly and I have gotten death threats, and now the bank has its eye on me. This changes the game."

"You're in the business of making deals, Patrick. Changes in the game don't change the deal."

"Deals are rewritten all the time."

"I'm not particularly motivated to rewrite this one."

That was a fair point, but I didn't belong on Wall Street if I couldn't find some incentive. Fortunately, I had a few cards to play.

"I went to Central Prison this morning," I said.

She glanced my way and folded her arms tightly. It was getting colder by the minute, and so was her tone. "That is a complete violation of our agreement. Tony Martin is off limits."

"Technically, you're right. But as of yesterday I got tired of playing by your rules."

"That doesn't give you the right to hop on an airplane and visit Tony Martin in violation of our agreement. Unless you have my direct authorization, anytime you contact anyone who had anything to do with Abe Cushman and Gerry Collins, you compromise the assignment. For obvious reasons, Tony Martin is absolutely out of bounds."

I ignored the reprimand. "The warden told me that he passed away last night. My money says he's still alive."

"I can't discuss that, Patrick."

"You relocated him for protection, didn't you? Created a phony death certificate for Tony Martin, may he rest in peace, and gave him another name?"

"Like I said: I can't discuss it."

"We need to talk about it," I said. "I went to Raleigh because I'm more convinced than ever that the wrong man is sitting in jail for the murder of Gerry Collins."

"Who put that idea in your head? Lilly?"

"I have a right to know the truth."

"Your job is to investigate Lilly Scanlon. So far, she has managed to take you completely off your assignment, first by sleeping with you, and now by putting ideas in your head that the wrong man is sitting in jail."

"What you just said is so inaccurate that you should have Tweeted it. My decision to go to Raleigh was my own."

Her legs were shaking up and down—anything to stay warm—and watching her was enough to make me shiver.

"Okay," she said, "I can't discuss this with you, so we're not discussing it. But if Tony Martin was innocent, then why did he plead guilty?"

"False confessions are more common than you folks in law enforcement like to admit."

"Sure, it happens," said Andie, "but in every case of false confession that I'm aware of, the prisoner later recanted his confession. Tony has never recanted his. In fact, if you were to ask him today, he'd tell you he killed Gerry Collins. Why do you suppose that is, Patrick?"

"I don't know. But if you're not willing to help me find out, maybe Lilly will."

"Stop thinking of her as your ally. And stop playing homicide detective. Your theory makes no sense anyway. He pleaded guilty to murder and accepted a life sentence. How is that better than having it exposed that his name is really Tony Mandretti?"

"Being Tony Mandretti is a ticket to a slow, painful death. Especially when you have cancer and don't have the energy to run. Spending the rest of your life in prison as Tony Martin and getting decent health care in your dying days is much preferable."

"Tony Martin killed Gerry Collins. He lost his entire life savings in the Cushman fraud. His fingerprints were found in Gerry Collins' car. He confessed to the crime. That's why he copped a plea."

"If the killer had simply pumped a bullet into the back of

Collins' head, your basic mob-style execution, maybe I'd be less skeptical. But Gerry Collins was murdered in a pretty unusual way, wouldn't you say? Wire saw. Cuts through flesh and bone like they're cardboard."

"I'd call it mob-style strangulation with an exclamation point."

"I call it an extremely personal killing. Lots of anger toward the victim. Not a clean hit."

Her expression tightened. "I believe this non-discussion has gone far enough."

I wasn't completely convinced that Lilly was right, but it seemed worthwhile to test her theory. "A guy told me I'd end up like Gerry Collins if he didn't get his money. Why would he do that, unless he killed Collins?"

"What happened to you is nothing like the murder of Gerry Collins. A gun to the back of the head is not this killer's style."

"And why would you be talking about a 'style,' unless the killer has the ability to strike again?"

"You're fishing," she said.

"Sometimes fishermen actually catch fish. The fact remains that my attacker threatened that I would end up like Collins."

"Copycats are everywhere."

"Maybe. But let me put it to you this way: suppose I report this incident to the police."

"You've reported it to me. That's enough. You know you can't go to the police."

I smiled thinly, knowing that I'd found her motivation to renegotiate our deal. "A full police report would surely trigger leaks to the press about the bank's possible link to Abe Cushman. Leaks to the press would mean that my work inside BOS would be over. Very bad for you and the FBI, no?"

"Yes. That would be bad."

"I'm so glad we've agreed to renegotiate."

She wasn't smiling, but she didn't seem too resentful of the angle I'd worked. She may have even respected it. "What are you proposing?"

"I'll stay on mission. But I want more protection. And I want protection for Lilly, too."

She scoffed so hard her breath steamed. "Lilly's the target."

"It's time to change the target. Collins used her. She's a pawn in this."

"You fell into bed with her. If you were an undercover FBI agent, you would have been fired long ago."

"We've already covered that ground, and I believe the bottom line is that I'm all you've got. Which puts me in the driver's seat. So here's the deal: I'll do what I can to help you and the FBI save face. One thing we know for certain is that Treasury isn't copying you on its internal memos. Assuming I don't get fired, I'll stay at BOS and help you gain back whatever ground the FBI has lost to Treasury in the great interagency race to unravel Cushman's scheme and be the first 'on the money,' so to speak."

"That's not what this is about."

"Stop. I'm only going to say this once. I'll also keep quiet about the threat I got in Times Square so that you and I don't have to waste all our time avoiding calls from the media."

"What's the catch?"

"I want two things. One: I want the FBI to help figure out who threatened me."

"Fine."

"I don't mean some abstract promise that law enforcement is doing everything it can. I want to be kept informed by *you*, personally."

"I'll see what—"

"No, there's no 'I'll see.' That's the deal. Second, I want protection for me—and for Lilly. Even more for Lilly."

Our eyes locked. She could have turned me down flat. But if she accepted, it would mean that Treasury's focus on Lilly and BOS/Singapore really had come as a surprise to her, and that my hunch was correct. For some reason, the FBI was out of sync with its sister agency, and Agent Henning needed me to stay involved if she was going to figure out what the heck was really going on.

"All right," she said. "I'll check with the bureau to see what kind of protection I can get."

"Thank you. And when this is over, remember that I was the one who told you that whoever wrote that Treasury Department memo is dead wrong: Lilly had nothing to do with Cushman."

"Sooner rather than later, you are going to have to open your eyes and help me see the real Lilly Scanlon."

I wasn't blind, and of course there was a corner of my mind that wondered if Treasury was right—that Lilly really did know something. But I wasn't going to share that with Henning. I felt guilty enough as it was for having spied on Lilly.

My gaze returned to Alice and her friends on the giant mushroom. "Sure thing," I said, "I love chasing down rabbit holes."

10

THE SUBWAY TOOK ME DOWN TO TRIBECA, AND ON THE SHORT walk to my apartment I stopped at the corner deli for takeaway. A couple of slices of pizza for me, a dinner salad for Lilly. I probably should have called to ask what she wanted, but I knew the chicken Caesar would be a winner. More to the point, I wasn't ready to talk to her yet, not even about something as mundane as, *What do you want for dinner?* Agent Henning's warning about "the real Lilly Scanlon" was playing on my mind.

My relationship with Agent Henning was complicated. Sometimes she felt like an adversary. Other times she seemed like someone I could trust. My first impression had been highly favorable, but only because I found it intriguing that such an attractive woman on the other side of the coffee bar seemed incapable of taking her amazing green eyes off of me. The second impression had been not so favorable. Getting cornered by an FBI agent is not exactly a banner day for a Wall Street banker. It was soon clear, however, that I was not suspected of any wrongdoing. The target was one Lilly Scanlon at BOS/Singapore. My immediate reaction had been that the FBI was overlooking an obvious point, which I'd laid right on the table.

"I work in New York."

"We have cooperation from an insider. She'll get you transferred."

"But I have no interest in going to Singapore."

"It will only be for a few months."

"That's a few months too long."

"We could be talking about billions of dollars for Cushman's victims."

"It's not that I don't care. But if this thing blows up and it comes out that I was a mole working for the FBI, my career is over."

"It won't blow up."

"Easy for you to say. Look, I don't mean to sound mercenary, but you're asking me to take a huge risk. I understand the point about helping Cushman's victims, but . . ."

"What's in it for you?"

"Back up even further. *Why me?* With eight thousand financial advisors at BOS, why are you sitting here in New York asking me, Patrick Lloyd, to help you?"

"Because I know you're not Patrick Lloyd."

The answer had hit me like ice water, but Henning was just getting started.

"Here's the deal . . . Peter."

Her invocation of my real name had done its job. Naturally, what had followed was the proverbial offer I couldn't refuse.

"Yo, dude," said the guy behind the counter. "You want the dressing on the salad or on the side?" He seemed annoyed, as if it was the third or fourth time he'd asked. I'd zoned out.

"On the side," I said.

A cold wind was blowing in from the river as I walked home. With no gloves, my right hand was glad for the steaming pizza in the paper sack I was clutching. My left was not so happy toting my overnight bag. I hurried down the sidewalk, passing a few pedestrians, then stopped short in front of my building. It was dark, I had things on my mind, and I was in a rush to get home—but I could have sworn that the man in the overcoat who'd just walked past me was the guy from Puffy's Tavern.

I pivoted and did an about-face. The man was walking briskly and had already reached the corner. He stopped to check for traffic, then glanced over his shoulder. The glowing streetlamp provided just enough light: there was instant, mutual recognition. I dropped the suitcase and the food and ran after him. He took off like a rocket.

"Stop!" I shouted, my arms and legs pumping. He ran even faster, heading west toward Hudson. I knew a shortcut through the alley and decided to head him off. I was at full speed when a truck backed out from behind a restaurant. I planted my foot, intending to cut like Reggie Bush, but I looked more like George Bush auditioning for *Dancing with the Stars*. My foot slipped, and I skidded into a pile of garbage bags.

"Beat it, pal," the driver shouted from his truck. "You can't sleep here."

I thought about continuing my chase, but the pain in my ankle trumped that inclination. I pulled myself up and hobbled back to my apartment, only to find a homeless man seated on the sidewalk enjoying my pizza and Lilly's salad. I grabbed my suitcase.

"Hey, that's mine!" he said.

I was in no mood to argue, and under the applicable urban laws of street survival, he probably had the better argument anyway. "How much you want for it?"

"Fifty bucks."

I gave him twenty, and he was happy. I dialed Lilly's cell on my way into the building. There was no answer, which concerned me. At Puffy's, the more I had thought about it, the less sure I was that I'd seen that man before in Singapore. This time, the opposite was true.

I dialed my apartment, but it went to the answering machine. "Lilly, if you're there, pick up the phone," I said.

She didn't answer. I hurried into the building and took the stairs, no time to wait for the old elevators to descend all the way from the penthouse. I dug out my key as I ran down the hall, turned the lock, and pushed open the door—pushed so hard that I nearly dislocated my shoulder when the chain lock engaged. It should have occurred to me that Lilly would have it secured. But if she was inside, why hadn't she answered the phone? I called out through the opening.

"Lilly, it's me."

I waited, then stepped back and rang the doorbell. No response. I dug out my cell and speed-dialed hers. Again, no answer. I dialed my landline and could hear it ringing inside the apartment, but it went to the answering machine, just like the last time.

"Lilly!"

Still no response. I dialed the front desk and spoke to the guard. "Gabriel, do you remember the woman I introduced you to last night?"

"Yes, sir."

"Did you see her go out today?"

"No, sir, but I've only been here since four."

I hung up and realized it had been a foolish question: my apartment had only one door, so if the chain was on, she had to be in there.

"Lilly, wake up and open the door!"

Lilly was a light sleeper, and it was odd that she would snooze right through the sound of the door catching on the chain, let alone a ringing telephone, the doorbell, and my shouting. I pushed my face into the opening, and this time I was struck by how cold it was inside—as cold as the outdoors. It was one of our longest-standing battles as a couple: I liked to sleep with the window open. Lilly never did.

Never.

Panic struck, fueled in part by having just spotted that guy from Singapore in my neighborhood. I feared the worst, and "the worst" had many faces, including the possibility that Lilly had done something stupid to extricate herself from a world that seemed to be crashing down upon her. I dropped my overnight bag and put my shoulder into the door, but that chain was serious hardware. I'd noticed a fire ax in the stairwell on my way up, right next to the alarm, and in a weird moment of life imitating art, I suddenly envisioned Kate Winslet in *Titanic* breaking Leonardo DiCaprio free from the handcuffs as water rose up around them. I ran and got the ax, racing down the hall as if the building were indeed on fire. I called out her name one more time, which drew only silence. One swing of the ax broke through the chain, and I rushed inside.

"Lilly!"

The apartment was as dark and cold as the night. I switched on the light and saw nothing out of the ordinary. I checked the bathroom, the closet, and then the loft. There was no sign of Lilly, but one window in the loft was wide open, which accounted for the cold wave that had gripped the apartment. I stuck my head outside. I'd never had to leave by way of the fire escape, but apparently Lilly had done just that.

Or did someone take her?

"Is everything okay in here?"

The old woman's voice drew me from the window, and I climbed down from the loft. My eighty-year-old neighbor was standing in the doorway, dressed in a bathrobe that looked to be at least her age. The fire ax on the floor and the busted chain on the door cried out for an explanation, but I offered none. Instead, I tapped into "the eyes of the building," as Mrs. Voss was known: she missed nothing, knew when her neighbors went to the bathroom, and could probably have made an intelligent guess as to whether it was number one or number two.

"Honestly, I'm worried," I said, understating it. "My girl-friend Lilly was staying with me. The chain was on the door when I came back, but she's gone and the window is wide open."

"She left three hours ago," said Mrs. Voss.

"With someone?"

"No."

"Are you sure?"

"I heard a noise on the fire escape and saw her climbing down. She was by herself. I don't know what strange things you have going on in here, young man, but this is a respectable building."

It occurred to me how bad this must have looked—an ax-swinging man breaking into his own apartment, a young woman fleeing by way of the fire escape. "This is not what it seems," I said.

She seemed skeptical, even a little afraid.

"Really," I said. "It's all fine."

She retreated quietly, muttering something about the guy who should never have sold me the apartment. I had the feel-ing that this was going to be prime grapevine material, if not a formal complaint to the condo association.

I picked up the fire ax, laid it aside, and closed the door. The heater hissed, overworked in the battle against winter. I climbed back upstairs and shut the window. When I returned, I noticed the rose petals on the floor. Three of them were just inside the door. Several more marked the way like bread crumbs to the kitchen. On the counter, next to the computer, lay a scattering of long-stemmed red roses. Not a neatly bound bouquet, but six single roses that appeared to have been tossed aside.

What the hell?

I turned and took a better look around the place, trying to reconstruct what had happened. Any number of shops sold fresh flowers in my neighborhood. It was possible that Lilly had been bitten by the decorating bug and gone out, but if the intent had been to brighten my apartment, a mixed bouquet would have done just fine. More likely, Lilly had received a delivery. And then something had scared her off in a big way. Something to do with red roses. It made me wonder what—or more precisely, *who*—Lilly was running from.

My eyes were drawn again to the roses on the counter, and then to my PC beside them, which was humming. I went to the computer and tapped the space bar. The screen saver vanished, revealing a typed message.

They're watching. Sorry I had to leave this way. Do not try to find me. Will let you know when it's safe.

I studied Lilly's words. No doubt about it: she'd given someone the slip by using the fire escape. My ax-swinging Kate-and-Leonardo episode could have been avoided if she'd simply removed the chain on the door before climbing out the window, but she must have been in too much of a rush. Maybe they were banging on the door as she was making her getaway. Whoever "they" were. I had no way of knowing, and my second sighting of the mysterious man from Singapore had given me nothing to go on. I was tired of guessing. I went to work on the computer.

My hunch was correct. The thought of Lilly cooped up all day in my apartment without going online was inconceivable, and either she didn't care if I saw her Internet search history, or she'd left in too much of a hurry to erase it. A quick review gave me a road map to her activity. She'd hit Facebook, of course, though only a complete idiot would post her destination online before making a run for it. There were visits to nytimes.com and other news Web sites. Amid the idle browsing activity was a visit to Google maps. *That* intrigued me. I pulled up the exact page she'd visited, and voilà. It was the high-tech version of the gumshoe detective who finds the notepad left behind and shades the top sheet with the side of his lead pencil to turn indentations into words and draw up the last message.

A street address popped up.

It was downtown, maybe a twenty-minute walk from my apartment. I jotted it down, then thought better of it. I committed the address to memory and tossed the note in the garbage. Then I thought of yesterday's ride through Times Square with a gun to my head.

I fished the note from the trash can, flushed it down the toilet, and headed out the door.

11

DO NOT TRY TO FIND ME. LILLY'S INSTRUCTIONS COULD NOT HAVE been clearer. Of course, that was like telling a six year old, Whatever you do, don't think about pink elephants. I was determined to find her, and not even that herd of pink elephants on the corner of Canal and Hudson was going to stop me.

"Where to?" asked the cabdriver.

I gave the address. The subway would have been just as quick, but my BlackBerry didn't always work down there, and a few minutes in the back of a cab gave me a chance to answer some e-mails and do my real job. One thread seemed particularly important. I'd been watching a company called Tatfree, a little-known medical-instruments manufacturer whose researchers were on the verge of developing a quick and relatively painless process for the removal of unwanted tattoos without scarring. It seemed like a wise investment in a world where my generation had gone tattoo crazy, seemingly oblivious to the fact that someday the girl with the dragon tattoo would be the old woman with a shriveled up reptile on her backside. My team leader wanted me to nail down rumors of plans for an initial public offering.

"Will make some calls," I wrote, "and provide color in the a.m."

I was starting to overuse that expression, but its utility was immense. Even if you hadn't done a damn thing, even if you didn't have squat to say, as long as you claimed to provide "color," your words had value on Wall Street.

"You can drop me here," I told the driver. We were way down on John Street, and if the cabbie hit one more pothole, I was going to shatter a molar. It was close enough for me to walk the rest of the way. I paid the fare and negotiated around two blocks of road construction by way of a temporary sidewalk.

Several of my favorite sandwich shops were on John Street, but they were closer to Broadway. This far from the heart of the financial district was unfamiliar territory. After nine P.M. the streets were deserted, and most storefronts were barricaded, which made some of the city's oldest buildings look even older. I had only an address, not a description of the building, so I did a double take when I reached my destination. It was a stone church, as tiny as it was old. I climbed the foot-worn granite steps out front—just three in all—and read the sign on the door. HOURS OF WORSHIP, it said, but nothing was posted. Beside it was a notice for an upcoming service to commemorate the first anniversary of the terrorist attacks of September 11, 2001. This did not have the feel of an active church.

"Looking for something?"

I turned to see a man standing on the sidewalk, his face barely visible in the faint glow of the streetlamp on the corner. He was wearing an overcoat, but even discounting that, he appeared to be of impressive stature. I climbed down the steps.

"I'm not sure I'm in the right place," I said.

"Then perhaps God has brought you here," he said, extending his hand. "I am the Reverend Manu Robledo."

"Patrick," I said, withholding my last name as we shook hands. "Is this your church?"

He chuckled. "*My* church? No, I'm merely the rector. This

building belongs to the faithful. It's the future home of the Church of Peace and Prosperity International."

And I work for the Swiss Bank of Love and Kindness, I wanted to say. But I held my tongue. "Where is the church's current home?"

"En todas partes," he said, the words rolling off his tongue in Spanish. "Everywhere."

"Is that so?"

"It is indeed," he said, seeming to detect my skepticism. "The church has tens of thousands of followers worldwide. We built ourselves from the ground up, but only in the figurative sense. Heretofore we've operated entirely in the virtual world, linked only by the Internet. This old building will be our brick-and-mortar headquarters, our first piece of terra firma."

"Congratulations," I said.

He thanked me, but he was suddenly studying the contours of my face. I took a better look at him as well, though the shadows made it difficult. The dark eyes and complexion jibed with his Hispanic surname, and he had the heaviest eyebrows I'd ever seen, almost as thick and broad as his black mustache. I was having trouble pinpointing the accent. I had enough international clients to know the difference between Mexican Spanish and, say, Colombian Spanish. But the rector's accent seemed to change from one sentence to the next. At times I also detected hints of Brazilian Portuguese. There was even a little Middle Eastern dialect. It had me stumped. And intrigued.

"You look familiar to me," he said. "Have we met?"

"I highly doubt it."

"No, I'm very good with faces. Even better with names. Tell me your last name, Patrick."

I hesitated to give too much information, but whenever people tried to guess my name it made me nervous, made me spit out the alias that the government had given me—anything to shut down the fishing expedition. "Lloyd," I said. "My name is Patrick Lloyd."

He snapped his fingers, smiling with recognition. "Yes, Patrick Lloyd. I *knew* I'd seen your face before."

"I'm quite certain we've never met."

"I've seen your photograph," he said. "On Facebook. You're Lilly Scanlon's boyfriend."

Lilly was the reason for my visit, but it still took me aback. "You know Lilly?"

"Very well," he said. "We spoke on the telephone not too long ago."

"How long?"

"Not long." His evasiveness seemed purposeful, and I had no way of knowing if "not long" meant ten weeks or ten minutes.

"Tell me, Patrick: Is everything okay with Lilly?"

"I'm not sure, to be honest."

"No one is, it seems. Such a shame. Lilly is one of our lost sheep."

"Are you saying that Lilly is a member of your church?"

He smiled again. "You say that as if we were some kind of cult."

If the shoe fits . . .

His cell rang, and he begged my pardon to check the incoming number. "I'm afraid I must return this call," he said. "But if you see Lilly, please tell her that we miss her. Will you promise to do that for me, Patrick?"

It came across not as a casual request, not mere idle conversation. He seemed to be sincerely soliciting my promise.

"Sure thing," I said.

"Good man," he said with a smile. "Lilly can't hide from us forever, you know. But I'm sure she knows that."

His friendly tone lent some ambiguity to his words. *Some.* "I'm sure she does," I said.

He bade me good night, climbed the steps, and unlocked the door. Then he turned and shot me another smile, adding a little wink before he disappeared inside the Church of Peace and Prosperity International.

I stood alone on the sidewalk, not sure what to think, but I had never seen a phonier smile or a wink less sincere. And that accent was so all over the place. I was having a hard time accepting that it was his real voice—that *anyone* actually spoke that way. It had me thinking that we had indeed met before.

But the Reverend Robledo didn't want me to know where.

12

IT WAS ALMOST MIDNIGHT, AND I WAS STILL WALKING. OLD "Tri-be-ca," named for the "triangle below Canal," wasn't that big. In the chilly night hours that followed my meeting with Manu Robledo I'd managed to cover virtually every square inch of my neighborhood. My best thinking was done while walking or while out for a run, and I had plenty to digest.

Lilly's possible connection to the International Church of Phony Baloney had raised a slew of questions. My subsequent conversation with Agent Henning answered none of them. Public parks were our preferred meeting spot, and this time I'd chosen "Position One": the stairway to nowhere along the Battery Park waterfront, basically an observation platform that rose up over the trees like a giant stuck horseshoe and offered killer views of Ellis Island and the Statue of Liberty. It was unusual for us to meet twice in a single day, but things were happening fast. In twenty minutes I recapped everything for her, from the reappearance of the stranger from Singapore to Manu Robledo's phony accent and thick, distinctive eyebrows. She gave me nothing in return, save for her assurance that I need not report Lilly as "missing" to the police. The FBI had it covered. I was grateful for that, and for the fact that Andie hadn't given me a big fat "I told you so."

"You want me to walk you to a cab?" she asked.

Even though I'd requested protection the last time we'd met, her offer was somehow emasculating. It made me realize that I needed to think through exactly what I meant by "protection." Maybe it was as simple as a panic button directly to the FBI. I wasn't sure—but a personal bodyguard definitely was not what I had in mind. This was my neighborhood, I loved living here, and I refused to let myself be afraid to walk home without an FBI escort. I was also fully aware that the park was patrolled at least until the piers closed at one A.M.

"You go ahead," I said, "I'll be fine."

Twenty minutes later I was still in the park, a short walk north of where Andie had left me, having found a peaceful place to let my thoughts gel. I simply wasn't convinced that Andie was right about Lilly. The last two days, however, had me seriously entertaining the possibility that I was blinded by . . . love . . . lust? Whatever it was that had kept me from asking the right questions during all that time I'd wasted in Singapore.

"Got a cigarette, dude?"

I was staring out at the black river, standing on the bicycle trail that snaked along the western edge of the Hudson River. The tennis courts behind me were dark. Equally quiet was nearby Chelsea Piers, where I'd paid through the nose for countless buckets of balls at Manhattan's only driving range. I was so wrapped up in my thoughts that I hadn't even noticed the man on the park bench.

"Sorry, I don't smoke."

I fought off the shadows for a better look, the thought occurring to me that beneath the homeless getup might lurk that stranger from Singapore, who seemed to show up everywhere lately. This man was huge, much too big to be that other guy, even bigger than Robledo, and it wasn't just the winter coat. His legs stretched out forever before him, and he had the hands of a man well over six feet tall. I turned and continued along the path toward the World Financial Center. The click of his heels followed.

"Just one lousy cigarette," he said. "That's all I want."

This, of course, was just what I needed: a homeless Paul Bunyan with nothing better to do than hassle me. I ignored him, but he didn't go away.

"Don't try and tell me you don't smoke," he said, still following.

I quickened my pace, but he kept stride.

"You Wall Street tight-asses all smoke," he said, still trailing me. "I see you hanging out every day by the barricades outside the stock exchange."

I wasn't a smoker, but he was right, in a general sense: no matter how cold the weather, you could find refugees from smoke-free office buildings puffing away in the pedestrian-only stretch of Wall Street off Broadway, right outside the exchange.

But how did he know I had anything to do with Wall Street?

I stopped and turned. He stopped, too. I looked him in the eye, which only reconfirmed that he wasn't the guy from Singapore. I was trying not to panic, but my thoughts raced with the even more disturbing possibility that this might be the guy from Times Square. That armed escort from Agent Henning was looking pretty good in hindsight.

"Who are you?"

He was silent, didn't move. I turned and continued on my way, listening carefully for the click of his heels behind me. We were coming up on a forested stretch of the path, and the darkness beneath nature's canopy made me extra cautious. His rant continued.

"Just as well," he said, "cancer sticks are what did in Tony Mandretti."

That got my attention. I started to turn, but before I could react he had me from behind. The cord around my neck made me freeze. Anyone who could move that quickly was definitely no random homeless person.

"Stop!" I said, but he was in control.

"Be still!"

The wire around my neck was taut enough to scare me, loose enough for me to breathe—barely. It was hard to focus. For the second time in as many days I was the victim of an attack, but I was having difficulty remembering the sound of the man's voice in the back of the SUV. Maybe that was because this voice was different. I wanted desperately to compare the two, but I just wasn't sure.

"Stay away from Lilly Scanlon," he said.

That was the opposite of what the guy in the SUV had told me, and with the conflicting agendas I could suddenly discern a difference between the voices. This was definitely not the same guy from the SUV.

"Okay, you got it."

"Stay away from the FBI, too."

I swallowed hard. He hadn't mentioned Agent Henning by name, and before he could, I suddenly felt the need to protect myself, or at least to deny any connection to anyone who was off limits.

"I honestly don't know—"

He tightened the wire and held it, which sent me into survival mode. I kicked backward and nailed him in the shin, but he pulled me to the ground and rolled me onto my belly. I swung my arms over my head, pried with my fingers at the wire around my neck—but the man was a bull. He had me, and he kept squeezing—not long enough to make me pass out, not so tight as to cause permanent injury. It was the perfect length of time and the precise amount of pressure to send a clear message:

I was dealing with a professional. Finally, he allowed me some slack, and I coughed for air.

"Just stay away," he said. "It won't be pretty if you don't."

Before I could answer he delivered a crushing blow to the back of my skull—a head butt, maybe. My chin hit the pavers, and I was barely conscious as the taste of blood filled my mouth. I tried to lift my head, but the side of my face might as well have been glued to the cold bike path. The groan I let out was completely involuntary, and the next thing I heard was the sound of his heels echoing in my mind—a quick pace, a man running, my attacker getting away.

Then all was black.

"Are you all right, sir?"

My eyes blinked open. The voice was a stranger's, and I was gazing up at a woman I didn't recognize. She was wearing a uniform. *A cop?* No, she was a park ranger, and only then did I even begin to remember what had happened to me. I sat up slowly. The ranger was at my side, down on one knee, and she braced my shoulder to steady me. My head was pounding, and it was a struggle to focus.

"Do you know your name?" she asked.

I was sure that I did, but the answer wouldn't come. I was suddenly blinded by a flashlight, and the ranger apologized, saying something about checking my pupils.

"Do you know what day it is?" she asked.

Never had such a simple question seemed so complicated. It was still night, that much I could tell. I was fading in and out, but for a moment I managed to comprehend that I was exactly where Mr. Congeniality had delivered a head butt with sufficient force to drop a rhinoceros. "What time is it?" I asked.

"Two twenty A.M."

It hurt to think, but I forced myself to do the math. I'd been out cold for a couple of hours. Or had it been twenty-six hours? I wasn't sure. "So, today is . . . Wednesday?"

"Can you tell me your name?"

There she went again, asking me that simple, impossible question. The answer was stuck somewhere between my brain and my tongue.

"Sir, can you tell me who you are?"

The night around me started to swirl. The ranger propped me up.

"Sir, what's your name?"

I fought to remain conscious. "My name," I started to say, but my train of thought was barely on the tracks. I drew a deep breath, reached inside, and yanked out the truth.

"It's Peter," I said. "My name is Peter Mandretti."

13

SHE WAS ALIVE. HE COULD FEEL IT. WITH TWO LATEX-COVERED fingers pressed against her neck, he detected a heartbeat. She was unconscious but slowly coming back. He'd taken her to the brink of death, but not beyond.

He hadn't lost his touch.

Wisely, he'd decided to hang around the riverfront after taking down Patrick Lloyd. The nearby marina offered dozens of hiding places. Himself a sailor—if you called a former Navy SEAL a "sailor"—he'd chosen the fifty-foot Morgan in slip E–35. The lock on the cabin door had been child's play, and while enjoying some rich investment banker's twenty-year-old scotch, he had peered through night-vision binoculars—standard equipment in his tool kit—as the park ranger came to the aid of the fallen target. He saw her revive him and watched them have a conversation before Lloyd blacked out again. The only problem was that he hadn't been able to hear what they were saying. All problems had a solution.

The ranger worked the graveyard shift, which ended at six A.M. He'd followed her to the subway, rode in the car behind hers, and got off the train ten seconds after she did. She'd had no idea he was tailing her, and by seven A.M. she'd unwittingly led him all the way to her apartment in New Jersey. Officially, sunrise was just minutes away, but the overcast sky was black with a hint of purple. Rows of barren elms cast long shadows in the glow of burning streetlights. He had the advantage of darkness, but he needed to be careful as the neighborhood came to life with morning commuters. Pretending to wait at the bus stop across the street, he'd watched the lights inside her apartment switch on and off, a silent trail that broadcast her trip from the front door to the bathroom to the bedroom. He'd imagined her undressing—there was definitely one hot body beneath that unflattering uniform—but he shook off the distraction. That wasn't what this was about. He'd allowed her forty minutes to fall asleep, then made his move. The window in the alley had been his point of entry.

"What . . . do you want?" she asked in a voice that quaked.

She was almost completely conscious now, revived if not refreshed, but at least coherent enough to ask a valid question. It amused him that she would even entertain the possibility of a response. He would ask the questions, and having taken her to the brink of death, he was assured of the truth.

He buried his knee firmly into her kidney. She was flat on her stomach, facedown on the bathroom rug, hands cuffed behind her waist, unable to move beneath his two-hundred-plus pounds of sculpted muscle. A man of considerably less strength could have obtained the same results. Control was more about technique than brute force. The strangulation stick was a simple but lethal device, a two-foot loop of nylon rope attached at both ends to a ten-inch wooden handle. It allowed him to twist with one hand and choke his victim, leaving the other free to control her.

Her legs twitched with each futile kick against the white tile floor. Some degree of fight remained inside her, but experience told him that he couldn't take this one to the edge again and be certain of her return. Three such journeys seemed to be her limit. Each twist of the noose around her neck had made her groan and squirm up until the point of lost consciousness. At precisely the right moment he would release. The loop at the end of the stick would loosen. Her swanlike neck would lose the hourglass effect. Her breathing would resume. Blood would bring oxygen to her dying brain. The purple ring of bruises around her neck would swell, then throb. Slowly, her near-dead body would return to life. As an interrogation tactic, the garrote was riskier than waterboarding, but when done properly it was far more effective.

Again he gave her a moment to catch her breath, then spoke in the stern voice that had elicited secrets from subjects much tougher than this one.

"Tell me what he said to you!"

"What who said?"

"The man you helped in the park."

"He didn't tell me anything."

"I saw you talking before he blacked out. What did he say?"

"I—I don't remember."

"Tell me!"

"Honestly, I don't re—"

A twist of the stick tightened the rope. She gasped, and he released. He leaned closer, breathing his words into her ear. "Tell me what he said. Or you die right now."

Her body shook, but her feeble resistance concerned him. She should have been pleading for her life. He feared he was losing her. He grabbed her by the hair and raised her head off the floor. Her eyes had rolled back into her head. Time was running out. He grabbed her by the shoulders and sat her up against the bathtub. The faucet was close enough for him to soak a bath towel, and he splashed her face. It was like trying to keep a druggie from slipping into a coma, but he was making some headway.

"Tell me what he said. *Right now.*"

"He, uh . . ."

He splashed her again with cold water. "He *what*?"

"He made no sense," she said.

"Just tell me what he said, damn it!"

She breathed in and out, but it was beyond a struggle. The wheezing told him that her throat was crushed, and she wasn't getting enough air.

"He said . . . his name . . . Peter," she said, her eyes closing.

"Peter what?"

She didn't answer, but he was determined to get it, even if he had to shake it out of her. "Peter *what*?" he said, prying her eyes open.

"Mandretti," she said.

Her voice was little more than a whisper, and he might not have caught it if he hadn't heard that surname before.

"Like Tony Mandretti?" he asked, but she didn't answer. Her shoulders slumped, and her chin hit her chest.

Peter Mandretti. Tony Mandretti's son. It made perfect sense to him. It was as he had suspected: the son was driving the car, but the father was navigating him down the road to Cushman's money.

He allowed the deadweight of her torso to slide to the right, and her body became a heap of collateral damage on the bathroom floor.

The interrogation was over, successful beyond his wildest dreams.

14

I WOKE IN A STRANGE BED WITH SIDE RAILINGS, A WHITE
fluorescent ceiling light assaulting my eyes. An angled mattress
had me somewhere between the upright position and flat on my
back. Squinting, I propped myself up further on one elbow and
peered through a crack in the white curtain before me. It wasn't
a window curtain. It was a room divider that separated my private cubicle from the busy common area beyond, where nurses
and doctors wearing green hospital scrubs darted about. I was
alone and still in my street clothes, no shoes. I had no memory of
coming to the emergency room, but my mind was clear enough
to recall a conversation with a park ranger before blacking out a
second time.

She must have brought me here.

Details of that conversation suddenly came flooding back—
"My name is Peter Mandretti"—and in a moment of panic, I
checked the hospital ID bracelet on my wrist.

PATRICK LLOYD, it read.

I breathed a sigh of relief. The park ranger had apparently
dismissed my "Peter Mandretti" slip of the tongue as the inco-
herent ramblings of an assault victim. Presumably, the hospital
had checked my driver's license upon admission.

My BlackBerry rang, but it wasn't in my pocket. I was still

gathering my wits and adjusting to my surroundings, and I was having trouble locating the phone. I sat up and listened more intently, but by the time I focused on the bag of personal belongings hanging from the bed railing, the ringing had stopped.

I checked the phone. It was 8:35 A.M. The call was from my team leader at BOS, and the history told me that I'd slept right through four earlier calls from him. I suddenly recalled that the first thing on the day's agenda had been a 7:30 breakfast meeting with a client who was wealthy even by BOS standards, and it was my job to recommend changes to his portfolio.

The ringing resumed—call number six in the last twenty minutes. With a sense of dread I answered, only to get an earful.

"Where the hell are you, Patrick?"

"I'm sorry. I—"

"I don't want to hear your excuse. Unless you're dead or dying, there is none."

How about under threat of death? I decided not to go there. "I'll grab a cab and be there in—"

"Forget it," he said. "I was able to wing it this time. But if you ever do that to me again, I will fire your ass. Period. Do you hear me?"

He hung up before I could answer. Jay was my best friend when things were going well, my worst nightmare if I screwed up. The harsh tone was a stark reminder that there was plenty to lose even if I didn't lose my head—literally. Not that it would have helped to explain things to him or to anyone else at the bank. A gun to my head, a cord around my neck, threats with tentacles reaching back to Abe Cushman—all brought about by my decision to become the eyes and ears of the FBI inside the very bank that employed me. Even I was having trouble comprehending it.

The curtain parted, then closed, giving me a start. It wasn't a doctor or a nurse. Lilly spoke before I could get a word out.

"I know who you are," she said. Her voice was just above a

whisper; her tone, somewhere between pain and anger. "Why did you lie to me?"

I could have played dumb. Lying in an ER bed, I could have turned it right back on her and demanded an explanation of all that had happened since she'd shown up and dragged me into Puffy's Tavern. But the look on her face left me powerless to do anything but put aside the last forty-eight hours and say what I'd wanted to say for months.

"I'm sorry," I said.

She stood there, silent, just looking at me. I wasn't sure what she was going to do, but an *I'm sorry, too* would have been nice.

She breathed in and out, then said, "I don't even know why I'm helping you."

Not exactly the mutual exchange of apologies I had hoped for. "Helping me? What do you mean, *help—*"

She shushed me, gathered my shoes from a chair in the corner, and told me to put them on. "We need to get out of here," she said, her tone urgent.

"Do you know what happened to me?"

"You're fine. They did a CT scan two hours ago."

"How do you know?"

"I read your chart when the nurse was away from the desk. Trust me, they wouldn't have you lie here by yourself sleeping if they thought you had a serious head injury."

"Hold on a second," I said.

"No, we need to get going before the nurse comes by to check on you again."

I took her hand. "Just *wait*, okay?"

She stopped, and our eyes met. If we were going to embrace, this would have been the moment. But things had gotten way too complicated, and it didn't feel right—not to me, and, I sensed, not to her, either. I let go of her hand.

"Three days ago I would have given anything to see you again," I said. "You've shown up twice since then, which coincides exactly with the number of times someone has tried to kill me."

"Please, Patrick—or should I call you Peter?"

The dig triggered another pang of guilt. "How did you find out?"

"Don't turn this around and make it about me," she said. "When did you intend to stop lying?"

"Lilly, do you have any idea what I've been through?"

"All I can tell you is that it wasn't the people who are after the Cushman money who did this to you."

"How do you know that?"

She pulled on my shoe, no time to waste. "It's like I told you at Puffy's: when they had you in the back of that SUV in Times Square, I promised to deliver their money in one week, instead of two, if they didn't hurt you. It would make no sense for them to put you in the ER after cutting a deal like that. They'd already made their point."

That made sense, I supposed. But there was still one major problem. "So, are you any closer to meeting the one-week deadline?"

"Nope."

"Then how do you plan to keep your promise?"

She stopped and looked me in the eye. "I have absolutely no idea. I'll figure that out once I get you out of here."

"I don't understand. You still have time to get their money. What are we running from?"

"*We* aren't running. *You* are."

"Me? No. Forget it. I'm not going on the run from some thug who jumped me in the park."

Lilly peeked out the curtain, then glanced back at me. "You're talking like Patrick Lloyd. It's Peter Mandretti who needs to run."

Her expression was deadly serious, and the fact that we were even having this conversation chilled me.

"How much do you know?" I asked.

"More than I want to. We need to go. *Now.*" She handed me my coat. "We're going to walk out of here, turn left—*away* from the main desk—and follow the hallway to the exit doors on the other side of the ER. Got it?"

"Sure."

"Just walk like you're a visitor and stay with me."

Lilly stepped out first, and I did exactly as told. We passed several cubicles. Some had the curtains drawn for privacy. Others were open. We passed a man with a broken arm and an old woman with an ice pack to one knee. Another patient was hunched over a bucket with his head down. The odor left no doubt that it was flu season. We passed two nurses as we rounded the corner, but they were too busy to stop and question us. The pneumatic doors opened automatically, and they closed behind us as we exited the ER. We passed the Radiology Department, and the sign on the wall indicated that we were headed in the opposite direction of the main entrance. In fact, this hallway was marked EMERGENCY PERSONNEL ONLY.

"I'm guessing you have a plan," I said.

"You guessed right."

Actually, I was tired of guessing. She'd put me on the defensive with talk of Peter Mandretti, but she wasn't the only one entitled to an explanation.

"Lilly, why did you climb out the window of my apartment?"

"Long story," she said.

She quickened her pace, and I kept up. We were leaving through the chute that received patients brought in by ambulance. The long corridor was deserted at the moment, no emergency in progress.

"I'm listening," I said.

"I left you a note on your computer. Didn't you see it?"

"Yes. It didn't explain anything. Don't change the subject."

We'd gobbled up a hundred feet of polished tile floor and were near the end of the corridor, ten feet away from the sliding glass doors and the driveway beyond. The walk was clearing my head, but I wasn't completely myself. I probably should have started with questions about Manu Robledo and the Church of Peace and Prosperity International, but my head was pounding, and honestly the name just wasn't coming to me.

I stopped her, laid my hands squarely on her shoulders, and looked her in the eye. "Lilly, are you involved in some kind of cult?"

"Cult?" she said, scoffing. "Seriously, do I strike you as a cult personality?"

"No, but . . ."

"But what?"

"The more I get to know you, the less I know you."

"Well, isn't that the pot calling the kettle black," she said.

"Stop avoiding the question. Why did you run away?"

A white commercial van pulled up in the driveway outside the sliding glass doors. "That's our ride," said Lilly, pulling me along. "Let's get out of here. I'll tell you on the way."

The glass doors slid open, and a blast of cool morning air hit me in the face. Lilly opened the rear door of the van and managed to get me to climb in first. The door slammed behind me.

Lilly was still in the driveway.

"Lilly!"

I tried to open the door, but there was no handle on the inside. The only windows were in the cockpit, so I couldn't see Lilly, but I heard her slap the side of the van and shout, "Go!"

The driver put the van into gear, and we pulled away.

I was alone in the cargo hold amid blankets and cardboard boxes. A wire grate separated me from the cockpit, and I pushed away a stack of boxes to get right behind the driver.

"Stop!" I shouted.

"Relax and be quiet."

I immediately recognized the driver's voice, and a moment of eye contact in the rearview mirror confirmed it.

"Connie?"

My sister glanced over her shoulder and said, "Who else can you count on to save your butt?"

I caught her drift: certainly not our father.

"Get under the blankets and sit tight," she said.

I hesitated.

"Do it!" she said. "We have to make sure no one sees you leaving the hospital."

If Lilly was right—if the danger was to Peter Mandretti, not to Patrick Lloyd—I could see the wisdom in the plan. I grabbed the nearest blanket and found a spot by the wheel well in the cargo hold. The ride out of the parking lot was smooth and steady, not too fast and not too slow—nothing to arouse the suspicion of whoever was waiting to see if and when I walked out the hospital's front door.

The tires hummed below me as I wondered exactly how Lilly and my sister had teamed up for this stunt. I wondered how long they'd been a team. More than anything, I wondered why Connie would have told her that our last name wasn't Lloyd.

15

"I HAVE TO GET THE VAN BACK TO THE ZOO, PRONTO," MY SISTER said over the hum of the engine. She was driving through lower Midtown, and the zoo accounted for both the funky odors in the cargo hold and the metal grate between the cockpit and me.

Working with exotic animals was the perfect job for Connie, a childhood dream she'd held since the same family trip on which Tony "The Snitch" Mandretti—our dad—had butchered Lewis Carroll's poetry and offended every East Side nanny within earshot of the Alice in Wonderland sculpture. For all his flaws, Dad was big on family events. That one had turned out to be his last before putting on a wire for the FBI, testifying against the Santucci family, and disappearing into witness protection. Mom had refused to join him. Only after her death—more precisely, after the parole of a certain under-boss who literally had an ax to grind with "The Snitch"—did my sister and I enter the program as Connie Ryan and Patrick Lloyd. The different surnames were for added protection. I was a young teen at the time, and my sister acted much older than her twenty-three years. I suppose it didn't take a psychiatrist to explain why, years after that final family trip, Connie would end up working at the Central Park Zoo, and I would designate Alice in Wonderland as a place to meet my FBI contact.

The van stopped at a red light. Connie reached back, opened the metal grate between us, and offered me the passenger seat.

"We're a good twenty blocks from the hospital," she said. "I think it's safe to say that no one saw you sneak away."

I buckled up as she steered through the intersection, heading north through Midtown. Even in traffic, the zoo was just minutes away. I had a slew of questions for her, but logistics came to the forefront.

"What's the plan after you return the van?" I asked.

"Don't have one. Lilly called and said you were in trouble. Step one was to get you out of the ER. We didn't get to step two."

I glanced out the window, then back at my sister. "I didn't realize that you and Lilly stay in touch."

"We don't. The last time I talked to her was when the two of you Skyped me from Singapore."

"And she just called you out of the blue this morning?"

"She said she didn't know who else to call. She was pretty much in a panic."

"Exactly what did she tell you?"

"Basically that you got roughed up in the park last night, and that if we didn't get you out of the ER immediately, someone would likely stop by and shake hands with your Adam's apple."

"That doesn't sound like something Lilly would say."

"I'm paraphrasing."

I circled back to the "they" question. "Did she tell you who 'someone' might be?"

"After what happened to Mom, I don't need to have it spelled out for me."

The buzz of city traffic filled the silence between us. Mom was a complicated subject. She'd always told us how brave Dad was for turning against the mob, and yet she'd refused to join him in the witness protection program. She'd probably still be alive if she had.

"You're saying it's the Santucci family?"

"Who else?" she said. "It seems like every six months one of the thugs Dad put in jail is paroled. They refused to believe Mom didn't know how to find Dad, and they killed her. What makes you think they'll stop there? They are never going to stop looking for us."

The Cushman connection had turned the Santucci family into old news in my mind, but I didn't think Connie was ready to swallow what this was really about. For the moment, I stayed with her theory, since it provided a nice segue to my visit to Central Prison.

"What if we could convince them that Dad is dead?" I asked.

Her response caught in her throat, and the pained expression puzzled me to the point of concern. "Are you okay?" I asked.

"Sorry," she said. "It's just weird that I wasn't prepared for that. All these years he's been gone, and I've never thought of him as anything but being very alive, the way I remembered him. It's upsetting to think of him as dead."

"I'm just saying, theoretically, if Dad were dead, then these guys he put in jail would stop, wouldn't they?"

"The key word there is 'theoretically.' There's no way to prove he's dead or alive. We don't even know who he is."

"Well . . . what if we did know?"

She glanced over and immediately caught my drift. "Holy shit. You found him? How? No, don't tell me," she said as her hands instinctively covered her ears, "I don't want to know."

I grabbed the wheel and steered around a stopped cab.

"Damn it, Patrick! You are going to get us both killed!"

"We're more likely to be done in by your driving, sis."

She swatted me and took back the wheel, but she was beyond angry. "We agreed that we would never do this," she said. "We promised Mom that we would never look for him."

"Listen to what I'm saying. If I can convince the Santucci family that he's dead, their search is over. There would be no reason for the mob to chase us, threaten us, kill us, or do any-thing else to us ever again."

"Is that what you're telling me: Dad is dead?"

"Actually, I'm virtually certain he's still alive. But I can prove he's dead."

"Stop playing with me!" she said as she stood on the brake. Behind us, tires screeched and horns blasted. It was a bona fide miracle that we weren't rear-ended. Connie steered the van to the curb and slammed it into park, her face beet red.

"It wasn't my intention to rip into you so soon," she said, "but you obviously don't understand how furious I am with you. Do you realize what you've done? Our only option may be to go back to the Justice Department and get ourselves re-processed in the program. New location, new identity: square one. That makes me mad, it makes me want to kick your ass, it makes me just want to cry. I like my life. Finally, for the first time since Mom died, I'm happy with who I am. And now I may lose everything all over again because you had to go and stir things up."

"I didn't stir up anything."

Connie looked away. She was trying to hold her emotions inside, but tears were coming, and it was tearing me up to watch her fall apart. I had to tell her. Finally, I had to tell *someone* the truth.

"This whole fear of the Santucci family rearing its ugly head is like being afraid of the bogeyman."

"The bogeyman doesn't put you in the emergency room."

"That had nothing to do with the Mafia. But it does involve Dad. I didn't want to go looking for him. I really didn't. It was the FBI who came to me."

"What are you talking about?"

I took a breath, not sure where to begin.

"Patrick, talk to me."

She was using her stern maternal voice, the one that made

me feel like the fifteen-year-old boy who went to live with his twenty-three-year-old sister. This wasn't skipping school or getting drunk on prom night, but I felt the same need to come clean.

"Her name is Andie Henning," I said. "About eight months ago she came to me and said she needed my help with an investigation."

"What kind of investigation?"

Anyone who had watched the news in the twenty-first century was generally familiar with the Abe Cushman story. Beyond that, I was so far ahead of Connie and the rest of the world that I had to stop and remind myself that the name "Gerry Collins" would probably mean nothing to my sister. More to the point, she had no idea that Tony Mandretti—our father—was Tony Martin, and that Tony Martin had pleaded guilty to killing Cushman's right-hand man.

"The FBI believes that a big chunk of the Cushman money was funneled through BOS in Singapore. We're talking about billions of dollars."

"The FBI asked you to spy on your own bank? Why on earth would you agree to do that?"

"That was exactly my reaction. Until Agent Henning mentioned the name Tony Mandretti."

I could see her anger rising all over again. "Please don't tell me that you got suckered into working for the FBI in exchange for some promise of a family reunion. That is the craziest thing I—"

"Dad's dying," I said.

She blinked hard, absorbing the blow.

"Not tomorrow, not next week," I said. "But it's coming. The good news is that he's getting decent treatment. That was the deal. I helped the FBI and went to Singapore; they arranged for Dad to get the kind of treatment he couldn't get in prison."

"Wait a minute. He's in prison? For what?"

I paused to soften it, but that seemed only to make her more anxious.

"*For what?*" she asked again.

"Murder."

She closed her eyes in anguish. "I really wish you hadn't told me."

"He didn't do it."

"Then why is he behind bars?"

"He pleaded guilty to the murder of Gerry Collins."

Her eyes closed again. More anguish. Or maybe it was a massive headache. "You are not making me feel better."

"Connie, I'm telling you: Dad didn't do it."

"Did the FBI tell you that?"

"No. In fact, Agent Henning is adamant that he's guilty."

"Did Dad tell you he's innocent?"

"Not directly."

"Don't be cute. Have you talked to him or not?"

"No. That was one of the conditions of my assignment: no contact between us. This wasn't about a family reunion, as you put it. The deal was simply to get Dad the medical treatment he needed. He doesn't know I had anything to do with it."

She drew a breath. "Patrick, it's understandable that you would want to help Dad if he was sick, and I can see how it would make it easier to help him if you thought he was innocent. But—"

"That's not it," I said. "I didn't agree to the FBI's terms and risk my career just to get medical treatment for a deadbeat father who had killed another man. What drove me is that I *knew* he was innocent. I'm not asking for your help or approval. I'm simply telling you that it's my intention to get him out of prison and let him live his last days the way he wants to live them."

"We haven't seen Dad in years. How could you possibly know anything about him, much less whether or not he's sitting in prison for something he didn't do?"

I started to talk, then reconsidered. It was beyond my persuasive powers to convince her in this setting. "Let me borrow
your phone."

She handed it to me but asked, "What's wrong with yours?"

I didn't have time to get into it fully. "I only have my
BlackBerry, and I'd rather not send this message on a bank-
issued phone if I can avoid it."

"Why not?"

"Just drive," I said.

"Drive where? To the zoo?"

"No, go through the circle and head up Central Park West,"
I said, while tapping out a text message on her phone. "Take
Terrace Drive through the park. There's someone you need to
meet."

"Who?"

Connie's phone chimed with Agent Henning's response to
my text. She was on her way.

"Alice in Wonderland," I told Connie. "I think it's time we
all got acquainted."

16

ANDIE WAS ALONE IN HER OFFICE WHEN THE TEXT ARRIVED. She didn't recognize the incoming number, but the message was clearly from Patrick.

Position Three. ASAP.

It was his third message in less than twenty-four hours, his second selection of Position Three. She sensed that something was wrong. She rose from her desk, closed the door, and hit Call Back. Speaking on the telephone was a total break in protocol, and Patrick sounded surprised, but he answered in Spanish—*Hola*—which was their previously agreed-upon code for *I'm OK, no gun to my head.*

"Are you sure you're okay?" asked Andie.

"Yeah, other than the fact that I got mugged in the park after you left and spent the night in the ER."

Andie wanted to follow up, but Patrick was on a cell she didn't recognize. "I'm on my way."

She grabbed her coat, then on second thought went back to her computer. The Parks system was part of the automated incident report database, and in less than a minute she had the full report of last night's incident. She printed a copy, skim-reading as she hurried to the elevator.

. . . white male found unconscious. . .

She stopped, relieved that Patrick had reported that he was okay, but anger was coursing through her veins. She blew right past the elevators, hung a quick left at the end of the hall, and found her supervisor alone in his office.

"Got a minute?" she asked.

Wayne Teese was the assistant special agent in charge of the Manhattan field office. Andie was his direct report on the FBI's money-laundering investigation at BOS. He didn't micromanage, but Teese had the final word on the broad parameters of Andie's relationship with the principal informant in the operation—Patrick Lloyd.

Teese grimaced at the sight of Andie standing in his open doorway, as if he knew what was on her mind. With some reluctance, he waved her inside. It wasn't that he disliked Andie. An overload of administrative responsibilities simply made any intrusion unwelcome. Andie closed the door and took a seat, his gunmetal, government-issued desk between them.

"I'm on my way to meet with Patrick Lloyd right now," she said. "I'm asking you to reconsider your position on protection for him."

"Denied," he said.

"But—"

He raised a hand, stopping her. "You've already stated your case."

She had indeed. Rather convincingly. The bureau's intransigence was baffling.

"He's been attacked twice," said Andie, holding up a copy of the police report. "This last one landed him in the emergency room. I don't see how we can expect him to continue in this role if we don't guarantee his protection."

"We have at-risk informants all over the world. It's cost prohibitive to protect every last one of them."

"Patrick Lloyd is different. This is not a situation where a target cooperated in the investigation to avoid prosecution.

Patrick is not suspected of any criminal conduct, much less the kind that would justify putting him in this much personal danger."

Teese folded his hands atop his desk. He had just a few years of seniority on Andie, but the worry lines aged him. With so much of the FBI's funding earmarked for homeland security, the shoestring budgets for more traditional operations had stretched the office and his supervisory capacity to the limit.

"We agreed to provide medical treatment for his father from one of the most prestigious cancer centers in the world. I don't have resources to essentially provide him with a personal bodyguard. We kept our side of the deal. He needs to keep his."

Andie knew exactly what he meant. "I realize that he has not delivered much."

"It's been the better part of six months, and he's delivered *nothing*."

"Patrick never agreed to be the FBI's all-purpose eyes and ears and give us carte blanche access to confidential banking information. He promised only to befriend Lilly Scanlon and tell us if she admitted to criminal conduct that fits our theory of the case."

"He certainly befriended her," Teese said, scoffing. "So either he's holding out, or he doesn't understand our theory."

"Or maybe there's something wrong with our theory."

Andie braced herself. The theory was one that Teese himself had developed. He was known for defending his brainstorms the way he defended his beliefs: with the vigor of a combat-tested Marine.

"It's been three years since Cushman's scheme blew up," he said. "Banks, lawyers, private security firms, and just about every law enforcement agency in the world have searched under every rock for the supposed sixty billion dollars that was lost. Only a fraction of that amount has been recovered. There's a good reason for that: most of the funds on Cushman's books never actually existed, except as a bogus entry in Cushman's records."

"I'm not saying the theory is implausible," said Andie. "There's no end to the creative ways to launder money."

"It's beyond plausible," said Teese. "If I'm a drug dealer with ten million dollars in dirty money from cocaine sales, a Wall Street crook like Cushman is my best friend. I give him my ten million. He records an 'investment' of a hundred million dollars. In a few months, maybe a year, he pays me a return of ten percent on my bogus hundred million dollars. Presto, change-o: my ten million, less a cut for Cushman, comes back nice and squeaky clean as investment proceeds. But the bottom line for Cushman's Ponzi scheme is that the fraud is overstated tenfold—sixty billion is more like six billion."

"I'm not debating the theory in the abstract. I'm just saying: maybe the reason we're getting nothing from Patrick Lloyd is that it wasn't drug money that flowed through BOS/Singapore to Cushman Investment. Or if it was, maybe Lilly Scanlon had no idea it was dirty."

"You're being naïve. The reason we've gotten nothing out of Patrick Lloyd is that he hasn't been given the proper incentive to talk."

"What do you mean?"

"I mean the element of added danger may be the added incentive that Mr. Lloyd needs to give us the information we're seeking."

"That incentive means putting an innocent person in danger."

"I hate to sound like a broken record, but I keep coming back to the deal."

"I understand the technical terms of our agreement. But by cooperating, he may have blown his witness protection coverage. The bank is digging deep into his background. We have at least a moral obligation to protect him . . . and his sister."

He was suddenly six inches taller in his chair, literally getting his back up. "Moral obligation? You're overlooking the fact that it was Patrick Lloyd's father who killed Gerry Collins and, in the process, eliminated the best source of information about the Cushman scheme."

"So, pox on the entire family? Is that it?"

"I'm saying it's a morally ambiguous situation."

"It's not ambiguous to Patrick. He firmly believes his father didn't kill Collins. He thinks his father was coerced into a confession."

Andie braced herself again, this time for a forceful denial, or at least a hearty guffaw. She got neither.

"I have to get back to work," said Teese. "Deliver this message to Mr. Lloyd: it's time he kept his end of the bargain. Deliver something. If he does, we'll take another look at protection."

Andie felt like she was back where she'd started. There was definitely no point in going around the same circle. "It would be helpful if I could tell him that we are continuing to keep our end of the deal."

"You mean tell him that his father is still alive and receiving treatment?"

"Yes."

Teese pondered it. "I don't see a problem with that."

"He'll also want assurance that the new treatment facility is comparable to the Duke center."

"You can tell him that in general terms. But you can't disclose the new location."

"That's going to be awkward," said Andie. "It's only natural for him to ask why his father was moved, what his new name is, why I can't tell him where he's gone—all of that."

"We can't tell him."

"Okay. But it would be easier for me to accept that decision if *I* knew the answers to those questions."

"That's on a strictly need-to-know basis."

"I find it interesting that there's enough money allocated to this operation to create a new identity for Patrick's father, move him to another facility, and arrange for medical treatment from a new facility. But there's not a dime in the budget to protect Patrick, who happens to be the only person helping us in the BOS investigation."

"Sorry," said Teese. "Strict need-to-know basis."

"Got it," said Andie.

Teese turned in his chair and faced his computer screen. Andie rose and started for the door, then stopped.

"You know, Patrick is very emphatic that his father is innocent. I can't overstate how strong his feelings are on that."

Teese was typing and staring at his computer screen, never looking up. "Strictly need to know," he said.

Andie nodded, not in agreement, but merely acknowledging his words as the FBI's final position. She left the office, her thoughts awhirl as she walked down the hall toward the elevator. No doubt about it: Andie *needed* to know.

17

SNOW STARTED TO GATHER ON THE GIANT MUSHROOM. I WATCHED the first few flakes fall from a gray sky and rest on the bronze heads of Alice and her friends. Connie was beside me on the park bench. We had hot coffee and one of the smelly zoo blankets to keep us warm on a day that was turning colder by the minute.

"My snow monkeys are absolutely loving this," said Connie.

I smiled. Huddled beneath that blanket in the middle of Central Park, we must have looked like a couple of lost little monkeys.

"Do you remember that summer we came here with Mom and Dad?" she asked.

"I think of it often," I said.

"Remember when Dad walked over and read the poem out loud?"

"Mmmm, no. Dad read a poem?"

"You don't *remember* the time—"

"Connie, I'm kidding. How could I forget? It was the only time in my life that I heard Dad recite something more literary than a menu, and he managed to punctuate it with the f-bomb."

We laughed, then it faded. I wrapped my hands more tightly around my extra-tall cup of coffee, trying to draw the last bit of warmth through the paper sleeve. Connie sniffled back what sounded like the beginnings of a cold. I hoped it wasn't snow monkey flu, or some such thing.

"Patrick?" she said, her tone more serious. "Why are you so sure Dad didn't kill Gerry Collins?"

"Do you think he did it?"

"I asked you first."

Sibling talk. Connie could shift from stand-in mother to big sister in a heartbeat, when it suited her.

I glanced again at the sculpture. The snow was falling harder, making the bronze a blur. Strangely, it seemed to make the past clearer. "About six months before Mom died, we had a talk."

"What about?"

"At first it was about me, the kind of talk any single mother might have with her son about gangs. Madison High changed a lot after you graduated. One of the gangs there had ties all the way up to the Crips. I was getting pressure to join one of the rivals. Mom wanted to make sure I stayed clear of it."

"Were you actually thinking of being a gangbanger?"

"Not really. But she was afraid that I might, because of the things Dad did when he was young."

"She didn't want you to make the same mistakes."

"That was a big part of it. But she wasn't preaching. As the talk went on, I think she just wanted me to know Dad's story. The truth."

"The truth about what?"

I put down my coffee—it was ice cold—and folded my arms to fight off the chill. "Do you know why Dad turned against the Santucci family?"

Connie paused. Her expression told me that she had never thought of it in terms of a trigger event, that she'd simply accepted Mom's mantra over the years that our father had searched his soul and finally found the courage to do the right thing.

"I'm not sure I do," she said.

"An underboss ordered him to whack a guy."

"You mean a genuine mob-style hit?"

"Yup. It was like an initiation rite. The natural progression of things on his way to a made man."

"I assume he didn't do it."

"No. But the family wasn't going to take no for an answer. They kept up the pressure for him to prove his loyalty, and he found himself in a kill-or-be-killed situation. He didn't see a way out. That's when he went to the FBI."

"So, 'doing the right thing' was just an exit strategy?"

"Not exactly. It was a matter of principle. It's how I know Dad didn't kill Gerry Collins."

"I'm not seeing the connection."

"Dad gave up everything—his wife, his kids, his *existence*— because he refused to whack some two-bit thug who probably deserved to die. Yet we're supposed to believe that he killed Gerry Collins for losing his money?"

She considered it. Connie was a bright woman, but she thought things through before rendering a verdict. "It doesn't compute," she said.

"It sure doesn't for me," I said.

Connie sighed, her breath steaming in front of me. "I wish Mom had packed us up and we had all disappeared with him."

I shook my head. "Mom was right. The marriage wasn't strong enough to survive that kind of trauma. Why would any woman take her kids into witness protection, away from ex- tended family and friends, only to go through a divorce?"

"It would have been safer."

"That's easy to say in hindsight. She had good reason to believe that no one would touch a woman whose maiden name was Santucci."

"What has the world come to? Not even the Mafia plays by the old code of conduct." It was an unusual bit of sarcasm from Connie, who normally had the optimism of an Eagle Scout.

I checked my BlackBerry for the time. Almost forty minutes since I'd texted Andie. She was taking her sweet time about getting here.

Connie said, "I don't want you going anywhere near the Santucci family."

"I'm not going to join them, if that's what you mean." Sarcasm came more naturally to me.

"No, smart ass. I understand what you were saying earlier in the van. I agree it would be nice if you could convince them that Dad is dead. That might put an end to all this. But it's too dangerous to make any contact with them for any reason."

"Connie, you must not have been listening. Let me say it again: the Santucci family is the bogeyman. Operation Clean House reduced them to almost nothing."

"Never underestimate a convicted mobster who wants revenge and finally gets paroled."

"I just don't believe it's the Santucci family who roughed me up in the park last night."

"How can you say that? Lilly called me this morning and said you might be dead before breakfast if we didn't get you out of the ER."

"That's the whole point: Lilly is mixed up with something else entirely. Something big enough to get her fired from the bank. I think it's tied to a guy named Manu Robledo, who heads up a phony-sounding church downtown that has to be a front for something. It could be a cult. I'm not sure."

"How much does Lilly know about the Santucci family?"

"I don't know. When you told her my real name is Peter Mandretti, did you talk about the Santucci family?"

Connie's expression was one of complete incredulity. "When *I* told her? Patrick, I didn't tell her anything."

"Then how did she find out my real name?"

"Cut the crap. For now I'll accept the fact that if she hadn't given me a heads-up to get you out of the ER, something really bad could have happened. But at some point you and I are go-ing to have a talk about how ticked off I am that you told her."

It took a moment before I could speak, but finally my re-sponse came. "I *never* told Lilly anything about us. From begin-ning to end I've led her to believe that I'm Patrick Lloyd, and that I've always been Patrick Lloyd."

"Oh, come on," she said.

"I didn't tell her. I swear."

We sat in silence, and finally Connie seemed to believe me, but her expression turned to one of grave concern.

"We got a problem, brother. I'm telling it to you straight: Lilly knows. Based on what we talked about on the phone this morning, I'd say she knows the whole story."

"I don't understand how she could."

Connie reached over and put her arm around my shoulder. "I hate to bust your chops, dipshit, but who the heck is this woman?"

I shook my head slowly, focused on nothing in particular in the falling snow. All was a blur.

"Apparently, I have no clue."

18

LILLY ENTERED THE CHURCH AT ELEVEN TWENTY A.M. THE entrance on John Street was unlocked, as promised. She was a few minutes early for her meeting with Manu Robledo.

The heavy oak door closed behind her, and it took a minute for her eyes to adjust to the dim lighting. The old church had a dusty odor, but there were more obvious signs of disuse. All religious artifacts had been removed, and a few indirect spotlights that had once displayed them were the nave's only illumination. Brass chandeliers hung from the cathedral-style ceiling, spiderwebs clinging to the unlit bulbs. Lilly walked tentatively down the center aisle, the click of her heels echoing on the old stone floor. She took a seat in the third pew on the left, just as Robledo had instructed her to do. A deep breath, followed by another, did nothing to calm her nerves.

Getting his name had been like hitting the jackpot. She had risked everything for it. Just one little peek behind the veil of bank secrecy, she'd thought, would reveal the client Gerry Collins had brought to BOS/Singapore. She could match a name to a numbered account. She would know the source—or at least a crucial link in a hidden chain—of funds she had routed to Abe Cushman's Ponzi scheme. She would know who had threatened to kill her if she didn't give it all back. A simple plan, but one that had failed. The bank had fired her before she could get the name Manu Robledo.

A visit from a stranger had been the answer to her prayers.

She started to say another one—she was in church, after all—but her mind was restless. It was cold within these old stone walls, and she started to shiver, not just from the cold, but with a fear that chilled her. It was partly her fear of Robledo. Mostly, it was fear of the stranger who had found her alone in Patrick's apartment. An all-consuming fear that kept her looking over her shoulder. A fear that she'd relived in her mind over and over. A fear that gripped her again in the darkness of the old church, taking her back to the knock on Patrick's door that had changed everything.

"Who is it?" asked Lilly.

"Flower delivery."

The chain and deadbolt were secure. Lilly peered through the peephole. The man in the hallway was holding a bouquet of red roses.

"Just a minute," she said.

Flowers. With all that had happened, she, of course, had to consider the possibility that it was a ruse—a clever way for someone to gain access to the apartment.

"Who are they for?" she asked.

"Lilly Scanlon."

Hmmm. No one knew she was in the apartment except Patrick. It would have been sweet of Patrick to send flowers to make up for running off after last night's reunion. But a girl who was under threat of death unless she coughed up two billion dollars could never be too careful.

"I'm leaving the chain on the door. Hand the flowers to me through the opening."

"They'll get crushed."

"Then hand me one rose at a time."

She turned the deadbolt, opened the door, and let it catch on the short length of chain. He handed her the first long-stemmed rose, then another. She had the fifth in hand when he grabbed her wrist and pressed a blade to her veins.

"Scream and you'll bleed out in two minutes," he said.

Lilly gasped and swallowed her scream. "What do you want?" she asked, her voice quaking.

"Just listen to me," he said in a rushed, husky voice. "I know why you got fired. I know why you ran from Singapore. I know why your boyfriend was attacked. I know all those things."

Lilly closed her eyes, then opened them, but she couldn't stop the trembling.

The man continued. "There's only one way for you to get out of this alive, Lilly. But you have to follow my instructions to the letter. If you don't, they'll kill you. Do you understand?"

She didn't. Not in the least. This was all too crazy. "What are you telling me to do?"

"Trust me."

She could barely form a response. "Trust you?"

"Yes. Here's my first show of trust: go to the Church of Peace and Prosperity International on John Street. Ask for Manu Robledo. Tell him you know who opened BOS numbered account 507.625 RR. Tell him you know it was him."

It was almost too much to remember, not because of the quantity, but because of how important it was—if it was true.

"Tell him he'll get his money," the man said, "but tell him you're in control."

"I can't—"

"*Tell him*," he said, squeezing her wrist so tightly that Lilly had to bite her lip to stop the pain. "You *must* do exactly as I say."

"Okay," she said. "I will."

"Good. And tell him you got his name from Patrick."

"No!"

"Do it!" he said, stern but not quite shouting.

"Please, keep Patrick out of this."

"His name isn't even Patrick. It's Peter Mandretti."

"What?"

"His father testified against the Santucci family, which means that your boyfriend has much bigger problems than Manu Robledo. The mob is breathing down his neck. Don't make his problems yours, Lilly. I'm here to help you."

"I don't want you to help—"

His grip was like a vise around her wrist, and this time the pain dropped her to her knees.

"Okay, okay," she said, "whatever you say."

He loosened his grasp, but not completely. "It's possible you're being watched. We have to make sure no one follows you. Don't leave this building through the main entrance. Use the fire escape."

Again she blinked, barely comprehending. "Okay. I'll do it."

He gave her wrist a final squeeze. Not a threatening one. It was as if he were trying to reassure her. "Trust me, Lilly. You deserve to live."

He released her. She pulled her hand inside, closed the door, and instinctively withdrew to the center of the apartment. Her emotions rushed forward, a combination of fear over what had happened and relief that he hadn't slashed her wrist. Fighting off tears, she went to the peephole. He was gone. She collected herself, trying to decide what to do. There seemed to be no right answer.

She went to the computer and found directions to the church.

"Don't turn around."

Robledo's voice ripped her from the past. He was seated in the pew behind her, and she was having trouble following his command.

"Eyes forward!" he said.

She obeyed, but it wasn't easy. It was the same voice she'd heard on the phone when Patrick was threatened in Times Square. The same voice that had threatened her in Singapore when she saw the Treasury memo. The same voice she'd heard day after day when receiving transfer orders for numbered account 507.625 RR at BOS. She wanted so badly to put a face with it.

"How did you find my name?" he asked.

"None of your business."

She felt a cold, round point of pressure at the base of her skull. "How about now?" he asked, nudging her with the pistol. "Still none of my business?"

Lilly tried to keep her voice from shaking. "It doesn't matter how I found out."

The old church was silent, save for the unmistakable sound of a pistol cocking.

"It matters to me," Robledo said.

Lilly searched for the words her source had fed her, but her delivery failed her. "I'm . . . I'm in control."

He grabbed her by the hair, yanked her head back against the pew so that she was staring at the ceiling. The muzzle of the pistol was at her temple.

"You got my first warning shot in Singapore," he said, speaking so close that she could feel his breath in her ear. "Your boyfriend got the second one in Times Square. That's it. No more *mock* executions. The next bullet goes in your pretty little head. I'm giving you five seconds to answer my question: How did you get my name?"

Thinking under this kind of pressure—caught between one

man threatening to slash her wrist if she breathed a word about his existence, and another who threatened to blow her brains out if she didn't—just wasn't part of her constitution.

"I don't know," she said, agonizing. "I don't remember, I just don't—"

"Patrick told you, didn't he?"

Lilly froze. That was exactly what the man who'd delivered the flowers had wanted her to make Robledo believe.

Robledo didn't wait for her response. "Patrick came to see me," he said.

He couldn't see her face, but Lilly wondered if Robledo could nonetheless sense her surprise. She wondered if that was the reason Patrick had at the hospital, seemingly out of the blue, asked about her possible involvement in a cult.

"I didn't give Patrick your name. I swear."

"That's what I'm saying! He gave it to you. *Didn't he?*"

"No," she said, searching for another explanation, anything she could think of to keep Patrick out of it. A lie finally came to her. "I got your name before I left Singapore. That's why the bank fired me."

"I almost believe you, which makes you one lucky girl. I'm not convinced that it takes both you and Patrick to find my money, but I'm not sure that it doesn't. So you've bought yourself some daylight. For a while."

"I need more time to find the money."

"No."

"I'm not going to beg."

"Wouldn't make a difference anyway."

"This is not a bluff. The snags are real. Don't worry. It's nothing we can't handle. We'll get there."

"Then get there," he said. "No extensions."

"I'm not asking for an extension. You gave me two weeks originally. I said I could do it in one if you kept your hands off Patrick. Just go back to the two weeks you gave me."

"No."

"It's just another week."

"I said *no*!" He pushed her head forward with so much force that her chin hit her chest. "And never come here again. You got that?"

Lilly felt as though she were suffocating, trapped between her fear of Robledo and an even greater fear of the deliveryman who had told her what to say to him.

"Yes," she said. "I got it."

19

IT HAD STOPPED SNOWING, BUT A FEW FLAKES STILL SWIRLED IN the sky, blown from treetops by a chilly north breeze. My toes were freezing in an inch-deep blanket of white that had fallen since breakfast. Alice and her friends looked almost edible, a chocolate bronze topped with cream-cheese icing. Snow in Central Park was the perfect antidote for my six months in steamy Singapore.

The last two days were another story.

Barely forty-eight hours had passed since I'd skulked out of the wrong meeting in the Paradeplatz Conference Room, only to face an executive-style grilling from Joe Barber about Lilly Scanlon and Abe Cushman. Not exactly what I'd hoped for on my first day back in the New York office. How had so much gone wrong so quickly? It was almost as hard to swallow as "the official response of the bureau" that Agent Henning had just announced to me.

"What do you mean you can't protect me?" I said.

She was standing before me, no time to brush the snow from the bench and take a seat. It was just the two of us. Connie had tired of waiting and insisted that she needed to return the van, presumably before her boss called upon Curious George and the zoo police to retrieve it.

"I'm sorry," she said, "but my hands are tied."

Andie had a copy of the Parks police report with her, and I'd added the details about my visit to the emergency room. The FBI's quick rebuff on protection wasn't what I had expected.

"So, that's it? Too bad, so sad, you're on your own, Mr. Lloyd?"

She glanced away, then back. "Can we walk? I'm freezing."

Always cold. I kept forgetting that the bureau had tapped her from Miami for this operation. I matched her stride, and the new snow squeaked beneath our feet as we followed the path around the sculpture.

"Part of the problem is my supervisor," she said. "He thinks you haven't been all that forthcoming."

"The information I agreed to pass along was very limited. Essentially, I promised to tell you if Lilly confessed to money laundering."

"The deal was broader than that. You agreed to tell us if Lilly made *any* admissions that are consistent with our theory of money laundering."

"If that's the FBI's view, then you should have told me more about your theory."

"We told you what you needed to know. I would have liked to tell you more, but like I said—"

"Your hands are tied, I know. That can be a highly convenient predicament."

"It's the truth."

"Maybe it is," I said. "But if you want the truth *from me*, tell your supervisor he needs an attitude adjustment."

We stopped walking, and our eyes locked. A moment of sunlight broke through the clouds, forcing Andie to squint, which made her expression even harsher.

"Is that some kind of threat?" she said. "*Are* you holding out?"

I was thinking of Manu Robledo. "I may have a name for

you. I don't have anything in writing, but it may well turn out that he's the holder of a certain numbered account at BOS/ Singapore."

"Who?"

"I'm not prepared to share."

"Don't be an ass."

"We're playing by my rules now. My six months in Singapore were payment enough for what you did for my father. Going forward, anything you get from me is strictly on a quid pro quo basis."

The sun disappeared, but Andie's eyes continued to narrow as she studied me. Finally, she said, "We're still helping your father."

I was already of the firm belief that Dad was alive, but it was hard not to react to official confirmation. I struggled to play it cool. "I knew he was alive," I said.

"I gave you more than that," she said. "I told you we're still providing specialized medical treatment for him. Don't ask me where or under what name. I can't tell you."

"If your supervisor thinks I haven't kept up my end of the deal, why are you continuing to provide treatment to him?"

She blinked. It was Andie's first flinch in the eight months I'd known her, and it was as if she had looked me in the eye and said, *That's a very good question, Patrick, and I wish I knew the answer.*

"Because it's the right thing to do," she said.

"Nice try." I said. "Quid pro quo. I'll give you the name of the numbered account holder when you tell me the following: What is my Dad's new name? Where did you send him? And why is the FBI still helping him even though your supervisor thinks I've been holding out?"

"I can't do that."

"Make it happen," I said.

She paused, but I didn't get the impression that the answers to my questions were on the tip of her tongue. In fact—and this was just more of my gut—I wondered how much she personally knew about Dad's situation.

"I'll work on it," she said.

"Work fast."

She didn't answer, but the silence confirmed that the conversation was finished. For now. Our footprints in the snow showed us the way back toward the bench.

20

IT WAS MORE WIND THAN SNOW THAT FORCED LILLY INDOORS FOR cover. She found a deli down the street from the church, but a nervous stomach made eating impossible. She ordered a camomile tea to calm herself down.

"Anything else?" asked the cashier.

How about a Xanax?

"Just the tea, thanks," she said.

Lilly broke one of her last remaining fifties. She'd fled Singapore with $9,990 in cash, just below the currency reporting requirement. Burning through money was easy in Manhattan. Her wallet was getting thin, but she didn't dare use a credit card. Cash wouldn't leave a trail.

The only open seat was near the entrance at the storefront counter. She claimed a stool and gazed out the plate glass window, watching a sidewalk construction crew stand around and do nothing. An hour of snow flurries was enough to block out the company name on the truck. Lilly wondered if it was one of the Santucci firms. Construction was a staple of the family's many mob-run businesses—at least that was what her source had told her.

A construction worker noticed her and winked. Definitely

not one of those ripped and gorgeous hotties on *Desperate Housewives* who sweated out pheromones. Lilly averted her eyes.

Steam rose from her cup. A quick sip scalded the roof of her mouth. It was a little thing that, cumulatively, was a big thing. She almost started to cry. Lucky for Gerry Collins that he was already dead. If he weren't, she would probably have killed him.

Thank you, Gerry. Thank you for using me.

Or had he?

Again, her mind replayed that three-year-old phone message he'd left on her voice mail just before his death: "It's blown up. I'll call you when I can. Talk to no one until I reach you."

Was it possible that Collins had thought she was aware of the scam? The arrangement had certainly been sweet. She'd essentially done nothing, and BOS had still given her revenue credit for over $2 billion in private banking activity. Perhaps Gerry had simply assumed that she was smart enough to recognize a deal that was too good to be legit. Since his death, the Treasury Department had certainly operated under that assumption, had even put it in an internal memo.

Her cell rang. She didn't recognize the incoming number, but she knew it was him—her source. He'd promised to follow up after her meeting with Robledo at the church. "Promised" was probably the wrong word. Everything he said sounded more like a threat. She was tired of getting hit from every direction—from him, Robledo, BOS, Treasury. It was time for her to find her spine and push back. She walked out of the noisy deli, found cover beneath the sidewalk bridge scaffolding, and answered her cell phone. He began with a question.

"Do you trust me now, Lilly?"

She didn't answer.

"Admit it," he said. "I steered you right. Robledo is the man you talked to on the phone every day at BOS, isn't he? The same man who threatened you in Singapore and your boyfriend in Times Square."

"Yes. I recognized the voice."

"So, do you trust me?"

"You nearly got me killed!"

"Watch your tone," he said.

She didn't back down. "Robledo put a gun to my head and told me no extensions on the deadline."

"Did you tell him you're in control?"

"He knew I wasn't in control."

"Did you tell him that you know he was the numbered account holder at BOS?"

"Not directly."

"What does that mean?"

"I told him I got his name before I left Singapore. That's why the bank fired me."

"Lilly, Lilly. You have to be clearer. His connection to the numbered account is the whole point; *that's* your control."

"It wasn't my fault."

"I can only tell you what to say. It's your job to be convincing."

"You're the one who wants me to drag Patrick into this. Robledo didn't believe a thing I said about him."

"What are you talking about?

"Robledo knew right away I was lying. Patrick went to see him before I even got there."

"*What?* Did you give Patrick his name? I told you *never* to share any of our secrets with Patrick!"

Lilly had indeed been warned, and the accusatory tone put her on the defensive. "I didn't say anything to Patrick. I don't know how he got it."

There was silence on the line, and Lilly felt the construction guy watching her again. She walked around the barricades and started down the sidewalk.

"We can work with this," her source said finally. "Actually, the fact that Patrick is meeting on his own with Robledo makes it even easier for me to help you."

"I don't want your help."

"You *need* it, Lilly."

"No, I don't need anything from you. I can't sleep, I can't eat, I can't even drink a cup of tea without scalding my mouth. Just leave me alone!"

"Lilly, you are in serious trouble. You helped Gerry Collins funnel two billion dollars to Abe Cushman, and from the get-go, Treasury refused to believe that you were unaware of the scam when you did it. They still don't believe you're innocent."

"Oh, and I suppose you have some kind of direct pipeline to the Treasury Department, is that it?"

"Maybe I do."

The way he said it, so matter of fact, gave her pause.

"It's all fitting together," he said. "Patrick Lloyd is Tony Mandretti's son. Mandretti killed Gerry Collins. We need to show Treasury that the real crook here isn't you. It's Patrick. If he's dealing with Robledo on his own, that's the missing link we need."

"What do you mean *we*? And anyway, all they had was a conversation. That doesn't mean there's a link."

"The link was there before you even met Patrick."

"You're making that up."

"You're in denial, sweetheart."

"Don't call me that."

"If there was no link between your boyfriend and Manu Robledo, why did he suddenly drop everything in New York and go to Singapore?"

"Singapore is a BOS stronghold in Asia."

"Really? And why did he immediately take to you like a fly to honey?"

"Patrick and I . . . we hit it off."

"Come on, Lilly. You're a beautiful woman, but let's get real. He lied to you two days ago when he pretended not to know that Tony Martin was really Tony Mandretti. If Patrick didn't know Robledo before going to Singapore, you can bet his father did. How else could Patrick have tracked Robledo down at his church and met with him before you did? We can't let him get away with this."

The cold wind chilled her—or maybe it was the sickening realization of where his plan was headed. "Oh, my God. It's not the mob who is chasing Patrick."

"Lilly, listen to me."

"It's *you*. You're keeping Patrick around long enough to take the blame for everything."

"He deserves the blame."

"I won't do this to Patrick."

"He would do it to you."

"Patrick loves me."

"Yes, so much that he left you all alone in his apartment two hours after your reunion."

"He had to catch a flight. It was a business trip."

"Another lie. He went to see Tony Mandretti in prison."

Lilly tightened her grip on the phone. "I don't believe you."

"You don't know a thing about him, Lilly! If it wasn't for me, you'd still think his name was Patrick Lloyd. I told you he's Tony Mandretti's son. That's the truth. The mob is after him and his father, and it was the mob who put Patrick in the hospital. That's why I told you to stay away from him, but of course you didn't listen. That scheme you cooked up to sneak him out of the hospital was idiotic!"

"What did you expect me to do, just leave him there, a sitting duck, waiting for the Santucci family to come and finish the job?"

"I expected you to stay *away* from him! Do only what I tell you to do, Lilly!"

"I don't believe you anymore. *You* put him in the hospital. Not the mob. I'm going to the police."

"And tell them what? You didn't know Abe Cushman was a fraud? You didn't know Gerry Collins was a thief? You had no idea Patrick Lloyd was Tony Mandretti's son? Face it, Lilly. Patrick has caused you enough problems. Treasury has already decided that the best lead on the Cushman money is the Lilly Scanlon/BOS connection. Robledo shoved the memo in your face."

Lilly stopped so short at the curb that she nearly slipped on the ice. "How do you know about that?"

"I know everything, Lilly."

It seemed as though he did. She was suffocating with fear all over again. "I don't understand why they're targeting *me*."

"You've been played," he said, his tone softening. "First by Gerry Collins, then, even worse, by Patrick Lloyd."

She had a green light to cross Broadway, but she didn't move. "No one could be worse than Gerry Collins."

"At least Collins was genuinely interested in you before he drew you into Cushman's scheme. Patrick played you from beginning to end, on *every* level. Do you remember when you were on Changi Beach in Singapore and that seagull came out of nowhere and dive-bombed right on top of his head?"

Chills cut through her. "You can't possibly know about that."

"I saw it happen."

"You were watching us on the beach? That's beyond creepy."

"Don't worry, I'm not some love-sick puppy who's been following you around for six months. I was only doing my job."

"Your job? Who *are* you?"

"Never mind that. Get back to my point about Patrick and his lies: it was sunscreen."

"What?"

"When you were looking up at the birds in the sky, your poor, heartbroken boyfriend slapped himself on top of the head with a glob of sunscreen. You had finally found the courage to dump him, and he wanted to make you feel really bad about it."

A passing bus forced Lilly to jump back onto the sidewalk. The snow was ten minutes old and already turning to brown slush. "That can't be true," she said.

"Trust me. The only shit on that beach was Patrick's BS. There's so much more I could tell you."

It was tempting to listen, but she reminded herself that she was dealing with a sick son of a bitch. "Stop. I don't want to hear another thing."

"Okay. That's enough for now, love."

"Stop talking to me like that!"

"You're confused. I understand. But admit it. Deep inside, you don't really think I'm lying, do you?"

"I—I don't know what to believe anymore."

"Believe this: I'm here to lead you out of this mess. You should live."

He was making her skin crawl, but she resisted the urge to hang up. "Should Patrick?"

He didn't respond.

"Your list of people who should live," she asked, "does that include Patrick?"

There was silence, but Lilly sensed that he was still there. Finally, he answered: "That's entirely up to us, Lilly."

"What do you mean *us*?"

The line went silent, and he was gone.

21

LOVE WAS IN THE AIR. THE LITTLE SNOW MONKEY WAS MAKING EYES at the big, strong male. Nothing like fresh snow around the steamy cove to simulate the après-ski, in-the-hot-tub experience. All they needed was a bucket of ice, a bottle of Chardonnay, and Michael Bublé on the loudspeaker.

"That's Boo-Boo," Connie told me. "The big guy is Yogi."

"Cute, like the cartoon," I said. "But I always thought the animated Boo-Boo was a boy."

"So is this Boo-Boo."

I took a closer look. If snow monkeys had a pop culture, Boo-Boo would be Sir Elton John. "Ah, now I get it."

The Japanese macaque (aka snow monkey) exhibit was Connie's primary responsibility at the zoo, and it was one of my favorites, especially in winter. I could have watched them all afternoon, but I actually did have a day job. I'd been doing my best by e-mail for the past two days, but sooner rather than later I needed to figure out if, when, and how I would return to my office at BOS. But not before I gathered some intelligence on Manu Robledo.

"Did you find anything?" I asked.

Connie leaned against the exhibit rail with arms folded, her back to the snow monkeys. The tribe had no interest in us, their attention focused on a pair of black-neck swans that had apparently asserted squatters' rights on monkey island.

"I'm very nervous about this," said Connie.

"Is Robledo that scary?"

"Well, possibly. But I mean, I'm uncomfortable about using Tom to check up on people like this."

Tom was her fiancé. He was a trained but unpaid volunteer in the Auxiliary Police Unit at the Central Park Precinct, which meant that he wore the familiar blue uniform and seven-point shield, carried a standard-issue radio that linked him to regular NYPD officers, and patrolled Central Park as the civic-minded "eyes and ears" of the sworn members of the service. It did *not* mean that he had access to law enforcement databases to run background checks—unless he pulled strings and called in favors.

"I'm reasonably confident that Tom isn't the first person to run a name through the computer for a friend."

"But . . ." she said, her expression pained, "he's a scoutmaster."

So was Connie. They'd met while leading a group of aspiring Eagle Scouts on a ten-day hike through New Mexico. Rumor had it that Connie had flung Tom over her back and carried him the last eight miles. I wasn't even aware that women were allowed to serve as scoutmasters, but Connie was totally committed. It seemed like the theater of the absurd: my life had been threatened, and it was still possible that my girlfriend had perpetrated a $2 billion fraud—but there I was before God and the gay snow monkeys, trying to console my sister about a possible violation of the Boy Scout pledge. A witness protection family was as dysfunctional as the next, I supposed.

"Connie, really. Just this once, it's okay."

"What's done is done, I guess."

"Tell me what you got."

She took a breath, then let it go. "Manu Caesar Robledo.

Born in Argentina. Forty-one years old, never been married. Travels between Miami and South America dozens of times a year. Owns a condominium on Brickell Avenue in Miami."

"Interesting," I said. "Gerry Collins' office was in the Financial District on Brickell."

"You're thinking maybe Collins handled the finances of his so-called church?"

"Or his own finances. His condo on Brickell has to be pricey. That's where you'll find all those glamorous high-rises on the bay in the opening credits for *CSI: Miami.*"

"He wasn't born rich, I can tell you that," said Connie. "He's from a little town called Puerto Iguazú. That's in the Tri-Border area where Argentina, Paraguay, and Brazil meet."

"That may explain the bizarre accent he was able to patch together when I was at his church."

"Could be. It's an interesting part of the world."

"You know it?"

"The zoo has a couple of endangered armadillos from that region. Ciudad del Este in Paraguay is right in that same neck of the woods. My supervisor went there on research three years ago. Said she felt safer in the jungle with the pumas and jaguars. It can be pretty lawless."

"What about our friend Robledo—any problems with the law?"

"Nothing in this country or as an adult. He did get into some kind of trouble as a juvenile in Buenos Aires in the early 1990s, but Tom says he couldn't tell anything about it from the computer entry."

"Could be worth exploring."

She looked like a nervous scout again. "We agreed that I would ask Tom this favor just *once.*"

"I meant *I* would explore it," I said, but my words were drowned out by a piercing scream. My gaze shifted to the snow monkeys, where Boo-Boo was standing atop a boulder and throwing a hissy fit at Yogi.

"You tell him, Boo-Boo," said Connie. We shared a laugh, but my sister was suddenly serious. My back was to the red panda exhibit, and Connie was gazing past me in that direction. "Don't turn around," she said.

"What's wrong?" I asked.

"About a hundred feet behind you, standing beside a tree at about two o'clock from your left shoulder, there's a man with a telephoto lens. At first I thought he was photographing the snow monkeys. But now it looks like he's taking pictures of you and me."

I immediately thought back to Puffy's Tavern and the guy wearing the rapper's hat who had come and gone without drinking his beer—who looked just like the guy who had photographed Lilly and me in the Singapore Mall, and who'd shown up again outside my apartment.

I couldn't help turning my head, and Connie grabbed me.

"I told you not to look!" she said, but there was no stopping me. I wheeled around completely, and like a laser my gaze locked onto the photographer by the tree. The lighting was flat on such a gray afternoon, and he was wearing a heavy winter coat, but his reaction alone confirmed it.

"It's him," I said.

"Who?" asked Connie, but I was off like a track star.

"Patrick!"

I was at full speed, my legs churning, defying the ice and snow beneath my feet. The man with the camera ran for the exit, jumped the turnstile, and hoofed it up the hill toward East Drive. I jumped the same turnstile, slipped on a patch of ice, and skidded on my knees across the salted pavers. It hurt like hell, and my pants were torn. Worse, I was down long enough for the guy to put another twenty yards between us.

It occurred to me that he might have a gun, that I should give Connie a shout to call for security or dial 911. But he'd committed no crime, and I dismissed the thought. It was still daylight, and I had him in my sight. His lead was less than fifty yards. With everything I had been through in the past forty-eight hours, I could have closed the gap on Usain Bolt—even with my knees bloodied.

I pushed myself up from the cold walkway and was off like a rocket. The fool was running away from Fifth Avenue, the taxis, the subway, and other means of escape. He was trying to lose me in the park. This time, he was not going to get away. This time, he was mine.

"Patrick, stop!"

Connie was trailing far behind, but I could hear the concern in her voice. Strangely, it only propelled me. I was inside of twenty yards, and closing, as he darted in front of a horse-drawn carriage on scenic East Drive. The driver cursed and reined in his big draft horse, then cursed even louder at me as I, in hot pursuit, cut off the horse a second time. My target was slowing down, and adrenaline was pushing me even faster. He followed the sidewalk down a ramp and into a pedestrian tunnel. Wollman Rink was directly ahead, and I couldn't let him get all the way there and disappear into a crowd. I went the other way, up and over the hill, and was dead even with him when he came out the other end of the tunnel. He glanced back into the tunnel and probably thought he had lost me as I dived like a hawk from the hill above him. He went down hard, breaking my fall like a human mattress beneath me. He writhed and squirmed, but he was exhausted from the run, and I was easily the bigger dog in the struggle. My knee was throbbing from the tumble over the turnstile at the zoo, but I drilled it into the small of his back anyway. He let out a miserable groan as I pinned his face to the frozen ground.

"Who are you?" I shouted.

He didn't answer, but I wasn't feeling much from him in the way of resistance.

"What's your name?" I asked, harsher.

His resistance weakened even further. He was completely spent from the chase.

"Don't hurt me!" he said, pleading.

"Tell me who you are!"

He started to cry—upper lip quivering, huge tears streaming down his cheeks. I had yet to slug him, and he was turning into gelatin. This was bordering on pathetic.

"Please, please, don't hit me."

It felt like I was beating up one of Connie's Cub Scouts. "Start talking and no one is going to get hurt," I said.

He drew a breath, then another. The crying was under control, but his body continued to tremble.

"Talk!" I said.

"My name is Evan," he said with a sniffle, "and I can help you, Mr. Lloyd."

22

THE BLACK LIMOUSINE PASSED A SECOND TIME. OR WAS IT A different one? Lilly wasn't sure. They all looked alike. On any given workday, thousands of limos must have cruised down Broadway in the Financial District. That call from her source was making her paranoid. Or maybe she was just more alert. No, this was definitely paranoia.

Damn you, Patrick.

She shook off that thought. She didn't want to jump to conclusions. Not everything her source had told her could be true. Not all the blame could be laid on Patrick Lloyd. Even though his name was really Peter Mandretti. And his father was in jail for murdering Gerry Collins. And he went to see Manu Robledo without any help from her.

"You've been played," her source had told her. *"First by Gerry Collins, then, even worse, by Patrick Lloyd."*

A pigeon waddled past her on the sidewalk. Lilly thought of its cousin in Singapore—the seagull that had swooped down from the sky and dropped a direct hit on Patrick's head. *Allegedly* swooped down. The timing of it—right in the middle of her breakup speech—had been rather unbelievable. *Sunscreen.* What kind of jerk would slap himself on the head with fake bird shit to make it even harder for his girlfriend to dump him?

"Patrick played you from beginning to end," he'd told her, *"on every level."*

Loser. That's what you are, Patrick: a lying loser.

A black limo with dark-tinted windows passed. Lilly stopped as it turned at the next block. Very similar to the last one that had turned off Broadway at the same cross street. It was hard to say if it was the same one she had seen before, but the mere possibility was making her so nervous that it felt like she had broken glass in her stomach.

This is all your fault, Patrick, Peter—whatever your name is.

She jaywalked across Broadway, avoided the piles of slush at the curb, and cut down the narrow side street at St. Paul's Chapel. Changing course made for a little longer walk, but she could get the subway at the World Trade Center. She thought about grabbing one of the cabs outside the Hilton, but her cash was running low, and the station was only two minutes away. She stopped at the crosswalk for the red light, glancing again at the chapel. She hadn't attended services in years, but she was suddenly back in elementary school and reciting the Golden Rule, guilting herself into being the bigger person and doing the right thing.

You have to call Patrick.

His lies were hurtful, no doubt about it. But that bizarre phone conversation had, in the end, come down to the question of whether Patrick should live or die: *"That's entirely up to us,"* the caller had told her. Whatever lies Patrick had told her didn't change that fact. She had to tell him.

The traffic light changed at Church Street as she reached for her cell, and she was stepping off the curb when the limo cut her off in the crosswalk. Lilly jumped back onto the sidewalk as the rear door opened. It startled her, but she recognized the man in the backseat. Even though she no longer worked at BOS, photographs of the new head of private wealth management at BOS/America had been all over the news lately.

"Get in," said Joe Barber. He was alone on the bench seat, directly behind the driver.

Lilly was more confused than afraid—but fear was definitely part of the equation. For a moment she couldn't move, her mind and body trapped between the eerie, urban silence of old St. Paul's Churchyard behind her and the incessant buzz of construction at the World Trade Center site across the street.

"Get in the car," said Barber.

Lilly froze, her eyes locking with Barber's. To say that she didn't know who to trust anymore was a gross understatement; she trusted no one. She certainly didn't know Barber, except for what she'd read about him. But the newest addition to BOS/America's top management—a former Treasury official who wasn't even working for BOS when Cushman had come crashing down—seemed low risk. And worth a listen.

But how did he know how to find me?

"Lilly, get in the car, or the next sound you hear will be FBI handcuffs closing around your wrists."

The broken glass was churning, clawing away at the inside of her stomach. Lilly's war was being fought on too many fronts. Her legs didn't have another run in them. She climbed inside and closed the door.

Barber signaled to the driver, and the limo pulled away.

23

CONNIE MADE ME FEEL LIKE THE CLASS BULLY AS I DRAGGED EVAN Hunt to the nearest park bench and sat his ass down. She started screaming at me about taking the law into my own hands, but I told her to save it for her scout troop.

"Taking a picture is not a crime!" said Evan.

"Then why did you run?" I said, shoving him.

He looked stunned. "You're assaulting me."

I shoved him again. "Yeah, you're right."

"Patrick, stop," said Connie. "I won't be part of this."

"Then go back to work."

She gnawed her lip, straining to find the perfect comeback, but in the end she settled for the standard sibling contrarianism. "Fine, you want me to leave? Then I'll stay."

She took a seat on the boulder behind me. Evan stared back at me like a scared rabbit, though he did seem relieved to have a strong woman around to control me. I grabbed him by the lapels of his trench coat, pushed him back onto the bench, and gave him thirty seconds to explain himself.

Five minutes later, he was still jabbering. To me, it was stream-of-conscious nonsense, but Connie seemed to be following it.

"Some people say I have a mind like a computer," said Evan, "but to me, that's an insult."

"I feel the exact same way," said Connie.

I shot her a look that said, *Connie, please.*

"You know anything about trading options, Mr. Lloyd?"

I was facing him, seated on the boulder beside Connie. "We trade thousands of options every day."

"So, you know every once in a while you have to calculate a second derivative, called a gamma, which is the rate of change in the first derivative, delta."

My knee was throbbing from my wipeout during the chase, but Evan was starting to make my head hurt even worse. Connie was totally with him, but it was like another language to me. "That's what computers are for," I said.

"*No!* That's what you guys in the expensive suits don't understand. There are still calculations in this business that are so math intensive that computers choke on them."

"I find that hard to believe."

"It's true," said Connie, chiming in. "He's absolutely right about that."

I was beginning to wonder if Connie's boyfriend Tom was on the bubble. I threw her another look—this time something along the lines of *Who asked for your help?*

Evan continued. "When you're in a situation where prices can move at an infinite rate, it's time to throw out the computer and look at the price of a stock or the market and calculate your own option price. I can do it faster than any computer."

"That's impressive," said Connie.

"That's his job," I said, making a rather easy deduction. "You're a quantitative analyst, I presume."

"Please," he said, "I prefer 'quant.' Synonymous with nerd. And proud of it."

It suddenly occurred to me that getting chased down in

Central Park and tackled on the run was a minor skirmish compared to the bruisings Evan had undoubtedly taken in middle school. At least I hadn't given him a wedgie.

"Enough with the mathematics double talk," I said. "You need to answer my questions. Was that you at Puffy's Tavern two days ago?"

"Yes. You and Lilly Scanlon."

"You know her name?"

"Of course."

"Were you the same guy who took our photo in Singapore last July?"

"Yup, that was me, all right."

His response bordered on glib, as if he was showing off, seemingly energized by the interest Connie had taken in his impressive mathematics background. I rose, leaving Connie alone on the boulder. Evan watched warily as I came closer, leaned toward him, and placed my foot on the front edge of the bench beside him. I was merely tying my shoe, but he had nearly wet his pants. I was back in control.

"Why have you been following me around and snapping pictures?"

"You and Lilly Scanlon are a key part of the analysis."

"What analysis?"

"My Abe Cushman analysis. See, when you're a quant, all you have to do is look at the numbers in Cushman's returns, and you can see he was running a Ponzi scheme."

"It's not exactly a secret that he was running a Ponzi scheme."

"Sure, *now* it's no secret. But I knew it ten years ago."

I couldn't help but smile. "Yeah, you and all the other Wall Street geniuses who came out of the woodwork the day after Cushman confessed. Suddenly, everyone and his brother knew it five years ago, ten years ago. In fact, CNBC has an interview scheduled next week with an ob-gyn who figured out that Cushman was actually planning his scheme while still in his mother's womb."

"You're making fun of me," he said.

A bigger jackass probably would have told him that if he had a problem with it, he should cinch up the twenty-year-old trench coat and hide the bright orange dress shirt and the Mickey Mouse neck tie. But something about the guy made me pull my punches. Or maybe I was trying to avoid more flack from Connie.

"Sorry," I said, "but I don't give much credence to your after-the-fact analysis."

"My analysis was not after the fact. I did my calculations before Cushman was exposed as a fraud. It's only the pictures that came later."

"I don't get the point of the pictures."

"People don't look at numbers the way I do. They need pictures to help them connect the dots. When I had nothing but numbers to show them, nobody listened."

"When you say nobody listened, you mean . . . who?"

"I mean the dickheads at the SEC."

"You shared your analysis with the Securities and Exchange Commission?"

"I wrote it up and spoon-fed it to them. They ignored me. All they had to do was read the damn thing, and the SEC could have shut Cushman down five years before he admitted he was a fraud. I'd be a very rich man now."

I studied his expression. He was deadly serious. "How would that have made you rich?" I asked.

"You don't think I did this analysis and wrote up a report for nothing, do you?"

"Are you working for somebody?"

"No, it's nothing formal like that. I'm talking about the

whistle-blower statute. I was entitled to ten percent of the scheme if the SEC shut him down. Ten percent of sixty billion . . . probably even you can do that math."

Technically, he was correct. By law, whistle-blowers were entitled to get paid for rooting out fraud. Reality was another matter entirely. "Do you realize that the SEC whistle-blower program doesn't apply to Ponzi schemes?"

His expression tightened. I got the impression that he was fully aware of the program's severe limitations, but he was still bitter about the fact that he hadn't realized it until after investing countless hours into Cushman.

"Doesn't matter," he said. "I'm done dealing with the government. Plenty of law firms will pay me a pretty penny for a road map to the Cushman money."

"Is that why you've been following me and snapping pictures? I'm part of your road map?"

He flashed a clever smile. "Say cheeeez."

He was gaining confidence as the conversation went on, even smug about himself. *Keep it up, and a wedgie is not out of the question.*

"You said you could help me," I said, reminding him of the promise he'd made while facedown in the snow and begging me not to slug him. "Exactly what did you mean by that?"

"Simple. Based on my analysis, I've come to the conclusion that you don't know squat about Cushman's money."

I suddenly liked him better. "You're the first person to say that. But there are others who seem to disagree."

"Others don't know what I know."

"I'd be curious to get educated," I said.

"Then you should read my report."

He seemed proud of what he knew, or at least empowered by the fact that someone was actually interested in listening to him.

"Where is it?"

"My place. Ten minutes from here on the subway."

"I honestly don't have ten minutes to waste."

"This will not be a waste of your time. I guarantee it."

It was his sincere belief that he could help me; I would have bet money on it. The question was whether he was dealing with a full deck.

His smugness returned. "You should feel honored that I've made this offer to you. Other than the SEC, there's only one person I've ever shown my report."

"Is that so? Who would that be?"

"Three years ago. A guy named Tony Martin."

It was clear that he expected me to know the name. It was not at all clear if he knew that Tony Martin was Tony Mandretti—or that Tony Mandretti was my father.

"How do you know Tony Martin?" I asked.

"I'll be happy to tell you that," he said, "right after you tell me how you know him."

Connie and I exchanged glances. She looked wary, but I sensed a reluctant green light from her.

"First things first," I told him. "Let's take a ride on the subway and have a look at that report."

24

MANU ROBLEDO UNLOCKED THE SOUNDPROOF DOOR TO THE church basement.

The workers had left for the day. Eventually, they might get around to restoring the two-hundred-year-old sanctuary to its former splendor. For the past month, however, the priority had been the basement. It was just days away from a complete rewiring, everything top of the line.

Robledo started down the stairs and switched on the handheld video camera. His tech team leader had assured him that encryption capabilities were in place to stream video safely across the Internet. Timely progress reports kept Robledo's investors happy, and there was nothing like narrated video. He went to a section of the basement where the floorboards had yet to be laid, where the wires between joists were still exposed.

"We've run literally miles and miles of cable," he said for the recording, "just like you see here. Think of it as a personal information pipeline that sucks in names, Social Security numbers, passport numbers, driver's license numbers, addresses, phone numbers, and IP addresses. For basic searches we link one or more of those core identifiers to records on age, marital status, race, ethnicity, employment, home values, estimated income. But we can take it much further than that. We can break people down by the medicine they take, the books they read, the cologne they wear, the flights they've booked, the music they download—virtually any piece of personal information that is out there in cyberspace."

Robledo could have gone on to explain the significance of that function, but his investors were smart people. They understood that purchase behavior and lifestyle data were invaluable in the perpetual quest to identify new recruits.

The camera continued to roll as he opened another door and entered a separate room of stacked computers.

"This is our grid," said Robledo, "a state-of-the-art network of supercomputers. Lightning fast, and they hold more information than you can fathom. In just a few weeks' time, we'll be operating twenty-four/seven to analyze and match the information we gather, which will allow us to create a detailed portrait of hundreds of millions of adults—and, more important, young adults."

He switched off the camera. Enough video. Tonight he would have his tech guy—an expert in steganography—embed it into a presentation on cookware or some other benign subject matter that would mask its true content. Then Robledo could transmit the file securely to the investors.

If I still have investors.

Robledo was all too aware that their patience was thinning. Three years was a long time to wait. Periodic reminders that most of Cushman's victims had given up hope of recovering all of their losses had done absolutely nothing to reduce their expectations. That was his fault, really. He had promised them too much, raised their hopes too high. It wasn't that he'd misled them. There had been good reason for Robledo to believe that his investors would get their money back, even if others lost every penny.

Gerry Collins had given him that assurance.

Robledo put the video camera away and pulled up a chair.

Long days and too little sleep had left him drained and exhausted, but that didn't stop the anger from rising. Years of networking and hard work were at stake. A loss of funding now would be disastrous. He was so close to becoming operational—would have been entering his third year of operation, if not for Gerry Collins. It was bad enough that Collins had steered him toward Cushman in the first place. Robledo had actually trusted him a second time.

Fool me once, shame on you. Fool me twice, shame on me.

The worst part was that Robledo was still paying for that second mistake, unable to get it out of his mind. It was especially bad at times like these—when the investors demanded to know when they were going to see the money they'd lost and why the recovery was taking so long.

He closed his eyes to suppress his anger. It wasn't working. The ghost of Gerry Collins came back to haunt him—taunt him—as that last meeting in Miami replayed in his mind's eye. It had gone down on the last day of November, just weeks before Cushman confessed his massive fraud, jumped off his balcony, and left feeders like Gerry Collins to fend for themselves.

Robledo reached the Coconut Grove Marina just after nightfall. A cool breeze blew in from the bay, making it cold enough for a cotton turtleneck and a peacoat. Each puff of wind brought the ping and twang of taut halyards slapping against the tall, barren masts of countless sailboats. Hundreds of yachts slept silently in their slips, side by side. Somewhere in the distance, a diesel engine rumbled toward home, a lonely growl in the darkness. Robledo walked alone to the very end of the long, floating pier, where he boarded a forty-six-foot Hatteras Convertible.

Technically a fishing boat, *Easy Money* was more like a floating lap of luxury. The salon had been entirely redesigned for parties and entertainment, complete with club chairs, a wet bar, hand-crafted teak cabinetry, and even a flat-screen television. Eight months earlier, on this very yacht, Robledo had first met Gerry Collins, introduced by the owner Niklas Konig, a wealthy German businessman. Tonight's reconvening had been at Robledo's request, and Konig had graciously offered his boat.

"*Bienvenido, mi amigo,*" said Konig. His Spanish wasn't terrible, but it bugged Robledo that the man who had introduced him to Gerry Collins would call him a "friend." Konig led him into the salon.

"Something to drink?" asked Collins, standing at the bar. He made the offer with a smile, but it seemed strained. The bags beneath his eyes were new, and they made him look much older than he was. His skin, too, had taken on an unhealthy ashen hue since that first meeting, before the entire financial world had turned upside down. Clearly, this was a man under enormous pressure.

"Nothing for me," said Robledo.

Collins took another stab at congeniality and small talk, but Robledo wasn't biting. "I'm here to talk money."

Money was what most of Cushman's investors wanted to talk about. Since the collapse of Lehman Brothers and Saxton Silvers, Cushman's clients had requested $7 billion in redemptions. Cushman had stopped honoring them.

"My favorite subject," said Collins, taking a seat on the couch. "Let's talk."

Konig joined him, seating himself in the club chair. Robledo remained standing.

"Take your coat off," said Collins, "have a seat."

Robledo did neither. He reached inside his peacoat, removed a thick envelope, and tossed it onto the cocktail table before his hosts.

"What's this?" asked Collins.

"An analysis," said Robledo.

"Of what?"

Robledo's eyes narrowed. "The biggest fraud in the history of Wall Street."

Collins' phony smile evaporated. "Surely you don't mean Mr. Cushman."

Robledo jerked his arm forward, and the .22-caliber pistol that was strapped to his forearm beneath his coat slid into his hand. His next move was like lightning, giving his victim no time to react. The silenced projectile slammed into Konig's chest, dropping him to the floor.

"Don't!" shouted Collins.

Robledo took aim at his forehead.

"Please, I can fix this!"

Robledo hesitated, his finger poised to pull the trigger. He hadn't come to listen, but there was poetry in watching a scumbag beg for his life.

"I can get the money back for you," said Collins. "And more."

"How stupid do you think I am?"

"Your funds never went to Cushman."

"What?"

"You're right," said Collins. "Cushman is a Ponzi scheme. I figured that out eight, maybe ten months ago. But that's good news for you."

Robledo took sharper aim.

"No, please! Listen to me. I was one of Cushman's biggest feeders for three years. After a while, it was obvious to me that he was a fraud, but here's the thing," he said with a nervous chuckle. "My clients didn't want to hear it. I think half of them even knew it was smoke and mirrors, but nobody wanted the bubble to burst. So I kept taking their money, and I kept telling them that I was investing it with Cushman. But I lied. I haven't sent money to Cushman in over six months."

"I don't believe you."

"It's the truth, Manu. The last three quarterly statements I sent out showing investments with Cushman were all fakes. And here's the best part. When Cushman blows up—which is right around the corner—all my clients will think they lost their money. They have no idea I've been stashing it away."

"You're lying."

"It's absolutely true! Not a single penny of what I funneled through BOS/Singapore ever reached Cushman. It's all safe in offshore accounts. It won't go down when he goes down. Get it? When Cushman blows up, the big winner is *me*."

The scheme made too much sense to have been made up on the spot by a coward staring down the barrel of a gun. Robledo asked, "How much are we talking about?"

"Ten figures. Almost a third of that is yours."

"A third?" he said, scoffing. "Wrong, my friend. *All* of it is mine."

Collins stared back at the gun, which was still aimed at his face. "Let's talk," he said. "All I have to do is get my banker to unwind everything, and then everybody will take his fair share."

"What banker?"

"Put the gun down so we can talk."

"What banker?"

"Please, I'm begging you. Don't throw this opportunity away. Don't pull that trigger."

Robledo's encrypted telephone line rang. It was the weekly call he dreaded. The one that made him wish he had ignored Collins' pleas and pulled the trigger. It was from Ciudad del Este—from his investors. Robledo swallowed his anger and answered with the respect that was due his chief funder.

"I'm very sorry, *Doctor*," he said, using the Spanish pronunciation. The "doctor" wasn't a medical doctor. He claimed to
hold a *doctor en derecho*, though Robledo had never verified his
law degree.

"Sorry for what, Manu?"

"I need a little more time."

"Time has run out."

"Please. I have upped the pressure. I should see results soon."

"Upped the pressure how?"

Robledo paused, not sure if he should even mention Patrick
Lloyd. True, he had threatened the boyfriend with the intent
of doubling up the pressure on Lilly, but somehow Patrick
had found the church, and Robledo wasn't convinced that his
overly affected accent had kept Patrick from realizing that the
Reverend Robledo and the gunman in the back of the SUV
were one and the same. He confined his remarks to Lilly.

"I made it clear to her today: no more stalling, or I put a
bullet in her head."

There was silence, then a chilling reply: "Don't make me
call you again, Manu."

"No, of course not, *Doctor*."

More silence, and then a final warning. "If I have to make
just one more phone call, then take my advice, Manu. Put that
bullet in your own head. It will be much more pleasant for you
that way."

The call ended, but Robledo continued to hold the phone
to his ear, absorbing the threat, even after his funder had disconnected.

"Don't worry," he said, thinking aloud, "I have plenty of
bullets."

25

I WAS STARVING, AND THE STEEP CLIMB UP THE BACK STAIRCASE TO Evan's second-story apartment made me even hungrier. We were in the heart of Chinatown, and I smelled moo goo gai pan and sweet-and-sour something or other wafting up from the busy restaurant directly below.

"Smells good," I said.

"For about an hour it does," he said, leading me up the narrow stairway. "The day after I moved in I got so nauseous that I thought I was going to have to move out. But the rent's cheap, and when your research takes you to places as far away as Singapore, money is definitely an issue. After about six weeks, I hardly even noticed the smell anymore."

Evan was breathing heavily as we reached the landing at the top of the stairs. A small window overlooked the Dumpsters in the alley. A chain-link gate extended the full width and height of the dimly lit hallway, blocking all access, and behind the gate was a heavy metal door. It was painted black, and the only way to get to it was through the gate, which was padlocked. Evan unlocked it, then used another key to unlock the deadbolt on the door.

"Is the neighborhood really that bad?" I asked.

"It is when you have the road map to two billion dollars."

Two days earlier a remark like that would have sounded utterly loony to me. *What a difference two days make.*

Evan locked the gate behind us and pushed open the door. I noticed two peepholes, one high and one low. It struck me as odd, and Evan picked up on my curiosity.

"You can tell a lot from a person's shoes," he said. "If somebody from the Salvation Army comes knocking on your door wearing a pair of A. Testoni calfskin boots that set him back at least a G, then . . . well, maybe he's not from the Salvation Army."

He directed me inside, closed the door behind us, and secured the deadbolt. The remark about the expensive Italian footwear begged for a follow-up: Did he think the Mafia was after him? But before I could go there, he switched on a lamp, which literally threw a whole new light on things.

"Holy cow," I said, taking it all in.

A tiny kitchen was to the left, behind a half-closed curtain, and the twin-size mattress on the floor told me that it doubled as his bedroom. The rest of his one-room apartment was the interesting part. An armchair, the television, his desktop computer, and few other pieces of furniture had been pushed to the center of the room so that there was nothing against the walls. The lone window had been covered over with brown butcher paper. Scores of unframed photographs dotted the walls from floor to ceiling, each connected by a thick hand-drawn line. The lines were in various colors—red, blue, green, and yellow—and sometimes more than one colored line connected one photograph to another. Where there were no photographs or colored lines, someone had gone to work with a thick black Sharpie. It was one long narrative, much of it boxed or circled to contain separate thoughts. Hand-drawn arrows directed the flow from left to right, from the kitchen, past the window, around the door, and then back to the kitchen—a 360-degree flowchart of some sort.

"Here's my analysis," he said.

"It looks like hieroglyphics."

"This is a working draft."

I noticed a number of red flags—literally, flags drawn in red marker on the walls. I approached one at random. "What are these for?" I asked.

The question seemed to engage him. "There are thirty-eight in all," he said. "These are all the red flags I pointed out to the SEC—each one sufficient in and of itself to prove that Cushman was running a Ponzi scheme."

I looked closer at the one in front of me. It appeared to have something to do with Cushman's purported trading strategy—that is, a bogus explanation of trades he had never actually made.

"Cushman claimed that his success was based on trades of S&P 100 Index Options," said Evan. "A simple call to the Chicago Board of Options Exchange would have confirmed that the total S&P 100 Index Options that Cushman claimed to acquire at any point in time exceeded the total open interest in S&P 100 contracts at the stated strike price."

I knew what Evan meant, but there was an even simpler way to think of it. "So basically Cushman claimed he was buying filet mignon when anyone with second-grade arithmetic skills could plainly see that the only thing left on the menu was ground chuck."

"Well put," said Evan. "But unfortunately the rigors of second-grade addition and subtraction are beyond the SEC."

A photograph near the window beckoned, and my shadow moved across the wall as I approached.

"This is the shot you took of Lilly and me in Singapore," I said.

Two lines, one yellow and one green, fed into our photograph. I followed the yellow one backward, right to left, which led me to Gerry Collins. The green line, extended backward, led to a question mark.

Evan said, "I haven't quite figured out how you teamed up with Lilly Scanlon."

Apparently, he knew nothing about Andie Henning and the FBI, and I wasn't there to educate him. My focus turned to the red line flowing out of the photograph of Gerry Collins, which traced back to another photograph. This one gave me chills. It had been a long time since I'd seen my father, but I recognized him instantly.

"Why is the line from Tony Martin to Gerry Collins red?" I asked.

"Why do you think?"

My gaze swept the room. Again, the red flags caught my attention. The line between Collins and my father was the only red one in the entire flowchart, and apart from those flags, there was not another red mark on the walls. Evan was still waiting, but I could only guess why.

"Because he killed Collins?"

"No," said Evan. "Because it's sort of a red flag, at least for me."

"What do you mean?"

"I don't believe for one minute that he did it."

I turned and faced him. I liked the way he thought. "How do you know Tony Martin?" I asked.

"You mean Tony Mandretti?"

I didn't pretend to be surprised, but his knowing that Tony Martin was Tony Mandretti did not equate to knowing that Tony Mandretti was my father. I had to play it cool.

"Okay," I said, "how do you know Tony Mandretti?"

He removed his coat and hung it behind the door. A cheap brown suit and orange dress shirt make it difficult to come across as serious, but somehow Evan was pulling it off. He stepped closer, looked me in the eye.

"I'm alive today, thanks to Tony."

"How's that?"

"I'm the guy Tony Mandretti was supposed to whack."

I had not seen that coming, and my expression must have shown it. I was face-to-face with the living and walking confirmation of the story my mother had shared with me—that my father had turned against the Santucci family after refusing a direct order to carry out a mob-style hit.

"I did some bookkeeping for the Santucci family when I was just a neophyte accountant. They thought I was skimming, and those guys have no sense of humor at all when it comes to money. I owe Tony my life. That's why I shared my report with him."

"I don't follow."

"I can never pay him back for what he did, but I thought a fifty-fifty split on the biggest whistle-blower payout in the history of Wall Street would be a nice gesture."

"So it was you and Tony who presented the report to the SEC?"

"Actually, it was just Tony."

"Why just Tony?"

He made a noise like a chicken.

"You were scared?" I asked.

"Hell, yes. Take a look at these red flags," he said, pointing. "The money from Europe, especially. Billions and billions of dollars came through offshore accounts. Now, I suppose there are legitimate reasons to have an offshore account. But any moron would know that a good chunk of that belongs to the Mafia, drug lords, or worse. These are people who would think nothing of rubbing out a quant like me who runs to the SEC screaming Ponzi scheme."

"Tony wasn't scared?"

Evan scoffed. "Tony Martin, Tony Mandretti. Doesn't matter what his name is. The guy's a total ballbuster."

The apple doesn't fall far from the tree. I was thinking of Connie.

"Anyway," said Evan, "you probably see my point. Tony put his own life at risk and gave up everything he had—including his family—because he drew a firm line in the sand. He refused to be a triggerman, even if the hit was on a worthless quant. That makes it hard for me to believe that he killed Gerry Collins, nearly tearing his head off in the process, over money."

It was exactly what I'd been saying all along. "I definitely see your point," I said.

"Good. So tell me, Patrick. How do you know Tony Mandretti?"

I hesitated. Evan apparently didn't *know* that I was Tony Mandretti's son, but surely he suspected it. *Strongly* suspected it. There was no better explanation for the way he'd been following me around and snapping photographs.

Evan said, "I've more than kept my part of the deal."

He meant the report on the wall, which he'd shared with me on the condition that I give something in return. He'd already filled a major hole. I had the feeling there were others he could fill. His rapport with Connie had been almost instantaneous, and now that I'd spent time with him, I trusted the guy, too.

"You've been very helpful," I said.

And then I told him.

26

THE NEW YORK STOCK EXCHANGE WAS CLOSED, THE TRADING day was over, but Joe Barber gave me forty-five minutes to meet him in his Midtown office—or I was fired. I left Evan's apartment and immediately called Connie.

"I'm headed over to BOS," I told her.

"Can't you lie low, at least for a few days? I just snuck you out of the ER to keep the Santucci family from putting a bullet in your head."

"That whole rescue was based on bad information from Lilly. What's happening has nothing to do with the Santuccis. I'm sure of it, now that I've talked to Evan."

I quickly told her who Evan Hunt really was, then explained my thinking. "He invested countless hours to expose Cushman's fraud, and he's put in even more time tracking the money. He's like an encyclopedia, and in all the information he's gathered, the only place the Santucci family shows up is when he and Dad first met—when Dad was still Tony Mandretti."

"He's a quant, not a private investigator."

"He's definitely right about one thing: if last night in Battery Park had been a hit on Peter Mandretti ordered by the Santucci family, I'd be dead now. The guy who attacked me didn't say a single word to suggest that he knew my real name."

"But Lilly was explicit when she called and asked me to help get you out of the ER: the Santuccis have figured out that you are Peter Mandretti."

"Someone injected the mob into the equation to drive a wedge between Lilly and me. To make her stop trusting me. Or to make her trust them."

"And you think that's Robledo?"

"No. Robledo is only a part of the big picture."

"According to Evan, you mean?"

"Connie, the man is a quant. You met him. He processes information better than a computer. More important, *Dad* trusted him. They teamed up on the Cushman report."

Her response came with a sigh of resignation. "You told him, didn't you?"

I took her meaning: the fact that I was Tony Mandretti's son.

"Yes. We need him. He doesn't think Dad killed Gerry Collins, either. Even better, I think he can help us prove it."

She didn't shout, didn't even groan. My final point—that Dad had put *his* trust in Evan—seemed to have been the clincher.

"I need to get back to the bank," I said. "Not just because the head of private banking says so. It's the only way to find out what's really going on."

She realized there was no changing my mind. "Be careful," she said.

I assured her that I would try.

Going back to BOS presented a host of concerns, ranging from the questions that corporate security had raised about my identity to the fact that I really hadn't done squat on the job since my return from Singapore—under "Patrick Lloyd" or any other name. I addressed the one problem that I could actually fix: my appearance. The combination of zoo blankets in Connie's van and the Chinese restaurant below Evan's apartment had me smelling like a snow monkey smothered in Szechuan sauce. Borrowing one of Evan's orange dress shirts and Mickey Mouse ties—he had a closet full—was not going to cut it. My apartment was roughly on the way, and the cabdriver waited at the curb as I ran upstairs and did a five-minute Wall Street makeover. I reached the BOS/America executive suite with all of thirty seconds to spare. Barber's assistant ushered me into his office, where I was hit with an immediate surprise.

"Lilly?" I said.

She was seated in the armchair facing Barber's desk. "Yes," she said coolly. "Lilly is my name. Always has been."

The "always has been" remark was a clear indication of her anger toward me for lying about my past. I had sensed some of that in the ER, but it seemed to have escalated since the morning.

"Have a seat," said Barber.

I took the leather armchair beside Lilly. She was no longer shooting daggers at me; she avoided eye contact altogether.

We waited in silence as Barber flipped through a document. There was no telling what it contained, but I suspected it had nothing to do with our meeting—that a man who enjoyed his power and position was simply making me sit, stew, and speculate about what kind of trouble I was in. It would have been easy to freak. Barber had a naturally hard look, and nothing about his office suggested that he was a man of mercy and compassion. Not a single photograph of his wife or kids anywhere. It was more of a shrine to his own achievements, a collection of plaques, honorary degrees, and photographs of him with everyone from the late Charlton Heston to three past presidents. A glass-encased issue of *Fortune* with his picture on the cover hung on the wall directly over his Bloomberg terminal.

Barber laid the mystery document aside and looked at me from across his desk. I knew I was not going to be fired, since it was corporate policy that at least two BOS representatives be present at the dismissal of any employee. It was a sad state of affairs when termination might well have been less troublesome than the actual purpose of the meeting.

Barber looked at me and said, "Lilly won't tell us."

"Tell you what?" I asked.

"Your real name."

"I don't know his real name," said Lilly.

I knew that was a lie, but I took it as a positive sign that, at least in front of Barber, she was pretending not to know that I was a Mandretti.

Barber tightened his stare. "We know your name is not Patrick Lloyd."

I opted for silence.

"I don't know who you are," said Barber, "and I'm guessing that you don't want me or anyone else to find out."

I continued to listen, saying nothing.

Barber rose, speaking as he walked to the window. A sea of city lights twinkled across Midtown, most of them below his fiftieth-floor vista. "I'm sure that if I kept digging, I would find out." He turned away from the view and faced me. "But, frankly, I don't care who you are."

I stole a quick glance at Lilly, trying to see if she was as confused as I was, but her gaze was cast at the floor.

Barber stepped away from the window and leaned on the edge of his desk, facing us. "How would the two of you like to help me solve a little problem?"

Lilly said nothing. "Sure," I said, not knowing what else to say.

"Great," he said, rubbing his hands together. His sudden upbeat manner was laden with sarcasm. "Here's the challenge: we need to find two billion dollars."

I shot another quick glance in Lilly's direction, but I got nothing back from her.

"What two billion dollars?" I asked.

"The two billion that was supposed to go to Abe Cushman, but that the Treasury Department seems to think was squirreled away with the help of BOS/Singapore."

"I don't know anything about that," I said.

"Of course you don't," said Barber, his sarcasm even thicker, "and neither does Lilly. That's why I'm through asking Lilly if she was complicit with you. And I won't even bother asking if you were complicit with Lilly. In other words, I'm sick and tired of wasting my time."

He walked around his desk and picked up two large manila envelopes. They'd been hiding beneath the document he'd laid aside earlier.

"Here's what we're going to do," said Barber. He handed me one of the envelopes, unopened. I could tell from touch that it contained several CDs or DVDs in jewel boxes.

"Patrick, I'm giving you full access to Lilly's records for the past three years." He handed the other sealed envelope to Lilly. "Lilly, I'm giving you complete access to Patrick's records. Everything you need is there. Trading confirmations, e-mails, electronic data of every form imaginable. I want you to comb through it. Find that money."

I tried another sideways glance, and this time Lilly looked as confused as I felt. "I'm not sure I follow you, sir," I said.

"No worries," he said. "One or both of you knows exactly what I'm talking about. One or both of you knows where the money is. My guess is, only one of you will come forward. The other will probably go to jail.

"Work hard," he said. "Search your conscience. Do the right thing. At the very least, save your own ass."

Barber walked to the door. Lilly rose, and I followed. I

could see from the way she moved that her stomach was in knots. Stress had always taken a toll on her body, and I was feeling more than responsible for this bout.

"Good luck," said Barber, showing us out of his office. "You're going to need it."

27

LILLY WALKED BRISKLY DOWN THE HALLWAY, NOT QUITE AS IF the building were on fire, but almost. There was no wait for an elevator, and it was just two of us inside when the doors closed.

"Can we talk?" I asked.

She kept her eyes fixed on the lighted numbers above the doors. I couldn't tell if she simply didn't want to talk while we were still inside the bank or if she hated my guts and never wanted to speak to me again. The range of possibilities seemed that broad.

It was an express ride from the executive suite to the lobby. Lilly got out first, and I nearly had to break into a trot to follow her out of the building. It was the tail end of rush hour, but even a crowded sidewalk didn't slow her down. I found myself dodging to and fro to avoid head-on collisions with oncoming pedestrians as I pleaded with her.

"I need to talk to you," I said.

"You lied to me," she said, never breaking stride.

"A legal name change for reasons of personal safety is not a lie," I said. "I've been Patrick Lloyd my entire adult life."

She stopped cold. "I came halfway across the world out of concern for your safety. I told you that the real name of the man who killed Gerry Collins is Tony Mandretti. You acted as if you'd never heard of him. Then you told me you had a business trip, got on a plane, and went to visit him—your father—in prison. *That's* a lie."

I would have liked a killer comeback, but I supposed she was right. "It wasn't as if I was never going to tell you the truth."

"That is so lame." She turned angrily and started down the sidewalk. I took her by the arm, stopping her.

"Let go of me," she said.

"Lilly, be reasonable."

"Reasonable? You want *me* to be reasonable? I had no idea Gerry Collins and Abe Cushman were a fraud. Now, even the Treasury Department thinks I'm hiding billions in dirty money. The bank fired me, thugs are chasing me, and my stomach feels like I swallowed a box of roofing tacks. Mind you, all of this came to pass after you arrived in Singapore."

"Are you suggesting *I* had something to do with all that?"

"Are you suggesting you had *nothing* to do with it?"

If this conversation was going to continue, there was only one way to answer such a broad question: "No, I'm not suggesting any such thing."

My veracity caught her off guard. Slowly, the anger in her expression transformed into curiosity. We drifted out of the flow of pedestrians, crossed the sidewalk, and took a seat on the lip of a huge granite planter outside the office building. Overhead, a decorative strand of leftover Christmas lights twinkled in the bare branches of a potted maple tree. Our breath steamed in the chilly night air, the blinking lights coloring our little puffs of conversation.

"I've made mistakes," I said, "and I'm sorry you're the one getting hurt."

She didn't answer.

"But," I said, "there are two sides to the story here."

"What do you mean by that?"

"It's true that I didn't tell you my real name was Peter

Mandretti. But somehow you knew that, and a whole lot more, when you called Connie this morning and told her I had to get out of the ER and run for my life. You want to tell me how you got that information?"

"Why does it matter how I found out?"

"It matters because you're getting bad information."

"Don't even try to convince me that you're not Peter Mandretti."

"That part is accurate. But you're being led down the wrong path if someone told you that the Santucci family has figured out that Patrick Lloyd is Peter Mandretti and is after me."

"How do you know it's wrong?"

"Because I'd be dead by now if they were after me. My mom is proof enough of that."

"Your mom?"

Lilly obviously didn't know that part of the story. I digressed to fill her in. I wasn't fishing for sympathy by bringing my mother's murder into it, but the effect was there nonetheless.

"I'm sorry about your mother," she said. "I really am. But hearing about her doesn't make it any safer for me to tell you how I got your real name."

Our eyes met, and I saw genuine fear in hers. "Talk to me," I said.

"The man is scary, Patrick. Really scary. He knows every-thing. He knows about your family. He knows about Gerry Collins. He knows about Manu Robledo."

"What did he tell you about Robledo?"

"That he opened the numbered account at BOS."

"And you're saying that's the truth?"

"Yes. I knew it as soon as I went to the church and spoke to him. It was the same voice."

"I knew that accent of his was phony," I said.

"What accent?"

"He put on a weird voice when I went to see him at the

church. At first it made me think he was some kind of cult leader. But it also made me think that maybe he was trying to keep me from recognizing him."

"He must have realized how weak it was," said Lilly. "He didn't even bother trying to fool me."

"So it is definitely Robledo who is threatening us, demanding the money."

"And warning us that we're dead if we go to the police. So *don't*."

"I just told you what happened to my mother when my dad went to the police. I'm not going to run and tell the police anything without a quid pro quo—protection, information, something. You know I wouldn't negotiate without telling you."

"Really? Right now, all I know is that you went to see Robledo and didn't tell me a thing about it."

"How did you know *that*?"

"How do you think? There's only one person who tells me anything, and your reaction just confirmed that he told me the truth. What do you have going on with Robledo?"

"Nothing. I only found out about him because you left a map to his so-called church in the search history of my Internet browser. I pulled it up after you climbed out the window of my apartment—which is another thing you haven't explained to me."

The anxious expression returned to her face. "The apartment," she said, almost stammering. "I had to leave. Right away. It was him. The guy I've been telling you about. He showed up, pretending to deliver roses."

"I found them."

"I'm not kidding when I say that he's scary, that he knows everything. He even knows stuff about *us*."

"What kind of stuff about us?"

"He was watching us in Singapore."

So was Evan Hunt, I thought—but I kept that to myself.

"He knows the littlest details, like how we broke up on the beach," she said. "He witnessed the whole incident with the seagull pooping on your head."

"Wonderful. I suppose that will end up on YouTube."

It was a stab at levity, but she remained deadly serious. "He said it was all a stunt. He saw you splatter yourself with a handful of sunscreen."

"What?"

"He said you were just trying to make me feel worse about dumping you."

Apparently, my joke about YouTube wasn't far from the mark. "Lilly, I Facebooked about the seagull after we broke up. I got about a hundred comments. I'm sure that's how he found out about it. He wasn't on the beach watching us. This sunscreen story is ridiculous. It just proves that he's a liar who wants to turn you against me. Who is this idiot?"

She ignored my question, her eyes narrowing. "He said your transfer from New York to Singapore wasn't just a career move. He said it was part of a plan."

"Really? He actually said that?"

"Getting to know me, getting me to trust you, was part of your plan."

I was starting to squirm. Lilly had been right—this guy's breadth of knowledge *was* scary—and I wasn't sure how deep a hole I was in. Honesty had been paying dividends so far tonight, though I wasn't sure how much was too much. I gave it a shot.

"Let's clear some of this up," I said.

"Aren't you going to deny it?" she asked.

"It wasn't just a career move, but let me explain."

"Are you saying there *was* a plan?"

I struggled with this one, measuring my words. "My trip to Singapore was part of an official investigation."

Her mouth fell open, and finally she spoke. "You went there to spy on me?"

"Spying is a strong word."

"So it's true?"

"I can't say it's true, because I don't know what he told you, but—"

"Oh, my God. You are such a liar."

"I'm not lying. I'm being completely honest."

"*Now* you are. But you played me for months."

"That's not true."

"All your talk about love at first sight—that was just a line to make me trust you. All part of an *official investigation.*"

"Lilly, just calm down."

"An official investigation for *whom*? Some warring faction of the Santucci family run by your father from a prison cell?"

I couldn't mention the FBI. "Lilly, please. That's not it at all."

"Go to hell, Patrick."

"You've got it all wrong."

She clutched the envelope Barber had given her, her glare shooting back at me like lasers. "We'll see what the data says."

She turned and joined the late rush-hour flow, disappearing into the night.

28

"IT'S ALL ENCRYPTED," SAID EVAN.

My package from Barber contained eight DVDs. After watching Lilly storm off to examine my data, I returned to Evan's apartment and enlisted some added firepower to examine hers. My instincts had been dead on: I officially needed Evan more than he needed me.

"Can you break the code?" I asked.

Evan looked up from his computer screen. I followed his gaze as it swept the flowchart of arrows, photographs, and handwritten narrative on his walls.

"What do you think?" he asked.

It wasn't arrogance; it was just a fact: Evan's first language was numbers. He spoke through numbers, read through numbers, looked for stories in numbers. Evan didn't simply make sure his checkbook and credit card statements balanced *to the penny*—which was weird enough. He was the kind of guy who, just for grins, would extract the raw data from his monthly statements and create an intelligent computing algorithm to analyze the dynamics of the prices he'd paid for his daily cup of coffee, accounting for his cost of transportation to each coffee bar, "cost" expressed as a function of both actual out-of-pocket expense and travel time.

"I think I've come to the right place," I said.

Evan went to work. I walked around the room and examined the flowchart more carefully. I noted the question marks attached to his reference to a numbered account at BOS/ Singapore. Clearly, he was unaware of what Lilly had just confirmed for me—that it was Manu Robledo who had opened the account. But even as I filled in blanks, I realized that the more I studied the analysis, the more questions I had. One of his "red flags"—the thirty-eight obvious signs that Cushman was running a Ponzi scheme—was simply dollar signs. I hated to interrupt him, but it was too cryptic for me to decipher.

"What do these dollar signs mean?" I asked.

Evan looked up. No doubt he was in the middle of a mathematical calculation that stretched out at least thirty decimal places, but he switched gears with remarkable ease.

"Red flag number twelve," he said.

"I can see that," I said, "but what does it mean?"

"Cushman Investment maintained accounts at two different banks. At the end of every reporting period, Cushman had his CFO convert all of the firm's holdings to cash equivalents— Treasury bills—to avoid SEC disclosure requirements. That should have been a tip-off to the SEC."

"That was in your report?"

"Yup. That and three dozen other red flags."

"And you gave all that to the SEC?"

"Well, not me, personally. Your dad did." Evan went back to work, then stopped and looked up again. "That's why I think he's in jail."

I turned, confused. "How's that?"

"I don't have the proof—yet—but I believe your father was framed for the murder of Gerry Collins because he put the report in the hands of the SEC and had the power to tell the world that the SEC knew that Cushman was a fraud. They locked him up and shut him up."

I thought about it, but I was still confused. "That doesn't really make sense. He could still talk from prison."

"Yes," said Evan. "If he wanted to. Clearly, he doesn't want to."

"Why not?"

"That's the missing part of the puzzle."

I could have strained my brain trying to figure that one out, but there was another problem. "I just don't see it," I said. "It wasn't simply a frame-up. My dad confessed."

"No one said it was a voluntary confession."

I shook my head. "Forcing a man to confess to murder is going way too far to protect the SEC's reputation. Do you really think my dad is sitting in jail just so the industry won't think the SEC is incompetent?"

"That's the point," said Evan. "It wasn't incompetence."

I glanced back at the flowchart—the thirty-eight red flags that proved beyond any doubt that Cushman was running a Ponzi scheme. "If that's not incompetence, I don't know what is."

"Nobody is *that* incompetent," said Evan.

"So what are you saying?"

His expression turned deadly serious. "They knew," he said. "They positively knew Cushman was a fraud. They didn't miss it. They overlooked it."

"You mean they knowingly looked the other way?"

"Yes."

"Why would they do that?"

"To advance some other agenda."

"Wait a minute," I said. "You're saying that the SEC could have shut Cushman down, but they let it play out because—"

"Because it advanced another government agenda. Yes. That's exactly what I'm saying. I don't know what that agenda is yet, but I think your father does. That's what got him in such a jam. Your dad kept my name out of it when he presented my report to the government, which I believe is the only reason I'm still alive. That makes twice your father saved my life. So I'm making it my business to find out what that other government agenda is. And when I do, everyone had better run for cover."

I didn't answer. This one was taking a while to sink in.

Evan looked away. "Okay, fine. Now you're exactly like everyone else. You think Evan Hunt is some kind of crackpot who sees a conspiracy brewing in every government office."

I was still thinking, still trying to wrap my mind around the full implications of what Evan was saying.

Evan got up from the computer, walked to the refrigerator, and got a soda. "I should have kept my mouth shut," he said, grumbling.

"No," I said, "I don't think you're a crackpot."

"You don't?"

"Not at all."

"Then what do you think?"

I didn't view the world entirely through the prism of old movies, but sometimes the fit was too perfect.

"Evan," I said, "I think this could be the start of a beautiful friendship."

29

BY EIGHT P.M. IT HAD BEEN DARK IN THE BOSTON AREA FOR OVER three hours, and Tony Mandretti was fading in and out of sleep.

Lemuel Shattuck Hospital Correctional Unit is a medium-security facility in Jamaica Plain. Twenty-three acute-care beds serve inmates from across Massachusetts—and, in the case of Tony Mandretti, from North Carolina.

Tony's treatment for non-Hodgkins lymphoma was an uphill battle. Unfortunately, his participation in a clinical trial at the Duke University Medical Center had proved that, at least for Tony, monoclonal antibodies were not the answer. Since then, he'd received chemotherapy and radiation, which was debilitating enough even under ideal circumstances. He was in a rest phase of the treatment cycle, and the trip from North Carolina to Massachusetts had completely worn him out. Hospitalization wasn't essential, but the plan was to keep him at Lemuel Shattuck for a week or so, until permanent reassignment to a correctional facility.

"Wake up, Carlson," the guard said.

It took a full minute to recall where he was, and only then did he remember that *he* was Carlson. Sam Carlson, to be exact. Tony Martin was no more, having gone the way of Tony Mandretti.

"Let me sleep," he said.

The guard switched on the fluorescent light, brightening a small room that was about as homey as a prison cell—no more, no less. A bed, tray table, and a chair were the only furnishings. No rug on the gray tile floor, no pictures on the beige walls. There was a small mirror over the sink, but as a rule he avoided mirrors. A kindly nurse had told him that the hair loss made him look like Bruce Willis, but he didn't feel remotely like a movie star. The bars on the window were definite overkill; it was highly unlikely that an inmate undergoing cancer treatment would escape from an eighth-floor unit.

"You have a visitor," the guard said.

"Who?"

"The FBI."

Tony wasn't expecting anyone, let alone an FBI agent. He realized, however, that Sam Carlson hadn't been in existence long enough for the visit to be for him. The FBI had come to see Tony Martin—or, more likely, Tony Mandretti. He didn't bother asking the guard what this was about; a corrections officer would have no idea.

"All right, I'm awake," said Tony.

With the push of a button, he raised the mattress to an upright position. The guard told him to sit tight for a few minutes—Tony didn't bother to tell him that he wasn't going anywhere—and then he stepped out, leaving the door open. Tony heard voices in the hallway, but he couldn't make out the conversation. He was still shaking off sleep, and as his mind cleared, it occurred to him that he hadn't asked for the agent's name. A visit from the FBI raised several possibilities, some better than others.

There was only one that he considered friendly—only one agent who had earned his trust.

Tony had first met Agent Scully in Operation Clean House, the undercover sting that had sent eleven members of the

Santucci organized crime family to prison. Scully had been Tony's contact throughout the assignment, and the relationship had continued after the trial, in witness protection, when Tony Mandretti became Tony Martin. Years later, Scully again had been Tony's chosen contact—when Tony had the goods on Abe Cushman.

Evan Hunt had been trying to pay back Tony Mandretti for years, ever since Mandretti had spared his life. Tony had explained many times that his refusal to carry out the hit was based on personal principle, devoid of any consideration of who Evan was or whether he deserved mercy. Evan could have just left him alone, and Tony would have called it even. Then Evan had shown him the Cushman red flags—and he had explained the whistle-blower program. He'd promised a fifty-fifty split of the bounty if Tony would present his analysis to the feds. After a visit to Scully, all indications were that Tony and Evan would be two very rich men. Then something had changed. Something on the government's end had changed radically. It had left Tony dumbfounded. He'd asked Scully to explain it, and Scully had stumbled through an apology for his complete inability to do so.

Not even the side effects of chemotherapy could erase the memory of that conversation. Scully's words came back to him as he lay there, waiting. He wondered if the only FBI agent he'd every really trusted had finally come back to tell him what in the world had gone wrong—before his cancer made it too late.

"I'm sorry," said Scully. "It's absolutely mind-boggling to me. I can't get anyone to bite on this."

They were in a dark booth, practically alone in a bar in Soho. Tony took a long pull from a bottled beer, then scratched his head.

"You realize it's all there in the report, right?" said Tony.

"Everything you need to bring Cushman down is laid out on a silver platter. I didn't write it, but I didn't make this shit up. It's all true."

"No one's saying you made it up," said Scully.

"You need to make them understand it."

"It's not a lack of understanding," said Scully.

"What is it then? They choose to ignore it?"

Scully didn't answer.

Tony said, "The fucking regulators *choose* to ignore the biggest Ponzi scheme in the history of the world?"

Scully looked around, uneasy. "Lower your voice, dude."

Tony breathed in and out. He needed a cigarette.

Scully said, "I told you all I know, Tony."

"You told me they aren't listening. You're not telling me why."

"I don't *know* why."

"Then find out."

"I tried."

"Try harder," said Tony. "You owe me that much. Without me, you had no case against the Santucci family. I gave up everything—my name, my family, my existence. I've never asked for nothing in return."

"Don't ask for this," said Scully.

"I'm asking. What's the deal?"

Scully looked away, then back. "It's classified."

"What's classified?"

Scully's expression turned very serious. "There's something else going on with Cushman. Something that has me beating my head up against the wall trying to get the regulators' attention."

"Are they embarrassed that they weren't the ones to figure it out? Is that it?"

"No, these guys have no shame. They'd figure out a way to take credit."

"Well, whatever their reason is, they can't make me go away by ignoring me. If they won't pay me a bounty, I'll sell the report to the *Wall Street Journal*."

"The *Journal* isn't into checkbook journalism."

"Then I'll find someone who is."

"No rag sheet is going to pay you a million dollars for a financial story."

"I don't need a million. All I want is my money back from Gerry Collins. Two hundred fifty grand."

Scully shook his head. "Tony, I tell you this for your own good: the chances of getting back the money you invested with Cushman are slim to none. Let it go."

"Let it go? That son of a bitch Collins has my life savings and won't give it back. Says he can't honor any more redemptions. What kind of crap is that?"

"Tony, I'm sorry, but—"

"This is for my kids," said Tony, "something from me to them, finally, for the way I screwed up their lives. It's all I got to make it good."

"I understand."

"I laid out everything the SEC needs to know, and you're telling me that you can't even get their attention? I expected you to come back and say there's some haggling over the amount of the bounty. I never expected this. What the hell's wrong with you?"

"Listen to me," said Scully.

"No, you listen. I couldn't care less about your government classified bullshit. I'm not going to let this die."

"Take it down a notch," said Scully, his tone ominous. "You need to be very careful with this."

"Are you threatening me?"

"Consider it friendly advice. This report of yours—it's like a financial weapon of mass destruction."

"What does that mean?"

"It means that Cushman and his feeders, guys like Gerry Collins, have been making a lot of people very rich. Those people are going to be very upset to find out that Cushman is a fraud. Some of those people would be very angry at anyone who says it's time to get off the merry-go-round. If I were you, I'd be very concerned about how those folks might express their anger."

"I'm not in this to win a popularity contest."

"I'm not talking about the typical whistle-blower backlash, Tony. Between you and me, Gerry Collins has some, shall we say, 'questionable' clients."

"I don't scare easily."

"It's not a question of scared. It's about smart versus stupid. Let me be clear: Gerry Collins has clients who would kill you if they thought you were trying to destroy the goose that lays the golden egg."

Tony considered the possibilities, and one of them brought a thin smile to his face. "Or they might take it out on Gerry Collins."

"What?"

"Say, for example, that this report landed in the lap of one of those 'questionable' clients—from an anonymous source, of course. I could see one of those clients going straight to Gerry Collins and giving him one fine ass kicking."

Scully smiled back. "Wouldn't that be sweet? Too bad that we can't—"

"Give me a name," said Tony, his expression very serious.

"What?"

"I want the name of one of those clients who would kick Gerry Collins' ass if he knew Collins was a fraud."

"Tony, I can't do that."

"I'm asking you this one favor: give me a name."

Scully struggled with it. Tony's stare only tightened.

"I lost my kids," said Tony. "My wife is dead. I lost my life. You owe me."

Tony hadn't come to the table with plans to play the payback mantra, but he could see in Scully's expression that it was working. Finally, Scully blinked.

"All right," he said. "But you didn't hear it from me. I'll get you a name. Just don't blame me if they do more than kick his ass."

Tony took another pull from his beer, then said, "I can live with it."

A gust of winter wind rattled the hospital window, startling him. The voices in the hallway grew louder, and Tony could count the footfalls in the tiled corridor as the guard approached with his visitor.

The thought of seeing Scully again presented a mixed bag. On some level Tony thought of him as a friend; but, at bottom, he was FBI. With all that had gone down in the past few weeks, Scully was probably coming to remind Tony of their agreement—the condition under which he had given Tony the name "Manu Robledo."

You didn't hear it from me.

"I'll be back in twenty minutes," the guard said. "Behave yourself, Carlson."

Tony turned his head toward the door as it closed. His visitor approached. It wasn't Scully. Not by a long shot.

"Special Agent Andie Henning," she said as she extended her hand over the bed rail. "I've come to talk to Tony Mandretti about his son."

30

CONNIE'S REGULAR WEDNESDAY-EVENING SCOUT MEETING RAN
from seven to nine P.M., and right after it ended, she caught
up with me at Evan's apartment. His 360-degree mural of
Cushman's fraud blew her away, but Evan was far more interested
in hearing how her troop was ready to smash the competition in
the upcoming Pinewood Derby. By ten P.M. I'd heard enough
about graphite axles and other ways to make a five-ounce block
of wood zip down an eight-lane track in record time. If I hadn't
cut her short and put Evan back to work, he might never have
cracked the code on the BOS data files.

"Almost there," said Evan.

He was still in the center of the room, keyboard clacking,
matching wits with some other computer genius who had encrypted the BOS files from Lilly's computer.

"How much longer?" I asked.

"He just said he was almost there," Connie snapped.

Evan smiled at the way she'd come to his defense. Yet again,
I had to wonder if poor Tom, her fiancé, was destined to run last
in the proverbial Pinewood Derby of egghead romance.

Evan said, "The bank has different levels of security attached
to different files. Lilly's e-mails were relatively simple. You can

review those on my laptop while I keep working on the tougher codes."

Connie and I spent the next ninety minutes doing just that. The vast majority of e-mails were worthless or, worse, distracting. Our task was to unravel the trail of money from Gerry Collins through BOS/Singapore. Instead, I found myself reliving my relationship with Lilly through e-mails. It was funny to see how cautious the early communications had been.

How about lunch?

Coffee?

What Lilly didn't know was how many drafts it had taken to come up with such brilliance and finally hit Send. If I wrote *Starbucks* instead of *coffee*, would she think it was a hot stock tip? If I wrote *buy you a coffee*, would she think I was cheap and limiting her to just one? If I wrote *buy you coffee*, would she think I was making a run over to the Food Stop and offering to bring her back a bag of beans? I could have written *buy you a latte*. But maybe she hated lattes—or, more likely, pretentious men who drank them. *Coffee.* That was perfect.

Too bad she was in bed by the time you finally sent it.

"Aw, this is so sweet," said Connie. She was reviewing another group of Lilly's e-mails on her smartphone, and apparently she, too, had found the personal stuff. "I didn't know you had such a sensitive side, little brother."

I approached Evan and quickly changed the subject. "Are we there yet?"

"Don't rush me."

"I'm not rushing you. Just wondering when you think you'll be finished."

Evan's hair was standing straight up, shaped by the number of times he'd run his hands through it in frustration. "With this last group of files, it may not be a question of when," he said.

"Are you serious?" I asked.

He wiped the sweat from his brow, then ran his hands

through his hair once more. "I hate to admit it, but I'm not sure I can break this."

I glanced at Connie, whose mouth was agape. It was as if Evan had just confessed that he'd never actually seen an episode of *Star Trek*.

Connie pulled herself together and said, "I'll get Tom to look at it."

"Who's Tom?" asked Evan.

"My fiancé. He's a genius. Would have graduated from MIT with a degree in engineering if he hadn't skipped art class his last semester."

"No offense," said Evan, "but they don't kick people out of MIT for skipping art."

"Oh, yes, they do," said Connie.

"Whatever," said Evan. "The entire engineering department probably couldn't crack this code."

"Folks, can we focus?" I said. "It can't be that tough."

"Easy for you to say," said Evan. "So far the only thing I've been able to determine is that the sequence of letters B-A-Q occurs with unusually high frequency in the encrypted data, which, of course, doesn't mean anything."

"That could be a code for something else."

"Or it could reflect an error in my own mathematical computations," said Evan.

A quick run of "BAQ" through a search engine on Evan's laptop turned up a handful of hits, from trade names for pool-cleaning products to a Puerto Rican folk dance called *el baquiné*. Nothing meaningful.

Evan said, "I'm telling you, this last phase of encryption is of the highest order."

"Meaning what?" I asked.

Evan cleared his throat, and I had a feeling he was about to get professorial on me. "Well," he said, "the actual cryptographic process is generally a complicated mathematical formulation—

the more complex, the more difficult it is to break. A key is supplied to the recipient so that he can then decipher the message.
Keys for encryption algorithms are described in terms of the
number of bits. The higher the number of bits, the more difficult
that cryptosystem would be to break."

It was late, and my head was starting to throb. "Sorry, I
wasn't asking for a technical explanation of encryption. What I
want to know is, when you say 'highest order,' what does that
mean?"

"That's what I'm getting at," said Evan. "The one file that
has me stumped involves a level of encryption that is on an entirely different order than anything else here. It's as if it doesn't
even belong on the same computer as the BOS data."

"Where would you expect to find it?"

Evan sat back in his chair, glanced at Connie, and then
looked at me. "If you didn't think I was a conspiracy nut job
before, you will now."

"I didn't think it before," I said.

Evan sighed and said, "All right. The level of encryption I'm
seeing is more like something you would expect in a matter of
national security."

"In Lilly's files?"

He paused, as if all too aware that he might sound ridiculous. "Yeah," he said, "in your girlfriend's files. There, I said it.
You can start laughing now."

My sister and I exchanged glances. Then my gaze returned
to Evan, his face aglow from a computer screen filled with
mathematical equations.

"Nobody's laughing," I said.

I checked the time. It was past midnight. I was about to
suggest we break for the night when Connie shoved her smartphone in my face.

"Look at this!" she said.

The lead story for the online version of the *Daily News*

included a photograph of a woman who had been strangled and found dead in her apartment. A sick feeling came over me as I recognized both her face and the uniform.

"That's the park ranger who found me in Battery Park," I said.

The story reported "no known motive," and I couldn't think of one. But I wasn't foolish enough to think that her slaying and my attack, separated by a matter of hours, were disconnected. It wasn't easy coming to terms with the fact that the ranger would probably still be alive but for the misfortune of having found me in the park. The *Daily News* also said that police were urging anyone with information to come forward. I realized that I would have to follow up with Agent Henning and comb over the details of my own attack—though I had no doubt that the FBI had already connected the dots, since Andie had shown up at our last meeting with a copy of the Parks police report.

I walked a complete circle in the apartment and took another start-to-finish look at Evan's 360-flowchart of the Cushman fraud. I wondered where a photograph of the park ranger's killer might fit in. I wondered who he was. And I wondered if, in some perverse way, he was enjoying the destruction of so many lives.

"Nope," I said, revisiting Evan's fear that I might think he was nuts, "no one is laughing. At least not in this room."

31

CLOSE TO MIDNIGHT, THE BOS LIMO DROPPED JOE BARBER AT HIS estate in Greenwich. To him, the fresh blanket of snow on the wooded acre made his house atop the hill look like a Norman Rockwell painting, though he had to concede that there was little nostalgia in a twelve-thousand-square-foot mansion with seven bedrooms, twelve bathrooms, two swimming pools, a clay tennis court, and a bowling alley built on a special "floating" foundation to keep the subterranean vibrations from disturbing the priceless bounty of the wine cellar. His wife was asleep in bed when he got home. Miraculously, she wasn't on the treadmill. Metaphorically speaking, though, he sure was.

A management position with a troubled Swiss bank was not the capstone career move that Barber had hoped for after his tenure at Treasury as deputy secretary. BOS had barely survived the subprime crisis, its reputation forever tarnished. Its standing as the premier bank in Switzerland was in question, and in America, it was undeniably second tier. As his wife had so often reminded him, friends at firms like Goldman Sachs and Morgan Stanley had offered Barber dazzling compensation packages. When he told them he was joining BOS, they had been shocked. When the journal reported that he was going there for less money, they feared that he had lost his mind. No one knew the real reason for his decision. No one could know that he was just following orders.

Most important, no one could *ever* know who was telling him what to do.

"Did you give them the data, Joe baby?"

Barber wondered why the question even needed to be asked, and he was getting fed up with the condescending tone and insulting nicknames like "Joe baby."

"Exactly the way you told me," said Barber.

They were in the first-floor study, just Barber and a man he knew only as Mongoose. He didn't have any of the weasel-like features of an actual mongoose, but, of course, it was the point of any good cryptonym to bear no resemblance to its subject. This Mongoose had short blond hair and the rugged good looks of a movie star, with broad shoulders and muscles so thick that his neck bulged.

"So you called them into your office and . . ."

"And I delivered the packages. End of story."

Barber shifted uncomfortably. He was seated in a chair that, tongue in cheek, he had always called "the hot seat," a boxy Chinese antique made of rosewood that had an upright back and no cushion. Another pair from the same set of four had once graced his office at Treasury, and they were so uncomfortable that no meeting had ever lasted more than twenty minutes—the intended effect. Mongoose was seated in the leather chair behind Barber's desk. Only Barber and the retired CEO of Saxton Silvers, who had passed it on to him, had ever sat at that desk. Until tonight.

"That's my boy," said Mongoose.

"You need to stop calling me 'boy,' 'Joe baby,' or whatever the insult of the day is. I'm tired of that shit."

"This isn't supposed to be fun, Joey. At least not for you."

"Killing innocent people? That's your idea of fun?"

Mongoose leaned back, put his feet up on Barber's leather-top desk.

"The park ranger was a regrettable piece of collateral damage. I needed to know what she and Patrick Lloyd talked about."

"What could she have possibly passed along to you that was of any value?"

"Exactly what your inept security experts couldn't: Patrick Lloyd is Peter Mandretti. Tony Mandretti's son."

The news didn't shock him. Barber's own intelligence was not as inept as Mongoose thought. But in some situations it was best to play dumb. "What do you want me to do with that information?"

"I want you to be very nervous. I want you to think about what could happen if I made a copy of the memo you wrote at Treasury and gave it to Tony Mandretti's son."

That thought chilled him. Mongoose laughed, clearly enjoying that Barber had gone cold.

Barber said, "I've done everything you've told me to do. You don't have to kill innocent park rangers. You don't have to bring Mandretti and his son into this. It's enough that you have the memo."

Mongoose smiled with his eyes. "You wish you had never written it, don't you?"

Barber didn't answer. But it was true: of all his regrets from his service at Treasury, the biggest was the classified internal memorandum he'd written about the Cushman Ponzi scheme.

Mongoose said, "That's one tough spot you put yourself in, Joey. You talk about *me* killing innocent people. What about you? Letting all those investors lose their money to a thief like Abe Cushman. Someone the government knew was a fraud. How do you justify that?"

Barber had no answer.

"It's the same old line, isn't it?" said Mongoose. "Every war has collateral damage—even a financial war, like this one. The investors who lost their money to Cushman are collateral damage. Pawns like Lilly Scanlon, who don't even know they're pawns, are collateral damage. A dedicated undercover agent whom you hang out to dry and who ends up with a bullet in his spine from Manu Robledo is collateral damage."

The antique chair was becoming more uncomfortable. Barber did not deny any of it.

Mongoose said, "It all comes back to you, Little Joe. Your name is on the classified memo. And it's crystal clear that Operation BAQ was your idea."

Again, no denial. Barber had even come up with the abbreviation, BAQ.

"Let's get on with it," said Barber.

"I'm tired," Mongoose said, rising. "We've covered enough ground for one night. I'll let myself out." He started for the door, then stopped. "Oh, by the way. I'm sure you don't have any delusions of stabbing me in the back or, more your style, hiring someone else to do it. But just in case, I wanted you to know: I have a safety valve."

"Meaning what?"

"Every blackmailer needs one. It's a way to make sure that if something happens to me, the trigger gets pulled. Everything I've threatened to do to you will come to pass."

Barber showed no reaction, not sure if he was bluffing or not.

Mongoose studied his expression, then said, "I'm not sure you believe me. But it's real. Your memo on Operation BAQ is mixed in with the BOS files you handed over today."

That was more than Barber could take quietly. "You son of bitch, if Patrick doesn't know enough to connect the dots, his father sure does."

"Relax," said Mongoose. "It's still encrypted. They don't have the key, and they don't have the resources to crack the code.

But here's how my safety valve works. If I don't log on to my computer every day and deactivate my safety valve, an e-mail will automatically go to Patrick and Lilly. The decryption key is in the e-mail."

There was no gun to his head, literally speaking, but Barber suddenly felt as if there were.

Mongoose said, "So unless you want your memo decrypted, unless you want the world to know about Operation BAQ and the role you played in it, then you need to be very concerned about my health. Understood?"

Powerlessness was a foreign feeling to him, but Barber knew who was holding all the aces. "Understood."

"Good. Now, stay on top of those two jokers," he said, meaning Patrick and Lilly.

"I will let you know as soon as I hear back from them."

"No. Don't wait. Follow up in the morning. Mandretti's son is going to crack. I can feel it. Even though Lilly doesn't know enough to make heads or tails of his data, Patrick has to be nervous that she might be able to make some sense of it. That's your leverage. I want a complete road map to the money."

"He isn't going to just knuckle under overnight."

"He will if you push the right buttons. That would make me very happy. In fact, if you get me an answer by tomorrow night, I might make you a partner. Wouldn't that make you happy, Joey?"

Barber was silent.

"Good night, partner." Mongoose laughed to himself. Then he turned, opened the door, and left the room. Barber listened as the footfalls of a blackmailer echoed in his own hallway. He heard the front door open, then close.

Mongoose was gone.

32

AGENT HENNING AGREED TO MEET ME AT EIGHT A.M. IT WAS HER idea to get out of Manhattan, in case I was being watched or followed. By default, that meant Position Four on my list of meeting spots, a thirty-minute train ride to my old stomping grounds on the other side of the East River.

I grew up in Queens, lived there till I was fifteen—until Peter Mandretti became Patrick Lloyd. I accepted the fact that Queens has its critics; I didn't accept the criticism. Yes, Brooklyn has more interesting housing, and there can be only one Manhattan, one Gotham-like center of the universe. The Bronx has the Yankees, and Staten Island has . . . well, as I might have told my friends in Queens, I've never had no freakin' reason to go there, so who the hell cares what they got? But I do know this: only Queens has the Lemon Ice King of Corona.

Trips to the Ice King on warm summer nights hold a special place in my memory. Rainbow was my favorite flavor, notwithstanding my sister's blunt reminders: "It's the *Lemon* Ice King, moron." The line could be long, but that was part of the experience, and with Shea Stadium a bike ride away, it was possible to snag a couple of last-minute seats for a Mets game on the cheap. Or you could just walk across the street to the park, where old

Italian men played bocce ball for hours. The Ice King had no dining area—it was a tiny joint on the corner that served only ices—so benches by the bocce courts were the primo spot for scooping out chocolate or fruity slush from a cup. In summertime, you were lucky to find a seat.

On a cold morning in January, I had no such problem.

Andie glared at me, arms folded, her breath steaming as she fought off the cold. "You know, Patrick, it would have been perfectly acceptable for your list of designated meeting places to include one or two indoor locations."

"My bad," I said. "I'll bring you back for a cherry ice in July."

It was nearly an hour past dawn, but the sun was nowhere to be seen in the gray winter sky. Andie wasn't getting any warmer, so I did a quick follow-up on the park ranger mentioned in the *Daily News*. Not surprisingly, the FBI was already aware that the victim was the same ranger who had found me unconscious and had sent me to the ER just a few hours earlier. Andie assured me that there was no need for me to speak directly to the detectives handling the homicide investigation—she had it covered—and then moved on to another subject.

"I met with your father last night," she said.

Her mention of Dad was a funny coincidence. Just moments earlier, my gaze had drifted to the tuxedo shop across the street where, according to my mother, Dad had rented a hideous, yet stylish, powder blue tuxedo for their wedding.

"How is he doing?" I asked.

She offered a few details about his treatment, then added, "I wish I could tell you he was better. But he's getting good care, and I can say he's a fighter."

"That's something, I suppose."

"I'm technically not allowed to tell you his new name or location," she said. "In fact, my supervisor wouldn't even give me that information. But I'm the curious type. And, frankly, I wouldn't be much of an FBI agent if I couldn't pinpoint a prison hospital that just admitted a sixty-year-old white male transfer patient who has non–Hodgkins lymphoma."

"What did you find out?"

"He's in Boston," she said, and then she mentioned the name of the hospital. "His new name is Sam Carlson."

As per our previous conversation, we were operating on a quid pro quo basis, and I knew this update was not gratis. She wanted something from me.

"I believe it's time for you to give up the name of the man who opened a certain numbered account at BOS/Singapore."

She meant the account that was at the heart of the search for Cushman's money, of course. I said, "As I recall, there was one more condition. You were going to tell me why the FBI is still helping my father, even though your supervisor thinks I've been holding out."

"I'll be honest with you," she said. "I don't know why."

I wasn't sure I believed her, which made me want to hold on to the name Manu Robledo until she really gave me something. "That's not good enough."

A wisp of wind sent a swirl of white powder across the frozen bocce court. I shifted gears and told her about my meeting with Barber and Lilly. The exchange of data piqued her interest.

"What would it take to get my hands on Lilly's files?" she asked.

"That's way beyond the scope of our original deal," I said, "and it's confidential bank data. But I might see my way toward sharing it with you if you can tell me what BAQ means."

"I have no idea what you're talking about."

"One of the files mixed in with Lilly's data is encrypted on a level that the federal government would use for a matter of national security. The only thing my tech expert can determine is that the letters B–A–Q appear in sequence with unusual frequency. It's possible that it's an abbreviation for something."

"Your tech expert?" she said.

I had no intention of bringing Evan into this. "Don't ask," I said.

"The abbreviation BAQ doesn't mean anything to me."

"I didn't expect an answer off the top of your head. Do some digging. Get me an answer, and I'll give you Lilly's files. Get it to me quick, and I'll throw in the name of the man who opened numbered account 507.625 RR."

It was the first time I'd mentioned the actual BOS account number, and it seemed to buy some credibility.

"Deal," she said.

Another breeze, which became a gust, cut across the bocce courts. Andie was downwind and took the brunt of it.

I said, "Why don't you go find someplace warm."

She brushed the icy powder from her eyebrows, muttered something about a fast plane back to Miami, and then looked me in the eye. "One last thing," she said. "I shared your father's new name and location because you wanted to know them. But after meeting with him, I feel like I should add one thing you probably won't want to hear: don't contact your father."

Her bluntness took me aback. "Would you tell me if he was going to pass soon?"

"It's not imminent, but that's not my point. I don't say this to be cruel or to hurt your feelings, but your father was moved and given a new identity at his own request. He doesn't want you to find him."

A reunion had never been my stated mission, but Andie's frank advice made me realize that it had indeed been a subconscious goal. I tried to absorb the blow. "Did he tell you that?"

"Yes. In almost exactly those words."

"Did he tell you why?"

"He has his reasons."

"That doesn't really answer my question."

She drew a deep breath of the cold morning air as she considered her response. "There are things that he doesn't want to have to explain to you."

"That's pretty vague."

"He'd prefer it that way. I'm sure of it."

"Did he kill Gerry Collins?"

"Patrick, I can assure you of one thing. It has absolutely nothing to do with your father's guilt or innocence."

"It's my mother, isn't it?"

Andie struggled. "I don't know if you're aware of this or not, but your mother tried to contact your father while he was in witness protection. He's convinced that's what got her killed."

"I didn't know it, but I always suspected."

"Now you know."

"That was a long time ago," I said. "The Santucci family isn't what it used to be. Who's to say it would be anywhere near as dangerous for his children to see him before he dies?"

"He doesn't want to take that risk."

Our eyes met, and held. The vibe between us wasn't about love and romance, but it suddenly occurred to me that I'd worked harder at this relationship with Andie Henning than I'd worked at any relationship with any woman who wasn't named Lilly. I didn't always trust her—not by a long shot—but at least, with respect to her advice about my father, I sensed that I could trust her completely.

"Thank you," I said.

"You're welcome."

There was compassion in her tone, and it was as if she was telling me that hearing the harsh truth was only part of the equation. Now all I had to do was deal with it.

Or, knowing myself, ignore her well-intentioned advice.

33

MONGOOSE TOOK THE EARLY TRAIN FROM NEW YORK TO BOSTON.
By nine A.M. he was at Lemuel Shattuck Hospital Correctional
Unit in Jamaica Plain.

Finding the right hospital hadn't been difficult. He'd already
confirmed that Tony Mandretti was Tony Martin, who had
been treated for non-Hodgkins lymphoma in North Carolina.
The number of correctional institutions equipped to render
quality treatment was not endless. He'd zeroed in on the facility
that had most recently admitted an out-of-state transfer.

"Right this way, Father," the corrections officer told him.

For purposes of this visit, Mongoose was Father Michael
Devane, complete with black shirt, white collar, dog-eared
Bible, and rosary beads. At three A.M. it had taken less than
thirty minutes to hack into the prison unit's computer records
and add the name of a nonexistent Catholic priest to the approved list of visitors for inmate Sam Carlson.

"Bless you," said Mongoose.

The correctional unit was on the hospital's eighth floor,
which was at full capacity with twenty-three inmates. Shattuck
was a medium-security facility, but medium did not mean lax.
Security cameras provided a continuous live feed to the unit
desk on the eighth floor and the main desk downstairs. Armed

corrections officers were posted at each end of the brightly lit corridor. Others stood guard directly outside the rooms of inmates who presented a heightened security risk or a possible threat to health care professionals. Mongoose followed the officer down the hallway, and they stopped outside an open doorway.

"Wait here," said the officer, and then he entered the room. Mongoose stood in the hall, opened his Bible, and pretended to read from it as nurses and orderlies went about their business, ignoring him.

"He's asleep," the guard said as he emerged from the room. "Not much else to do when you're on that much pain medication."

"I'm sure he needs his rest. Don't wake him. If I can't pray with him, I'll pray over him."

"Sure thing, Father. I'll be right here if you need me."

Mongoose tucked the Bible under his arm and entered the room alone. He stopped at the bed rail and cast his gaze downward at the man now known as Carlson. His face was thin, his hair was gone, and his pallor was more suitable for a corpse. Cancer had left him a mere shell of his former self, but Mongoose immediately recognized him as Tony Mandretti.

Some things from his days with the agency Mongoose would never forget.

Mongoose laid the Bible and his beads on the table, his gaze sweeping the room. Breakfast was on the tray table; Mandretti hadn't touched the scrambled eggs or the burned wheat toast. An IV hung from a pole beside the bed. A steady drip from three separate bags mixed to become a pharmaceutical cocktail that flowed through a single plastic tube, which fed into the veins of Mandretti's forearm. An even longer tube from a second IV pole disappeared beneath the sheets, presumably feeding into his leg or abdomen.

Mongoose hated hospitals. They brought back bad memories—or perhaps "memory" was the right term, since he'd been unconscious for most of his four-week stay in intensive care. He had no recollection of the triage in the emergency room, the rush to the OR, the surgery to stop the bleeding and repair the damage to internal organs. Luckily, it had not been hollow-point ammunition, which would have taken the internal injuries to another level. Even so, no one had expected him to survive—least of all the man who had shot him: Manu Robledo.

His supervisory agent hadn't sold the assignment to him as a particularly dangerous one, as far as undercover operations went. The blue eyes and fair skin that made Mongoose believable as an Irish priest tonight had also made it easy for him to play a German financier named Niklas Konig, a European mover and shaker in the nebulous international circles of Miami money. He would live on a confiscated yacht, a customized Hatteras Convertible that was fit for the lifestyle of the Colombian drug lord who had forfeited it to the DEA. Konig would introduce Manu Robledo to Gerry Collins and get Robledo to move his clients' money to a numbered account at BOS/Singapore, after which Collins would steer it through a maze of other banks on its way to Abe Cushman. Weird thing was, for a time he had actually liked Collins. Robledo, too. As Gerry used to say, online dating may be the trend, but nothing will ever replace plunking down a stack of Benjamins for thousand-dollar bottles of Crystal as *the* way to meet women. He was having a good time, totally outclassing those two jerk-offs. Until that night on the yacht.

He could still see the expression on Robledo's face. The way Robledo had raised his arm. The way the gun had suddenly found its way into his hand from inside the sleeve of his peacoat. He'd faced down gunmen before, but never unarmed, never so certain that the son of a bitch was actually going to pull the trigger. He would never forget the anger in those dark eyes, hooded by those thick brows, and then the flash from the muzzle. After that, there was a gaping black hole. His next memory—and he could see it clearly now, standing at Mandretti's bedside in this cold and sterile room—was waking up on his back in a hospital bed, looking up into the eyes of his supervisory agent.

"What the hell happened?" asked Mongoose. They weren't his first words, but he had no memory of the earlier mutterings that had marked his return from a coma.

His supervisory agent was at the bed rail. A doctor came quickly. Several doctors. Maybe some nurses, too. Mongoose wasn't sure who they were. The questions they asked seemed silly. *How old are you? Where did you grow up?* The pointless jabber was wearing him out. He wasn't sure how long it went on. It could have been minutes, could have been an hour or more. At some point, his mind cleared. He reached over the side rail and grabbed his supervisor by the arm.

"Get me out of here," he said.

The doctor stopped him. "Try to be still," she said. "It's important that you not make sudden movements."

Mongoose tried to sit up and protest, but the sharp pain in his back choked off his speech. It was as if someone had heated the blade of a steak knife and jabbed him in the spine.

"Holy shit," he said as he settled back onto the mattress. He overheard the doctor speaking to a nurse.

"We may need to increase the medication," she said.

"What is wrong with me?" asked Mongoose.

"You were shot."

"I know that, damn it. What is this pain in my back?"

The doctor leaned closer, speaking to him in a calm, even tone. "You were hit in the chest. Fortunately, we were able to repair all damage to your organs. But the exit wound was more problematic. The projectile fractured the left pedicle of the thoracic five vertebra in your spine. The spinal cord was indirectly damaged by what we call 'cavitation.'"

"Spinal cord injury?" That was not the news Mongoose wanted to hear.

"The good news is that the surgery was successful. We did a microscopically assisted posterior revision at T-four/five."

"Can you speak English, please?"

"Your motor function should be fine."

That hot knife was suddenly jabbing him in the spine again. He got through it with clenched teeth. "What about the pain?"

The doctor hesitated, then said, "There are some limitations there."

"Limitations?"

"The damage to the vertebrae can be addressed surgically only if we were to remove your internal organs. That's high risk. I recommend that we wait and see."

Another wave of pain took his breath away. "Wait and see what?"

"See if the pain subsides with time. It could."

"Could? Or should?"

"We'll just have to wait and see."

His supervisor gestured toward the doctors and nurses, and they left the two men alone. It was just Mongoose and his boss, who was speaking in a hushed voice. "Don't worry, Manu Robledo will get his. Cushman is going down before Christmas. Robledo's investors will take care of him once they find out he lost their money."

"You're not going to arrest him?"

"No. If we do that, all you worked for will be for nothing. Operation BAQ fails."

Mongoose closed his eyes, trying to absorb the pain shooting down his spine. "This is ridiculous."

"Listen to the doctor. Rest, and it should go away."

"Robledo will pay for this."

"Like I said: just let it play out. The FBI is all over Collins to find out if he was also part of the setup."

"Collins is *alive?*"

"Yes."

"Was he shot?"

"No. Robledo spared him."

"Spared him, my ass. If Collins is alive, he's in with Robledo."

"We're looking at that."

Mongoose grabbed him by the arm. "Robledo had a source. He came to the boat with a report, some kind of proof that Cushman was a fraud."

"A report?"

"An analysis, he called it. He was saying something about it right before he started shooting."

"This is the first I've heard of it."

"Collins didn't tell you?" asked Mongoose.

"No."

Mongoose blinked hard, trying to contain his anger. "It's the three of them. Collins, Robledo, and somebody who tipped off Robledo with that report. It's no coincidence that the only guy who got shot is the federal agent."

"Just concentrate on getting well."

"I want to know who tipped off Robledo."

"I want you to concentrate on getting better."

Mongoose propped himself up on an elbow, ignoring the pain, and looked his supervisor in the eye. "Get me that fucker's name," he said, "and then I'll get well."

The hum of an electric motor drew Mongoose from his memories. A blood pressure cuff automatically tightened on

Mandretti's bicep, and the reading flashed on the digital monitor alongside his bed. One thirty over one ten.

Mongoose's was much higher.

He leaned over the side rail and looked down at the patient. It was exactly the wrong move, and it triggered the pain in his spine—the excruciating pain that had never gone away, that had made him a slave to the pill mills that dispensed Percocet like candy. Mongoose worked through it, focusing.

Mandretti was breathing, but it was barely noticeable. Seeing him in such sorry shape only reaffirmed the decision Mongoose had made from the outset: there was no point in killing a man who was already headed for the grave. The better plan, the only route to true revenge, was to add to his misery in his dying days.

Mongoose leaned closer, his lips to Mandretti's ear. "Fight to stay alive," he said, caring not that Mandretti was unable to hear him. Then he stood upright, took hold of his Bible and beads, and resumed his priestly role. "May you live to feel a pain worse than mine," he whispered as he made the sign of the cross. "The pain of destroying your son's life. Forever."

34

CONNIE BORROWED THE ZOO'S VAN FOR THE DAY, AND WE HEADED to Boston. She drove. I tried not to breathe through my nose.

"Sorry. When one of our furry friends has an accident, it can take a week for the smell to go away," she said.

By "accident" she didn't mean fender bender. I rolled down the window a crack and drew in the cold air.

I hadn't decided to visit Dad on a whim. Connie was against it. Had Evan sided with her in opposition, they might have been able to talk me out of it. The idea had blossomed around midnight, as I was taking one last look at Evan's walls. The photographs he had taken over the years were an integral part of the Cushman timeline. Most required no explanation. Lilly with Gerry Collins. Lilly and me in Singapore. They prompted me to ask about the shots he'd snapped just before I ran him down in the park, the ones of Connie and me talking in front of the snow monkeys—where would they fit into the flowchart? "They don't," he'd said, which made me push for an explanation. The hour was late, and perhaps fatigue had caused him to drop his guard. Or maybe he had simply come around to the view that I deserved to know the truth: "Tony asked me to take those weeks ago, when he was still in North Carolina."

That Dad had asked for pictures of Connie and me was no

small thing. It was the reason Evan had suspected that we were Tony Mandretti's children, the reason my confirmation of his suspicions had come as no surprise. More important, for me it was proof enough that Dad wished his children were still part of his life.

"Coming here is a big mistake," said Connie.

We were driving through Brookline, ten minutes from Lemuel Shattuck Hospital. Connie had insisted on driving rather than taking the train so that she could talk freely en route—i.e., talk me out of it.

"We've been over this," I said. "I'm not changing my mind."

"What are you going to say to him?"

It was a good question. Maybe I was tired of being told that the people who mattered most to me were criminals and that I had to keep my distance. Dad. Lilly. It was time to claw back and take control of my personal life.

"I don't know what I'm going to say," I said.

We parked in the snow-covered visitors' lot and followed the freshly salted sidewalk to the hospital's main entrance. There was a separate registration window for visitation to the prison unit. Connie followed me to the desk, and I told the corrections officer behind the glass that I had come to see Sam Carlson.

"Visitation is by appointment only," she said. "Department rules require at least twenty-four hours' notice."

Connie was shameless in her sarcasm. "Oh, what a pity. Come on, let's go home."

"Forget it," I said. "We drove all the way here from New York. There must be some flexibility."

"On a normal day, maybe," the officer said.

It wasn't a holiday or a weekend. "Today's not a normal day?" I asked.

The officer didn't answer. She took our names and asked us to wait right there. A minute later she returned, buzzed us through a locked entrance door, and led us down the hall. We passed an express elevator that serviced only the prison unit on the eighth floor. Just beyond it was a small vacant room, where the officer told us to sit tight. The room had no windows, and Connie took the only chair. The officer left and closed the door, and both Connie and I heard her secure it with a key from the outside. I tried to turn the knob, but it was locked.

"I'm getting a bad vibe," Connie said.

"Brilliant, sis. It must be all the time you spend with zoo animals that gives you such a keen sense of danger."

"What is that supposed to mean?"

"Nothing."

"Don't you dare insult me, Patrick. Who knows what kind of mess we're in now? I told you we shouldn't have come here."

I heard *I told you so*, or words to that effect, several more times before the latch turned and the door opened. Andie Henning entered the room, closed the door, and glared at me with double-barreled death rays.

"What are you doing here?" she asked.

"What are *you* doing here?" I replied.

"There was a breach of security. Someone hacked into the hospital computers last night and added the name of a bogus priest to the list of pre-approved visitors. He came to see your father this morning."

"Is Dad okay?" asked Connie, blurting out my exact sentiment.

"He's fine," said Andie. "He's not even aware that he had a visitor. Needless to say, all visitation to the entire unit is suspended until we figure out what happened."

Connie rose and formally introduced herself. "I presume you're the FBI agent who arranged for Dad's medical treatment?"

"Sorry, I didn't mean to be rude," I said. Over the past few days Andie had been so much a part of my conversations with

Connie, and vice versa, that I had forgotten they'd never actually met.

"No problem," said Connie. "It's all that time I spend at the zoo that gives me such a keen sense of common courtesy."

Touché.

"Did I miss something?" asked Andie.

"Never mind," I said. "Do you have any idea who the visitor was?"

"Nothing definite yet, but we have two solid leads. Security cameras captured some clear footage. We're running images through a facial-recognition database, but that's a needle in a haystack. We also have a match on a shoe print."

"Match to what?" I asked.

"The floors on eight were polished clean last night, and the video surveillance showed us exactly where our suspect walked, so we were able to pull up a clear shoe print."

Connie said, "I would have thought you needed a soft surface, like carpeting, to pick up a shoe print."

"Actually, the best shoe prints are on hard surfaces, like tile," said Andie. "Or the polished marble floor of a park ranger's bathroom."

I caught her drift. As did Connie, who looked at Andie with concern. "So the man who strangled that park ranger was just here in my dad's room this morning?"

"I'm afraid so," said Andie. "You two should go back to New York. Even if you are going to ignore my advice to stay away from here, today is obviously not the day to push to see your father."

"She's right," said Connie.

I understood, but I was determined to make the most of the trip. "Andie, what about BAQ? Have you made any headway on decoding that?"

I could tell that she had, but she paused to measure her response. "Your instincts were correct," she said. "BAQ is not a random sequence of letters. It stands for Operation BAQ."

"What is Operation BAQ?"

"If I answered that question, I would have to turn in my badge."

"If it's a matter of negotiation, I'm prepared to share the name of a certain account holder at BOS/Singapore."

"Manu Robledo," she said.

"You know about him?"

"It's been a productive morning," she said. "At this point, I'm confident that I know more about Robledo than you do."

"Then I presume you're going to arrest him."

"For what?"

"For putting a gun to my head and threatening to send me the way of Gerry Collins if he doesn't get back the money he lost."

She shifted, uneasy. I sensed that the bureau's party line was coming, and that she wasn't entirely comfortable with it. "As of this point in time, the FBI doesn't have sufficient evidence to substantiate as a matter of fact that the attack took place."

As I'd expected: the party line. "You disappoint me, Agent Henning."

"I told you when it happened that you should have called me immediately. You even washed the powder burns away from your neck. There's no physical evidence."

"You could at least bring him in for questioning."

"I've told you all I can about the FBI's position on Robledo. There's nothing more to say."

I felt the need to convince her otherwise, to demonstrate that our mutual exchange of information was still worth her while. The memo was my best angle.

"BAQ is a Treasury operation, isn't it," I said.

I didn't expect her to confirm it, but clearly my educated

guess had piqued her interest. "Why would you say that?" she asked.

"It's a fairly easy deduction. My tech guy did his best to decode all the data in Lilly's files. He was able to extract the letters BAQ from a memo that was encrypted on the order of a national security memorandum. You just told me that BAQ is a government operation of some sort."

"I didn't say it was a Treasury operation."

"You didn't have to. The only government memorandum Lilly ever mentioned to me was a Treasury memo stating that she and BOS/Singapore represented the most promising lead in the search for the Cushman money."

"How would she know about a memo?" asked Andie.

"Lilly got the same threat I did: hand over the Cushman money or die. She told him she didn't know anything about it, but he showed her proof that she was lying."

"He showed her the memo?"

"Yes."

She seemed to credit what I was saying, but I could see her concern as the realization sank in: in the world of quid pro quo, she owed me.

"I want to see the memo," I said, getting right to the point.

"I can't do that."

"Lilly has already seen it. Why can't I?"

"My guess is that she didn't see the classified version."

"There are two versions?"

"One version has all the classified information concealed. There are black bars on the page wherever anything has been redacted."

"I want to see the classified, unredacted version of the Treasury Department's Operation BAQ memorandum."

"That's not going to happen."

"Sorry you feel that way," I said. "I suppose I could take the encrypted file to someone who knows how to decode it. Maybe the Russian embassy can help me."

"That's not funny," she said.

"I'm not laughing," I said.

"You're messing with treason."

"You're messing with my life and my family."

Neither of us had raised our voice, but I could feel the heat from the exchange.

"Clearly, the smart thing is for us to work together," Andie said.

"Agreed. I'm offering to hand over the encrypted file I have in my possession and to keep quiet about it. But I want to know what's in it."

"You're asking too much."

"You're giving too little."

Andie did not respond. I signaled to Connie that it was time to leave. "Think about it," I told Andie as I opened the door. Connie exited first, and I followed. "But think fast," I said. "I instructed my tech guy to be very careful with that encrypted file, but accidents do happen. I'd hate for him to hit the wrong button and send the thing viral over the Internet."

I closed the door, leaving Agent Henning alone in the room to consider the proposal on the table.

35

LILLY DIDN'T ANSWER MY CALL TO HER CELL PHONE, WHICH CAME as no surprise. I sent her an e-mail and hoped she would bite:

The Treasury memo was in your files. Give me a chance to prove you're innocent. Meet me at Puffy's, 2 p.m. today.

The message was clear enough—surely she would realize that "the Treasury memo" was the one with her name in it—and I thought I'd struck the right tone by offering to help. Puffy's was familiar territory, the Tribeca bar we'd stumbled out of singing *I need your cow.* Still, I had to catch my breath when she actually showed up.

"You came," I said, stating the obvious.

Lilly slid into the booth, no kiss or hug to greet me. None was expected, but seeing her so tense, seated on the other side of the table, made me wish that I could erase the last four days and start over.

She unbuttoned her winter coat but left it on. "I can't stay long."

She was trying so hard not to be the Lilly I knew that it came across as robotic. I would have liked to melt some of the ice, but there was a glacier in the room, and I didn't have ten thousand years.

"This won't take long," I said.

"Can I see the memo?"

"First, there's something I need to know. How did it get into your BOS files?"

"I had no idea it was there until I got your e-mail."

That made sense, and I realized that it was at such a high level of encryption that she wouldn't have been able to read it even if she had known it was there. But I had to discount my assessment of everything Lilly said by a serious I-want-you-back factor.

"Patrick, are you okay?"

Just seeing Lilly could do terrible things to my ability to focus. "Yeah, sorry."

"So now can I see the memo, please?"

"The short answer to that question is yes."

She was wary, the way most people react if they're smart enough to know that the long answer always swallows up the short answer.

"You don't have it, do you?" she said.

I drew a breath, and it was hesitation enough for Lilly to get up to leave. "You are such a liar, Patrick."

"Lilly, wait. I do have it."

She stopped, threw me a look that said *You'd better not be lying*, and slid back into the booth.

A waitress came, and we ordered coffee. Decaf for Lilly. The aversion to caffeine told me that she hadn't been sleeping well, which added to my own sense of regret.

"Lilly, I am really sorry that—"

"Stop," she said. "Let's not go there."

"Right," I said, pulling myself back together. "Here's the deal with the memo."

I paused, not sure where to start. Our talk outside the building after the meeting in Barber's office had ended in disaster, mostly due to the way I'd skirted around my involvement with the FBI.

"Go ahead," she said. "You were saying."

I leaned closer, as if to emphasize that I was sharing a secret. "Do you remember last time we spoke, when I said I went to Singapore as part of an official investigation?"

She rolled her eyes. Clearly, it wasn't a pleasant memory. "Yes."

"It wasn't an investigation for some warring faction of the Santucci family," I said, using her words. "It was for the FBI."

The waitress brought our coffee, which was a good thing, because it forced Lilly to keep her composure. The waitress left, and Lilly listened as I explained my deal with the FBI—cancer treatment for my father in exchange for any information I might find that Cushman was laundering money through BOS/Singapore.

"You mean information that *I* was helping Cushman launder money through BOS/Singapore," said Lilly.

I was getting no wiggle room. "Well, yes."

"So, the bottom line hasn't changed. You *were* spying on me."

"I didn't even *know* you when I cut the deal. Everything changed after I met you. And once we started seeing each other, I never lied about my feelings for you."

" 'Love at first sight' was not a lie?"

"Lilly, don't count this against my feelings for you now, but I never told you it was love at first sight." I nearly gasped, not because of my honesty, but because I was starting to sound like a reject from *The Bachelor.*

"I know you didn't," Lilly said, lowering her eyes. "When I said love at first sight, maybe I was channeling my own feelings to you."

She looked at me, and I at her, and after a moment I could see that we had come to the same critical realization: this was nauseating.

"Oh, baby, I need your cow," I sang.

Lilly smiled, and then we shared a little laugh. I wanted to reach for her hand, but the feel-good moment hadn't made our problems go away.

"So," said Lilly. "The memo?"

She was back to the heart of the matter, but her tone was softer. I told her about the trip to Boston to see my father, the conversation with Andie Henning.

Lilly asked, "Do you think Agent Henning will actually show you the decrypted memo?"

"There's a chance," I said. "But there's at least an equal chance that my tech guy will decode the encrypted version I already have."

My BlackBerry vibrated. I didn't recognize the number, so I let it ring through to voice mail. "Lilly, I know this isn't a pleasant memory, but I wanted to ask you about the day you were attacked. When you actually saw the memo."

"We went over this the last time we were here."

"I know, but so much has changed. Tell me not just what you read, but how he showed it to you, what he said to you. Everything."

She took a breath, then let it out. "Okay. It was my last week in Singapore. I went for a run early, like I always did, before it got too hot. There's a path by the beach that's really beautiful when the sun comes up. I was in the zone, cruising along, and suddenly, I was down on the ground, my face in the sand. Before I really knew what was happening, he was sitting on my spine and I was pinned underneath him. My instinct was to fight back, but I was tired from the run, and he was way too strong. When he grabbed me by the hair, it was like he was going to pull it right out. Then I felt the gun at the back of my head."

This version of events had more details than the one before, and her voice was starting to quiver. I gave her a moment.

"Then what?"

"It was a lot like what happened to you in Times Square. He said it was time to turn over the money that was funneled to Cushman through BOS."

"Did you say anything?"

"I said I didn't know a thing about Cushman. That's how I ended up with the powder burn I showed you the last time we sat at this table. He pulled the trigger, jerked the gun away just enough for the bullet to brush past my neck. The silencer probably kept me from going deaf, but it told me I was dealing with someone who knew what he was doing."

It was more than "a lot like" what had happened to me. It was virtually identical. "How did the memo come into it?" I asked.

"I kept saying over and over, 'It's not me, you've got the wrong person!' He pulled my head up by the hair again and . . ." She swallowed hard, then continued. "I thought he was going to put a bullet in my head. But that was when he put the memo under my nose, literally, right in the sand."

"You're sure it was a Treasury Department memo?"

"It was on Treasury letterhead. I supposed it could have been a fake, but why would he forge it? He'd only be fooling himself."

"Tell me everything you remember about it."

"It was quick, so what I remember most is the part that mentioned me by name. Something like: 'Treasury's most promising lead as to concealment of proceeds from the Cushman fraud remains Gerry Collins' banking activities at BOS/Singapore, and the key person of interest at BOS has been identified as Lilly Scanlon.'"

"Do you remember anything else?"

"Not really. He focused me on the key language. It wasn't like he gave me time to read it from start to finish."

My BlackBerry rang again, the same number as before.

This time I realized it was Evan, so I begged Lilly's pardon and answered.

"What's up?"

"Got some good news," Evan said.

"Tell me."

He chuckled, then did a really bad imitation of a Russian spy: "I broke the code, comrade."

36

BY MIDAFTERNOON ANDIE WAS OUTSIDE OF PHILADELPHIA. The small yellow house on the corner was old but well maintained, one of many just like it on this quiet, tree-lined street. It seemed perfect for a retired couple, except for the need to shovel four inches of new snow from the walkway. As Andie climbed the steps of the front porch, she noticed a plaque above the door from the Society of Former Special Agents of the FBI. LOYALTY, FRIENDSHIP, GOODWILL, it read. It reminded Andie of FIDELITY, BRAVERY, INTEGRITY, the motto on her own shield—the same shield that Frank Scully had carried for twenty-five years. He was just beyond the bureau's minimum retirement age of fifty, but well short of the mandatory cutoff at age fifty-seven.

He greeted Andie at the door, led her to the TV room, and offered her a seat. He took the other armchair, facing her.

"Thanks for meeting with me," said Andie.

"You didn't give me much choice."

Scully was right. The phone conversation had been short and to the point. At first Scully had refused to talk about Tony Mandretti. Knowledge was power, however, and her mere mention of a familiar name had put the power in Andie's hands.

Scully asked, "How did you find out about Manu Robledo?"

"Don't worry," she said. "Your secret is apparently safe

within the FBI. I can't find a single agent who even pretends to know about Robledo's connection to Gerry Collins."

Scully glanced at her sideways. He looked fit and younger than his years, more like an agent who would have worked right up until the moment he blew out fifty-seven candles, rather than take early retirement. "So if you didn't get it from the inside, who told you?"

"Tony Mandretti," she said.

"I don't believe you. Tony would never crack."

"He would if he thought his children were at risk."

Scully fell silent, but his expression confirmed that she'd struck a chord.

"Is that what you told him?" he asked.

"I did," said Andie, "because it's true."

"How do you even know Tony's kids?"

"Because I'm the agent who carried out the money-laundering investigation at BOS that you drew up before retiring."

"Ah," he said, as if things were falling into place. "How close did you stick to the way I drew it up?"

She told him about her arrangement with Patrick, the promise of cancer treatment for Tony Mandretti in exchange for Patrick's cooperation with the FBI. "At the time," she went on to say, "I presumed that the bureau had targeted Patrick because his father was in jail for the murder of Gerry Collins."

"That would seem logical," he said.

"I also had no reason to believe that Tony Mandretti was anything but guilty as charged," said Andie. "Now that Manu Robledo is in the picture, I'm not so sure."

Scully didn't answer.

"Let me ask you the same question you put to me," said Andie. "How did you find out about Robledo?"

"Sources," he said.

"Inside the bureau?"

"Operation BAQ was not an FBI operation."

"Then how were you able to get Robledo's name and pass it along to Tony Mandretti?"

Scully shifted in his chair, and Andie could see his discomfort.

"I'm waiting," she said.

He chuckled, but it was nerves. "I guess now you're starting to get a feel for why I took early retirement."

"You can answer my question," said Andie, "or I can report my full conversation with Tony Mandretti to headquarters, and you can explain it to them."

"Is that a threat?"

"You might prefer to think of it as having the power of choice."

His nervous smile vanished. Anger was beginning to rise up. "I was a damn good agent," he said. "Worked hard, did the right thing. I always kept my word, even when I gave it to a former mobster like Mandretti. It took a lot of courage for him to flip and testify against the Santucci family. It's no secret what he gave up—his wife, his kids, his life. It made me sick the way the bureau turned its back on him."

"What do you mean?"

"Tony went into witness protection and really tried to straighten out his life. He started up his own repo business, totally legit. He was the muscle that lenders hired to repossess expensive cars, boats, airplanes—all the toys the new rich guys played with until they burned through their dough like the fools they were and couldn't afford to play anymore. Every penny Tony made, he saved and invested. It took him fifteen years, but he had himself a pretty nice nest egg. Almost a quarter million bucks. He always said it was for his kids. It was his way of proving to them that he never forgot about them, never stopped caring. It was all good. Until he invested his money with Gerry Collins."

"Lost it all," Andie said.

"Every penny. Like everyone else."

"But Tony wasn't exactly like everyone else."

"No," said Scully. "That money was definitely more than just money to him. It was fifteen years of sweat from his own brow."

"And it was for his kids."

"More than that," said Scully. "I don't think you can understand unless you've lost touch with a child. It wasn't just *for* his kids, the way parents raise their children, watch them grow up, and then leave something for them in their will. This was Tony's only chance for any connection to the family he'd lost, and it was his kids' only chance to feel connected to him. At least that's the way Tony saw it."

"Collins lost his money, and Tony wanted him to pay for it."

"Not dead, necessarily. But he wanted Collins to feel the hurt."

"I would think that a guy like Mandretti might enjoy doing that himself."

"Tony was on parole. If he violated parole, he not only went to jail, he was out of witness protection. The Santucci family has long tentacles. How long do you think Tony Martin would last if it got out that he was really Tony Mandretti?"

"So you gave him the name of Manu Robledo, someone who would put that kind of hurt on Gerry Collins if he knew Collins was a fraud."

He nodded. "If he knew he was a fraud."

"Which brings me back to my question: How did you find out about Robledo?"

"That was part of a larger deal."

"By larger, you mean . . ."

"Operation BAQ was run out of Treasury. Years in the making. Manu Robledo was the key."

"How did you find out about it?"

"Tony gave me the analysis showing that Cushman was a fraud. I took it to the SEC, thinking this would be purely a regulatory matter. The hope was to get Tony a whistle-blower bounty for exposing Cushman's fraud. I heard nothing from them, which was pretty surprising. I started poking around, looking for information on Gerry Collins."

"That's how you came across the name Manu Robledo?"

"No. I found out Collins had drawn a lot of attention from law enforcement for business with offshore banks. After twenty years with the bureau, I hear offshore bank and I think organized crime, drug cartels, or both. That's when I went back to Tony and told him to be careful about bringing down Cushman through Gerry Collins."

"And that must be when he asked you for the name of someone who would give Gerry Collins a mob-style beating if they knew he was a fraud."

Another nervous smile. "My goodness, you and Tony did have quite the talk."

"Yes, we did. He's a dying man trying to protect his kids."

Scully said, "I take it that you promised to help him with that."

"Yes," she said, turning it right back on him. "Just like you did." Andie let her words sink in, and her explicit reminder of the role of "handler" that Scully had played for the Mandretti family seemed to strike a blow. She pushed even harder. "I heard you say you were a man of your word, even when dealing with a mobster like Tony. I'm sure you did all you could. But I've exhausted every avenue I have inside the bureau. I can't pick up where you left off—I can't help Tony or his kids—unless you tell me how you zeroed in on Manu Robledo."

Silence followed, the former agent and the younger one

locking eyes. It took a minute, and finally, without uttering a word, they reached an understanding that what was about to be said would not leave the room.

Scully started talking. "I kept poking around in Gerry Collins' offshore transactions, deeper and deeper. Too deep. Next thing I knew, I was flying to Washington for a meeting with the deputy secretary of the Treasury and two of his assistants."

"Joe Barber?"

"The one and only."

"Are you saying that Barber, personally, saw the analysis outlining all the reasons Cushman was a fraud?"

"I'm saying that Barber and everyone involved with Operation BAQ knew that Cushman was a fraud, and they knew it long before I showed them Tony's analysis."

Andie took a moment to absorb that revelation. "Was it Barber who gave you the name Manu Robledo?"

"His name came out in the negotiations."

"What do you mean?"

"Treasury wanted me to get Tony to sit on the Cushman analysis. I couldn't promise that Tony would just pretend like it didn't exist. So Treasury cut a deal with him."

"A deal?"

"Yeah. It was agreed that Tony would get his analysis into the hands of Manu Robledo. In essence, the fact that Cushman was a fraud would be laid out in black and white for a man who was identified by Treasury as Gerry Collins' dirtiest client."

"Dirty in what way?"

"I don't have that information. But there was no doubt in anyone's mind that Robledo would go straight to Gerry Collins and, shall we say, confront him."

"So Tony got exactly what he wanted."

"And more. Tony was allowed to stay in witness protection,

and he also got back the money he lost to Gerry Collins. Two hundred fifty thousand dollars."

"Treasury agreed to pay him a quarter million dollars if he kept his analysis of Cushman's fraud to himself?"

"Not exactly to himself. He was allowed to show it to no one but Manu Robledo—who, of course, would then confront Gerry Collins."

"That's a pretty sweet deal for Tony."

"There was one other component—a very important contingency from Treasury's standpoint. Like I said, there was a substantial risk that Robledo might do more than inflict a bruising on Gerry Collins. Tony agreed that if Collins ended up dead, then . . ."

He didn't finish, leaving it to Andie to fill in the blank. "Tony would take the rap."

"Yes."

"Why?"

"Tony was terminally ill with cancer."

"I understand that it might be easier for a man to agree to prison for the rest of his life if he knows it means three years instead of thirty years. But why would Treasury ask Tony to make that promise as part of their deal with him?"

"Clearly, it was important to Treasury that Manu Robledo not land in jail."

"Why?"

"Pretty obvious, don't you think?"

"Not to me," said Andie.

"How could Operation BAQ work if Manu Robledo was behind bars for the murder of Gerry Collins?"

"I can't answer that," said Andie. "I have no idea what Operation BAQ is."

Scully looked at her. "Neither do I."

"I'm not sure I believe you."

"Oh, you can believe me on that one," he said with a mirthless chuckle. "I *tried* to find out. That got me nowhere . . . except a ticket to early retirement."

It smacked of politics and cover-up, and nothing offended Andie more than a good agent getting a raw deal. "Where would someone start if she was interested in picking up where you left off?"

"You really don't want to do that."

Andie leaned closer, meeting his stare. "Try me," she said.

37

LILLY AND I HOOFED IT FROM PUFFY'S TAVERN, THROUGH Chinatown, to Evan's apartment. The restaurant on the first floor of the old brick building was gearing up for the dinner crowd. Even with the door closed and windows shut, the noise of a busy kitchen spilled into the alley, and enough heat radiated through the walls to melt away the snow along the building's curtilage. The entrance to the back stairway was unlocked, and as we climbed to the second story, Lilly realized that she had actually eaten at the restaurant below.

"Dim Some Lose Some," she said. "I love this place."

The news from Evan—that he'd cracked the code—had us feeling upbeat. I led her past the small window at the top of the stairs, which looked out over the Dumpster. A light was on in the hallway, and the chain-link gate that Evan had installed for added security was unlocked. It was hard for me to imagine Evan—a guy with two peepholes on his front door—leaving anything unlocked. But he was expecting us. I pushed the gate open, and Lilly followed me to the end of the hallway, where I stopped and knocked firmly on the black metal door to his apartment.

"Evan, it's me, Patrick," I said.

No one answered.

"Maybe he went out for dim sum," said Lilly.

"I'm pretty sure quants only eat millennium problems for lunch. More likely he's in a trance, staring at his computer screen." I knocked harder. "Evan, please open up."

I waited, even put my ear to the door, but there was only silence.

Lilly asked, "Are you sure he was calling from his apartment?"

"Yes. I told him we were on our way."

"Try the door."

I did, expecting the knob not to turn. But it wasn't locked. I paused, the knob still in my hand, but I hesitated to push the door open.

"Evan?" I called.

I gave him a moment, and when no response came, Lilly and I exchanged glances of concern. I pushed the door, this time expecting the deadbolt or chain to stop me. The door swung all the way open. I stood at the threshold and called into the dark apartment. "Evan, if this is your idea of a joke, it's not funny."

Silence.

"Let's leave," said Lilly.

"I just talked to him on the phone fifteen minutes ago. Something's wrong."

"Like I said: let's leave."

"He could be hurt."

"We could be next."

I took one step inside and flipped the wall switch. A ceiling light brightened the apartment, and our shadows stretched from one end of the room to the other. Lilly was peering around my shoulder. I'd told her about the flowcharts on Evan's walls, but she still seemed taken aback.

"Don't be alarmed. The place always looks like this." I left the door open and entered the room. Lilly came with me, and we stopped in the middle of the room.

"He lives here?" she said. "How bizarre."

My gaze swept the room, though my focus was not on the boxes, arrows, and photographs that had drawn Lilly's attention to the 360-degree flowchart on the walls. There was no sign of Evan; however, the curtain that separated the main living area from the kitchenette was drawn shut. Lilly clung to my arm as I approached, and I feared the worst as I flung it open.

There was nothing askew, no body on the linoleum floor.

"Patrick, I really want to go," she said.

"Let me check the bathroom real quick."

"I don't like this at all. Can't you put in a call to the FBI agent you've been working with?"

I could have, I supposed. But if Evan had wanted the FBI to see his prize project, he would have shown it to them long before now. I crossed the room, peered into the bathroom, and switched on the light. The brightness against white tiles assaulted my eyes. But again, there was nothing out of the ordinary, no sign of Evan. I turned, took another survey of the room, and then stopped.

"His computer's gone," I said.

"What?"

I went to the center of the room, where Evan had kept his desktop computer, next to the television.

"It was right here," I said. "Now it's gone."

"Is that the computer that had all the encrypted files on it?"

"Yes."

"Would that include the BAQ file?" she asked, with even more trepidation.

"That would be correct," I said, equally concerned. "Probably right along with whatever decryption algorithms he created."

A shrill scream from the alley gave me a jolt. Lilly and I ran from the apartment, out the open door, and through the gate.

I looked out the small window that was at the top of the stairs, down toward the alley below, where several people had gathered around the Dumpster. Earlier, when Lilly and I had arrived, the lid had been closed, but someone from the kitchen had flipped it open to dump the trash. Two men dressed like waiters were consoling the young woman who'd made the discovery. Inside the Dumpster, atop heaps of trash, a man's body lay faceup.

Even from the top of the stairs, dusk settling in, I knew that orange dress shirt and Mickey Mouse tie.

I knew it was Evan Hunt.

38

BY NIGHTFALL EVAN'S APARTMENT AND MOST OF THE NARROW alley behind Dim Sum Lose Some was a busy crime scene.

My first move had been to phone Andie Henning. I was able to answer her first question—"Are you sure he's dead?"—simply by looking into the open Dumpster. The crimson hole between his eyes, where the bullet had entered Evan's amazing brain, was confirmation enough. Andie had told me to touch nothing and to stay put until she got there, which had taken about ten minutes.

An hour later, Lilly and I were among the onlookers on the sidewalk, standing at the yellow police tape, beyond the outermost perimeter of crowd control. I counted eleven police officers, their uniforms transitioning from dark blue to shades of orange in the swirl of police lights. Portable vapor lights from NYPD turned the buzz of investigative work behind the restaurant into a glowing hive of activity. A second perimeter of yellow tape surrounded the Dumpster, where the medical examiner's van waited to receive Evan's body. Two male officers stood guard at the foot of the stairway that led up to the apartment. They looked formidable even from a distance. If ever they lost their jobs with the NYPD, they could easily have found work as bodyguards for rappers.

"What do you think will happen to Evan's flowchart?" asked Lilly.

"Don't know, but I wouldn't count on those two dudes to tell us," I said.

I spotted Andie coming down the stairs behind the restaurant. She spoke briefly to someone near the Dumpster, presumably a member of the forensic team, and then she started up the alley toward Lilly and me. A cold wind from the street funneled between the buildings and hit her squarely in the face as she approached. She cinched up her coat, ducked under the yellow tape, and told me to walk with her. I followed, and Lilly didn't seem to know whether to stay or come with me. Andie made herself more clear.

"You, too," she said.

Andie took us down Mott Street to a Chinese café called Tearrific. I'd heard of it before but had never gone. The name had always struck me as too gimmicky—like heading into Little Italy for real Italian and eating at the Ciao Hound or some such place. A waiter recommended a pot of bubble tea with sesame dumplings and then left us alone at a small table in the corner where we could talk.

"I'm very sorry about your friend," said Andie.

I thanked her, then asked, "Who is going to tell my dad?"

"I spoke to him by phone already," said Andie.

"How did he react?"

"Angry. Upset."

"I meant, who does he think did this to Evan?"

"He doesn't know."

Andie poured herself a cup of tea, breaking eye contact, as if she knew the next question I was about to ask.

"Who do you think did it?"

Andie shrugged and tasted her tea.

Lilly had been quiet thus far, but she was suddenly annoyed.

"Oh, come on," she said. "How many more people have to get killed before you arrest Manu Robledo?"

"He's definitely a person of interest," said Andie.

"Of *interest*?" said Lilly, incredulous. "He was cloaked in bank secrecy, thanks to his numbered account, but we all know that it was Robledo who was giving me the anonymous orders to move his money through BOS/Singapore."

"Actually, you're the only one who has confirmed the voice recognition, Lilly."

"Are you saying I'm wrong?"

"I'm just saying: you're the only one who heard the voice of the account holder on a daily basis, so there's no way for me to verify whether you're right or wrong."

"It's not just the voice. Who else but the account holder would have threatened to kill Patrick and me if we don't find his money?"

"You've hit the problem on the head," said Andie. "The entire case against Robledo is based on the allegation that he was the holder of numbered account 507.625 RR at BOS/Singapore. The Bank of Switzerland has never confirmed that it was, in fact, Robledo; and, according to my contacts at the Department of Justice, nothing short of a court order is going to make the bank budge. It takes time to pierce bank secrecy."

"Can't the FBI arrest him and hold him until the court order is issued?" asked Lilly.

"That's not the way things work in this country."

"But we were attacked," said Lilly. "The bank should be required to release that information if its own bankers have had their lives threatened."

"Swiss law does allow banks to cooperate with law enforcement where an account is being used to further criminal activity. Unfortunately, even if he threatened you, it's not clear that we could convince a judge that Robledo is *using the account* to commit a crime. Even if we get over that legal hurdle, it's like

I told Patrick: Other than your say-so, there's no evidence that those attacks ever took place."

"Well, there's plenty of evidence that Evan Hunt was attacked," said Lilly.

"That doesn't mean it was Robledo who did it."

"Didn't you see the walls inside his apartment?" said Lilly. "Evan Hunt knew more about the Cushman Ponzi scheme than Patrick and I could ever hope to know. Doesn't it stand to reason that Robledo made the same threats against him—find my money, or end up like Gerry Collins?"

Andie paused. In my eight months of dealing with her, I'd seen virtually every facet of the bureau side of her personality, so I felt confident in concluding, beyond a shadow of a doubt, that Lilly was not going to get a direct answer to her question.

"Lilly, how closely did you look at the writings on Evan's walls?"

"Not very. I barely had time."

"Do you remember seeing the name Manu Robledo anywhere on those walls?"

Lilly searched her memory, but I spared her the effort.

"It's not there," I said. "Evan knew a lot about Cushman, but it was clear to me that he didn't know anything about Manu Robledo. That was one of his holes."

Andie said, "And by the same token, Robledo had no reason to know about him. Don't you agree, Patrick?"

"I suppose I do."

Her gaze shifted toward Lilly. "Or could it be that there was some link between Evan Hunt and Manu Robledo. Something that might have put Evan Hunt in the kind of danger that could get a man killed. What do you think, Lilly?"

Her tone was more accusatory than inquisitive. Clearly, Henning was trying to push a button with Lilly, but I wasn't getting it.

"What are you suggesting?" I asked.

"I'm suggesting that your girlfriend knows something you don't know, and I'm counting on her to be honest with us. Lilly, you know how Manu Robledo got his hands on Evan Hunt's analysis, don't you."

It was an accusation, not a question. "Hold on," I said. "Lilly doesn't know anything about Evan's analysis, let alone whether Manu Robledo has it."

Andie's stare tightened on Lilly. "That's not true, is it, Lilly. You know he got it from Patrick's father."

I was about to rise again to Lilly's defense, but I quickly realized that the women at the table were way ahead of me. Andie pressed on, for my benefit, sharing the things she'd learned in the last twenty-four hours—that my father couldn't comprehend why the SEC had shown no interest in Evan's analysis, that in frustration he'd decided to use it against Gerry Collins.

"With a little help from a friend in the FBI, your father found a client on Gerry Collins' roster who would show absolutely no mercy to a man who dared to cheat him. A true badass who would deliver a beating he would never forget. Or worse."

"Are you saying that my dad hired Manu Robledo to kill Gerry Collins?"

"This was no murder for hire," said Andie. "In fact, what your father did isn't even remotely a crime. He simply gave Manu Robledo the truth and let him do with it as he may."

"Fully expecting that it would not end well for Gerry Collins," I said.

"That's a fair statement," said Andie. "Don't you agree, Lilly?"

Lilly averted her eyes, looking at neither me nor Andie. I knew where this was headed, but I asked the question anyway.

"Lilly, you knew all this?"

The expression on her face was one of complete misery, but the truth was undeniable. She knew.

"You found this out how?" I asked.

There was pain on top of her misery, which was transforming into fear. "You know how," she said.

It had been hard enough for her to tell me about her "source," and it was plain as day that she wasn't ready to talk about it in front of an FBI agent. Lilly pushed away from the table, ready to leave, but I stopped her.

"Lilly, you've got to tell Andie."

"That's not an option," she said as she gathered her coat.

Andie leaned across the table, forcing Lilly to look her in the eye. "Lilly, if you have a source—"

"I can't talk about it."

"There's no way for me to help you if you won't talk to me."

"Damn it, Patrick. Did you set this up?"

I hadn't, but I could see how she would think otherwise. "No, but Andie's right."

Lilly rose, and so did Andie, blocking Lilly's path to the door. "Sit for thirty seconds more," said Andie, "and hear me out."

Andie hadn't presented it as an option, and Lilly backed down.

"Here's the situation," said Andie. "Take it as a given that Manu Robledo has in his possession a copy of Evan Hunt's analysis of the Cushman Ponzi scheme. I can name three people who are alive today who could truthfully say that they saw the report in Robledo's hands around the time he got it, three years ago. Robledo, obviously, is one. Tony Mandretti, who gave it to him, is another."

"The third, I presume, is Evan," I said.

"No. I said people who are alive today. I don't think Evan knew anyway."

"Then who's the third?" I asked.

Andie hesitated, which underscored the importance of what she was about to say. "It's a former government agent."

"From the FBI?"

"No."

"Who is he?"

"An undercover agent who introduced Manu Robledo to Gerry Collins. He was at a meeting in Miami three years ago, when Robledo confronted Gerry Collins with the analysis showing Cushman was a fraud. I can't go into detail, but suffice it to say that things went terribly wrong. He was shot, but survived."

This was entirely new territory to me, and a string of questions came to mind. "When you say he was an undercover agent, would I be on track if I were to guess that the government operation had something to do with the letters B-A-Q?"

"You'd be right on track," said Andie.

"So he worked for the Treasury Department?"

"Slow down," said Andie. "We can talk more about this, but only if I know both you and Lilly are on board."

"On board what?" Lilly asked.

The color had drained from Lilly's face, and I knew that we were sharing the same thought. I put it into words: "Are you saying that this former government agent is Lilly's source?"

Andie leaned closer, tightening her figurative grip on Lilly. "You don't want to mess with this man," Andie said to her. "He's ruthless and has his own agenda. Trust me, your safety and well-being are not high on his list of priorities."

"I know that," said Lilly, her voice flat. "It's all very disturbing, the way he talks to me."

"What does he say?" I asked.

"He uses very affectionate language, which is totally out of place. He tells me all the time that he is protecting me. He'll call me 'Love,' or he'll tell me how much I need him."

"That's a ruse," said Andie. "I told you: he's a former government agent. He understands how psychological profiling works in law enforcement. If he comes across as a lovesick puppy, it's only to confuse us about his real motivations."

"'That would actually be a relief, if you're right," said Lilly.

"You should operate on the assumption that you can't believe a thing he says," Andie said.

"But that's not exactly right, either," said Lilly. "Apart from the lovesick stuff, just about everything he's told me has been right on the money."

"Like what?" asked Andie.

"He told me that it was Robledo who opened the numbered account at BOS/Singapore. That was true, whether the bank will admit it or not. He told me Patrick was really Tony Mandretti's son. That was true. He told me—"

She stopped, which brought Andie and me to the edge of our seats.

"He told you what?" asked Andie, pressing. "I want to know everything he's told you."

"And he promised to kill me if I tell anyone."

"That's not a threat to be taken lightly, given the intelligence that's been gathered on him. I can see what a toll this is taking on you, emotionally and physically. If you work with me, we can bring this nightmare to an end."

Lilly glanced at Andie, then at me.

"What do you say, Lilly?" asked Andie.

"First, I need to talk to Patrick," she said, "alone."

39

LILLY AND I FELT A BLAST OF THE COLD WINTER NIGHT AS ANDIE opened the door and left the Tearrific café. I watched through the plate glass window, and my gaze followed her across narrow Mott Street. She disappeared into the darkness, but I noticed the lighted red awning above the Fong Inn, which in bold white letters advertised PUTO and HOT TAO. Puto is a steamed rice cake, but under my rough understanding of Spanish slang and Chinese menus, linking it with "hot tao" created the literal multilingual equivalent of "way-hot male prostitute." Talk about lost in translation.

"What are you looking at?" asked Lilly.

I didn't even attempt an explanation. "Nothing," I said. "What did you want to tell me?"

Lilly sat up straight, preparing her words. "You heard me tell Agent Henning that my source claims to be protecting me, but it goes further than that."

"You mean all the lovesick remarks he makes?"

"No, not that. I think Henning's take on that is probably right: he's playing to a profile stereotype just to confuse me. What I mean is that he's not just protecting me: he blames you—wants to blame you for everything that happened at the bank. And he cautions me to keep my distance from you so that the blame doesn't spill over to me."

"Strange as that sounds, the notion of putting distance between us actually jibes with the warning I got in the park. The guy who attacked me told me to stay away from you."

"Basically he thinks that I got used. First by Gerry Collins. Then by you."

It was awkward to be among the "users," but it suddenly turned into one of those "lightbulb" moments. "Your source leaked the Treasury memo," I said, energized by the realization.

"What?"

"Robledo had to have gotten that memo from someone in Treasury. Your source is a former government agent. He leaked the Treasury memo, and Robledo showed it to you. Your source is the one who put you on Robledo's radar."

"But if he's the one who put me in danger, why would he be protecting me?"

"He's got your back," I said, as things suddenly came clear to me.

"What does that mean?"

"My bet is that he leaked the Treasury memo for some other purpose—to hurt somebody else. Putting you in danger wasn't his intention. Protecting you is what he's all about right now."

"I don't know."

"Think about it. Clearly, he doesn't believe the statement in the memo about your being the best lead on the Cushman money. He called Collins a user. Now your source thinks I know where the money is, and he says I'm using you to get there. In his eyes, I'm as bad as Gerry Collins."

"I still don't see how that adds up to his having my back."

"He was an undercover agent who ended up shot. He got *used* on the front end of Operation BAQ, just like you did. He's out to punish everyone who was behind Operation BAQ—the users. Leaking the Treasury memo was part of a bigger agenda. Putting you in danger wasn't. Collins got his punishment. He's here to make sure I get mine. He wants to make sure you don't get used in the process. He's not in love with you. He's got your back."

I could almost see her head spinning. "Give me that again," she said. "You're saying Collins was part of Operation BAQ?"

"That's exactly what I'm saying."

Her expression soured. "I knew Gerry. He was definitely not an FBI agent."

"Of course not. He was a scumbag who fed billions of dollars to the biggest Ponzi scheme in history. I can easily see a situation where someone in the FBI or Treasury came to him and gave him the option of going to jail for the rest of his life or playing along with Operation BAQ—whatever it is."

Lilly was suddenly with me. "That would be just like Gerry. Cut a deal, save himself."

"Save himself in spades. I'm betting that the federal agent assigned to handle Collins was told to take the bullet himself before he let Collins go down—before he let Operation BAQ fail. Collins bought himself a human shield. And now that shield is a rogue agent who thinks that he got used by his own government, who thinks that *I'm* using you."

Lilly's expression went cold, but it wasn't because she disagreed with me. "That's why he said it's up to me and him to decide . . ."

"Decide what?"

"Whether you live or die."

"He actually used those words?"

Lilly nodded. She reached across the table and held my hand. "What are we going to do?"

I withdrew my hand and poured more tea. "Stay right here," I said, "until I'm damn sure you've decided I should live."

"You're kidding, right?"

I breathed in the steam from my tea, catching her eye over the brim of my cup. "When did he tell you this?"

"Yesterday afternoon, when he listed all the lies you'd told me."

"Alleged lies," I said.

"Lies," she said.

"Okay, lies. But, shit, Lilly. The guy says it's up to you to decide if I live or die, and you're telling me now?"

"It's sounds horrible when you say it that way, but even as mad and hurt as I was, I literally was dialing your number when Barber pulled up in his limo and told me to get into the car. I was really scared, and in no position to call you. An hour later you were in his office, and he was telling us to look through each other's files for the smoking gun. I don't have to tell you everything that's happened since then. It's been crazy, and I'm sorry it's taken us this long to have this conversation, but . . ."

"But what?"

"Up until we had this last conversation with Andie Henning, you were the only person sitting at this table who had an FBI agent looking out for you."

"I've been trying to make that happen," I said.

"I've been trying, too, damn it. But it's been just *me*."

I could see it in her eyes, hear it in her voice: she really had been trying. And she'd raised a valid point. I had Andie. I had Connie. I'd even had Evan for a while. Lilly had no one.

"Patrick, we can let this get ugly and turn against each other. But we've both made mistakes. Please, can we just move forward?"

I still wished that she had told me sooner, but it was a fair statement that we'd both made mistakes—and the real truth was, the only one who had affirmatively lied to the other was me.

"That sounds like an excellent idea," I said.

"Really, Patrick. What are we going to do?"

The tea and our talk had cleared my thoughts. I took my phone from my pocket and removed the battery.

"What are you doing?" asked Lilly.

"Deactivating my phone to make sure I don't use it before a tech expert can tell me what spyware is on it. I suggest you do the same with yours."

"I suppose that's a reasonable assumption—that it's bugged."

"Beyond reasonable," I said. "Right here, right now, you and I are going to burn one indisputable fact into our brains: Evan Hunt was shot in the head fifteen minutes after he called and told me that he had cracked the code on an encrypted memorandum about BAQ."

"Okay. And exactly what does that tell us?"

"It tells us somebody was listening to that conversation. It tells us that we need to figure out what Operation BAQ is, and not end up like Evan Hunt."

"Does that mean we should take up Agent Henning on her offer to help us? You want to 'get on board' with her, as she put it?"

I leaned closer, hoping that it truly mattered what either one of us thought—wondering if either one of us had any real control.

"That's the question, isn't it?" I said.

40

ON A QUIET CROSS STREET IN LOWER MIDTOWN, AT THE DESIGNATED time and place, Andie Henning waited on the salt-stained side-walk beneath a burning streetlamp. A black limousine stopped at the curb. The driver got out, closed his door, and walked to the newsstand on the corner. The motor continued to run, exhaust swirling from the tailpipe and blurring the orange glow of tail-lights. Dark-tinted windows prevented Andie from seeing inside. The rear door on the passenger side swung open. Andie slid onto the black leather seat and pulled the door shut.

By phone Andie had requested a face-to-face meeting with Joe Barber, and he'd agreed to see her on his own terms. They sat facing each other on bench-style seats. Andie flashed her credentials to confirm her identity, but Barber waved them off.

"You're alone; I'm alone," he said. "Keep it unofficial."

She put her badge away. "Fine by me. Because it's clear now that, officially, you and I have been working at cross-purposes for the past eight months. FBI going one way, Treasury going another."

"You seem to forget that I'm no longer with Treasury."

"Fair enough. Up until your resignation, we were work-ing at cross-purposes. But we both ended up at the same place: BOS/Singapore numbered account 507.625 RR."

She waited for his reaction, but he showed none. Finally, Barber said, "I told you on the phone that I would listen. I didn't say that I would talk."

"You'll talk," she said. "Or you'll go to jail."

His eyes narrowed, his tone suitable for a lord speaking to a serf. "Just who do you think you're talking to?"

"The former deputy secretary of the Treasury who wrote an internal memorandum on Operation BAQ."

"And exactly what do you know about that memorandum?"

"I know that it was encrypted on a level that is reserved only for matters of national security. I know that a quant named Evan Hunt, who claimed to have cracked the code, ended up dead in a Dumpster. I know that your memo named Lilly Scanlon as Treasury's best lead to the whereabouts of billions of dollars that disappeared in Abe Cushman's Ponzi scheme. And after months of investigating Lilly Scanlon on suspicion of laundering money for Abe Cushman and Gerry Collins, I've come to the firm conclusion that she doesn't know anything about the location of those funds. In other words, I know that what you wrote was a lie."

"Government officials don't go to jail for putting inaccurate information in an internal memorandum."

"They do if the misinformation gets people killed. Especially innocent people who are used as bait."

"That's a very serious accusation, even for an unofficial meeting."

"I couldn't be more serious about it. I don't know exactly what Operation BAQ is, but I do know it's some kind of fishing expedition. The catch of the day is a rather dodgy character named Manu Robledo—or someone connected to him. Lilly Scanlon was the bait."

"Am I supposed to be impressed?"

"No. Ashamed. It was former FBI agent Scully who figured

out most of everything I just told you. That's why you forced him into retirement."

"You need to check your directory of government employees, sweetheart. I was at Treasury, not the bureau."

She paused before pushing beyond her sphere of knowledge, but suddenly, it felt like more than a hunch. "Operation BAQ goes way above your pay grade. Above Treasury. Above the FBI. Plenty high to send an overly inquisitive special agent packing."

Barber pulled his cell from his pocket, but he didn't dial. It was hard to tell in the dim light of the limo, but Andie was quite sure there was a smirk that needed wiping from his face.

"You look too young to retire," he said. "But with one call, I can have you working at far less interesting places than the FBI."

"I don't scare easily."

"I don't scare. Period."

He pushed a speed-dial button. A moment later, the door opened and the driver was at the curb.

He put his phone away. "Next time, I dial 'M.'"

"For murder? Are you actually threatening to kill me?"

"No, sweetie. For meter maid. You'd make a good one. Have a good evening, Agent Henning."

Andie climbed out and stepped onto the sidewalk. The driver went around to the other side and climbed inside. Andie watched the limo pull away, and as the orange taillights merged into traffic, she was sure of one thing: Operation BAQ did indeed reach higher than the former deputy secretary of the Treasury.

The only question was how high.

Andie pulled her scarf up to her chin and headed for the subway.

41

I TOOK A PATH TRAIN FROM MANHATTAN AND WAS IN NEW Jersey by dinnertime. Lilly came with me, which I took as a positive sign that I was indeed on her deserves-to-live list. Just as Lilly had wanted to talk to me before forming any alliance with Agent Henning, I also needed to speak to someone. I phoned Connie several times, but her machine picked up.

"Call me," I said, keeping my message short.

Connie had given me a key to her apartment with a standing offer to stay there. Lilly still had a hotel room, but with Evan Hunt's shooting, she didn't feel safe going back there. My place wasn't an option, either, since her last stay had ended with a phony deliveryman forcing her to escape out the window. After a three-minute walk from Journal Square Station, however, I was seriously wondering how she would feel safer in this part of Jersey City. Things changed block by block, and some streets were easily better than our old neighborhood in Queens. Some weren't. Connie's definitely wasn't. I had never asked my sister how much the zoo paid her, but if it was more than minimum wage, she was socking away a fortune in what she saved on rent. It was no wonder that she leaped at every opportunity to sleep in a tent on scouting trips.

Connie's building was like the others on her street. An old three-story unit in need of a paint job. No alley between neighbors. Sheets of plastic covered the windows for added insulation. The buildings were set back from the street, and once upon a time there had probably been a front lawn, but now there were only driveways. With cars parked side by side, two and three deep, it was a safe bet that more people lived in these one- and two-bedroom apartments than they were ever intended to house.

The sidewalk had not been shoveled, and the cold night air had turned the snow to a crusty ice that crunched beneath my shoes as I climbed the front steps. Lilly waited at the curb, her arms folded for warmth, her eyes darting left to right, as if she were expecting a drug deal to go down at any moment. I reached for the key but decided to knock first, just in case she was home.

To my surprise, the porch light switched on.

"Connie?" I called out.

The light switched off, leaving Lilly and me in the distant glow of the streetlamp on the corner.

"Probably a motion detector," Lilly said. "Open up and let's go in before we get mugged."

I heard Connie call out, "Be there in a minute!"

She wasn't right on the other side of the door; her voice was more removed, as if she were in another room, perhaps the bedroom. It made me wonder why she hadn't been answering her telephone, but I gave her a minute. I heard a door slam and what sounded like someone running across a wood floor.

I leaned closer to the door. "Connie?"

"Just a second!"

The door opened, and Connie invited me inside. She seemed out of breath.

"Is everything okay?" I asked.

"Yeah, fine," she said, though her voice cracked with nervousness. Lilly and I exchanged glances, clearly sharing the same impression that we'd caught Connie in a romp.

"Strong procreation gene," I said, still looking at Lilly. "Runs in the family."

Connie blushed. "Oh, you're thinking that I was . . . No. It's not that. There's no one here. Just me, myself, and I."

I heard a thud behind the closet door, followed by a ping and the sound of a penny rolling across a wood floor. I looked down and saw that it wasn't a coin. I bent down and picked up the bullet that had rolled up against my heel. "What the heck is this?"

"Nine millimeter, hollow-point," said Connie.

Either my hunch about sex had been dead wrong, or my sister was far kinkier than I had ever imagined. "You want to tell me what's going on?"

She drew a deep breath and then let it out, sighing. Slowly, with obvious reluctance, she turned the knob and opened the closet door. Wedged between an assortment of winter coats and camping gear, a man turned his head toward us and shot an awkward wave hello. The face was familiar, and when he stepped into the room where there was better lighting, I recognized him.

"Scully?"

I hadn't seen Agent Scully since I was a teenager, but there are certain people, certain situations, that a person never forgets. Scully had served as the handler for our entire family when Dad turned against the Santucci family. As my father testified before a federal grand jury in lower Manhattan—literally, at that very moment—Agent Scully and my mother sat down with my sister and me at our dining room table in Queens and told us what a courageous thing our father was doing, how important it was to the fight against organized crime, and how, frankly, our young lives would never be the same.

"What are you doing here?" I asked.

"I heard about your father's friend, Evan," he said. "So I reached out to Connie."

"He's concerned for our safety," said Connie.

"So he's hiding in your closet?"

"I can explain that," said Scully.

"No, let me," said Connie. "Patrick, I know how you feel about guns. But your big sister is one of those people who believes that a guy like Evan Hunt might have had a fighting chance if he had kept a gun in his apartment. So when Scully called and asked if there was anything I needed . . ."

I looked at Scully. "You brought her a gun?"

Connie groaned. "See, that's why I hid him in the closet when you came knocking. I knew you'd be against this."

Scully reached into the closet, retrieved a canvas duffel bag, and laid it on the floor. It clanged like an armory. "I brought an assortment, actually."

"What are we doing here, forming a militia?" I asked.

"We're protecting ourselves," Connie said.

"I haven't picked up a gun since Mom died," I said.

"You got pretty good," said Scully. "Just basic self-defense was all I wanted to teach you."

Connie reached inside the duffel bag, pulled out a Glock semi-automatic pistol, and shoved in the ammunition clip like a pro. "I stuck with it. You probably could use a refresher course."

Lilly backed away nervously. "I don't like this. Patrick, you need to regroup with Agent Henning and find a safe place for us to stay."

Scully said, "I can stay here as long as you kids want, if you don't feel safe."

It was odd to be called "kids," but things apparently hadn't changed from Scully's perspective, either.

"I can also teach you to use a gun, Lilly," Scully said as he pulled another pistol from his bag. "Maybe you'd be more comfortable with the Sig Sauer."

"Patrick, let's go," said Lilly.

The image of Evan, faceup in the Dumpster, ran through my mind, and the pain of each physical trauma my body had sustained over the past few days came roaring back—the gun to my head and powder burns to my neck in Times Square, the wire around my neck and my chin hitting the sidewalk in Battery Park, the knee I'd torn up chasing Evan in Central Park.

"Agent Henning has offered to help us, and that's the way I'm leaning," said Lilly.

She wasn't being unreasonable, but I looked at Scully and suddenly felt as though I'd found an old friend.

"Grab Connie's phone in the kitchen and let Henning know where we are, if that makes you feel better," I said. "But take off your coat. We should stay awhile."

42

THE SUBWAY RIDE FROM MIDTOWN GOT ANDIE BACK TO THE FBI field office in lower Manhattan before six P.M. Barber had called their limousine meeting "unofficial," but Andie intended to complete a formal interview report anyway. She was seated at her desk and about to start typing when Supervisory Agent Teese entered her office, closed the door, and delivered the news.

"We're pulling the plug."

Andie didn't have to ask, *On what?* After eight months of investigating the movement of Cushman's funds through BOS, however, she wasn't about to simply pack her bags and fly back to Miami.

"Who made the decision?"

"Washington."

"By 'Washington,' do you mean headquarters or someone outside the bureau?"

"The decision came to me from the director's office."

"That doesn't exactly answer my question."

He pulled up a chair and sat facing her, surprisingly contrite. "I'm sorry about this, Andie. It's not a matter of my backing down to the political will. It's embarrassing, is what it is."

"For the bureau, you mean?"

"For me, and for everyone else who's been trumpeting the theory that the actual money in Cushman's Ponzi scheme was one-tenth of the sixty billion dollars that most estimates put it at. I was certain that Cushman was a money-laundering operation with mostly paper losses."

"So you've changed your tune: Patrick Lloyd was not holding out on us."

"Not holding out," he said.

"So the final chapter on this investigation will read how?"

He thought about it, and the expression on his face was like that of a man writing his own obituary. "There was no evidence that Cushman funds were laundered by anyone at BOS/Singapore, least of all Lilly Scanlon."

"But getting back to the embarrassment factor: this is not just the shutting down of our investigation into BOS."

"No. It's a wholesale rejection of the theory that Cushman's Ponzi scheme was a money-laundering operation, and that the only real money was the phony ten percent return that Cushman pretended to pay his investors."

Andie was not one to say *I told you so.* "I think we both saw this coming."

"You did. I should have. The reason the 'paper loss' theory got any traction at all was because, at first, so little money was recovered for the victims. That's changing. Every day I get reports that lawyers are hot on the trail of real money—nowhere near the full sixty-billion-dollar loss, but much more than the ten percent that was posited by the money-laundering theory."

Andie said, "This probably doesn't make you feel any better, but there must be regulators feeling more heat than us for missing a sixty-billion-dollar fraud with real victims who lost real money."

"Yeah," he said, shaking his head slowly, as if he'd just heard the world's largest understatement. "The fallout is going to be huge."

"How so?"

"Nothing for you to worry about."

"I'd like to know. I think, after eight months of work, I *deserve* to know."

Teese met her stare, but he was the one to blink. Andie didn't take it as a sign of weakness. It was just a matter of fairness.

Teese said, "The view that the entire Cushman fraud was no bigger than six billion dollars of real money was an underlying assumption in the formulation of certain policies at Treasury."

"Do you mean Operation BAQ?"

He hesitated, as if to measure his response. "Operation BAQ dates back over three years—before Cushman's collapse."

Andie connected the dots. "So that means it was known that Cushman was not legit."

He didn't offer a verbal response. Andie didn't take his silence as a denial; he'd simply said all he could say, and she appreciated that. Even so, she pushed another button. "I met with retired agent Scully," she said. "The handler for Tony Mandretti."

"I know who he is. He worked out of this office for over twenty years."

"The things he said about Operation BAQ were frankly difficult to swallow. But this conversation would seem to confirm everything he told me."

Again, Teese didn't answer directly. "Be careful with Scully."

"That was my initial reaction," she said. "But now my impression is that he was simply saying things that a retired FBI agent would tell another agent to make sure she didn't become the bureau's fifty-fourth special agent killed in the line of duty."

"Scully is trouble," said Teese. "You'd do well to stay away from him."

Andie took the advice for what she thought it was worth. "What am I supposed to do now?"

"Wrap it up. Go back to Miami."

"What can I tell Patrick Lloyd?"

"That his cooperation is no longer needed. Nothing more."

"What about his father?"

"He'll receive medical attention until he passes. That satisfies our end of the deal."

Teese rose, and he seemed ready to apologize once more, but he didn't. Instead, he started for the door.

"Tell me something," Andie said, stopping him. "How high does Operation BAQ go?"

He stood there for a moment, showing no reaction. Finally, he turned away, no answer, and left the office. Andie turned back to her computer, the blank report of her conversation with Joe Barber still up on the LCD.

That high, huh? she said to herself, answering her own question.

43

SCULLY CLOCKED ME AT JUST UNDER EIGHT SECONDS.

"Not too shabby, Patrick," he said. "A shot-to-shot reload of two seconds or less would get you into law enforcement, but not bad at all for a guy who hasn't touched a gun since he was a teenager."

We'd started with basic gun safety instruction, and for the next hour it was a series of dry-fire drills: draw, reload, target transition, and visualization skills. The Sig Sauer had felt a bit small in my hand, so we went with the Glock 9 millimeter. The fit was right, and it was much lighter weight than I'd expected. Everything was still step by step for me: Is the slide locked back? press magazine release → magazine is clear → grab new magazine → insert new magazine with correct orientation → release slide. But with enough practice I would store procedural memory, and the operation would become second nature. At least that was the theory.

"Tomorrow morning we can get to a range and do live fire," said Scully.

"Patrick, don't you have a job?" asked Lilly.

Her continued disapproval of firearms came through in her tone, but the question did remind me of the e-mails that were piling up on my BlackBerry since I'd removed the battery.

Scully dug into his duffel bag again. "Lilly, do you want to try the Sig Sauer?"

"No, I don't. As far as I'm concerned, you can put away your Glock, your Smith and Wesson, your bazooka, and whatever else you've got in there. I'm serious, Patrick. Are you going into the bank tomorrow?"

I didn't know the answer, didn't know much about tomorrow at all.

A knock at the door broke the tension. Our pizza had arrived, a thin-crust, New York–style marvel from Gino's on Central Avenue. Maybe not the best pizza in the entire universe, but definitely the best in the neighborhood. At Connie's suggestion, we gathered around the kitchen table and turned the evening into more than just a weapons tutorial. We talked as the slices of pepperoni with extra-gooey cheese disappeared. Connie had a box of brownie mix left over from her last scout meeting, so she put a batch in the oven. None of us had room to eat them after knocking off a pizza, but there was nothing like the smell of brownies baking to change the mood in a room. Soon we were deep into Abe Cushman and Gerry Collins, four separate threads weaving into a single tale. Much of the focus was on Agent Henning, from my first communications with her eight months earlier, to Scully's recent conversation. The honesty between Scully and me seemed to loosen Lilly's tongue, and she opened up about her source. Her voice didn't quake the way it had the first time she'd talked about him, but I could hear her throat tightening at times.

"Agent Henning told us that he's a former government agent," said Lilly. "He was shot by Manu Robledo."

"She heard that from me," said Scully.

"What else did you tell her?" I asked.

"Basically everything I know. He survived the gunshot, but a spinal injury apparently left him in horrible chronic pain. He got addicted to painkillers to the point that he was permanently disabled."

"That explains the anger, I suppose."

"Henning has offered us protection," said Lilly.

"Is that so?" said Scully.

"You sound skeptical," I said.

"You look even more skeptical," he said, firing right back.

"Don't get me wrong, I like Henning," I said.

Scully waited for me to say more, then gave me the appropriate prompt. "But . . ."

I drew a breath, long enough to focus my thoughts. It was the FBI's promise of first-rate treatment for my father's illness that had drawn me into this mess, and at bottom this was still all about my father. Connie and Lilly already knew my position, and I wanted Scully's view on the fundamental issue that had kept Henning and me from seeing eye to eye.

"I've never been able to get Henning to seriously consider the possibility that my father didn't actually kill Gerry Collins."

Scully wiped a glob of pizza sauce from his sleeve and said, "That's probably because he confessed."

Connie jumped in. "There's absolutely no physical evidence."

"His fingerprints were at the scene of the crime," I said, playing devil's advocate.

Scully scoffed and shook his head. "Collins was murdered in his car, and Evan Hunt's written report was found on the front seat. Your father's fingerprints were on Evan's report. To me, the only thing the fingerprints prove is that your father handed the report to Manu Robledo, and Robledo gave it to Collins."

"*That's* the fingerprint evidence?" I asked.

"That's it," said Scully, "lock, stock, and barrel."

"Oh, my God," said Lilly.

She looked at me from across the table, and I could see the

change. Scully and his stash of weapons had temporarily pushed her away from me, but his explanation of the fingerprints seemed to bring her back to my side—perhaps further into my camp, the *Mandretti* camp, than she'd ever been—as if the last obstacle had been cleared.

"Your dad really is innocent," she said.

No one spoke for the next minute, and Lilly's words—the conclusion of the only person in the group who could remotely qualify as an outsider—seemed to hang over us.

"Does that mean that the man who killed Gerry Collins also shot Evan?" asked Connie.

"Maybe, maybe not," said Scully.

I had my own theory. "Like I told Lilly at Tearrific, I'm convinced that whoever killed Evan was listening to our phone conversation right before he was shot. Evan told me that he cracked the code on the encrypted data we got from Barber. Fifteen minutes later he was dead, and his computer was gone."

"Then add my source to the list of suspects," said Lilly. "But Manu Robledo is still at the top."

I reached for my BlackBerry and laid it on the table. "The list is growing," I said. "There's a reason I carried both an iPhone and a BlackBerry. Love the apps and the Internet on the iPhone, but my BlackBerry is issued by BOS with enhanced security, as hacker-proof and impenetrable to spyware as the largest Swiss bank in the world can make it."

Scully said, "Your point being that anyone who eavesdropped on your BOS BlackBerry . . ."

"Is probably working from inside BOS," I said, finishing Scully's thought.

"You mean Joe Barber?" said Lilly.

"Maybe I do."

"That doesn't make any sense," Lilly said. "Why would he call us into his executive suite, *give* us the files that contain the encrypted memorandum about Operation BAQ, and then kill Evan for cracking the code?"

"He gave me your files, Lilly. You didn't know the BAQ memo was in there. Maybe he didn't know, either."

Lilly considered it. "Two billion dollars is a lot of money to most of us. But we're talking about Joe Barber and the Bank of Switzerland. I just don't see Barber at the heart of a BOS conspiracy to kill Evan Hunt over money."

"Barber was deputy secretary of the Treasury. Your source is a former government agent who was working on a secret operation for Treasury. I'm not saying they're working as a team, but it would appear that there is much more than money at stake."

"Money or no money, killing Evan Hunt would be a very desperate act."

Scully said, "Desperate men do desperate things. Let me borrow your phone for a couple of hours, Patrick."

"For what?"

"I have a tech expert I work with. Former FBI. If there's spyware on your BlackBerry, he can unravel it."

I slid the phone across the table to him, along with the battery I'd removed at Tearrific.

Scully said, "Lilly, let's check yours, too, just in case."

"My phone isn't issued by the bank. I had to give up my BOS BlackBerry when they fired me."

"Let's check it anyway," said Scully.

She gave it up, the battery separated from the phone, just like mine. "I suppose if Patrick's comes back with spyware and mine doesn't, that would tell us it was a BOS job."

"Good point," I said, "but I have a sixth sense about how this is going to play out. Scully, let's do the target practice another time. I'm going into the bank tomorrow."

"I wouldn't put it off," he said.

"I know, but—"

Connie's landline rang, cutting me short. I checked the number. "It's Agent Henning," I told the group.

"She must have heard you say that you're going into the bank tomorrow," said Connie. She was kidding, but only half kidding.

"You told me I could call her on Connie's phone," said Lilly, "so I left her a voice mail and told her we were here."

"Take it," said Scully.

I answered the call, and with just a few words from Andie, I knew that something had changed. I could hear it in her voice.

"First, let me say that what I'm about to tell you will have no impact on your father's health. Nothing has changed in that regard. He will remain at Lemuel Shattuck Hospital as long as necessary, and he will continue to get first-rate medical treatment as long as he needs it."

"Okay, thank you for that. But I'm getting the feeling that something is definitely wrong."

Andie hesitated, and I glanced at the concerned faces around the kitchen table. Finally, Andie's voice was in my ear.

"I'm sorry, Patrick. I hate to do this on the phone, but things have happened fast. There is going to be a major change in our working relationship."

44

TRAFFIC OUT OF THE CITY WAS WORSE THAN USUAL, AND BARBER was stuck in a limousine that was barely moving. He would have preferred to make the phone call from his home, but there was no telling when that would be. He raised the soundproof partition between him and the driver, then dialed from memory on a special encrypted line to the West Wing of the White House.

Barber had first met Brett Woods at Saxton Silvers, when they were making their mark and earning tons of money as young bond traders at what was then the premier investment bank on Wall Street. They were friends but highly competitive, not just in their work but in thousand-dollar side bets on everything from whether the next unescorted woman to walk into the bar would be blond or brunette to which drop of rain clinging to the window outside their trading floor would be the first to trickle from top to bottom. The twentysomething cowboys eventually grew up, and the last two decades had seen them in and out of public service, though on very different tracks. Barber worked his way up in Treasury, eventually reaching the number two post. Woods parlayed his international business skills into matters of state, serving as ambassador to Turkey, then deputy director of the Central Intelligence Agency, and finally national security advisor. Woods probably had the most solid business background of any national security advisor since Frank Carlucci in the Reagan administration, and both Woods and Barber had been savvy enough to cash out of Saxton Silvers before the subprime crisis drove the bank into receivership. Some said Barber was jealous of his old friend for snagging such a prestigious White House appointment. Others acknowledged that Barber's position was one that his friend could never have attained—that it had been hard enough to secure Senate confirmation for Woods' ambassadorship to Turkey, and that more recent controversy had virtually ensured he could never be named deputy secretary of the Treasury, or anything else that required confirmation by the Senate.

"I have a meeting with Mongoose later tonight," Barber said into the telephone.

"Nothing has changed," said Woods. "Until we eliminate the threat, it's business as usual."

"Meaning what?"

"Meaning that until you hear otherwise, he's got our backs to the wall. Give him what he wants."

"He wants two billion dollars."

"Once upon a time, that was a lot of money."

"You're missing my point. He wants *Robledo*'s two billion dollars."

"Better it goes to Mongoose than back to Robledo."

"That money is *gone*. The Gerry Collins–to–Lilly Scanlon pipeline is a dead end. She doesn't know squat. I've tried everything, even pitting her against her boyfriend—which backfired, to say the least. It's time to face facts: Gerry Collins scammed Robledo *and us*. You've heard the tape."

Barber was talking about the recorded conversation of Gerry Collins pleading with Robledo for his life after Mongoose had been shot on the boat. The yacht, taken from a drug lord in a forfeiture proceeding and commissioned for use in Operation BAQ, was fully wired for eavesdropping.

"Yes, I've heard the tape," said Woods.

"I haven't been with the bank long, but it's been long enough to confirm that Collins wasn't bluffing when he said that Robledo's money never went to Cushman, that he'd stashed it all away. He brought in Robledo's money, just like he was supposed to, but he didn't funnel it to Cushman. He used Lilly Scanlon—made her, Robledo, and us think she was part of the pipeline to Cushman—but he moved the money offshore."

"Do your job, Joe."

"What is that supposed to mean?"

"It may have been pressure from Mongoose that made us find a place for you in BOS management, but that doesn't necessarily make it a bad idea. You're inside. Find the money."

"I can't! It looks like Collins took that information to the grave."

"Forensic accounting can do wonders. Unwind it."

"There's no way. Collins used *hawalas*. Southeast Asia *hawalas*, as best I can tell. There's no paper trail."

Barber didn't have to elaborate. For all the politically correct rhetoric about the value and legitimacy of the informal "non-banking system" that operates across the globe in the Islamic world, even some Muslim countries had made *hawalas* illegal because of the way they allowed money to "move" without actually moving, without any paper trail, without any way for law enforcement to detect money laundering. The national security advisor knew better than anyone that *hawalas* were much more than an efficient way for taxi drivers in Manhattan to send funds back to their family in Pakistan.

"Shit," said Woods.

"We're teetering on disaster," said Barber.

"Don't get all Chicken Little on me."

"We're in a situation where no one can trace the money, but Robledo has seen a redacted version of my memo identifying

Lilly Scanlon and the bank's Singapore office as Treasury's best lead."

"How do you know he's seen it?"

"Mongoose told me that he sent it to him. That was his first threat: play ball, or next time I send the full decrypted version of your memo and blow the lid off Operation BAQ."

There was silence on the line. Then the NSA spoke, his tone beyond serious. "The fallout would be bad enough if the American public were to find out that its government knew Cushman was running a multibillion-dollar Ponzi scheme but let it happen."

"No one understood the scope of Cushman's fraud when we formulated Operation BAQ. Sixty billion dollars still sounds like a fantasy world. Our estimates were one-tenth that amount."

"There are all kinds of excuses," said Woods. "No one expected Cushman to kill himself before the feds could swoop down and recover at least *some* money for the innocent investors. No one anticipated that Cushman would collapse at a time when the entire world economy was in crisis and the financial system itself was teetering on the brink of ruin."

"Those are all true statements," said Barber.

"This isn't about the truth. What do you suppose a special congressional oversight committee is going to say about those excuses when it comes out that a certain deputy secretary of the Treasury and the president's national security advisor not only knew about Cushman but actually *wanted* him to collapse, in furtherance of Operation BAQ?"

Hearing the NSA ask the question aloud had conveyed the gravity of the situation. "Go to jail," said Barber, "go directly to jail."

"Exactly," said Woods. "So, we need to deal with the problem at hand. At this point, Lilly Scanlon is at risk."

"Let's not mince words," said Barber. "Robledo is going to

kill her if she doesn't come up with that money. And Mongoose is going public with Operation BAQ if I don't deliver it to him."

"So it's either us or Lilly Scanlon."

"Knock off the sarcasm. People have already died over this. The money is *gone*."

"Fix it."

"How do you expect me to come up with that kind of money?"

"Oh, I don't know. Weren't you one of the geniuses over at Treasury who decided to give BOS about eight billion dollars in stimulus money? Maybe you can go to the board of directors and claw back the bonuses they paid to themselves."

"Bite me, all right?"

"Just find the money somewhere and give Mongoose what he wants."

"Then what is your decision on Lilly Scanlon?"

"Whatever happens there is not our fault. It was Gerry Collins who identified her as his point person, not us."

"But *I* put her name in the memo. I'm not exaggerating here: Robledo will kill her if he doesn't get his money. He may kill her boyfriend, too."

"I've said it before, and I don't think I can be any clearer about this: Robledo can't get his money back."

"Then neutralize Robledo. Or put him in jail."

"If Robledo is out of the picture, we'll never find out who his funders are. Phase two of Operation BAQ fails."

"So you're saying . . ."

"The bureau is already on board with this. In fact, it's already taken care of. I think you know what I'm saying."

The NSA wished him luck. The call was over—and, yes, Barber knew what he was saying:

Lilly Scanlon and Patrick Lloyd were on their own.

45

AROUND ELEVEN O'CLOCK I WENT OUTSIDE AND SAT ON THE FRONT stoop. Every unit on Connie's block had the same facade—a couple of concrete steps leading to a storm door with duct tape on the cracked glass. On such a frigid January night I was the only lunatic in the neighborhood sitting outside as if it were mid-July. Connie's tiny one-bedroom just didn't offer a place to escape, and after three hours, I desperately needed time away from her and Scully. I was alone for only a few minutes when Lilly joined me.

"Good news," she said as she sidled up next to me on the top step. "We finally got the sleeping arrangements figured out."

By "we" I knew she meant Connie. "What was the scout-master's decision?" I asked.

"Connie and I will take the bedroom. The men are in the living room: Scully gets the couch, and you get the air mattress on the floor."

"Ah, the air mattress. I knew we'd break out the camping equipment. When do we start the campfire and make the s'mores?"

"Be nice," said Lilly.

I smiled, but Lilly was right. As we sat together in the cold,

Lilly's head against my shoulder, it occurred to me that I had yet to give Connie a proper thank-you for all she had done.

"Something bothers me about Scully," she said.

Lilly's remark had taken me aback. We were seated side by side, so I couldn't read her expression, and my attention had been drawn across the street, where a kitten seemed to be losing the race against time to find a warm place to spend the night.

"Bothers you how?" I asked.

"It's mostly a feeling I get."

"There must be something behind it."

"Well, for one, I don't like the way he's been trying to talk you into a gunfight."

"He's training me to protect myself so that I don't end up like Evan. That's all."

"Maybe. But even more than the guns, it worries me the way Agent Henning cut you loose tonight—just like that. Two hours after Evan was shot, the three of us were in Chinatown trying to figure out how the FBI could help us and how we could help the FBI. Another two hours later, we're sitting at the kitchen table with Scully—whom you haven't seen since you were a teenager—and Agent Henning calls to tell you that we're on our own."

"Scully didn't have anything to do with that."

"I'd hate to think he did," she said. "But why does it keep gnawing at me?"

I didn't have an answer, but she didn't seem to be waiting for one. It was just something she wanted out in the open, off her chest. I was about to suggest that we rescue that kitten across the street, but a neighbor opened his front door and called the nearly frozen feline inside.

"Don't you love happy endings?" asked Lilly. She'd been watching, too.

"Yeah, I guess I do."

She paused before asking the follow-up, but I could feel it coming.

"Patrick, what do you think is going to happen with us?"

No easy answer came to me, so I ducked it. "I think Shia LaBeouf will play me and Jillian Michaels will play you in a summer blockbuster that will spin off into a reality show called *Wall Street Three: The Biggest Losers.*"

Her puff of laughter crystallized in the night air before me. "Seriously," she said. "So much has happened in the last few days, but we haven't really talked about us. I'm just asking: assuming we don't get shot, strangled, or arrested, where do you and I end up?"

"That's a pretty big question," I said.

"That's a pretty vague answer."

She was right. "The fact that after four full days of hell we're sitting here next to each other says a lot, don't you think?"

I had intended to speak from the heart, but I could feel from her reaction that my words had fallen short. Maybe I was too tired to do better. Maybe she wished I wasn't so afraid to say the wrong thing at the wrong time. Maybe all the stress since Lilly had dragged me into Puffy's Tavern on Monday morning had made our six months in Singapore seem like the distant past— made us seem like two different people, even.

Lilly squeezed my hand gently as she rose and said good night. The cold metal hinges creaked as she pulled open the storm door.

"Lilly?" I said.

She stopped and looked at me.

"I'm glad you're here," I said, then tried to do better. "I'm glad you're with me."

There was warmth in her eyes, but she offered no words. She pushed open the front door, and I heard the loud slap of the metal storm door as she went inside. I was alone on the stoop, and the night felt colder without her. I started a mental list of perfect responses to Lilly's question, but I fought off the second-guessing. It suddenly occurred to me why I was having so much trouble with the thrust of her question—*What's going to happen to us?* It wasn't that I didn't care about Lilly and me, the relationship.

I was more worried about Lilly. Really worried.

46

ANDIE DUCKED UNDER THE YELLOW PLASTIC TAPE IN EVAN Hunt's doorway and reentered the apartment. Two hours of decoding Evan's walls had left her bleary-eyed and in need of coffee. She was recaffeinated and rejuvenated, ready for the second leg of a Tour de France–like journey through the mind of a quant.

Even though the body had been found in the Dumpster, the living space of Evan's apartment was the focus of the crime scene investigation. Members of the team, some on hands and knees, aimed LED flashlights at anything of potential interest, bagging and tagging everything from suspicious hairs and fibers to traces of dirt that may have come from the killer's shoes. A ballistics specialist scoured the walls for stray bullets that may have missed their target and buried themselves in the plasterboard. Two other investigators collected fingerprints. The investigation team was exclusively NYPD. The FBI's investigation into BOS money laundering had officially ended, and homicide was technically outside the jurisdiction of the FBI. Technically. There was no doubt in Andie's mind that Evan Hunt was caught up in a financial crime of federal proportions, and until she was on a jet flying back to Miami, she would spend every waking hour trying to prove it.

"How long you staying?" the lead detective asked. He was a young guy, full of confidence, with eyes that roamed Andie's body as he spoke.

"Just wanted to take one more look at the wall for my final report," Andie said.

He glanced at the jumble of words and photographs on the only wall with a window—the window that Evan had covered with butcher paper in order to keep his flowchart continuous. "Good luck," he said. "Looks like the work of a class-A nut job to me."

Andie shrugged and smiled, but the detective's words struck a deeper cord. Indeed, he'd hit precisely on the reason she'd returned to Evan's apartment. The suspicion was unavoidable that certain people in Washington—the powers who had abruptly shut down her BOS investigation—wanted the world to dismiss Evan's analysis with similar disparagement.

Just the work of a class-A nut job.

The detective checked her out one more time as he started away, then stopped himself. "We're ordering Chinese from the restaurant downstairs. You interested?"

"No, thanks."

He handed her the menu. "If you change your mind, there's a bit of a trick to reading this thing. The restaurant saves trees by making double-sided copies, but it's all screwed up. Page four is page one, page two is page two, page three is page three, and page one is page four."

Andie gave it a look. "Wow, that is confusing."

"The hostess said it happens all the time. The busboy they send to the copy center to run off the takeout menus speaks no English and always forgets to hit the collate button. It's become a running joke—kind of a signature of their takeout business. The regulars dig it."

Information you dug up, no doubt, while hitting on the hostess.

"If you don't want takeout," he said, "maybe later you and I could—"

"Four, two, three, one," said Andie, noting the wedding ring on his finger. "I got it."

"Suit yourself," he said.

Andie walked to the middle of the room, turning slowly to take in the 360 version of the Cushman world through the eyes of Evan Hunt. A photographer was on the scene to capture it in segments. A videographer recorded the panoramic version. They were working too fast to appreciate the details. Andie allowed herself a long, studied view.

It would have been easy to dismiss Evan's walls as the work of a disturbed, paranoid genius. At first blush they were a jumble of unframed photographs connected by hand-drawn lines in a variety of colors. The rest of the story was told in words, a handwritten narrative in which each independent thought was expressed inside a separate oval, rectangle, or other seemingly random shape. It reminded Andie of a crude version of an LCD that was connected to a computer with no pop-up blocker. The arrows, however, were the key. If Andie followed the color sequence, she could follow the story. She couldn't blame NYPD for not seeing it. Andie's investigation of Lilly Scanlon and BOS/Singapore had given her at least a glimpse into Evan's world. But these walls supplied pieces that even the FBI didn't have. Until now.

Evan Hunt was definitely no nut job.

Andie stepped closer to the wall near the kitchenette. She was following a long yellow line that had puzzled her all night. It started near the bathroom, rose up and over the closet that held Evan's collection of orange dress shirts, and continued down the other side of the wall. There were various forks in the line along the way, but the main thread ran to a small, hand-drawn rectangle just above the baseboard near the kitchenette. It was no bigger than a standard index card. Inside the rectangle

was a list of dates, all from the same period of time: the last six
months of Gerry Collins' life.

Andie stepped back again for a broader view. She knew the
dates had to be important, falling so close to Collins' murder
and Cushman's collapse. But the rectangle contained no other
information, and the dates bore no apparent relationship to the
surrounding clutter of information on the wall. The long yellow line that stretched halfway across the room also suggested
that the dates were significant, but it connected the rectangle
to nothing.

"Last call for food," the detective announced. "You change
your mind yet, Henning?"

"No, I'm okay," she said.

"One of us dumb locals can help you decode the menu, if
that's the problem."

Clearly, he fancied himself a smooth operator, and when all
else failed, there was self-deprecation. "I got the sequence," said
Andie. "Four, two, three—"

She stopped herself in midsentence, and she remembered
what he had said earlier about the screwed-up menu.

*The hostess said it happens all the time. It's become a running
joke—kind of a signature of their takeout business. The regulars dig it.*

There were four pages in the "signature" menu. Four walls
in Evan's flowchart. Andie turned and faced the flowchart again.
She'd studied that rectangle long enough, looked at it from
enough different angles, to recall where it fell in the seemingly
endless sequence of squares, rectangles, circles, ovals and other
hand-drawn shapes in Evan's narrative. It was a hunch, but Evan
was a quant, and numbers were his entertainment. She counted
again, just to make sure, and her hunch proved to be correct.
The little rectangle that had seemed so randomly placed, that
contained such an important list of dates, that was tethered to
a long yellow line that led to nowhere, was indeed the fourth
rectangle on the wall.

Turning clockwise in the center of the room, Andie shifted her gaze to the next wall. Following the pattern—four, two, three, one—she located the second rectangle on the wall. This one, too, seemed out of context, though the information in it didn't cry out for Andie's attention the way the dates had. There was no reason to notice it, unless she was following the pattern. It contained the names of several business establishments—Precious Jewelry Exchange, Discount Diamonds, and the like. She jotted down the names on a notepad, then turned and faced the next wall.

Andie found the third rectangle just above the baseboard. Like before, the information inside the rectangle bore no relationship to the information around it. Andy recognized it as a list of towns and regions in Singapore: Woodlands, Bedok, Hougang, Jurong West, and Bukit Merah. Andie scribbled them all into her notepad next to the dates and the list of businesses.

Finally, Andie faced the fourth wall, which was the one with the papered-over window. The first rectangle—the last in the four, two, three, one sequence—was enormous in comparison to the others. The wall was basically a person-by-person profile of key players in the Cushman fraud.

Rectangle number one was all about Gerry Collins.

Andie reread her notes. Four, two, three, one. It only seemed logical that each date in rectangle number four marked a business transaction of some sort. She'd investigated enough financial crimes to sniff out bogus transactions, however, and she noted that each establishment identified by name in rectangle number three appeared to be in a line of business that lent itself to the creation (fabrication) of big invoices—tens or even hundreds of thousands of dollars a pop. Rectangle number two confirmed that the businesses operated in Singapore, not exactly a model state of tight financial regulation. And it all went back to rectangle number one in the cast of characters: Gerry

Collins. Phony business transactions were one way to launder the fruits of criminal activity, and it was no leap of logic to conclude that jewelry invoices from Singapore that bore Gerry Collins' fingerprints—actual or virtual—were probably fakes.

Four, two, three, one.

It happens all the time. It's become a running joke—kind of a signature of their takeout business.

Of all the ingenious codes that a math whiz could have devised to stop a stranger from breaking into his apartment and uncovering key information in his Cushman flowchart, Evan Hunt had simply borrowed the pattern established by the consistently screwed-up pagination of the takeout menu from the Chinese restaurant below him. Evan was one of the regulars who liked the "running joke." It was as if he was making fun of every movie, every TV show, every book that had ever strained to find "codes" in meaningless number sequences. The quant had a sense of humor.

Who knew?

Andie stepped back from the wall, and the broader perspective confirmed her hunch: There was indeed no line of any color connecting these 4–2–3–1 boxes to Cushman. Andie was beginning to feel the excitement of a multibillion-dollar lead on missing investment funds—funds that, she suspected, Gerry Collins had never actually fed to Cushman.

She went into the bathroom and closed the door, then dialed the number of a colleague she had worked with on another financial crimes investigation. He worked in the Office of Law Enforcement Support at FinCEN—the Financial Crimes Enforcement Network—and she didn't have to remind him that he owed her a favor or two.

"Andie, hey, it's good to hear from you."

"Sorry to call so late," she said.

"No problem. How can I be of help?"

"I've come across the names of a few business establishments in Singapore, and I was hoping that you could check to see if any have shown up on your radar screen."

"You mean in suspicious-activity reports?"

"Not exactly."

Andie paused, knowing that she had to be careful, since the plug had been pulled on her investigation. What she wanted was some very specific information about the oldest informal banking system in Southeast Asia. One that often operated as a side business to jewelry stores, rug dealers, and other going concerns in local communities from New York to Karachi, from London to Dubai. A $300 billion-a-year system that relied on an unregulated global network of personal relationships and trust, and that involved no actual exchange of money or formal record keeping—definitely nothing electronic. Unrecorded conversations were king—conversations in Arabic, Hindi, Urdu, Gujarati, and Farsi.

For Andie's present needs, English would do, and it was perhaps best to speak in generalities.

"I want to talk to you about *hawalas*," she said. "*Hawalas* in Singapore."

47

I COULDN'T SLEEP. THE AIR MATTRESS WAS PLENTY COMFORTABLE, but my mind would not shut off. Scully's snoring didn't help.

I got up quietly, tiptoed to the kitchen, and raided the refrigerator. There was one slice of pizza left over from dinner, and it had my name on it. I brought the Gino's box to the table and pulled up a chair. Connie's PC was humming on the counter, and the only light in the kitchen was the dim glow of the screen saver on the LCD. Snow monkeys.

What else?

The pizza wasn't nearly as good cold, but Connie's apartment was so small that I feared even the hum of a microwave would wake the others. I ate half of the remaining slice and decided it wasn't worth the extra sit-ups I'd have to do in the morning. The rest went into the garbage. But I still wasn't sleepy.

I felt the urge to reach for my BlackBerry. Separation anxiety, I supposed. My BlackBerry was in the hands of Scully's tech expert. Lilly's phone had come back clean—no spyware—but it was taking longer to scan my BOS BlackBerry. In truth, I didn't need a tech expert to confirm that Evan's killer had eavesdropped on my last conversation with Evan and heard him say that he'd broken the encryption code. Not that any tech expert could tell us who was doing the eavesdropping. Good spyware was typically installed remotely, no way to trace it back to anyone.

The snow monkeys called to me, in a manner of speaking, offering a quick e-mail fix to an addict without his "crackberry." I'd already used Connie's PC to log onto my e-mail server four times since dinner. I got up from the kitchen table and made it five. Dozens of messages loaded. I read the latest thread from my team leader, Jay Sussman. It was only my fourth day on the job since returning to New York, but that was more than long enough for slackers to get fired on Wall Street. Jay had breathed not a word about the Cushman money to me, which I took as a positive sign: the pressure I was getting from Barber truly was between him, me, and Lilly. Jay's latest message was to confirm a meeting with a private equity group in Chicago that the bank needed me to attend. It was scheduled for Monday at ten A.M. That gave me three days, including the weekend, to pull my life together. I had no idea how to make that happen. I told Jay I'd be there, hit Send, and then did a double take. The next message in my in-box gave me chills.

It was from Evan. The time posted in the Sent block was 5:14 P.M.—minutes before his death. It had apparently been floating around in cyberspace for the past seven hours, finally hitting my inbox at 11:55 P.M. The reason for the delay was evident: the attached file was enormous. I clicked to open it. The hourglass started spinning. And spinning. Whatever was inside was going to take a while. I was beginning to wonder if Connie's computer was actually powered by snow monkeys. I read the message while the file downloaded:

"Freaked. Someone is at the door. Very suspicious shoes."

It took me a second, but then I remembered the second peephole on Evan's door. I read on:

"I am getting the hell out of here as soon as he leaves. The work we talked about is attached. Really big file for e-mail. Hope it comes through."

I checked the hourglass on the file download. Still spinning. The message continued:

"Be careful with Lilly. Can't understand how T memo on BAQ got in her data."

Evan's message ended there.

Connie's computer was still struggling, the hourglass spinning as it tried to open Evan's file attachment. Like Evan, I, too, had no idea how a Treasury memo on Operation BAQ had ended up in Lilly's data, but if I had to wait another ten seconds to read Evan's decrypted version of it, I thought I would burst. The screen flickered, and my heart nearly stopped.

Do NOT crash!

Another flicker across the screen, and my e-mail program suddenly shut down.

"Shit!"

A message box popped up. Inside, the hourglass continued to spin round and round. Connie's computer was still trying to open Evan's file.

Please, God.

My hand shook as I waited on the work that Evan had died—literally—trying to send me.

"Is everything okay?" asked Lilly.

I turned as she entered the kitchen. My outburst had apparently woken her, or perhaps sleep had been equally elusive for her. I started talking, my tongue racing, but I couldn't have made much sense to her.

"It's from Evan, an e-mail, and the attachment is so ginormous that Connie's computer is about to—"

I caught my breath as the computer screen flickered one more time. Another box popped before my eyes. It was a long message with some kind of code attached, but this code was not from Evan, it was from Microsoft. Two words caught my attention:

FILE CORRUPTED.

The screen went black, and the PC fell silent. I clicked the mouse, I tapped the keyboard, I pressed the main power button again and again. Nothing.

"You can't be serious!"

"Patrick, what is going on?" asked Lilly.

"Where's your phone?"

"Charging," she said, "right over there."

I spotted it by the toaster, hurried over, powered it on, and went straight to the Internet, where I pulled up the remote access program for my e-mail account. I scrolled down the in-box to where Evan's message had been. Then I tried the trash bin.

"It's gone," I said, my heart sinking.

"What's gone?"

I couldn't believe it. The message and the e-mail—both were gone, wiped clean from the in-box and the trash bin.

"Patrick, what is it?"

I closed my eyes and then opened them slowly, hoping to wake up and find that this had all been a dream, a nightmare. It wasn't.

"Disaster," I said. "A total disaster is what this is."

48

ROBLEDO'S TWIN ENGINE CESSNA LANDED AT ELEVEN THIRTY P.M. There were no runway lights. There was no runway. The unscheduled flight from São Paulo, Brazil, had touched down on an unofficial landing strip. Hundreds of such strips cut through the remote woods and grasslands of the Tri-Border region, a landlocked patch of jungle and rough country that lies along the Tropic of Capricorn, where Argentina, Paraguay, and Brazil meet.

Robledo was in the eleventh hour of a southward journey that had started on a commercial jet out of JFK airport. Even though he'd slept on the flight to São Paulo, and even though he'd lost only two hours with the time change, he felt jet-lagged and was glad to have a driver. His name was Oscar, and he spoke only Spanish.

By midnight the four-wheel-drive SUV was approaching Friendship Bridge, a sixteen-hundred-foot span that connected Brazil to Paraguay. A sign posted at the bridge's entrance announced that crossers were prohibited from throwing merchandise off the side. Midnight, however, was the regular shift change for the customs officers. Crews on the Brazilian side were thin, and as usual, bribes had been paid to the Paraguayan naval police at the other end of the bridge. As Robledo's SUV rolled across the bridge, smugglers by the dozen worked fast and fluidly, taking advantage of the window of opportunity that came three times daily with every shift change. Scrambling but still drinking beer, working within a couple hundred meters of Brazil's customs and immigration outpost, smugglers harnessed boxes of goods to long nylon ropes that dangled from the railing and lowered them onto the forested riverbank. Below, teenage boys armed with flashlights sorted through the packages in litter-strewn, knee-high grass.

"Bienvenido a la Ciudad del Este," his driver said with a smile. "Welcome to Ciudad del Este."

Robledo knew the place well. The nightly commotion on the bridge was business as usual in a city of two hundred thousand thieves, swindlers, whores, hit men, gangsters, kidnappers, drug runners, drug addicts, extortionists, smugglers, counterfeiters, terrorists, and well-armed revolutionaries—some with causes, most without. Ciudad del Este was a veritable festering urban sore in the jungle on the Paraguay side of the Paraná River. Not even the pop and crack of semi-automatic weapons in the distance was cause for alarm. More than likely, it was a test firing by just another buyer of AK-47 assault rifles from China or submachine guns stolen from the Mexican army.

"Which hotel?" the driver asked in Spanish.

"Hotel Hamburg."

"Hamburg, *sí*," he said, chuckling. The German name was a bit of a running joke among some of the locals. Ciudad del Este drew a wide range of Hispanics and native South Americans from neighboring countries, and it was home to sizable Muslim, Japanese, Taiwanese, and Korean communities. Few of them realized that the first Western settlers in nearby Colonia Independencia were retired German military from World War I—which explained the disproportionate number of places in the region with names like "Hotel Hamburg" or "Restaurante de Munich." Robledo understood that bit of history, and not just because he'd grown up in the area. Café Berlin was where he had first met Niklas Konig, the German investor who had later introduced him to Gerry Collins.

I'd shoot him again if I could.

The SUV stopped in front of the hotel, and Robledo stepped out. His goal on every trip was to keep a low profile. A thirty-dollar-per-night flophouse like Hotel Hamburg blended right in with the fume-filled traffic jams and bazaarlike shops on Avenida Monseñor Rodríguez, the main drag in the center of town. From there, another five thousand shops fanned out in all directions for a twenty-block area.

Robledo's only luggage was an overnight bag, which must have seemed odd to the late-night attendant behind the registration desk. Guests often checked into the hotel with a half dozen or more empty suitcases, leaving the next day with their take. Cheap electronics equipment and cigarettes were popular items, but only for the casual buyer. Little or no luggage was a sign of a serious player with a serious agenda—cash for weapons, sex, sex slaves, pirated software, counterfeit goods, cocaine by the ton, murder for hire, and just about everything else illegal—from phony passports to human body parts for medical transplants. Delivery could be arranged for all of it. For a price.

Robledo picked up a room key, which came with a handwritten message: his contact was waiting across the street at the bar. He dropped his bag in his room and then followed the directions in his message to the Fugaki Bar.

Late January was the height of the summer rainy season. Even after midnight, the potholes in the street remained filled with the muddy remnants of the afternoon downpour. Some of the puddles were like sinkholes, seemingly big enough to swallow up everything from an unsuspecting tourist to a truckload of counterfeit Mont Blanc pens. Robledo stepped around them, passing a restaurant called Lebanon. It was a reminder that the Tri-Border Area was home to an estimated twenty-five thousand residents of Arab descent. Born and raised in Argentina, Robledo was often taken for Hispanic, and his Spanish was perfect. Not many people were aware that Robledo's first language was actually Arabic.

Ironically, coming off as Hispanic had actually worked to his advantage in cultivating Lebanese wealth. Robledo was the golden boy who had found a way around Abe Cushman's unspoken refusal to take Arab money. Robledo and his contact, Gerry Collins, had found a way to slide under Cushman's radar and bring Saudis to the Cushman trough—investors with whom Cushman could never have done business without jeopardizing his stature in the Jewish American community, and without alienating the Jewish charities that would become his unwitting principal victims. For a time, Robledo's Arab clients loved him.

Lately, not so much.

"I don't like to be kept waiting," said Fahid.

He spoke in English, their common tongue, as Fahid's Arabic and Robledo's Lebanese were not a perfect mesh. Fahid was a badass—in any language, any culture, any country. He was the spokesman for Robledo's largest consortium of angry Saudi investors.

"I'm very sorry," Robledo said as he took a seat on the barstool beside Fahid. "We had some difficulties getting over the bridge. The usual midnight chaos."

Fahid tapped the rim of his shot glass. The bartender poured him a refill and also brought one for Robledo. They belted them back in unison. Robledo's throat burned, and his eyes hurt. He wasn't sure exactly what it was, but it must have been the drink of choice for the guy who had coined the word *firewater*. It was bad enough that the Fugaki had no air-conditioning. The liquor had Robledo's face glistening with sweat, and the conversation had not even started.

Fahid said, "That 'chaos,' as you call it, pays the light bill."

"My apologies," Robledo said. "Chaos was a poor choice of words. I meant 'business.'"

Big business. The official GDP of Paraguay was about $17 billion. The money moved illegally through banks in Ciudad del Este on an annual basis was estimated to be at least double that amount, much of it connected to *hawalas*. There was another $14 billion in black market trading of goods, from cigarettes to counterfeit designer watches. Fahid and his consortium held a 10 percent share, mostly in smuggling. Simple math dictated that the $2 billion Robledo had lost in the Cushman Ponzi scheme—the pipeline from Gerry Collins in Miami, through Lilly Scanlon at BOS/Singapore, to Cushman Investment in New York—was the financial equivalent of flushing months of profit down the toilet.

"I reviewed your latest videotape from the church," said Fahid. "Very impressive operation you are building."

"Thank you. Our computers should be targeting potential recruits by the end of the month."

"Not much good if there's no money to train them."

"I hear you."

"No. You're still hearing the message I delivered six months ago—that our patience is coming to an end. The message is different now: our patience has ended."

"You're putting me in an impossible situation."

"You put yourself there."

"No. This was not my fault."

"Are you suggesting it was *my* fault?"

"Not at all."

"Don't blame this on Abe Cushman and Gerry Collins. *You* were the one who put our money with them."

"I accept that," said Robledo. "But, please, listen to me. I have scoured the earth for our money. I have applied force at every conceivable pressure point. After three years, I am convinced that there is more at work here than Cushman's Ponzi scheme. There is a much bigger reason for our losses. I beg you to make the consortium understand that this was not within my control."

Fahid looked at him like a judge about to pronounce sentence. Finally, he gave another tap to the rim of his shot glass. The bartender poured refills, which Robledo took to mean that he had another minute or two of Fahid's time.

"This may sound crazy," said Robledo, "but it is my firm conclusion that we lost our money because the U.S. government *wanted* us to lose it."

Fahid stared at him for a moment. Then he burst out in laughter. Laughed so hard that he nearly fell off his stool.

"I'm serious," said Robledo. He removed Evan Hunt's report from the inside pocket of his blazer and laid it on the bar, which brought Fahid's laughter under control.

"What's this?" asked Fahid.

"An analysis of thirty-eight reasons why Abe Cushman was a fraud. A friend of Tony Mandretti prepared it years before Cushman blew up. Mandretti gave it to me before I met with Collins."

"Does Mandretti's friend work for the government?"

"No. But if some quant in Chinatown was able to come up with this, can anyone seriously believe that the federal regulators were unaware?"

Fahid took a moment to absorb what was said. "So they knew."

"Yes, they knew," said Robledo. "It's my belief that they took that knowledge and cut a deal with Gerry Collins. They could have promised him anything from a reduced sentence to better food in the federal penitentiary he was headed for. I don't know what he got. But it's clear to me what Collins gave them: *us.* Collins and his friend with the boat in Miami—Mr. Konig, whom I took care of personally—lured me into the scheme just in time for us to lose two billion dollars."

Fahid belted back another Paraguayan firewater. "Mandretti gave you this three years ago. Why am I hearing this government conspiracy theory just now?"

Robledo reached into his pocket and removed another document. "Do you remember the Treasury Department memo I told you about?"

"Of course."

Robledo laid the memo on the bar, then read the key language: "'Treasury's most promising lead as to concealment of proceeds from the Cushman fraud remains Gerry Collins' banking activities at BOS/Singapore, and the key person of interest at BOS has been identified as Lilly Scanlon.'"

"Yes, I remember. This memo is what put that girl Scanlon and her boyfriend in the crosshairs."

"I think this memo is part of the government's plan," Robledo said.

"How?"

"It came to me so out of the blue, like a gift from Allah. Now I know it was no gift. It was leaked to me to keep me chasing after the money."

"Why would the U.S. government want you to keep looking?"

"Because it was one thing to lose my clients' money in the Ponzi scheme. It is quite another for the U.S. government to actually find out the names of my clients."

Fahid studied the Treasury memo, took another look at Evan Hunt's analysis, and then shook his head. "This troubles me," he said.

"It should."

"My concern is that if the U.S. government wanted us to lose our money, then they must have known the true identity of your investors."

Robledo paused. He knew the consequences of any breach of client confidentiality. "No, you are jumping ahead. It has to be the case that the Americans simply had suspicions about my investors. That's why they are using this girl Scanlon. She's the bait they want me to chase. The longer I chase, the more chances they have to find out who I represent."

"That may be. But I'm sure you will agree with me that if that information did get out, neither Gerry Collins nor the U.S. government is to blame."

Robledo swallowed hard, but he knew there was only one correct response. "I wouldn't blame anyone but myself for that."

"Nor would I," Fahid said, his stare cutting right through him. He took Robledo's shot glass, tipped it back, and slammed the empty glass on the bar. Then he left a hundred-dollar bill and said good night.

Robledo was alone at the bar, watching through the Fugaki's plate glass window as Fahid made his way out, crossed the street, and passed another busload of Brazilians checking in at the Hotel Hamburg.

49

"WHO ATE THE LEFTOVER PIZZA?" ASKED CONNIE.

I had no idea that the city that never sleeps extended all the way to New Jersey. Her kitchen was like an active crime scene, more like two o'clock in the afternoon than two in the morning. Before we'd gone to bed, Scully's tech expert had called to confirm that there was indeed spyware on my BlackBerry, which would have allowed someone to overhear my conversation with Evan before he died. Scully called him in again after the computer crash, so there were five of us in a cramped kitchen trying to figure out what had happened to Connie's outdated PC, though Connie's immediate concern was the case of the missing slice.

"I ate it an hour ago," I said.

Connie grumbled as she closed the refrigerator door, then pulled up a barstool next to Lilly. I stole a quick glance, and all that kept Lilly from doing a face-plant on the floor was her elbow on the Formica counter and her chin resting in her hand. All of us were exhausted, but Lilly especially was struggling to focus on what Scully's friend was telling me.

"The attempted download completely fried the motherboard and the hard drive along with it," he said.

Zach Epstein was the same former FBI tech expert whom

Scully had called upon to find the spyware on my BlackBerry. Zach was definitely not "retired." A good techie with as little as two years of "FBI" experience on his résumé could easily land a job in private security that paid ten times his former government salary.

"Exactly what does that mean?" I asked.

Zach said, "Ever see that old public service announcement on TV with the egg in the frying pan: This is your brain on drugs? That's pretty much Connie's hard drive."

"Can we recover Evan's file?"

"I've run every diagnostic test I can run," said Zach. "The file is not there to recover, is what I'm telling you. The download failed, and in the process it fried the hard drive. I could recover Connie's address book and probably 80 percent of whatever data was there when you attempted the download. But I can't recover a file that never made it to the hard drive."

"There has to be a way to recover that file," said Scully. "People are always saying that e-mails never really go away."

"Normally the surest route would be to access Evan's e-mail account and retrieve his sent messages."

"Then let's do that," said Scully.

"Already tried," said Zach. "Not only has the account been shut down, but there's a monster security wall around it. No doubt that's part of the homicide investigation."

"Or part of the continued cover-up of Operation BAQ," I said. "There has to be another option."

"Just to make sure we're not overlooking the obvious, is there any way for me to get my hands on Evan's actual computer?"

"Gone," I said. "Whoever killed him took it."

"That's what I figured," said Zach. "The other possibility is that even though the message is no longer in your in-box, we could recover it from the bank's server. Do you think the bank's IT people would work with us on that?"

"I wouldn't even ask," I said.

"I get paid to do things the hard way, but it would be a whole lot easier if I had the bank's cooperation."

"That's not possible," I said.

"Why not?" asked Zach.

I glanced at Scully, who gave me a little nod that said Zach was cool and that it was okay to share my theory with him. "You said before that the BlackBerry is a highly secure smartphone, less vulnerable to spyware than most. And my BlackBerry was made even more secure by enhancements from BOS security."

"That's right," said Zach.

"Someone still managed to load spyware without ever having touched my phone. It was a remote implant, which makes me think it was the bank that put it there."

Zach said, "That would be a likely source, at least from the standpoint of technical ease and opportunity. But 'the bank' is a big place."

I didn't see a reason to be more specific, but Scully overrode me.

"We think Joe Barber authorized the spyware," said Scully.

Zach was like a walking computer, and I could almost see his mind working as he processed the various puzzle pieces we'd fed him: the phone call from Evan telling me that he'd decrypted the Treasury memo; the e-mail with his decrypted attachment sent minutes later; Evan's body in the Dumpster minutes after he'd hit Send.

"You're saying that Joe Barber killed your friend and stole his computer to stop you from getting a decrypted copy of the Treasury memo on Operation BAQ?"

"To keep *the world* from seeing that memo," I said. "I'm not saying he physically pulled the trigger. But, yes, I believe he's behind it."

Zach glanced at Connie, as if he were suddenly interested in the family consensus. "You agree with him?"

"That depends," said Connie. "I would need to know more about how that spyware you found on Patrick's BlackBerry actually works. It's just hard for me to imagine someone—especially someone like Joe Barber—eavesdropping on Patrick's BlackBerry in real time, twenty-four hours a day, just in case something of interest came along."

Zach smiled, as if the statement were naïve. "That's not the way it works. Virtually all spyware is programmed to alert the master when the target—in this case, Patrick—is actually using his telephone."

"But I use my phone a lot," I said. "Someone would have to listen to hours and hours of crap in the hope of getting ten seconds of meat, unless there's a way to refine it further."

"There is," said Zach. "More sophisticated spyware can be programmed to alert the master only when you communicate with certain phone numbers."

"So it's possible that when Evan called to tell me about the decryption, the 'master,' as you call him, received an automatic alert that I was on the phone with Evan."

"That's right."

"Can you tell by looking at my phone if that alert system was, in fact, part of the spyware?"

"No. That would only be in the master's equipment."

"Damn. Nothing's ever easy," I said.

"You got a plan to deal with someone like Joe Barber?" Zach asked.

"Is that spyware on my BlackBerry still active, even though you've analyzed it?" I asked.

"Yeah, sure," said Zach.

"Then the answer to your question is yes," I said. "I do have a plan."

50

LILLY DIDN'T LIKE WHAT SHE WAS HEARING. TOO MUCH SCHEMING, too much at stake, too much *former* FBI involvement.

Ex-FBI, ex-lover, ex-anything. They all have an ex to grind, pun intended.

"Excuse me," she said as she pushed away from the kitchen counter. Her smartphone was fully charged, so she unplugged the cord and took everything with her. Patrick didn't even notice her get up. Scully and his tech buddy were talking over each other, and Patrick was in the middle.

"You're not going to bed, are you?" asked Connie, surprised.

"Bathroom," said Lilly. She left the kitchen, taking little steps. The official Boy Scouts of America 100th Anniversary sweatpants that Connie had loaned her for the night were long enough to cover her feet like footies. She was virtually sliding across the tile floor to the master bathroom off Connie's bedroom. She could hear the strategizing in the kitchen right up until she switched on the light and closed the bathroom door.

Lilly went to the sink and looked in the mirror. *Frightful.* Weeks of worry had left bags beneath her eyes that were way beyond the miracle of any concealer. But that was merely the superficial toll. The youthful gleam in her eyes, the sparkle from within, had completely vanished. Fear had replaced it, the fear of being trapped. It had been a while since she'd heard from her source—the ex–federal agent who wanted to protect her. Another ex. Another ax to grind. Lilly knew it was just a matter of time before he gave her another assignment.

A sharp pain gripped her abdomen. It was her "funny tummy," as she called it, but there was nothing funny about it. This episode was so bad that she doubled over, unable to stand, and sat on the tile floor. Leaning against the wall was the only way to hold herself up. She breathed in and out until the pain subsided.

I can't do this anymore.

Lilly closed her eyes to consider her options. There weren't many—and the really good ones totaled zero. She chose the least of the worst. She powered on her telephone: 2:13 A.M. That didn't matter. The invitation had been to "call me any-time." Lilly had committed the number to memory. She dialed and counted the rings until she heard the voice on the line. A sleepy voice that simply grunted out the word "hello."

"It's Lilly Scanlon, please don't hang up."

There was a pause on the line, perhaps a moment to check the clock on the nightstand and see what godforsaken time of day it was. "Lilly, is everything okay?" asked Agent Henning.

"I'm sorry to call you at this hour, but I—I don't know who else to turn to."

"It's fine. I'm glad you reached out to me."

The pain cut through Lilly's abdomen again. She gritted her teeth and struggled through it. "I can't talk here."

"Where are you?"

"Still in New Jersey. Can we meet somewhere? Just you and me?"

"Not Patrick?"

"No. Not Patrick."

There was another pause, as if Agent Henning were thinking through the schism. "Okay, that's fine," Henning said. "I can meet you anywhere, anytime. Right now, if you want."

"No, not now. Patrick is going into the bank in the morning. I can't get away until then."

Get away? Lilly wondered how that must have sounded to an FBI agent, but there was a light knock on the bathroom door before she could clarify.

Connie asked, "Lilly, are you okay in there?"

Lilly's heart raced. She tightened her grip on the phone, whispered the meeting place she had decided upon prior to making the call—"Septuagesimo Uno Park, nine A.M."—and quickly hung up.

"Lilly?" called Connie.

She kicked herself for having chosen a park with a Latin name, the pronunciation of which she'd mangled. No way Henning had understood. Lilly banged out a clarifying text message, adding for good measure that it was on Seventy-first Street at West End.

Another knock. "Lilly?"

Lilly pushed herself up from the floor, took a deep breath to calm her nerves, and opened the door. She was face-to-face with Connie.

"Were you on the phone?"

Lilly didn't know whether to lie or tell her the truth. "No," she lied.

"Oh. I thought I heard you talking."

"No," said Lilly—but it was a squeak, her nervous helium voice. She tried to cover with an explanation. "I was just checking my voice mail."

Connie gave her a funny look. "Whatever. Anyway, Patrick has a question for you. Can you join us?"

Join us. Of all the simple questions Lilly had heard in her lifetime, that one had to be the most complicated.

"Sure," said Lilly, "whatever you need."

51

MONGOOSE WAS ON THE MOVE. HE DID HIS BEST WORK AT FOUR A.M.
More than three years had passed since his last visit to
Ciudad del Este. That one had been the capstone in a string
of nine visits over a four-month period, all paid for by the
U.S. government, all under the name Niklas Konig, a wealthy
investor from Berlin. German was only one of five languages
he spoke fluently, and on his first visit with Manu Robledo
he'd spoken mostly Spanish. By their fifth meeting, he had befriended Robledo. By the eighth, they'd forged a business relationship. After the ninth, Robledo had traveled back to Miami
with him to meet his Cushman connection, Gerry Collins.
Collins had already been brought on board: Mongoose, personally, had sat him down, told him that Treasury was fully
aware that he and Cushman were running a Ponzi scheme,
and promised that Collins could get off with a prison sentence
of ten years—as opposed to ten decades—if he cooperated.
Operation BAQ had launched without a hitch. Manu Robledo
and his highly suspect clientele would take a $2 billion loss
without ever knowing that they'd been set up. A thing of
beauty, and a perfectly acceptable result under a public policy
cost-benefit analysis, if only Cushman's scheme had, in fact,

been worth the mere $6 billion that Treasury had estimated, not $60 billion.

Morons.

Mongoose climbed another step in the dark stairwell, then stopped. A bumpy puddle-jumper flight from São Paulo had left him with a nearly unbearable pain that radiated down his leg. Another painkiller would have been useless. After three years of living on pills, his system had built up a tolerance. Excruciating pain was a way of life, though sometimes it was so bad that it was impossible to stay on task. The pain—more specifically, the pills—had definitely made it impossible for him to remain with the agency. At least that was what the psychiatrists and pain-management specialists had told the bureaucrats on the disciplinary review panel. Shitheads, all of them.

Focus, damn it!

He closed his eyes and breathed in and out, slowly, letting his mind conquer this useless part of himself. After a minute or two, the pain lessened; it never completely went away. Pain was always somewhere, in his spine, in his lower back, in his hip. The worst was the pain down the back of his leg that felt as if some sadist had heated a knife with a blowtorch, jabbed him in the ass with the white-hot blade, and sliced him open from hip to heel. Pain on some level was with him every minute of every day, ever since he'd awakened in the hospital three years before and heard the doctor say that his motor function was unimpaired and that, in time, the pain could possibly go away. Possibly. The doc had been only half right. There were days when Mongoose would swear that there was something to be said for paralysis—for no feeling at all.

Only the promise of revenge kept him going. Sweet revenge.

Mongoose lifted his right foot, the less painful option under the current pain pattern, and took another step. He knew the

Hotel Hamburg well. He had stayed there before, and he had climbed the back stairwell many times. The elevator would have been easier, but there was a security camera inside it, and the last thing he wanted was a digital recording of his visit. He knew the doors to the stairwell were never locked, knew that there were thirty-two steps from ground level to the second floor. He climbed the last eight slowly, then opened the door at the top of the stairway.

The hallway was empty.

Without a sound, Mongoose let the door close behind him, and he started toward Room 217. Carpeting muffled his footfalls. He needed to go only as far as the fifth door on the right. His stealth was merely a precaution to prevent any light sleepers from checking out a noise in the hallway and laying eyes upon him.

He stopped outside the fifth door. The rooms on either side of 217 were vacant. Mongoose had paid the desk clerk to make sure of it. He had the key to 215, which was an adjoining room to 217. He also had Room 219—just to make sure no one would overhear what was about to happen in 217.

He entered Room 215 and locked the door behind him. He did not switch on the lights. The glow of the moon between the parted draperies, through the window that overlooked a parking lot, was the only light in the room. He closed the drapes and waited for his eyes to adjust. Then he stepped farther into the room and laid his bag on the bed. It was his tool kit. He unzipped it and found the serrated diver's knife. Just enough moonlight shone through the crack between drapery panels for the blade to glisten. He fastened his tool kit to his belt and stepped closer to the door to the adjoining room—the door to Room 217.

He took a deep breath, adjusting his mind-set, reminding himself that his actions were justified by more than just revenge. His old "friend" Robledo had shared much about himself—

about his grandparents coming to the Tri-Border Area in the major wave of Lebanese-Muslim immigration that followed the Arab-Israeli conflict in 1948; about his father, though an Argentine citizen, returning to battle the Israelis in the 1982 Lebanese War, only to fall alongside another 17,000 Lebanese killed. The war was considered an Israeli victory, with one major footnote: Hezbollah took control of southern Lebanon and southern Beirut. Mongoose was quite familiar with rumors that it also controlled the Tri-Border Area. One of many unsettling rumors. He'd also heard that the homicide rate in Ciudad del Este was more than five times that of New York City.

Mongoose wondered how many men had boosted the rate in both cities in the same week.

Mongoose threw his weight against the door and busted through to the adjoining room. Before Robledo could move, before he was even fully awake, Mongoose grabbed him, cuffed his hands behind his back, and threw him down onto the floor. He drove his knees into Robledo's spine, shoved one side of his face against the carpet, and put the knife to his neck.

"Don't move," said Mongoose.

"Please, don't!"

"Quiet!" he said, making sure that Robledo felt the cold steel of the knife as he reached into his bag with his other hand and removed his tool of choice. Not the garrote. This time, it was the same class of tool that had been used on Gerry Collins.

"I can make you a rich man, I promise," said Robledo, his voice shaking. "Just don't do this, please!"

"Begging already, Manu?"

Robledo's body stiffened, as if perhaps there were a spark of recognition. "Do I know you?"

Mongoose leaned closer and hissed into his ear. "Don't you remember me, Manu? It's your old friend, Niklas Konig."

"No, no way! Konig is dead."

It was the one thing the Central Intelligence Agency had

done right after his shooting—the certificate of death issued for Niklas Konig.

His hands a blur, Mongoose dropped the knife and, with the speed of a trained assassin, wrapped the wire saw around Robledo's neck. With enough back and forth, it was fully capable of beheading a man. Eventually.

Dead, you thought?

"You wish," said Mongoose as he jerked the wire saw.

"Please, stop! *Please!*"

Another jerk of the wire deepened the flesh wound, enough to reveal that Robledo was a screamer.

"Stop!"

His begging made it all the more satisfying for Mongoose, but clearly a gag was essential. He quickly taped Robledo's mouth shut, but as he tucked the roll away in his bag, Robledo squirmed and managed to kick over the cocktail table. Mongoose brought him under control with a tug on the wire, taking care not to inflict fatal injury, the tape muting Robledo's cries of pain.

The upended cocktail table lay a few feet away, the four legs pointing upward like a dead animal with rigor mortis. For demonstrative effect, Mongoose went to work on one of the table legs, the saw cutting through solid pine in seconds. It dropped to the floor just inches from Robledo's eyes, which were wide with fright, as big as saucers. Mongoose leaned closer to his prey, adding a touch of poetry to his sense of justice: "NATO-approved commando wire saw, Manu. Purchased right here in Ciudad del Este. Just like the one you used on Gerry Collins."

Robledo groaned, but, again, the duct tape did its work.

Mongoose checked the thickness of the carpeting. Things would surely get messy, and his mind flashed with thoughts of sleeping guests in the room below waking to the steady drip, drip of blood seeping through the ceiling.

The bathtub.

With one hand Mongoose drew the wire tighter, and with the other, he grabbed Robledo's shirt and dragged him across the floor to the bathroom.

"Be a good boy, Manu. Do exactly as I say, and I promise to make this quick."

As quick as paint drying.

52

I WAS IN THE BOS MIDTOWN OFFICE BEFORE NINE A.M. I DIDN'T
have to pretend to be busy. My team leader had reams of finan-
cials for me to review in preparation for Monday's meeting with
the private equity group in Chicago—the one I had promised
to attend, no problem, "my plate is clear." Not until after lunch
did things settle down enough for me to make my move, which
was okay. Joe Barber was out of the office most of the day and
couldn't see me until four forty-five. It was clear that his assistant
had penciled me in only because she thought it was adorable
that a junior FA thought he could ring the executive suite and
schedule a meeting with the head of private wealth management.
There was definite surprise in her voice when she called me back
at four thirty.

"This is to confirm your four forty-five meeting with Mr.
Barber," she said.

"I know. I have an appointment."

"I mean, he really is going to see you."

I thanked her and rode the elevator upstairs. As the doors
opened and I stepped out onto the polished marble floor, it occurred to me that I was probably setting a bank record for the
number of times a junior FA had set foot in the executive suite
in a single week.

Amazing what the inside track on $2 billion will do for you.

Barber's assistant offered me coffee or a soda, which I declined, and then she led me down the hall to Barber's office. He was behind his desk, pacing as he spoke into his headset on a phone call, and he waved us in. His assistant directed me to the armchair, and then she tiptoed out of the office and closed the door.

"We need to hit the links again soon," Barber said into his headset, about to wrap up his call.

My focus was on my plan—not just what I would tell him, but how I would deliver it. I'd been doing dry runs in my head since dawn, however, and I was starting to fear that it would come across as too rehearsed. I allowed my eyes to wander across the cherry-paneled walls, a quick survey of the trappings of Wall Street success. Some would have regarded the shrine that Barber had erected to himself as clutter, but there was indeed order to the plaques and mementos encased in glass and gold-leaf frames. His early days at Saxton Silvers. His service at Treasury. His elbow rubbing with the right politicians. I'd noticed much of it on my last visit, but this time I was struck by the contrast to what I'd seen in Evan's apartment. If Evan's walls told the story of Wall Street thievery, Barber's walls told the story of . . . well, maybe it wasn't such a contrast.

Barber ended his phone call and laid his headset atop his desk. It had been a pleasant call, judging from his expression, but all sign of pleasantries faded as he came around to the front of his desk, leaned against the edge, and faced me.

"I assume this is about Lilly Scanlon's banking files," he said.

Less than forty-eight hours had passed since his Wednesday-evening meeting with Lilly and me, when I had sat in this very armchair, when Lilly and I had received each other's data with the challenge to find the missing $2 billion.

"That's correct," I said.

He folded his arms, a smug smile creasing his lips. "I feel it's only fair to tell you that I've already received Lilly's report on your data. Very interesting."

It was a weak bluff. "I don't believe you."

"Of course you don't. But that doesn't surprise me."

There was a light knock on the door, and Barber's assistant poked her head into the office.

"I'm very sorry to interrupt, but Mr. Lloyd has a family emergency."

Even Barber was taken aback, and it wasn't his emergency. "What is it?" asked Barber.

"I have a doctor on the line from Lemuel Shattuck Hospital in Boston." Then she looked at me with sadness in her eyes and said, "It's about your father."

It was the kind of news no one wanted to receive, but I was checking Barber's reaction. Under my witness protection profile—the life I had been living—Patrick Lloyd's father was deceased. I wondered if Barber realized that we were talking about Peter Mandretti's father. If he did, he did not let on.

"Would you like me to forward the call again?" his assistant asked.

I had my BlackBerry with me; confronting Barber about the spyware was part of the plan I had discussed with Scully.

"Yes, please do," said Barber. "Forward it to his BlackBerry."

The way he'd said it confirmed in my mind that Barber was behind the spyware, or that he at least knew it was installed. But in a "family emergency" it wouldn't have made sense to insist on using another phone, anything less expeditious.

His assistant went back to her desk. My BlackBerry vibrated in my pocket. "I can take it in the lobby," I said.

"Please, use my study," said Barber.

His offer of privacy was, of course, pointless, since he would hear it anyway through spyware. But after the doctor's call, my actions were those of a son anxious for news about a family emergency that involved his father, so I stepped into the study that was adjacent to his main office and took the call. The woman on the line introduced herself as an oncologist, Dr. Alice Kern.

"I'm calling about a patient named Sam Carlson," she said. "Is he . . ."

"No. But the situation is grave. We don't have any family information on file, but he tells us that you are his son."

I took a deep breath. "So he's conscious?"

"Yes."

"How long does he have?"

"You should come immediately. Special arrangements have been made for you to stay at his bedside until it's time."

"Thank you for that."

"You're welcome.

"Does he know I'm coming?"

"Yes. He specifically asked for you."

"He did?"

"Yes," she said. "He indicated that there is something he wishes to tell you face-to-face."

Enough had been said on a phone with spyware. I didn't push the doctor to speak further. "Tell him I'm on my way."

The call ended, and my knees felt like rubber. I knew that I had to hurry, but for a moment I couldn't move. I was scared for my dad, for my sister, for myself. I felt sorry for Evan Hunt and his family. I wanted to call Lilly, but I didn't dare use the BlackBerry that the Wall Street bully in the next room had essentially converted to his own use with spyware. His ego was everywhere, even in this private study, the walls of which were covered with still more glass-encased articles about him from newspapers and magazines. It was sickening—and then, suddenly, it was an epiphany.

The *Forbes* article on the wall caught my attention—almost slapped me in the face. I stepped closer and locked eyes with the tough, take-no-prisoners persona of "Joe Barber, deputy secretary of the U.S. Department of Treasury" staring back at me. Standing to his left in the photograph was the assistant secretary for Intelligence and Analysis, charged with overseeing the production and analysis of financial intelligence for use by policy makers in combating illicit financial activities. To his right was the assistant secretary for Terrorist Financing, responsible for developing anti–money laundering and counterterrorist financing policy.

But what snagged my full attention—what reached out, grabbed me by the neck, and shook me—was the subtitle in small but bold letters:

Is al-Qaeda broke?

"Holy shit," I said aloud.

I suddenly knew who Robledo's clients were, knew why an undercover agent had duped him into investing $2 billion through Gerry Collins, knew why Treasury had ignored Evan's thirty-eight red flags and allowed Cushman to collapse, knew what BAQ meant. I knew everything.

Most of all, I knew that I was running out of time.

I tucked away my BlackBerry and hurried out the door, apologizing to Barber on my way, though surely he didn't deserve one. There was an express elevator from the executive suite, so I didn't bother stopping for my overcoat. In less than sixty seconds I was in the ground-floor lobby, pushing through the revolving doors at the bank's main entrance. The sidewalk on Seventh Avenue was bustling with nine-to-fivers headed for the subway, eager to start their weekend. The zoo's white van was at the curb, where we had agreed last night that Connie would meet me, and I jumped into the passenger seat.

"We need to go to Lemuel Shattuck right now. It's an emergency."

"Is Dad okay?"

"A doctor called saying that I needed to get there as soon as possible, that there's something Dad wants to tell me."

"Oh, my God, he's dying."

I hated to see such pain in her expression, but we had to move. I took my BlackBerry from my pocket and removed the battery.

"What are you doing?

"The spyware in here could have GPS tracking. Taking out the battery disables it."

"If there's spyware on that phone, they already know you're headed to the hospital."

"Call me paranoid, but I don't want the guy who killed Evan Hunt knowing exactly where I am on the road between here and Boston."

"Okay, but if it's a tracking chip, it has its own power source. Removing the main battery won't disable it."

I figured a scoutmaster would know. I rolled down the window and tossed the phone into the street. A passing bus ground it into the pavement.

"That will," I said.

"If you were a scout, I'd pull your world conservation badge."

"Drive, Connie."

53

THAT FRIDAY, JUST AFTER DARK, MONGOOSE'S FLIGHT TOUCHED down at Westchester County Airport, a two-runway operation that served one of the largest fleets of corporate jets in America. The other passengers on board worked for the same hedge fund in Greenwich, just across the Connecticut state line in affluent Fairfield County. Mongoose didn't know them, didn't care why they were flying back from Ciudad del Este before dawn, and hadn't said a word to them since takeoff. Commercial nonstops from Ciudad del Este to New York were nonexistent. With $2 billion in the pipeline, Mongoose had jumped all over the open seat on a chartered Gulfstream jet, even if the car ride from White Plains to Midtown was over an hour.

"Your luggage will be on the tarmac," said the flight attendant.

"Got none," said Mongoose. No bags would naturally prompt a few questions at customs, but that was easier than trying to explain traces of blood, bone, and soft tissue on a commando wire saw.

The "enhanced interrogation" of Manu Robledo had taken about two hours. Using the nylon rope from his tool kit, Mongoose had completely immobilized his prey, flat on his back, in the bathtub. Robledo's arms were up over his head, his wrists tied to the plumbing fixtures. The assistance rail on the wall at the other end of the tub was strong enough to secure his feet, shoes off. The drain could handle any amount of blood, but just to make sure that Robledo didn't bleed out too soon, Mongoose had fastened a tourniquet around both wrists. Then he'd gone to work.

The left thumb had been first. Ignoring the muffled pleas for mercy, Mongoose had wrapped the wire around the base and pulled in rhythmic fashion: left, right, left right. All Robledo could do was grab the wire, but the result had been a severed index finger along with the severed thumb. As a general proposition, a wire saw took anything that got in its way—and Robledo's right thumb was next. Had it not been for the gag in his mouth, Robledo's screams would have awakened the entire hotel. But he was powerless to resist, save for the futile grasp of the wire saw, and the result was the same: simultaneous severance of his thumb and index finger. Mongoose had paused to allow Robledo to get a full grasp of his condition, making sure that Robledo watched as, one by one, he'd flushed the digits down the toilet. Then he'd tied another tourniquet to Robledo's ankle. The big toe would have been too predictable. He wrapped the wire saw around the middle of the foot, through the center of the arch, pulling it tight. From the look in Robledo's eyes, he'd begun to feel the pain even before the wire had torn into his skin. An opportunity had presented itself. Before starting the back-and-forth, Mongoose had looked Robledo in the eye and said, "I'm going to give you the chance to tell me everything. Do you want that chance?"

Robledo had nodded eagerly.

Talk, talk, talk. The starting point had been the Church of Peace and Prosperity International, which Robledo explained was a front for a data-mining operation that would identify and then recruit angry young Islamic extremists who were already in the United States and who could be persuaded to blow themselves up in shopping centers. There was nothing that Robledo would not have told him. At some point, however, the risk of someone hearing his screams was too great. Not that anyone in Ciudad del Este would bother to call the police, not that the police couldn't be bought off even if they came. As it was, Robledo had even confessed to participation in the worst terrorist attack ever against an Israeli diplomatic mission, the bombing of the Israeli embassy in Buenos Aires on March 17, 1992. False confessions were a definite hazard of wire saw interrogation. But it was a fact that no one had ever been prosecuted for the murder of twenty-nine and wounding of dozens more, many of them schoolchildren, in that bombing.

You never know.

Mongoose was through airport customs and immigration before six o'clock. He was walking toward the taxi stand when his cell phone rang. It was Barber.

"Joey baby, how are you?"

"I told you to stop calling me that. Listen to me."

Mongoose waved off a taxi and stood at the curb as Barber filled in the details of his meeting with Patrick Lloyd. The fact that Tony Mandretti had called for his son, had something to tell him from his deathbed, was of special interest.

"What are you afraid of, Joey? That Daddy is going tell his little boy about the crooked man who lives in a crooked house and runs a crooked bank?"

"No, asshole."

"Oh, I know," Mongoose said, his voice laden with even more sarcasm. "You're afraid Mandretti's going to tell his son that he didn't kill Gerry Collins, and that our own government paid him to confess."

"I know you believe that, but it's simply not true."

"Bullshit. You don't have to know everything about Operation BAQ to understand that it couldn't work unless

Robledo was on the outside leading his investors down the road we'd paved for them."

"You believe that. Mandretti believes it. Patrick Lloyd will believe it once he hears it from his father. I'm telling you that it is absolutely not true, but somebody planted that seed, and this is going to be a classic case of 'perception is reality' if I don't crush this right now."

Mongoose said, "It's just not clear to me why this is my problem to fix."

"Try this on for size: you won't see ten cents of the re-covered money if this father-son reunion blows the lid off Operation BAQ. You got nothing on me if that secret gets out."

Mongoose considered it. "Funny how life works, isn't it? I remember sitting in your study not too many hours ago, offer-ing you a partnership."

"Don't go there."

"Our interests actually seem to align here, partner."

"Brilliant. Just don't call me your partner."

"That's fine, Little Joe. Where is Lloyd now?"

"He and his sister are driving to Boston."

"I'll head them off."

"No."

"Excuse me?"

"You and I may be forced to sleep together, but I am not going to roll over and put myself in the position of having to explain the sudden disappearance of two young and perfectly healthy people like Patrick and his sister. Work from the other end: silence the sixty-year-old man who's already on his death-bed."

"That actually makes sense," said Mongoose, "but I'm not sure there's time."

"Use the corporate helicopter. It will have you in Boston at least two hours before Patrick and his sister can drive there."

"It's not just a race between Patrick Lloyd and me. We're talking about the hospital's prison unit. The place is on high alert since that phony priest got through security."

"Yeah, and I wonder who the phony priest was," Barber said.

"Never mind that," said Mongoose. "You said special arrangements were made for Patrick to be at his father's bedside. The question is, how do *I* get at his bedside?"

"Don't worry, I'll take care of that," said Barber.

Mongoose smiled. "Still have friends in high places, eh, Joey?"

"Just get on the helicopter," said Barber. "I said I'd take care of it."

"One more thing," said Mongoose, his tone very serious. "I understand that whomever you hired to take out Evan Hunt also took his computer with the encrypted Treasury memo."

"I didn't hire—"

"Spare me the lame denial," said Mongoose. "I just want you to know that it doesn't matter what you did with that computer, my safety valve is in place. Every day, your memo on Operation BAQ is automatically reset to go straight to the media at midnight, unless I manually deprogram the e-mail blast. The day I die is the day that memo launches. Is that clear?"

"Yes," said Barber.

"Good," said Mongoose. "Make sure it's crystal clear to your friends in high places."

54

CONNIE AND I DROVE NONSTOP TO BOSTON AND REACHED Lemuel Shattuck Hospital around nine o'clock. It was after the prison unit's regular visitation hours, but this wasn't a regular visit. Even so, the corrections officer at the ground-floor entrance told us that only one visitor at a time was allowed in the room.

"You go," said Connie. "He asked for you."

I completed the visitation paperwork, and my sister returned to the main lobby, where the Celtics game was playing on a flat-screen TV so small that Kevin Garnett looked like a Lilliputian, albeit one who could dunk. Searches were mandatory for all visitors, but in my case it was made all the more necessary by the fact that the metal detector showed no cell phone on my person, which the guard found utterly unbelievable for anyone whose work address was on Wall Street. He rode with me in the express elevator to the eighth floor, where another officer was posted at the locked entrance to the prison unit. Dr. Alice Kern met me in the waiting area, on the visitors' side of the security doors, and introduced herself.

"How is he?" I asked.

"We had to give him something for his pain, which, of course, makes him drowsy. He's asleep."

"But he asked me to come because he had something to tell me."

"Honestly, you got here much faster than I expected. You'll have your time with him. He'll come around in an hour or so."

"So, his passing is not . . . imminent?"

"It's not a matter of hours, no. But it could be any day. You can stay here as long as you like." She glanced at the corrections officer, adding, "It's been approved."

I signed my name on the register, and the guard inside the glass booth buzzed Dr. Kern and me into the unit. I followed her down the brightly lit hallway, my heart pounding. Once the secured entrance was behind us, the prison unit looked much like any other hospital, with the exception of the corrections officers posted at each end of the corridor. There were probably a few more security cameras than in a regular hospital, but this was definitely not San Quentin. We passed several more rooms and finally stopped outside an open doorway.

"When is the last time you saw your father?" she asked.

"When I was fifteen years old."

She arched an eyebrow. "In that case, I guess what I was about to say goes double: you should be prepared for a change in your father's appearance."

I had thought I was prepared, but hearing her say it made me realize that I wasn't. "You're right, I should be."

"Do you want me to go in with you, or do you prefer to be alone?"

I had not yet thought about it, but the answer came quickly. "Alone."

"That's fine. If you need anything, you can push the red call button by the bed."

"How much longer will you be here?" I asked.

"Don't worry, I'll be around."

I thanked her, which she acknowledged with a supportive nod. Then she retreated down the long corridor, and I turned to face the dark opening to my father's room, where he lay deep in drug-induced sleep. After one tentative step forward, I stopped, the prognosis replaying in my mind.

It could be any day.

I was suddenly wracked with guilt, my feet nailed to the floor. The last five days had been all about my father, and this was the third time since Monday that I'd tried to see him. That made for a grand total of three such attempts since my fifteenth birthday. Did that make me a lousy person? An angry young man, forever bitter that in finding his conscience, my father's choice to turn against the mob had ended in the death of my mother? Or was I a good son who respected the courage of a father who had come to the painful realization that the only way to protect himself and his children was never to see them again? The answer was complicated, but I had no doubt that guilt was the reason I had jumped at Agent Henning's offer to arrange for first-rate cancer treatment in exchange for six months of spying on Lilly in Singapore. I wondered if my father knew what I had done. I wondered if he would care.

I wondered, too, if guilt was the reason I felt the way I did about Lilly—that I was so desperate for *something* good to come out of a bad situation.

"Sir, you can't hang out in the hallway," the corrections officer said. I hadn't even heard her come up behind me. "It's not allowed. You either have to go into the room or go back to the waiting area."

"Sorry," I said, breathing out some of my anxiety. "I guess I'll go in."

55

BARBER'S MIND WAS ON ANYTHING BUT CHARITY, BUT HE WAS stuck hosting a table for ten at a black-tie gala for yet another organization that had conferred "philanthropist of the year" honors on his wife and his checkbook. Vanessa lived for these events, and it annoyed her to no end when he checked his BlackBerry in the middle of one of her stories. But he might well blow his brains out if, yet again, he had to hear about Todd, "the world's most fabiola-amazing decorator," who had raced across Midtown, loaded up Vanessa's Range Rover, and rescued $11,000 worth of ice sculptures that had been mistakenly delivered to the Waldorf instead of the Pierre.

Barber froze. Finally, the message he'd been waiting for: "Mr. W. will take your call now." It was from the office of the national security advisor. He rose quickly, angry for many reasons, not the least of which was the fact that an intellectual inferior like Brett Woods had the power to make him jump.

"Excuse me, everyone," he said to his table guests, loud enough to be heard over a twenty-piece band that was playing Gershwin.

Vanessa shot him a death ray. She hadn't even gotten to the part where a sudden stop on Fifth Avenue had broken a swan's neck, but "clever Todd" had just told everyone it was a stuffed turkey.

"My apologies, but this may take a while," said Barber.

"The White House calling again, Joe?" his tennis buddy asked with a smile.

Barber forced a little laughter. "No, those days are over."

"Please hurry back," his wife said flatly.

Barber walked quickly through the ballroom, weaving between banquet tables, avoiding eye contact with anyone who might grab him by the sleeve and corner him for a networking opportunity. He exited to the hotel's mezzanine level, at the end of a long row of carved oak doors, leaving the buzz of the band and the crowd behind him. A staff member directed him down the hall to a vacant room, where he could make a call in private. It was a cozy, windowless business suite with a conference table, a fireplace, and a brass chandelier. He tipped her a twenty, closed the door, and dialed Brett Woods.

"I've been trying to reach you for three hours," said Barber. "Did they not tell you it was urgent?"

"I was in a meeting with Clark," he said, meaning the CIA director. "More trouble with Operation BAQ. The collateral damage is much broader than we thought."

The innocent investors were collateral damage. "I thought all of Cushman's investors had been accounted for."

"Different kind of collateral damage. It seems that our intelligence on the terrorist connections of some of our targets was faulty."

"Meaning what?"

"A number of the 'suspected' terrorist funders that were pulled into the Ponzi scheme had nothing to do with terrorism."

Barber leaned against the marble mantel, not quite believing his ears. "The whole justification for Operation Bankrupt al-Qaeda was that these investors were financing terrorism. Are you telling me that we targeted a bunch of rich Arabs with no terrorist connections?"

"To some extent, yes."

"Damn it! I should *never* have listened to you in the first place. I conceived this as a Treasury operation—but, *noooo*, you had to bring in the CIA. Thanks to your stroke of genius, we have a rogue CIA agent named Mongoose putting the screws to us. And now, to top it all off, you're telling me that the CIA didn't even have the intelligence right."

"I didn't say *none* of the investors had links to terrorism. But it now appears that many were, well, like I said: collateral damage."

"You assured me that the CIA had nailed down the terrorist-financing connection. I would never have given the green light otherwise."

"That's bullshit, Joe. Now that we got bin Laden, everybody wants to forget how desperate the administration was to strike a deathblow against al-Qaeda."

"I wasn't desperate. I wanted to get this right."

"You knew this was an ambiguous situation. That's the reason I recommended that we go to the CIA instead of the Justice Department. Justice couldn't simply freeze their accounts under the Patriot Act—we *suspected* they were terrorist financers, but we couldn't *prove* it."

Barber took a seat at the conference table, nearly collapsing into the leather chair. "The fallout from this will be unbelievable."

"Only if it gets out," said Woods.

"That's why my call was so urgent. Mandretti is on his deathbed. He summoned his son because he has something to tell him."

"He might just want to say good-bye."

"Or he wants to be at peace before he dies. My guess is that his son will come out of the meeting believing the same BS that his father believes—that the government forced him to confess."

"Is Mandretti's son with him now?"

"They're in the hospital room together, but my sources tell me that Mandretti is not conscious."

"What are the chances that he will regain consciousness?"

"I don't know. But I don't want to take the risk."

Woods did not respond, and Barber sensed the need to address his apparent reservations. "Don't get sanctimonious on me, Brett. We're talking about a little acceleration for a terminally ill man who has a matter of hours to live. A man who, by the way, is clearly talking out of school about his role in Operation BAQ."

"What are you proposing?"

"I've already sent Mongoose."

"What do you mean you *sent* him? You can't send a rogue agent to do anything."

"I had no choice. If he thinks we're taking out Mandretti without his involvement, he'll smell a rat. I'm living under a standing threat from Mongoose: If I double-cross him, the decrypted version of my memorandum outlining Operation BAQ will go viral over the Internet."

"You said taking Evan Hunt's computer would eliminate that threat."

"I said reduce, not eliminate."

"A civilian casualty is a high price to pay for threat reduction."

"Nobody expected a ninety-eight-pound weakling to fight to the death over his computer."

Woods was silent, but an aura of acquiescence came over the phone. "Where is Mongoose now?"

"In Boston, one block away from the hospital," said Barber. "Got him there by helicopter but had to put him on hold. I need you to pull a few strings to get him inside the room."

"What's the plan?"

"Mandretti is receiving a variety of potent medications intravenously. Mongoose will simply make an adjustment to the IV, and Mandretti won't be talking."

Woods considered it. "You said the son is there. Can you trust Mongoose to confine his mission to the old man?"

Barber didn't respond right away. "That's impossible for me to answer."

"I want to know what you think."

"Here's what I think," said Barber. "If Mandretti wakes up and talks to his son, I can guarantee you that Mongoose *won't* confine his mission to the old man. Mongoose wants his money."

Woods seemed to appreciate the conundrum. "All right. Let me make a phone call."

"Call me right back."

"Yeah," said Woods. "Give me five minutes."

56

I COULDN'T BELIEVE I WAS IN THE SAME ROOM WITH MY FATHER.

I'd been standing at his bed rail for several minutes, unable to move, watching him sleep. I wasn't sure what to do.

Do I lean over and give him a kiss?

Do I touch his hand?

Do I even know him anymore?

The room was quiet and dimly lit. It felt more like a hospice than a hospital, which had made the first thirty seconds even more painful. The last time I'd seen him, my father had been a handsome man in his prime. The image of him sharply dressed, not a hair out of place, ready to take my mother out on a Saturday night was firm in my memory. Even after I'd learned he was sick, my mind had never allowed me to conjure up what my father would look like when he was dead. Now, it wasn't much of a stretch to picture someone pulling the sheet up over his face.

That initial shock faded sooner than I would have guessed. I began to see little signs that reminded me of how full of life he'd once been. I laid my hand on his head, covering the baldness from his treatment, imagining him with jet black hair. That alone helped. I smiled at the sight of the scar that was still on his forehead. It had happened during our reenactment of the seventh game of the World Series. Connie had been at the plate. I was pitching. Dad was the unlucky catcher who'd learned the hard way that Connie threw her bat.

"Any signs of coming around?" asked Dr. Kern as she entered the room.

"Still sleeping," I said.

"You can try to wake him, if you like. But as I said, he's likely to be quite confused if you do."

"I'll wait," I said. "This quiet time is giving me a chance to adjust."

She went to the IV. "Let me just shut this thing off. I had him down to twenty-five milligrams, but that doesn't seem to be doing the trick."

"I don't want him to wake up in pain," I said.

"He can't get more than six hundred milligrams every twenty-four hours anyway. We're there." She walked around to the side of the bed and made the adjustment.

"If there's anything you need, let me know."

I thanked her, and she left the room. Then I looked at my father, reached through the railing, and touched his hand. His breathing was steady, but quiet.

"If there's anything *you* need, let *me* know," I said.

57

THE WHIRRING BLADES OF A SIKORSKY S-76B BLEW PUFFS OF snow across the heliport as the BOS corporate helicopter touched down in Boston. Touchdown was delayed more than thirty minutes due to weather. Mongoose hurried into the terminal and retrieved a detailed voice mail message from Barber. It laid out the plan.

As instructed, Mongoose took a taxi to Lemuel Shattuck Hospital and went to the food court on the ground floor, an enclosed mall-like area that was completely separate from the prison unit. He sat away from the crowd, alone at a table outside a sandwich shop that had already closed for the evening. From there, it was a classic case of "hurry up and wait." The package arrived twenty minutes later. The courier didn't introduce himself, but Mongoose recognized an operator from a private military firm when he saw one. He'd dealt with dozens of them when he was with the CIA. He assumed that Barber had hired the same private firm to pay Evan Hunt a visit while Mongoose was in Ciudad del Este; Hunt's job had "contract" written all over it. Mongoose took the package, no questions asked, and went into the men's room.

Three minutes later, he emerged wearing hospital scrubs

and a photo-identification badge that bore the name Henry Bozan, Nurse Anesthetist.

A nurse? Really?

As he passed a doughnut shop, he checked his reflection in the plate glass window. He hadn't liked the plan from the beginning but, seeing himself in nursing scrubs, he really didn't like it.

You are a disgraceful waste of talent.

Those words, buried in his memory, were suddenly burning in his brain. It was the blunt answer he'd gotten after confronting his platoon leader and demanding to know why he wasn't recommended for advancement to SEAL Team Six, the elite of the elite. Raw talent had never been an issue. He'd been one of many incredible young athletes, all former high-school and college stars in their own right, who'd entered basic underwater demolition/SEAL training in California. Six months of intense training—everything from two-mile ocean swims and "drown proofing" in frigid water to four-mile timed runs in soft sand and mountain endurance runs wearing forty-pound rucksacks— had whittled down the field of 250 candidates. Mongoose had emerged as one of nineteen who'd actually finished. But his platoon leader had never liked him—or maybe he'd just seen through him. It was often said that men who survived the rigors of training to become SEALs possessed much more than physical strength. Under any adversity, even in unbearable pain, they had the depth of character to put aside their own pain and fear to help a struggling buddy. There were always one or two who lacked that commitment to higher purpose, a few who managed to beat the odds in service of their own ego. A SEAL, however, was no tenured professor. The bad fits were inevitably rerouted, forced to stand aside as their former platoon performed "kill or capture" missions in the "sea, air, and land" war on terrorism, from the elimination of Iranian-trained snipers at the bottom of the pyramid to the takeout of bin Laden at the top. For

Mongoose, the bitter irony was that his reroute to the Treasury Department's financial war on terrorism had led him to the end of the road—a bullet to his spine, disabled by chronic pain.

He was the expendable pawn in Joe Barber's Operation BAQ.

"Excuse me, which way is the nurses' lounge?"

Mongoose turned to see a blue-haired senior citizen staring at him, a hospital volunteer.

"Hell if I know, lady."

He continued around the corner and found an alcove beyond the elevators. Barber's voice mail message had told him not to call, but he didn't care. He dialed the private number.

"I'm not in a place where I can talk," Barber said.

Mongoose heard the crowd noise in the background, could even hear a band playing "Stardust." "You've got two minutes to call me back," he said, then put away his phone and waited.

Two minutes more to consider his place in history. Rare indeed was the former SEAL and CIA agent who murdered civilians and turned against his own government. Some might put him in the category of Jeffrey MacDonald, the Green Beret who butchered his two daughters, ages five and two, after stabbing his pregnant wife thirty-seven times. Others would equate him with Robert Hanssen, the FBI counterintelligence agent who acted as a paid spy for the Soviet Union and Russia for two decades, telling the FBI after he was caught that his only motivation was the money. Mongoose saw himself as neither. It wasn't really about the money. He hadn't snapped under pressure. He was making idiots like Joe Barber pay for their arrogance, their narrow-mindedness, their sweeping definition of "collateral damage."

Some might even say he was a patriot.

Mongoose checked the time, and his phone rang. Barber was back on the line with ten seconds to spare on his deadline.

Mongoose pulled no punches. "I'm not going in as a nurse,

completely unarmed. If I go in as a corrections officer I can at least pack a sidearm."

"It's too risky to involve the Department of Corrections," said Barber. "This way we need no one's approval, no one's co-operation to get you in."

"Are you saying that I'm going in without anyone from corrections knowing anything about this?"

"Correct. Our techies have already hacked into the prison-unit records to add Henry Bozan to the list of approved practitioners on the pain-management team. You'll sail through security check-in."

A naked undercover mission. That made things more interesting. "You could have at least made me a physician."

"Going in as a nurse anesthetist gives you another layer of protection. If anyone questions what you're doing, tell them that you're following the directions of the anesthesiologist in charge of the team. The only treating physician in the prison unit right now is a general practitioner named Alice Kern. If she has a problem with anything you're doing, she'll have to follow up with the anesthesiologist. You can be in and out of there by the time she gets any answers."

This discussion was making him all the more aware of his own chronic condition, the pain that never stopped running down the back of his leg. "All right. I've seen enough pain-management specialists to pull this off."

"Not that this is a complicated assignment. You go straight to room eight thirty-four and check on the patient. The prison unit typically uses Demerol in an IV to manage pain for cancer patients. The maximum dosage for someone his size is one hundred milligrams every two hours. Whatever he's getting, adjust the drip to one hundred every hour. Leave before his breathing begins to slow. By the time you're outside the building, the patient will be in fatal cardiac arrest."

"What if Mandretti's son is still in the room?"

"It doesn't matter. He doesn't know who you are or what you look like. He has no reason to believe that you're not simply there doing your job."

"I still don't like going in unarmed."

"You can't adjust the IV dressed as a corrections officer. If someone were to walk into the room, or if a security camera were to pick up a corrections officer messing with medication, the only way out would be a gunfight. It's much cleaner this way. And it's too damn late in the game to change plans."

Mongoose couldn't argue, but he was naturally suspicious. "Fine," he said, "but remember what I told you. If I don't come out of that hospital alive—"

"My memo goes viral. I understand."

"Be sure you do," said Mongoose.

He ended the call and crossed the food court, following the signs marked Authorized Personnel Only on his way toward the prison unit.

58

I COULDN'T STOP TALKING. I WAS LEANING ON THE BED RAIL, MY father's hand in mine, telling him stories.

The minutes had passed too slowly in silence, and I'd suddenly felt the need to tell him everything I'd been doing for the past fifteen years. The stories kept coming, evaporating the gloom, and it didn't matter that he couldn't hear me. Maybe he could, on some level. I wondered how deep and restful his sleep actually was. My poor mother had married a man who snored like a grizzly bear. This was clearly drug-induced sleep, something altogether different. Quiet. Quiet awareness, maybe. Who knew?

I was telling him about my graduation from college when the door opened.

"Hello, I'm from the pain-management team."

The man didn't introduce himself as a physician, but he acted like one. Even after introducing myself, I still didn't get his name. He walked around to the other side of the bed and checked the monitors. If Dr. Kern was a model of bedside manner, he was more in line with my preconceived notion of prison-unit health care.

"Are you a doctor?" I asked.

"Henry Bozan, nurse anesthetist. How long has the patient been sleeping?"

"He was out when I got here. That was around nine."

"I thought I heard you talking."

It was an odd tone, almost accusatory. "I've been telling him stories as he sleeps," I said.

"So he hasn't told you anything?"

Another odd question. "No," I said.

"You may want to get some rest yourself. He probably won't come around until morning."

"Hopefully sooner than that. Dr. Kern reduced the Demerol."

He checked the drip hanging from the IV pole. "That's not a good idea. This patient is in serious pain."

"Dr. Kern said he's already at the daily maximum."

"I'm following the direct orders of the chief physician on the pain-management team."

"I'd prefer that you talk to Dr. Kern about that."

I heard voices in the hallway, someone approaching. The door opened. Dr. Kern entered with a distressed expression on her face and a corrections officer at her side.

"That's him!" she said.

The ensuing moments were a complete blur. The corrections officer rushed past Dr. Kern and drew his weapon. I dived forward, shielding my father. The nurse anesthetist was suddenly like a gymnast on a pommel horse, pushing himself up on the bed rail with two strong arms, swinging his legs over the bed—over me and my father—and propelling himself feet-first into the oncoming officer. Dr. Kern screamed as the gun flew from the officer's hand, slammed into the wall, and fell to the floor. The nurse-turned-gymnast got there first and emptied two quick rounds into the officer's chest, dropping him to the floor in a spray of blood. Then he slammed the door shut, grabbed Dr. Kern, and put the gun to her head.

"Don't move!" he said, meaning me.

59

ALARMS SOUNDED THROUGHOUT THE PRISON UNIT. DOOR AFTER door slammed in the hallway as the unit went into the hospital equivalent of lockdown.

Andie Henning raced down the hall from Room 826.

Andie's plan had started with Patrick's father. "Call Patrick," he'd told her, knowing the end was near, "and let him know that there's something I need to tell him, man to man." With his approval, Andie had taken it a step further, the key to her plan being that she would call Patrick on his BlackBerry—a phone compromised with spyware. It was a virtual lock that the eavesdropper would hear the news and take the necessary steps to stop Patrick's father from making a deathbed confession to his son about Operation BAQ. The FBI's plan had been hatched on the quick, but Andie's instructions to the Department of Corrections had been specific. Watch for red flags: a new corrections officer, a new nurse, a new doctor, a new janitor—anyone trying to enter the unit who had never entered before. Someone had obviously screwed up.

Idiots!

It was like riot control in the hallway, a team of corrections officers rushing to Room 834 in response to the gunshots.

"He could have hostages!" Andie shouted, but she was too late.

The first officer smashed through the door, weapon drawn. Shots erupted. The lead officer went down and fell into the room, his feet motionless in the open doorway. Three other corrections officers crouched into positions of cover, their backs flat against the walls in the hallway.

"Officer down!" Andie shouted as she came up behind them, the alarm continuing to sound as she positioned herself near the intercom in the hallway.

60

THE GUARD WENT DOWN HARD TO THE FLOOR, DROPPED BY TWO quick shots that left him motionless. His pistol skidded across the tile toward the bed. I dived for it as the gunman took Dr. Kern and moved away from the window, toward the closet. I grabbed the pistol and took aim, but he was using the doctor as a human shield.

"I have hostages!" he shouted in a voice that was loud enough for the officers in the hallway to hear him.

A voice crackled over the speaker box on my father's bed: "We hear you."

I recognized the voice as Andie Henning's.

The alarm went silent, and an eerie stillness came over the room. Two guards shot, my father barely alive. Andie's voice continued over the intercom speaker:

"We want to get medical treatment for the injured officers."

"They're dead! And if you make another run at this room, they're all dead!" Then he looked at me, his gun pressed to Dr. Kern's head, and said, "Drop your gun!"

I held my aim, my finger on the trigger.

"Do it!" he said as he shoved the pistol even harder against the base of the doctor's skull.

I didn't move. Andie's voice was on the speaker again.

"Patrick, do as he says. We don't need your help." She paused and then addressed the gunman directly. "Mongoose, there's no escape. We know who you are."

"Mongoose," I said quietly, a reflex, as if there were at least partial closure in knowing what he called himself.

"It's hopeless, Mongoose," said Andie. "Joe Barber is being arrested as we speak. Drop your weapon and surrender now."

Mongoose glared at me from across the room, his eyes like lasers. "Put the gun on the floor and slide it toward me," he said in a calm, but threatening tone.

The doctor's eyes widened with fear. I should have done as I was told, should have followed Andie's direction. But there was no guarantee that my father would ever wake, and I had Mongoose's attention—a chance to get some answers. I couldn't let go.

Mongoose tightened his stare on me and said, "There's no one here worth dying for, Patrick. Your father is a traitor to the U.S. government."

"You're reaching," I said.

"Your father cut a deal with terrorists."

"Right. And yo' mama eats worms. Now, put down the gun, asshole!"

"You think this is a joke?" he said, pressing the pistol even harder against Dr. Kern's head.

It had been a knee-jerk effort to show Mongoose that he wasn't in control, that I wasn't afraid to shoot him. But the doctor's terrified expression made me regret my words. "Not a joke," I said, backpedaling. "Let's put away the weapons and talk."

"Just shut up and listen! I heard the truth last night from Manu Robledo. If not for your old man, Manu Robledo never would have seen the quant's analysis showing that Cushman was a Ponzi scheme."

I held my aim. Mongoose kept talking.

"Your father wanted to get someone riled up enough to kill Gerry Collins, and he didn't care who else Robledo took out along the way. Didn't care if he took *me* out."

The anger in his voice was palpable. He seemed to hold as much animosity toward my father as he did toward Robledo—and, by extension, toward me.

Mongoose continued his rant. "For three years I was convinced that the government had forced your father to confess as part of Operation BAQ. Nobody *forced* him. Your father took the rap so that Robledo could stay out of jail and find the money that Collins had stashed away. We're talking billions of dollars from terrorist financers who would have killed Robledo unless he got it back. Your father confessed for a cut of that money—money that he would leave to you and your sister."

I had actually been with him right up till then—until the part about a cut of terrorist seed money. "You're making this up."

"Robledo spilled his guts last night."

"I doubt that Robledo has ever told the truth in his life."

"Trust me, he was in no position to be less than truthful."

"I don't believe you."

"I just spoke with Joe Barber. Even *he* can't figure out who started this fiction about a government-forced confession."

"Oh, now, there's an honest politician."

"I know a traitor when I see one. Your father is a traitor, Patrick."

"You're lying."

"He *is* lying," my dad said.

It happened in a split second. The Demerol wasn't enough to force sleep through a gunfight, and the sound of my father's voice had startled Mongoose more than me. I was standing in the marksman's pose, holding a Glock that was identical to the one that Scully had taught me how to use in Connie's apartment, the sights lined up, my finger on the trigger. Dr. Kern dived for safety, and I squeezed the trigger. The shot erupted like thunder, and in a crimson explosion, Mongoose's head jerked back. His gun dropped to his feet as his body collapsed in a heap. Dr. Kern raced into the arms of the first officer to burst through the door.

I dropped the gun, fell on the bed, and squeezed my father so hard that I could barely breathe. Fifteen years of emotional confusion collided with a week of stress, anxiety, and my own near-death experiences to create a long, cathartic embrace. "I'm fine, it's over," I said. "Mongoose is gone."

He laid his arm across my back, not really holding me, but doing the best he could with the strength that remained.

"'Yo' mama eats worms'?" he said.

His muted chuckle was little more than a tremble, and I broke our embrace long enough to see a hint of a smile crease his lips. I wanted to laugh and cry in the same breath. It was beyond comic relief. It brought a moment of humanity to years of sorrow and separation.

And then it faded.

"Dad?"

I didn't want to lose him. Holding on tight seemed like the only option.

"Go get your sister," he whispered into my ear.

I took a breath and released him. I knew what he was telling me. "I'll be right back," I said, catching one last glimpse of Mongoose in a puddle of blood as I hurried out of the room.

61

I RAN TO THE ELEVATOR. ANDIE FOLLOWED. I HAD NO CELL PHONE, but she was able to dial Connie's number on hers.

No answer.

I didn't know how much time my father had left, hours or minutes, but standing around waiting for my sister to pick up her cell was not an option. The lockdown had triggered additional security, but Andie cleared us through it, and the express elevator took us to the main lobby. I went straight to the spot where Connie had been sitting. The television was still playing in the corner, but the lobby was deserted, no sign of Connie. The gunfire had clearly triggered an evacuation.

"Come with me," said Andie.

She led me outside to the parking lot, where a group of people was waiting for the all clear to come back inside. It was a cold night, and falling snow flickered in the cones of yellow-white glow beneath the lampposts. People in the crowd were shifting their weight from one foot to the other, arms folded or hands in pockets, trying to stay warm.

"Connie!"

A few heads turned in response to my call, but no one responded. I went from person to person, searching. My sister was nowhere.

"Has anyone here seen a woman named Connie Ryan?" I asked in a loud voice.

A few people shook their heads. Most glanced in the other direction, ignoring me. Finally, a high school kid dressed in a hoodie and smoking a cigarette came forward.

"White chick?" he asked. "Blue coat?"

"Yeah."

He took a drag from his cigarette. "Me and her was watching the Celtics game on the TV. She left with some dude about a half hour ago."

"Are you sure?"

"Yeah. They was arguing, like she didn't want to go. I was gonna say something, but I guess they worked it out. Better not to get involved, you know?"

"What did the guy look like?" I asked.

The kid shrugged. "Big guy, kind of old for her. Fifties, I guess. An asshole, if you ask me."

I looked at Andie, and she read my mind. "Scully," we said to each other.

62

A PAIR OF HEADLIGHTS PIERCED THE NIGHT AS THE WHITE SUV rental headed down the highway toward Providence. Connie rode in the passenger seat, her hands tied behind her back. Scully drove. The dashboard rattled with the tinny sound of an over-worked defroster struggling to clear the windshield. The *whump-whump* of the wipers pushed the falling snow from one side to the other.

"We trusted you, Scully," Connie said.

His eyes narrowed. Some idiot driver in an approaching car had his high beams on, nearly blinding him. Scully flashed him back.

"Dad trusted you," she said.

"Shut your trap, Connie. Your father was no Boy Scout."

"He changed."

"No, he didn't. Your father lost everything in a Ponzi scheme, so he asked me for the name of another victim who would take Collins for a one-way car ride if they knew he was a fraud. I gave him Robledo's name."

"It wasn't a crime for Dad to give Evan Hunt's report to Robledo."

"Robledo wasn't *given* anything. I sold it to him."

"My father wouldn't have taken money from a man like Robledo. Not after everything he gave up."

"You're right. All your old man cared about was getting even with Collins for stealing his nest egg. But that report gave Robledo something that no one else in the world got. Robledo got a heads-up on Cushman's fraud, and the chance to recover his money. Why shouldn't I get a cut?"

"A cut of *what*? The money was already gone."

He shot her a quick glance, and for an instant, Connie thought she almost saw the old Scully—a man who surely understood that Connie would never agree with what he'd done, but who didn't want her to think he was evil. "There's my dilemma, Connie."

"Dilemma?"

His gaze returned to the icy road, but he kept talking. "One percent of two billion dollars is a lot of money. But I got one percent of nothing if Robledo couldn't track down his money. It didn't take a genius to see that Robledo would never recover a dime if he went to prison for killing Gerry Collins."

Connie knew exactly what he was saying. "You pig! *You* forced my father to confess!"

"Your father was already sick with cancer. It wasn't like he was going to be locked up forever."

"You bastard! You used his kids against him, didn't you? You were our handler. How could you threaten to out Patrick and me unless he confessed to something he didn't do?"

He slapped her with the back of his hand. It landed with so much force that Connie's head slammed against the passenger's-side window.

"Connie! Oh, my God, I'm sorry. Are you okay?"

She blinked hard, trying to shake off the blow and take the blur out of her vision. Scully's apology left her equally dazed. Clearly he was at war with himself over his betrayal, the FBI version of an abusive spouse who returns home with a bouquet of flowers after pushing his wife down the stairs. The salty taste of her own blood trickled from her mouth as she spoke.

"That's what Dad wanted to tell Patrick today, isn't it?" she said. "That Scully is dirty."

Scully was no longer smiling. His audience of one was spitting the vitriol of an angry mob. He focused on his driving, the tires humming on the snow-covered highway.

"I still don't hear a denial," Connie said.

"He doesn't know."

"What?"

"If it's any comfort to you, your father never knew I stabbed him in the back. When I got Treasury to pay him some money for agreeing to sit on the Cushman report, I told him that it was compensation from the CIA for his confession—that if he didn't take the deal, and that if he ever claimed he was framed, it was the CIA who would hand his kids over to the Santucci family. As far as he knew, the CIA had to keep Robledo out of prison for Operation BAQ to work. To this day, he thinks I was just the messenger."

"You're even worse than I thought you were."

"Hey, at least I let him have the money."

"Yeah, money he couldn't even use to pay for his own cancer treatment once he was in prison."

Scully kept one hand on the wheel and dialed his cell.

"Who are you calling?" asked Connie.

"Your dumbass brother," he said. "Be still and behave yourself. You ain't seen nothin' yet."

63

I HAD NO PHONE, BUT MY NUMBER RANG TO ANDIE'S CELL. IT HAD taken a tech agent in the Boston field office all of thirty seconds to program the wireless hijacking and reroute my calls to Andie.

"It's Scully," she told me.

We were still in the parking lot, seated in the back of an FBI van that had arrived on the scene. Andie quickly plugged her phone into the mobile audio system. Her phone rang a second time—this time over the van's surveillance speakers.

"You want me to take it?" I asked.

"Yes. Play this exactly the way I told you to play it. And keep Scully on the line as long as possible so that our techies can triangulate a location."

On the fourth ring she hit Talk and handed me the phone.

"Scully, where are you?" I asked.

Andie gave me a quick thumbs-up, letting me know that she could hear the conversation just fine.

"I have your sister," he said.

"Good. Bring her back. Dad wants to see her."

He was on to my act. "Don't play dumb," he said. "I *will* hurt her."

I'd never heard that tone from Scully, and it chilled me. The man was clearly desperate.

"Okay," I said. "What do you want?"

"For starters, you need to keep your mouth shut. If you go to Agent Henning or anyone else with any of the things your father told you, Connie's dead."

Again I felt chills. It was clear that Scully had no idea that the FBI was involved and that it had all been a setup—that my trip to Boston to see my father, the whole idea of a deathbed conversation, was something that Andie and my father had co-ordinated with me in order to draw out Mongoose and Barber. Andie slipped me a note: *Don't tell him you haven't talked to your father.*

"I hear you," I said into the phone.

"It would have been much better for everyone if he had taken his secrets to the grave. But he just had to share all the things Agent Scully told him, didn't he?"

I was tempted to play along and stall, but with Connie's safety on the line, I was afraid to wing it.

Scully pushed harder. "What did he tell you, Patrick?"

Andie handed me a note. I wasn't sure if I was just buying time for the tech agents to triangulate the call, or if it was another strategy, but I followed her script.

"Dad told me that he was forced to confess," I said as I grabbed a second note from Andie. "But it was Robledo who killed Collins."

"I know he told you more than that."

I looked again at Andie, who handed me yet another note. "He said Operation BAQ would fail if Robledo was locked up for murder. That's why—"

I stopped, bordering on panic. I wasn't sure that Andie had written down her thoughts correctly.

Scully said, "That's why *what*?"

Andie underlined her words, reaffirming the message. I delivered it as written: "That's why Dad believed you when you lied and told him it was the CIA that forced him to confess."

Scully paused, and when he finally spoke, he sounded a bit philosophical. "So the poor bastard finally figured out it was me."

It was confirmation of the theory Andie had scribbled out on her notes. She gave me a signal to keep him talking, but Scully had never really stopped.

"Payback's a bitch, isn't it, Patrick?"

I wasn't sure what he meant. Scully's betrayal had been difficult for me to comprehend—the way he'd turned against my father, against Connie and me, against the bureau. Money could make people do worse things, I supposed. But his mention of "payback" made me realize that something more personal was also driving him.

"My father was the stain on your perfect career. That's what this is about, isn't it, Scully?"

He answered in a low, angry voice. "I told him and your mother both: stay away from each other. The fact that her maiden name was Santucci didn't make it any easier for me to protect her. I made it crystal clear that the mob would put a gun to her head if they thought for one minute that she could reveal where your father was hiding."

"But Dad wouldn't listen."

"Neither one of them listened."

"So they killed her," I said, the words catching in my throat. But I had to push through this. "She was killed *on your watch*. Not a very career-enhancing move in the bureau, I suppose. Losing the mother of two children."

"Are you playing shrink on me, Patrick?"

"No. Just calling your 'payback' what it is. When Robledo waved all that money under your nose, it wasn't so hard for you to grab it at my father's expense, was it?"

"Not as hard as it might have been. But that's all in the past. Let's deal with the present. I don't want to have to hurt your sister."

"I don't want you to hurt her, either."

"Then forget what you know about your father and me. Forget that I gave him Robledo's name. Forget especially that I ever mentioned Operation BAQ or the CIA to him."

I didn't know the ins and outs of constitutional and criminal law, but I was pretty sure I recognized the voice of a former FBI agent who was looking at potential charges that ranged from obstruction of justice to treason.

"That's fine with me, Scully," I said. "Everything that was said in the hospital was between my father and me. Just don't hurt my sister."

"Good. Now, I need you to follow my instructions—to the letter."

"I'm not going to help you go on the run with an escape plan, if that's what you're asking."

"You will, or your sister pays."

I swallowed hard. Saying it would have sounded like heroic hyperbole, but I truly thought it: I wished he had taken me instead of her.

"I want to talk to Connie," I said.

"Shut up and listen."

"No. I need to know she's still alive. Put her on."

He didn't refuse right away, which I took as a good sign. I was about to prod one more time when he answered.

"Fine. I'll let you hear her voice."

Andie gave me the stretch sign, though she was openly frustrated that her tech agents needed still more time to pinpoint the call.

"That's not enough," I told him. "How will I know it's not just a recording? She has to talk to me—to answer a question from me."

Again, I took his hesitation to mean that he was considering it. I nudged.

"A former FBI agent should know my request is reasonable," I said.

"Fine. You can ask her a question. *One* question."

Andie gave me a signal that said her techies were almost there. But Scully was no dummy, and I had the sense that he knew exactly how long he could stay on the line without being triangulated. The thought of his hanging up seconds before his position could be determined was more than I could bear.

"Patrick?" said Connie.

I could hear the fear in her voice, but I knew Connie wasn't the type to be beaten by fear.

Scully was back on the line. "Ask your question, Patrick. You got ten seconds."

He was definitely timing the call. Andie gave me the stretch sign again, and I could see the angst in her expression. Triangulation wasn't the answer. It was time to take things into my own hands, and the right question suddenly popped into my head. I was thinking of a conversation that Connie and I had once had about our mother, after her death. We'd talked about what a terrible mistake it is to get in the car when you know it's a one-way ride. How you should kick, scream, pull hair, and gouge eyes—whatever it takes not to end up in the car.

And if the abductor still manages to force you inside the car, you do everything you can to crash it.

"Connie," I asked, "what should Mom have done?"

64

CONNIE WAS STARING STRAIGHT AHEAD THROUGH THE WIND-shield. The snowflakes were huge, and they splattered against the glass on impact, making it virtually impossible to see more than one or two car lengths in front of their SUV. It was not a night to be out on the road in New England.

What should Mom have done?

Connie's hands were tied behind her back. The side of her head was still throbbing from Scully's backhanded slap. She was at his mercy, but Patrick's question energized her. It gave her hope. It gave her a plan. She could hear the packed snow beating against the floorboard, drawn up from the road by the spinning tires. Scully was driving with one hand on the wheel, his right arm extended so that he could hold the cell phone to Connie's ear.

What should Mom have done?

Connie opened her mouth, but no words came. She bit down on his hand, her jaws locking onto him, her teeth digging down to the bone.

Scully screamed like a wounded snow monkey.

Connie leaned to her right, refusing to let go, hanging on to her prey with the tenacity of a hungry pit bull. She pulled so hard that she dragged his upper body halfway across the console, nearly into her own seat. Connie was in control—but their SUV was completely out of control, spinning, whirling across the icy highway. It slammed into the guardrail with too much force and at precisely the wrong angle. It hopped the rail and rolled over once, then again, continuing to roll all the way down the steep, snowy embankment.

More rolls than Connie could count before she blacked out.

65

I WAITED OUTSIDE THE HOSPITAL ROOM. CONNIE WAS INSIDE.
With my father.

Scully's telephone had remained on through the crash, even
after it. The FBI tech agents were able to triangulate the signal,
and emergency personnel were there within minutes. Scully
was pronounced dead at the scene. Connie was brought to
Lemuel Shattuck. Her arm was broken, and she was pretty beat
up. But she'd fought her way out of the ER to have a moment
with Dad. Her *own* moment. I understood.

Andie sat in the hallway with me, waiting.

"How are the two corrections officers he shot?" I asked.

"The second one just got out of surgery and should recover.
The first one . . ." She stopped, shaking her head slowly. "A
wife, two kids in preschool. Horrible."

She was right. The park ranger, Evan Hunt, and now a corrections officer. Their deaths were all horrible.

"This wasn't done right," she said. "We should have had
snipers on the roof, more agents. The problem was that I was
already supposed be back in Miami. It's just impossible to pull
together that kind of support when the plug has already been
pulled, but I should have—"

"Andie," I said, stopping her. "This was not your fault."

I probably hadn't convinced her, but she did seem to appreciate the sentiment.

We sat in silence for a moment. I was thinking about the ambulance ride with Connie. She'd recounted her conversation with Scully—how he'd cut a deal with Robledo, how he'd lied and told Dad that the CIA was behind the threats to expose his children if he didn't confess to the murder of Gerry Collins. He'd made my father believe that he was just more collateral damage in the financial war on terrorism. Andie suspected that it was fear of charges of treason—or perhaps some lingering loyalty of an FBI agent to his country—that had kept Scully from telling Robledo what he'd managed to piece together about Operation BAQ.

Still, there were things that confused me.

"Why did you pick me to investigate Lilly?"

To Andie, the question had probably seemed to come out of left field. But for me the FBI investigation into Lilly Scanlon at BOS/Singapore was where it had all started. Knowing where it had finally led, it made no sense that Andie would have picked me. I simply didn't believe in coincidences that big.

"This investigation was started before Scully retired," she said. "He picked you."

"Why?"

"The same reason he forced your father to confess: he didn't get a dime until Robledo recovered the money that Collins had diverted from Cushman. After all he did to keep Robledo out of jail so that he could hunt down the money, the last thing he wanted was for the FBI to find it first. Clearly, he thought you were someone he could control."

"What about you? You're the one who signed me up. Why did you use me?"

"The operation was already approved by the time Scully was forced to retire. They brought me in from Miami to take over. I inherited his pick."

"So it was just inertia?"

"You'd be amazed by the number of things that the bureau does for no other reason than that."

I was feeling scammed yet again—not for myself, but for Lilly. "So Scully steered the FBI investigation toward Lilly so that it would go nowhere?"

"Nowhere," said Andie. "You and I went there together, my friend."

My head rolled back. "Lilly," I said. "I don't even know where to begin with her."

"She'll be okay," said Andie. "We've been talking."

I was aware of that. Lilly's call from Connie's bathroom had prompted Andie to contact me—which had sparked the formulation of Andie's plan, the deathbed confession that had netted Mongoose and Barber.

"The question is whether Lilly will ever talk to me," I said.

The door to my father's room opened. Connie stepped out. Tears were in her eyes. My heart raced, as if knowing that it was about to be broken.

"What?" I asked.

She came to me, sat in the chair beside me, and took my hand. The expression on her face said it all, but she said it anyway.

"It's time to say good-bye," she said softly, pausing before she said my name, "Peter."

Epilogue

THE WEDDING WAS OUTDOORS ON A BEAUTIFUL AFTERNOON IN April. At the Central Park Zoo.

Connie was a radiant bride dressed in an official scout leader uniform—dark blue skirt hemmed below the knee, yellow shirt with epaulets, and a Tiger Cub den leader neckerchief. Tom, undeniably her soul mate, wore khaki pants, a safari hat, and a Hawaiian shirt that was hard to look at without sunglasses. The snow monkeys watched from their rocky perch, their dark eyes seemingly filled with a mixture of confusion and amusement as the preacher pronounced them husband and wife, looked at Connie, and said, "You may kiss the groom."

And, boy, did she.

For me, it was the first day since Dad's funeral that thoughts of him hadn't triggered pain or sadness. I felt as though he was watching, peering down at us from somewhere beyond one of the fluffy white clouds in the bright blue sky, happy for a daughter who deserved happiness.

Operation Bankrupt al-Qaeda had dominated the news for weeks. After Mongoose's death, there was no one to activate his computer's "safety valve," and the internal Treasury memorandum on Operation BAQ had gone viral over the Internet. The federal multicount indictment in Washington, D.C., against former deputy secretary of the treasury Joe Barber and National Security Advisor Brett Woods had laid out the damning charges: within days of Cushman's suicide, the national security advisor himself had made it clear that *no one* could ever find out that both Treasury and the White House had known about Cushman's fraud and let it happen, and *no one* could ever know about the biggest blunder in the country's financial war on terrorism. A congressional investigation was under way to determine how high knowledge and culpability ran in the White House, but the drumbeat was growing louder. Even those who weren't talking about impeachment were quietly conceding that they were defending a "one-term president." Barber's trouble reached beyond Washington. The Manhattan district attorney was planning a murder-for-hire prosecution in connection with the execution-style shooting of Evan Hunt, though it seemed doubtful that the world would ever know the identity of the actual triggerman.

Still, the public debate had developed an intriguing vibe. No one had seemed too upset when "the body of suspected terrorist financer Manu Robledo" was found in Paraguay, though there were plenty of sensational (albeit accurate) reports that the killer had used a commando wire saw, that Robledo's mutilated hands and feet were evidence of torture, and that his severed head had yet to be located. On a policy level, many in Washington decried Operation BAQ while, behind the scenes, breathing a sigh of relief that the $2 billion that might otherwise have funded terrorist operations was now . . . where?

Nobody seemed to know. Pundits speculated that it was buried deep in the *hawala* remittance systems run by Islamic extremists. Or in the vault of a "neutral" Swiss bank that had offices in Singapore.

"Very cool wedding," I said.

Connie hugged me. "Come on. It's time to throw the bouquet to my snow monkeys."

Honestly, it was the ugliest bouquet I'd ever seen, but I suddenly understood why: it was made of edible blossoms suitable for monkey tummies. Not that there was any danger of those monkeys ever going hungry. Although Dad never knew that the quarter million dollars in his account had come from Treasury to keep him quiet about Evan Hunt's report—not, as Scully had led him and Agent Henning to believe, from the CIA for a false confession—the fact remained that a nice chunk of money had passed through Dad's estate to Connie and me. We'd donated most of it to the zoo. The rest went to Evan's family.

I followed Connie along the stone walkway, but we were only halfway to her chosen spot for the bouquet toss when we stopped in our tracks.

"What's wrong?" asked Tom.

Connie and I were facing in the direction of the red panda exhibit, our gaze fixed on the woman who was standing in the shade of a Japanese fern tree.

I hadn't asked Connie if she was going to invite Lilly. This was her wedding, and I didn't want to use her special day as a vehicle to reconnect. Lilly and I hadn't parted on bitter terms, but we'd reached a mutual agreement that time apart was best. Last I'd heard she'd left banking. I wasn't even sure if she planned to stay in New York. Frankly, I wasn't sure I planned to stay.

"I invited her," said Connie, "but I didn't think she'd come."

"She looks amazing."

"Ya *think*?" said Tom.

Connie slugged him in the arm, then nudged me along. "Go say hello, dope."

I took a half step, and though Lilly was at least hundred feet away, our eyes met. I detected a smile. Didn't really see it. I just felt it.

"Okay," I said, "here goes nothing."

Oh, baby, I need your cow.

Acknowledgments

I DIDN'T THINK I WOULD EVER GET TO SAY THIS AGAIN, BUT I want to thank my editor, Carolyn Marino. Carolyn and I did fifteen novels together, the last of which was *Born to Run* in 2009. After a couple of novels without her, I'm thrilled to have her back, along with her assistant, Wendy Lee. I also want to thank my agent and friend, Richard Pine at Inkwell Management; Sally Kim for early edits on *Need You Now*; and two of the best proofreaders I've ever known, Janis Koch (aka Conan the Grammarian) and Gloria Villa. I can assure you that any mistakes in this novel are due to late changes I made after Janis and Gloria had already read the galleys.

Connie Ryan gets a big thank-you for lending her name and her love of scouting to the other Connie Ryan, who is a fictional character in *Need You Now*. She now joins her husband, Tom Bales, in the literary halls of immortality (Tom lent his name to a character in *Intent to Kill*). Their generosity at a character auction will benefit the children of St. Thomas Episcopal Parish School.

Finally, to my wife, Tiffany. Thank you. I love you. I need you . . . always.

JMG

May 14, 2011

About the Author

James Grippando is the *New York Times* bestselling author of nineteen previous novels, including *Afraid of the Dark*, *Money to Burn*, *Intent to Kill*, *Born to Run*, *Last Call*, *Lying with Strangers*, *When Darkness Falls*, and *Got the Look*. He lives in Florida, where he was a trial lawyer.